KB061776

# 일범의 특별한
# 영어 이야기

이 책을 소중한

_____ 님에게 선물합니다.

_____ 드림

# 일범의 특별한 영어 이야기

초 판 1쇄   2021년 10월 27일

지은이 손영징
펴낸이 류종렬

펴낸곳 미다스북스
총괄실장 명상완
책임편집 이다경
책임진행 김가영 신은서 임종익 박유진

등록 2001년 3월 21일 제2001-000040호
주소 서울시 마포구 양화로 133 서교타워 711호
전화 02) 322-7802~3
팩스 02) 6007-1845
블로그 http://blog.naver.com/midasbooks
전자주소 midasbooks@hanmail.net
페이스북 https://www.facebook.com/midasbooks425

© 손영징, 미다스북스 2021, *Printed in Korea*.

ISBN 978-89-6637-972-9 03810

값 35,000원

※ 파본은 본사나 구입하신 서점에서 교환해드립니다.
※ 이 책에 실린 모든 콘텐츠는 미다스북스가 저작권자와의 계약에 따라 발행한 것이므로 인용하시거나 참고하실
   경우 반드시 본사의 허락을 받으셔야 합니다.

미다스북스는 다음세대에게 필요한 지혜와 교양을 생각합니다.

An Ordinary Man's Special Living English

# 일범의 특별한
# 영어 이야기

일범 손영징 지음

"미국에서 살아남기 위해 좌충우돌 전투적으로 배운 살아 있는 생존 영어!"

미다스북스

## 책머리에

나는 영어공부를 하기 위해 나름 열심히 노력했다고 생각한다. 1971년, 중학교에 입학해서 A, B, C를 배우기 시작했는데, 그 당시 시골 중학교에서 원어민이란 있을 수도 없었고, 고등학교 졸업할 때까지 외국인과 자연스럽게 대화할 줄 아는 영어선생님도 드물었다. 영어공부 잘 하는 학생들이란 영어문법을 잘한다는 의미였다. 나는 고3 때 영어회화 학원에 등록하여 몇 달간 원어민으로부터 회화를 배운 적이 있었지만 꾸준히 이어지지를 못했다. 군제대 후 복학했을 때, 뜻한 바 있어 다시 영어회화 학원에 다니게 되었는데, 이 때 만난 영어강사들이 미국 선교사들이라, 좀 영어다운 영어를 배웠던 것 같다. 그러나 대화가 겨우 통할 정도였지 유창하지도 못했고, 특히 TIME 지는 물론이고, 영어신문도 사전 없이는 읽지 못했고, AFKN 청취도 불가능한 수준이었다.

1989년부터 공장을 지으면서, 설비공급사인 영국인과 프랑스인을 상대하게 되었는데, 되든 안 되든 영어로 대화할 수밖에 없었는데, 한마디로 전투 영어였다. 공장 준공 후에는 해외에 자주 출장을 다니면서, 클레임 해결 또는 기술지원을 했는데, 이 때에는 나는 내가 영어를 잘하는 줄로 생각했다. 사실은 영국 또는 프랑스의 수퍼바이저들에게는 내가 '갑'의 입장이었고, 내 말을 못 알아들으면 그들이 손해였기 때문에 어느 정도 통한 것이었고, 해외 출장 때도 내가 아쉬운 쪽이 아니었기 때문에 내가 영어를 제법 하는 줄로 착각했던 것이었다.

2000년, 미국으로 발령받아 나갈 때만 해도 가족들에게는 어깨에 힘 주고 갔는데, 철강공장 현장에서 진짜 미국인들과 마주쳐 본 이후부터는 모든 것이 달라지고 말았다. 그 사람들의 영어는 세미나에서 사용하는 표준영어가 아니고, 발음도 불분명한데다 일상으로 쓰는 속어(slangs)와 관용구(idioms) 범벅이었는데, 못 알아들으면 나만 손해였다. 당황할 새 없이 살아남기 위해서는 공부를 할 수밖에 없었다. 매일 만나는 사람에게서 새로운 표현을 들으면 양해를 구하고 무조건 메모를 했다. 가능한 많은 부류의 사람들을 만나고, 가능한 많은 주제의 얘기를 나누었다. 아침에 일어나면 미국 TV부터 켜고, 출, 퇴근시간에는 라디오를 들었다. 지역대학에 영어수업을 듣고, MBA 과정에 등록하여 공부도 하고, 1주일에 한 번씩 과외도 받았다. 3년 정도 열심히 했더니 많이 좋아지긴 했으나, 여전히 모자란다. 특히 그들만이 주고받는 농담 속으로 동화되거나, 미국 TV의 코미디 프로그램을 이해하는 것은 불가능하다.

영어로 인해 미국생활이 힘들수록, 나는 내가 경험했던 미국영어를 정리하여 내 후배들에게 미리 알려줘야겠다는 생각을 했다. 하나, 둘 모은 것이 책 한 권 분량이 된다. 불행히도, 내가 근무하던 회사가 미국으로 완전히 넘어가 버렸기 때문에 후배들에게는 전해줄 수가 없게 되었지만, 책으로 남겨두면 누군가에게는 조금의 도움이 되지 않을까 생각한다. 아무도 보지 않아도 그냥 기록이 되겠지.

2021. 10
일범 손영징

# 차례

## 3장 미국문화의 이해

# 제2부 만화로 배우는 미국, 미국영어

## 1장 주제별 만화

## 2장 작가별 만화

제1부

# 영어, 나이 들어
# 공부하기엔 참 어렵다

# 1장

# 미국영어에 대한 나의 생각

## 영어와의 전쟁
(2004년 포스코 신문에 기고한 글이다.)

"죽도시장 회비빔밥이 먹고 싶어요."

며칠 전 미국으로 이사한 지 3년째 되던 날, 아내가 한 말이다. 나도 힘든데 아내는 오죽하랴? 이 곳에서의 생활은 매일매일 온통 영어 때문에 받는 스트레스의 연속이라 할 수 있다. 미국으로 발령받기 전에는 영국, 프랑스 사람들과 싸워가며 공장도 지어본 경험이 있어서 나도 영어깨나 한다고 생각했다. 하지만 내가 이곳 UPI에서 근무한 지난 3년간의 생활은 한마디로 '진짜 미국영어'와의 전쟁이었다. 우선 현장 사람들과의 커뮤니케이션이 생각보다 쉽지 않았다. 지식과 경험이 있어도 현장에서 의사소통이 잘 안 되는 이유가 여러가지다.

첫째, 단위의 차이다. m, kg 대신 inch, lb에 익숙해지는 것도 쉽지 않은데, 두께를 지칭하는데 무게 단위를 사용하지 않은가. 예를 들어 호칭칫수 "0.21mm × 823mm"에 익숙한 나에게는 "Seventy five basis weight, Thirty two and a quarter wide"가 빨리 이해될 수가 없었다.

둘째, 용어의 차이다. 정수(定期修修)를 Down Turn, '길이방향반곡'을 Coil Set, '마찰흠'을 Gall, 냉연코일 또는 도금코일을 Sheet로 표현하는 것 등은 전혀 다른 말인 줄 알았다.

셋째, 나름대로 사용해온 약어나 설비명칭이다. TAC(Trim After Coating: 도금 후 트리밍), OSW(Outside Wrap: 외권부), BWL(Basis weight Light: 두께미달) 등은 그 자리에서 무슨 뜻인지 물어볼 수도 있었지만, 트랜자이트 롤(Transite라는 회사에서 납품한 Roll), 코우비모터(일본 Kobe에서 제작한 Motor) 같은 말들은 잘 알아듣지 못하고 얼버무렸다가, 나중에 영어사전을 찾아봐도 안 나올 때는 얼마나 황당했는지.

마지막으로, 미국인들은 어려서부터 발표력을 키우기 위해 꾸준히 훈련받아 오기 때문에, 누구나 자신의 의사를 더듬거리지 않고 정말 잘 표현한다. 그러나 그들이 사용하는 일상적인 표현들― Graveyard(야근), Hook up(설치), Bogey(목표), 24/7(항상), Skid row bum(노숙자) 등등―은 표준영어만 배워온 나에게는 너무나 익숙하지 않았다. 특히 철강현장 사람들에게는 일상화되어 있는 비어나 저질표현들은 미국생활문화의 밑바닥을 체험하면서 자란 사람이 아니고는 이해할 수 없는 것들이 많다.

현장영어는 세미나에서 들은 영어와는 다르다. 때로는 설비소음 속에서 주어, 동사도 없는 중얼거림, 때로는 쉼표, 마침표도 없는 속사포, 그리고는 그네들끼리 우스워 죽겠다는 듯? 이것 참 끼어들 수도 없고, 그냥 넘길 수도 없고―.

내가 근무하는 부서에 한국사람은 나뿐이니, 나야 스트레스를 낙으로 생각하고, 하루 종일 영어와 싸울 수밖에 없지만, 이렇게 주워 모은 표현들을 나 혼자 알고 있기보다, 다른 사람과 공유하면 회사의 귀한 자산이 될 수가 있기에, 나는 틈나는 대로 이 사람들이 사용하는 Slang(속어), Idioms(숙어) 및 Jargon(전문용어)을 열심히 정리하고 있다. 나와 똑같은 실수를 후배들이 또 겪을 필요는 없으니까.

어느 정도 마무리되면, 포항 가서 죽도시장 회나 실컷 먹어봐야겠다.

## American Slangs
(2001년 LMC에서 영어공부를 할 때 쓴 글의 번역본이다.)

지난 화요일 아침, 보스와의 아침회의 참석을 위해 서두르고 있었다. 보스의 사무실 앞에서 동료 한 명을 마주쳐 "Good morning, Lynnette."이라고 하자, 그녀는 "Good morning, how are you?"라고 했다. 내가 "Fine, Thanks. How are you?"라고 하니, 그녀의 대답은 "Hanging inner."였다. 나는 그 말을 이해할 수 없어서 순간 당황했는데, 그녀는 곧바로 'hanging in there'는 'pretty good'이라는 뜻이라고 설명을 해 주었다.

나는 일상생활의 대화에는 큰 어려움이 없었으나, 회사에서 회의시간이면 잘 알아듣지 못해 스트레스를 많이 받았는데, 잘 못 알아듣는 주원인은 그들이 속어(slang)와 비상식적인 토막영어(chopped English)를 너무 많이 사용하기 때문이었다.

오후에 동료 한 명과 Slang에 대해 어떻게 생각하는지 얘기를 나누었다. 대부분의 미국인들은 매일 많은 Slang을 사용한다. 나는 이러한 Slang들 때문에 그들의 대화에서 소외되는 느낌이다. 속어사전(slang dictionary)을 사 봤으나, 그들이 Slang을 말할 때 그 단어의 스펠링을 모르니 별 소용이 없었다.

다음 말들은 내가 작년에 미국으로 온 이후 내가 들었던 Slang의 일부다.

– cool: 아주 좋다(수년 전에는 'hot'도 같은 의미로 쓰였다)
– bad: 아주 좋다
– It's gross: 아주 나쁘다
– kick down: 주다, 허용하다
– kicked out: 고장 나다
– kicked to the curb: 버리다
– fire away: 먼저 해
– out of the blue: 갑자기
– buff: 닦다
– buffed: 근육질의
– freeze: 움직이지 마

내가 다양한 Slang에 익숙해지려면 많은 시간이 걸릴 것이다. 그러나 미국화 되는 가장 좋은 방법은 미국의 Slang을 이해하는 것이다.

＊LMC(Los Medanos College): California 주 Pittsburg에 소재한 Community College.

## American Expressions

(2002년 Golden Gate University에서 MBA 과정에서 발표한 영어 Speech의 일부를 번역한 것이다.)

안녕하세요? 손영징입니다. 여러분들 앞에서 발표할 수 있어 기쁩니다. 오늘 저는 제가 미국에 온 이후 저를 많이 당황하게 했던 미국식 표현에 대해 얘기하고자 합니다.

저는 2년 전에 미국으로 왔는데, 2년간의 미국생활은 겉으로는 행복해 보였지만 실제로는 제게 정말 힘든 시간이었습니다. 매일 매일이 영어로 인한 스트레스의 연속이었습니다. 저는 유에스스틸과 한국의 포스코라는 철강회사가 합작하여 설립한 UPI라는 회사에서 조업지원 담당 매니저로 일하고 있습니다.

미국인들과 함께 일하는 데 가장 힘든 점은 의사소통 문제입니다 – 듣고 상대방을 이해하기, 나 자신을 표현해서 말하기. 저는 한국의 중, 고등학교에서 영어를 배웠습니다. 제가 배운 영어는 정상적인 표준영어였습니다. 그러나 제 경험에 의하면 실제 생활에 사용되는 미국식 표현은 제가 학교에서 배운 것과는 너무 달랐습니다.
예를 들면, 사람이 처음 만나 인사를 하는 경우, 저는 이렇게 배웠습니다.

"How do you do, Mr. Smith?"
"How do you do, Mr. Kim?"

그러나 실제로 이렇게 인사하는 경우는 없었습니다. 대신에,

"I'm Mike, nice to meet you."
"I'm Linda, good to see you."

저는 처음 만난 사람에게 이름을 부르는 것은 예의가 아니며 무례한 것으로 알고 있었는데, 모든 사람이 이름으로 소개하고 상대방 이름도 바로 불렀습니다.

다른 예로, 미국인들은 "How are you?"보다는 "How are you doing?" 이라는 표현을 더 좋아하는 것 같습니다. 내가 길가다 마주친 누군가에게 "How are you doing?"이라는 말을 들었을 때, "I am doing well, how about you?"라고 대답하려고 했습니다. 그런데 내가 채 말을 끝내기도 전에 그는 벌써 저만치 멀어져 가고 있었습니다.

또 다른 예로, 어떤 사람은 그녀가 무슨 상황에 대해 설명할 때 내가 이해하는지 못 하는지 계속 확인하는 질문을 해댔습니다. "You know?", "Do you know what I mean?", "Do you know what I am saying?" 그러나 그녀는 내 대답을 기다리지 않고 자기말만 계속했습니다. 따라서 나는 그녀의 말을 가로채 "Yes, I do" 또는 "No, I don't" 라고 대답하지를 못했습니다. 많은 날이 지난 후에야 그러한 말들은 그저 의미 없는 'pet phrase'임을 알았습니다.

철강회사 작업자들이 사용하는 표현들은 더욱 이해하기 힘든 게 많습니다. 그들은 많은 속어, 비어, 심지어는 나쁜 말이나 뜻 모를 말을 하는 경우가 많습니다. 예를 들면,

"When was it hooked up?": 언제 설치했어?
"Top entry rectifier #2 kicked out.": 입측 상부 정류기 나갔어.
"Kicking ass, make money": 신나게 돈번다.
"What's the scoop ruddy poop?": 잘 지내?
"It's better to pissed off than pissed on.": 차라리 내가 미치는 게 낫지.
"Chilling like a villain.": 그럼 수고해.
"yadi yadi yada": 기타 등등

철강회사에서는 CB(Citizen Band) radio talks 용어도 사용하는데 처음에는 정말 당황했었습니다.

"Mike Ortiz, do you copy?": 마이크, 내 말 들리냐?
"What's your 20?": 현재 위치가 어디냐?
"10, 4": 알았다.

나는 외국에서 쇼핑, 여행, 세미나 참석, 심지어는 업무상 출장을 수행하는 것까지 아무런 문제가 없었습니다. 그러나 철강회사 현장 작업자

들과의 의사소통은 다른 외부활동과는 많은 차이가 있었습니다.

미국과 한국에서 같거나 비슷하게 사용하는 속담이 있습니다.

"One stone kills two birds(일석이조)"
"No news is good news(무소식이 희소식)"

이런 말은 완전히 똑 같습니다. 또 같은 상황에 대해 비슷한 표현도 있습니다.
버리자니 아깝고 가지고 있어도 별 가치가 없는 것을 미국에서는 "White elephant(흰 코끼리)"라고 하는데, 한국에서는 "Chicken rib(계륵)"이라고 합니다. 미국의 속담 "The squeaky wheels get the grease(소리나는 바퀴에 기름칠한다)."는 한국 속담 "The crying child get more cake(우는 아이에게 떡 하나 더 준다)."와 비슷합니다.

> ＊속담은 속담일 뿐 현실에서는 "The squeaky wheels get replaced(소리나는 바퀴는 바꿔버린다).", "The crying child get scolded(우는 아이는 혼난다).가 더 많은 것 같습니다.

어색한 미소가 적절한 대답을 대신할 수 없고, 부자연스러운 몸짓이 적절한 말로 설명하는 것을 대체할 수 없습니다. 사전에 상황을 이해해 두는 것이 보다 나은 커뮤니케이션에 도움이 되며, 말할 것을 미리 준비하는 것도 좋은 방법입니다. 그러나 외국인이 미국인처럼 듣고 말하기 위한 가장 좋은 방법은

"Listen, listen, and listen.": 듣고, 듣고 또 들어라
"Speak, speak, and speak.": 말하고, 말하고, 또 말하라


## Why am I so Poor in English?
(2004년 LMC에서 영어공부를 할 때 쓴 글의 번역본이다.)


원어민이 아닌 사람으로서 원어민처럼 말하기에는, 영어가 가장 어려운 언어라고 생각한다. 나는 열네 살 때부터 영어를 공부해 왔고, 미국에 온 지도 4년이나 되었다. 그러나 아직도 다른 사람들을 이해하고, 나 자신을 표현하는 데 많은 어려움이 있다.

내가 영어를 잘 못 하는 데는 몇 가지 이유가 있는 것 같다.
우선, 내가 영어를 항상(all the time) 사용하지 않는다는 것이다. 매일 영어단어의 뜻을 암기하려고 노력은 하지만 또 매일 그만큼 잊어버린다. 기억력이 안 좋을 수도 있겠으나, 보다 중요한 이유는 외운 단어들을 일상생활에서 사용하지 않는다는 것이다. 집에서 한국어를 쓰고, 한국동료들을 만나서도 한국어로 대화하지 않는가? 그러나 미국인과 말할 때는 머릿속에서 한글로 먼저 생각하고 영어로 번역하는 과정을 거치니 제대로 된 영어가 될 수 없다. 미국에 살지만 마음은 딴 데 가 있는 것이다. 영어로 생각하고, 영어로 꿈을 꾸어야 하는데, 이래서는 영어가 늘 수가 없다.

두 번째 이유는 미국인들이 말을 너무 빨리 한다는 데 있다. 나는 라디

오나 TV의 대담프로그램 내용을 거의 알아들을 수 없다. 내가 미국에서 자랐다면 그들이 말에 익숙해져 있겠지만, 그들이 말하는 속도와 불분명한 발음은 내 이해수준을 넘어섰다.

누군가가 아주 빠른 속도로 "I'm sorry if Anthony thod I w'z int'rested 'n 'im, b'd 'e w'z off-base when 'e thod 'e could kiss me."라고 말한다면, 누가 통역해 주지 않는 한 내가 그 말을 어떻게 이해할 수 있는가? 나는 그러한 속도로 말하는 영어에는 익숙하지가 않다.

세 번째 이유는 미국인들이 일상대화에서 속어(Slang)를 너무 많이 쓴다는 데 있다. 텔레비전 시트콤이나 드라마, 라디오 토크쇼를 이해하는 것은 정말 어렵다. Slang은 미국인들 사이에서는 아주 유효한 소통 수단이지만 내가 이해하기에는 절대적인 장애물이다. 처음에 'kicking ass, make money.', 'hooked up.', 'hanging in there.', 'what's up, doc?', 'kicked out.', 'bull shitter.' 이러한 말을 들었을 때는 정말 당황스러웠다. 나는 불분명한 말을 들을 때마다 말한 사람에게 무슨 뜻인지 확인하려고 노력하지만, TV나 라디오에 대해서는 방법이 없다.

마지막이자 가장 중요한 이유는 나의 어휘력 부족이다. 내가 어느 분야에 충분한 정보와 지식이 있다면, 다른 사람의 말을 쉽게 이해하고, 내 의견도 유창하게 표현할 수 있을 것이다. 풋볼의 용어를 잘 알면, 미국친구들과의 대화에 도움이 된다. 소송절차에 대한 용어를 잘 알면, Scott Peterson 재판을 이해하는 데 도움이 된다. 미국친구들과 대화를 잘하려면, 야구팀과 선수들에 대한 정보도 많이 알아 둘 필요가 있다. 미국의 정치, 경제, 세금, 군대, 사회보장, 이라크에 대한 지식은 대통령 후보자의 토론회(debate)를 이해하는 데 도움이 된다.

많은 미국인들이 내게, 더 많이 읽고, 듣고, 말하라고 충고한다. 나도 가능한 한 많이 읽고, 듣고, 말하려고 노력하고 있다, 그러나, 너무나도 자주 사전을 찾아보며 읽는다는 것은 너무 지루하고, 대화의 뜻을 잘 모르는데 듣다 보면 잠이 온다. 내 생각을 충분히 표현할 수 없을 때는 내 자신이 미워진다. 어디 영어 정복의 왕도는 없나?

# 2장

# 미국식 영어표현(American Expressions)

## 'How are you?'의 여러가지 표현

인사할 때는 "Hi." 또는 "How are you?"가 가장 많이 쓰이는 표현이지만, 조금 친해지면 "How are you doing?"이나 "What are you doing?" 또는 "What's up?", "What's going on?", "What' up, doc?", "What's up, bro?" 같은 표현을 쓰는 경우가 많다. 내가 알고 지내던 몇 녀석들은 "Yoyo, what's the dealio?", "What's the scoop ruddy poop?", "What's up, homes skill it?", "What's the dealing?"이라고도 했는데, 다 "What are you doing?" 또는 "What's going on?"이란 뜻이다. 'doc, homies, kid, bro, son' 등은 아주 친한 친구끼리 부르는 호칭이니 오해할 필요는 없다.

## 'How are you?'에 대한 여러가지 대답

우리는 학교에서 외국인이 "How are you?"라고 물으면, 'I'm fine, thank you. How are you?'로 답한다고 배웠다. 그러나 내가 미국인에게 "How are you?"라고 했을 때, 그렇게 대답하는 미국인은 한 사람도 없었다. 가장 일반적인 대답은 "Good, How about you?"였다. Good 은 Fine보다 더 많이 사용되었다. "Hanging in there."(그럭저럭 산다. 마지못해 산다) 또는 "Couldn't be better.", "Never been better."(더할 나위 없이 좋다)라고 하는 사람도 간혹 있었다.

참고로 옛날식 표현이긴 하지만 "groovy."(good이란 의미), "tight." (very good이란 의미)라고도 대답한다고 한다.


## 'Hand'가 들어가는 표현

박수는 영어로 Hand clapping이지만, '그에게 박수를 주세요'라고 하는 표현은 "Give him a big round of applause." 혹은 "Give him a big hand of applause." 또는 그냥 단순히 "Give him a hand."라고 하면 된다.

반면에 '도와주세요'는 "Give me a hand."라고 하면 "help me."라는 뜻이 되고, "Give my right arm for it." 은 '정말 그걸 갖고 싶다'라는 뜻이 된다.


## 동사가 풍부한 영어, 형용사와 부사가 풍부한 한글

영어의 특징은 동사가 많고, 한글은 동사는 단순하나 그 동사를 수식하는 부사가 풍부하다고 할 수 있다. 또 형용사의 경우 영어는 단순한 반면 한글은 너무나 풍부하다.

걷다(walk)라는 단어 하나를 영어표현과 한글표현을 비교해 보자. 물론 한글의 걷다 외에도 거닐다, 산책하다 같은 다른 말들이 있지만 영어가 그만큼 동사가 풍부하다는 의미이다.

Loiter: 어슬렁거리다

Strut: 뽐내며 걷다

Trod: 속보로 걷다

Tip toe: 발끝으로 걷다

Capper: 깡충깡충 뛰어다니다

Prance: 깡충깡충 뛰어다니다

Bustle: 활발하게 움직이다

Plod on: 터벅터벅 걷다

Shuffle: 발을 질질 끌며 걷다

Scurry: 종종걸음으로 걷다

Swagger: 뽐내며 걷다

Stride: 성큼성큼 걷다

Plod: 걷다

Ramble: 목적없이 거닐다

Saunter: 산책하다

Stroll: 산책하다

# 한 단어에 여러가지 의미를 가지는 영어

영어가 어려운 것은 하나의 단어가 전혀 다른 의미로 쓰일 때가 많다는 데 있다. 미국에서 자란 사람이 아니고, 늦은 나이에 미국 가서 살려면, 단어의 알고 있는 뜻 하나만으로는 바보되기 십상이다. 미국인들은 이런 단어의 이중의미로 말장난(Play on words)하는 경우가 많다. 안 속고 잘 적응하려면 그 때 그 때의 상황을 잘 이해할 필요가 있다. 이 책의 많은 부분은 'Play on words'에 할애했다. 간단한 몇 개의 예를 보자.

Husband: n.남편, v.절약하다

Stable: a.안정된, n.마구간(Stall)

Sewer: n.하수구, n.재봉틀

Fare: n.요금, n.음식

Pool: n.물웅덩이, 수영장, n.당구

Rail: n.철도, v.욕을 퍼붓다

Staff: n.직원, n.막대기

Bolt: n.볼트, n.번개

Fair: a.공정한, n.품평회, 장

Brooks: n.시내, v.참다, 허용하다

Crab: n.게, n.불평하는 사람

Lie: v.눕다, n.거짓말

Cram: v.억지로 채워 넣다, v.시험을 위한 벼락치기로 주입식 공부를 하다

# As ~ as Expressions

as busy as a beaver: 매우 바쁜(be extremely busy)

as cool as a cucumber: 매우 침착한(be calm and collected)

as wrinkled as a prune: 매우 주름이 많은(be extremely wrinkled)

as happy as a clam: 매우 행복한(be extremely happy)

as nutty as a fruitcake: 완전히 미친(be totally crazy)

as limp as a noodle: 매우 지친(be totally relaxed)

as easy as pie: 매우 쉬운(be extremely easy)

as blind as a bat: 전혀 볼 수 없는(be unable to see at all)

as sick as a dog: 매우 아픈(be extremely sick)

as gentle as a lamb: 매우 친절하고 유순한(be extremely kind and docile)

as poor as a church mouse: 매우 가난한(very poor)

as mean as a snake: 매우 비열한

as busy as a bee: 매우 바쁜

as inevitable as death and taxes: 피할 수 없는

as dumb as a horse: 우둔한

as safe as houses: 매우 안전한

as dead as a dodo: 완전히 죽은; 쇠락한; 죽은; 존재하지 않는

as sick as a parrot: 컨디션이 아주 나쁜

as white as a sheet: 백지장같이

as red as a beetroot: 홍당무처럼

as good as gold: 얌전한, 예절 바른, 아주 좋은

as bold as brass: 철면피한, 뻔뻔스러운

as thin as a rake: 말라빠진

as like as two peas: 매우 닮은

as fit as fiddle: 매우 건강한

as right as rain: 완전히 정상으로, 매우 건강하여

as crooked as politician: 사기꾼

as silent as an oyster: 대단히 과묵한

as pale as death: 매우 창백한


as long as: ~이면

as many as: 무려 ~나 되는

as good as: ~나 다름없는

as near as: ~하는 정도의


## 일상생활에서 잘못 사용하는 말과 올바른 영어

한국인이 영어인 줄 알고 사용하는 데 미국인들이 이해 못하는 경우가
많다. 이것은 우리가 쓰는 말이 올바른 영어가 아니고, 미국인들은 쓰
지 않는 말이기 때문이다. 미리 알아 두면 미국생활에 도움이 된다.
가장 흔히 틀리는 몇 가지 예를 들어 보자.

카레라이스는 curry and rice 또는 curried rice라 해야 하고, 오므라이
스는 omelet rice이다. 돈가스는 pork cutlet, 비후까스는 beef steak가

맞다. 프림은 cream이 맞는 말이다.

자동차와 관련된 말은 특히 많은데, 본네트는 Hood, 윈도우 브러시는 wiper, 백 미러는 rearview mirror, 크락션은 horn, 핸들은 steering wheel, 빽(빠꾸)는 back up, 빵꾸는 flat tire, 카 센터는 body shop이라 해야 알아듣는다.

미팅은 blind date, 올드 미스는 old maid, 쏠로는 single이 맞다. 사무 용품인 매직펜은 marker, 샤프펜슬은 mechanical pencil, 스카치 테이프는 adhesive tape, 코팅은 laminating, 형광펜은 highlighter, 호치케스는 stapler라고 한다. 의복 중에, 바지는 pants, 팬티 스타킹은 pantyhose, 와이셔츠는 dress shirts, 런닝 셔츠는 T-shirts이다. 의료 용어로 핀셋(Pincette)은 불어이고 영어로는 Tweezers, 바캉스(vacances)도 불어이고 영어는 vacation, 몽타주(Montage) 도 불어이고 영어는 Police sketch, 깁스(Gibs)는 독일어이고 영어로는 Cast, 링겔(Ringer)도 독일어이고 영어로는 IV 또는 Fluids, 아르바이트(arbeit)도 독일어이고 영어는 part-time job이라 한다.

이 외에도, 아이쇼핑은 window shopping, 콘센트는 a wall outlet, 믹서는 blender, 밴드는 band aid, 애프터 서비스는 After-sale service, 핸드폰은 cellular phone, 비닐 백은 plastic bag, 탤런트는 TV star라 한다.

# 영어와 한글의 비슷한 속담

미국 속담이 우리 속담과 너무 유사한 것들이 많아 정리해 보았다. 어디 가나 사람 사는 세상 비슷한가 보다. 다만 문화적 차이로 인해 뜻은 같아도 표현방식이 좀 다르니 비교해 보면 재미를 느낄 수 있다.

Everything you do comes back to you in time: 인과응보

A small bite of a big elephant: 낙숫물이 바위 뚫는다

Goes around comes around: 뿌린대로 거둔다

Too many cooks spoil the broth: 사공이 많으면 배가 산으로 간다

One stone kills two birds: 일석이조

Talk to a brick wall: 소 귀에 경 읽기

Add insult to injury: 설상가상, 엎친 데 덮친 격

The apple falls close to the tree: Like father, like son: 부전자전

A living dog is better than a dead lion. : 살아 있는 개가 죽은 사자보다 낫다

A misfortune turns into a blessing: 전화위복

Barking dogs seldom bite. : 짖는 개는 좀처럼 물지 않는다

Every dog has his day. : 쥐구멍에도 볕들 날 있다

Let sleeping dogs lie. : 긁어 부스럼 만들지 마라

Make a mountain out of a molehill : 침소봉대하다

Love me, love my dog. : 아내가 귀여우면 처가집 말뚝 보고도 절을 한다.

Still waters run deep: 잔잔한 물이 깊다. 벼는 익을수록 고개 숙인다.

Absent minded: 마음이 콩밭에 가 있다.

You're taking out your frustration on: 한강에서 뺨 맞고 종로에서 눈 흘긴다.

## 스포츠 관련 표현들

미국에서 살면서 사람들과 어울려 대화를 해나가려면, 풋볼, 야구, 농구에 대해 어느 정도의 지식을 갖고 있는 게 매우 중요하다. 다음의 몇몇 사례를 보자. 바로 이해할 수 있을 정도로 지역별 연고팀과 대표선수 몇 명쯤 외워 둘 필요가 있다.

49ers are dead beats, Raiders are class act.
  (49ers는 샌프란시스코, Raiders는 오클랜드 연고의 풋볼팀 이름이니까 이 말은 Raiders 팬이 한 말이겠다. Dead beats는 trouble maker라는 뜻이고, class act는 good team이라는 뜻이다.)

신문 Sports 란의 제목을 보고 내용을 바로 이해한다면 영어실력 톱클라스로 인정할 수 있다.

Pistons the Stars in Opener(디트로이트 연고의 농구팀 Pistons가 첫 게임을 이겼다.)

Bats and Arms come up big for A's, Giants(오클랜드 연고의 야구팀 A's와 샌프란시스코 연고의 Giants 팀, 둘 다 방망이와 투수가 끝내줬다.)

Flames, Lightening down to one-game finale(캘거리 연고 아이스하키팀 Flames와 템파베이 연고팀인 Lightening 이 마지막 한판으로 승부를 가리게 되었다.)

Martin gets breaks, stop winless slide(카레이서 Martin이 운 좋게도 마침내 우승했다.)

스포츠 얘기를 할 때는 속어를 사용하는 경우가 참 많다.
Hustle은 '내기에서 남을 속이다'라는 뜻인데, 내기 골프에서 Handie를 속일 때 "You hustle me"라고 하면 된다. Bull shitter는 '거짓말쟁이, 허풍장이'라는 뜻이고, Sand bagger는 '말로는 못한다고 하면서 실제로는 잘하는 사람'을 지칭한다.


## 저질 표현들

미국인들 중 특히 교육을 제대로 받지 못한 흑인이나 멕시칸 중에는 일상대화가 저질스러운 욕으로 가득 찬 경우가 많다. 우리가 이런 단어를 일상대화에서 사용해서는 안 되겠지만, 그들이 하는 얘기를 알아들을 수는 있어야 할 것 같아서 몇 가지를 소개한다.
우선 Fuck, Dam, Shit, Ass, Sucks 같은 단어가 들어가면 무조건 저질 표현이라 생각하면 된다.

You're horse's ass: 난 못 믿겠다

You screwed me: 너 나에게 잘 못 했어.

It sucks: 젠장

Blow smoke up your ass: 아첨해라.

I feel like going out tie one on: 밤새 맥주를 마시고 싶다.

I feel like shit in the morning: 아침에 숙취가 있을 것 같다.

You look like shit: 안 좋아 보인다.

Pain in the ass(PIA): 죽을 지경이다.

You know what burns my ass?: '정말 화나게 하는 것은….' 하면서 말을 시작하는 표현


주로 젊은 흑인들이 쓰는 저질 영어를 Ebonics라고 하는데, 아주 젊잖은 표현들도 이들은 일부러 저질스럽게 표현하는 것 같다. 절대 사용하지는 않아야겠지만, 들었을 때 이해를 할 필요는 있다. 몇 가지 예를 보자.


My! You're a lovely lady.(오! 당신은 사랑스러운 숙녀입니다.)

: Damn!! Yousa fine mother fucker!

Let's go for a ride, shall we?(우리 드라이브를 갈까요?)

: Hey baby, jump in my low rider and let's rotate dees tires.

You are beautiful. I'd like make love to you.(당신은 아름답습니다. 사랑하고 싶군요.)

: Damn bitch, you stupid fly, Lemme pull up that bumper and smack dat monkey.

Hello, Sir.(여보세요, 선생님)

　: Whaddup, dog!

May I borrow some money?(돈 좀 빌려주시겠습니까?)

　: Hey, Lemme hold some ends, I'll hit you back on dee first my
　　brother.

You don't have it, Thanks anyway.(안 가지고 있다고요? 어쨌든 감사
　합니다.)

　: Fucking you.

I admire yourfashionable shoes.(당신의 유행하는 신발이 참 좋습니다.)

　: Drop them Nikes off your ass before I blast you mother fucker.


## 철강회사 현장에서 사용되는 표현들

몇 번을 강조했지만, 미국 철강회사의 작업자들이 사용하는 용어는 아
무리 공부해도 끝이 없다. 그러나 모르면 대화가 되지 않기 때문에 어
쨌든 배워야 한다. 내가 20년간 현장에서 배운 표현들 중 심한 것들은
여과하여 여기 정리해 둔다.


Kick ass, take the names: 설비도 잘 돌리고, 출근부에 도장도 찍고
I came to kick ass and chew bubble gum, but I am all out bubble
gum.: 설비도 잘 돌리고, 여유도 가지려 했는데, 하루종일 껌만 씹었다.

The facility was fully cranking: 설비가 잘 돌아가고 있다

When was it hooked up?: 언제 설치했어?

They are off the hook: 그들은 책임이 없다.


Hump day: 수요일(Hump는 '낙타등'이란 뜻)

Over the hump day: 가장 어려운 단계를 지났다.

TGIF(Thanks God in Friday): 내일부터 주말이다


Yada yada yada: 기타 등등

Pee on: 밑바닥 인생

You're up: 네가 먼저 시작해라(회의에서)

You're nickel: 네 차례다(원래 의미는 '네가 지불해야 된다'라는 뜻)


Chilling like a villain: 우리말 표현으로는 '그럼 수고해'에 가까움.(Take it easy)

You are all mapped up: MAP 교육과정을 받고 온 사람에게 하는 말 만일 SAS 교육을 받고 왔다면 "You are all sassed up."

You da man: 잘 했어.

Are you just cruising around?: 그냥 돌아보는 거야?(Walking around)

Our bogey is 92% yield ratio: 우리 목표는 실수율 92 %다.

You killed the yield: 실수율 목표 달성했다.

TTM beat the tons: TTM은 목표 달성했다.

Low hanging fruit: 하기 쉬운

Long shot: 하기 어려운

Accrue the money: 회계용어지만 현장 매니저들이 자주 사용하는 말로써, 비용이 많이 발생하는 부품을 구입할 때 실제 구입하기 몇 달 전부터 미리 비용으로 인식하여 비용을 평준화시키는 방법.

There is a little screw at thing going out here: 뭔가 잘못되었다

I am not ruling it out: 아니라고 말하진 않는다, 그럴 수도 있겠다

You can rule that out: 그건 이슈가 아니다

Heard from horse's mouth: 어떤 사람에게 직접 들었다

# 3장

---

# 미국문화의 이해

## 미국을 이해하는 데 도움되는 표현

'Friendliness'는 얕은 우정으로, 미국인은 대부분 낯선 사람에게도 친절하지만,
'Friendship' 은 깊은 우정을 뜻하며, 정말 어려울 때 서로 도와주는 친구가 되기는 쉽지 않다.

Buy union: 노조(union)가 있는 회사 제품을 사고, 노조(union)가 있는 매장을 이용하라. 예를 들면, 월마트(Wal-mart) 대신 세이프웨이(Safeway)를 이용하라.

"Keep your slate clean": 더 이상 범죄 저지르지 마라
어원: 옛날의 학교에서는 slate(점판암) + chalk(분필)+ eraser(지우게)를 가지고 가르칠 때가 있었다. 한번 글씨를 쓴 slate는 깨끗이 지워야 다음 글씨를 쓸 수 있었다

Knock on woods: 일이 잘되고 있을 때, 계속 그 상태를 유지하기를 바란다는 뜻으로 나무를 서너 번 톡톡 침.

Wet back nation: 불법으로 국경을 넘어오는 멕시칸을 지칭. 강을 헤엄쳐 건너면 등이 젖게 마련이므로 불법 월경자를 이렇게 부르게 됐다. 철조망(Barbed wire fence)을 뚫고 넘어오는 사람 포함.

Advance directives: 주로 노인 환자에게 해당. 만일의 경우 어떻게 할 것인가에 대한 여러가지 설문, 산소 호흡기를 달거냐 말거냐 등

Grim Reaper: 저승사자(a messenger of the other world), 큰 낫을 들고 망토를 걸친 해골 모습의 사신(死神)

Society snobs: 지위·재산 등을 숭배하는 사람, 웃사람에게 아첨하고 아랫사람에게 거만부리는 사람

It's gonna blow over.: 큰 문제없이 괜찮아질 거야. 한국식 표현으로는 '부부싸움은 칼로 물 베기'

"I'll be pushing up daisies": 데이지 꽃(프랑스 국화, 묘지석 앞에 많이 자람)을 땅밑에서 밀어 올린다는 뜻이므로 죽은 지 오래됐다는 의미.

You are killing a lot of trees today.: 종이를 낭비하는 사람에게 하는 말. 종이는 나무로 만드니까.

Who raised you?: 대단히 무례한 사람에게 하는 말. '니 애비가 누구야?'
Keep my Rhetoric low key: 증거나 사실에 의하지 않고 너무 감정에

치우쳐 목소리 크게 흥분하지 말고, 차분히 냉정해라

Boys will be boys; men will be men. : 애들이 다 그렇지
That's a little creepy. : 무섭다
I'm kinda creeped out. : 편안하지 못하다
Cut-and-dried: 흑과 백처럼 아주 분명한
I don't buy the 'favorism' thing. : 동의하지 않는다

Top cookie: 머리가 좋고 유머감각도있는 사람(top duck)
Underdogs: 다크 호스
Top dogs: 우승 예상자
Skid row bum: 집 없는 노숙 건달

Day Light Saving Time: 여름에 1시간 당기는 시스템(썸머타임)
Spring forward: 봄에 한 시간을 당기다(set clock 1 hour ahead)
Fall back: 가을에 한 시간을 늦추다(set clock 1 hour back)

Split it in two. : 둘로 나누어 달라
I want two servings. : 2인분 달라, 곱배기 달라

Honey do list: 아내가 남편에게 해달라고 요구하는 일 목록. 일반적
으로 'Honey, baby, you do this for me.'라고 아양을 떨면서 얘기함.

Been there, done that. : 그만 얘기해라, 다 아는 얘기잖아

I have been around the block. : 경험이 많다, 잘 알고 있다

It's not my first BBQ. : 나도 초짜는 아니야

Be there, be square. : 가서 봐라


I'm sitting on my wallet. : 내 키가 큰 것이 아니라, 지갑을 깔고 앉았기 때문에 커 보인다, 즉 그만큼 내 지갑이 두둑하다.(여자들이 금방 좋아할 거다)


Young and full of beans. : 젊은 혈기에 버릇없이 말썽부리고 다니는


Stupid is as stupid does, Handsome is as handsome does : 외모나 지적수준으로 판단하지 말고 행위(행동, 생활)로 판단하라


Talking jive, jive talking : 기만적이고 과장된 의미 없는 말을 하다

Landslide : 선거에서 압도적으로 이기다(반대표현: by a whisker, by a nose)


Boot & boom : 농담에 대해 농담으로 되받아 치기

Wishy-washy : 우유부단한, 김빠진, 시시한


Buying in : 적극적으로 참여하려고 하는

Burning rubber : 신발바닥에 불이 나도록

Loosey goosey : 얼렁뚱땅, 좋은 게 좋은, loose goose(무리와 떨어진 거위)에서 유래

A slam dunk: 확실한 것

Pink slip: 해고통지서 또는 자동차 등록증

Kiss off: 해고하다

Butterflies in the stomach: 안달하다, 안절부절하다.

Elevator does not go to the top: 좀 우둔한 사람을 일컫는 말

He or she is not the brightest bulb in the chandelier: 좀 우둔한 사람

The light is on, nobody is home: 좀 우둔한 사람

He is missing the boat: 나는 준비가 되어 있는데, 상대방은 아직 관심이 없는 것 처럼 보일 때 쓰는 표현

24, 7: 항상(하루 24시간, 일주일 7일 동안)

I can make chicken soup out of chicken shit.: 난 뭐든지 할 수 있다.

I'm domestic now.: 현재는 집안일 하고 있다.(빨래, 청소…)

My gut feeling: 논리적인 방법이 아니고 그저 나의 감으로 느끼는 것.

Does it ring a bell?: 뭐 생각나는 것 없으세요?

Now I have seen everything: 별일 다 보겠네, 해가 서쪽에서 뜰 일이네.

Over my dead body: 내가 죽기 전에는 안 돼, 내 눈에 흙이 들어가기 전에는 안 돼.

Stop dogging me: 험담 좀 그만해라.

You talk in trash: 말도 안되는 허풍 떨고 있네.

10 % cross the board: 모든 항목을 일괄적으로 10 %씩
Vocal minority: 목소리 큰 소수
Tie up any loose ends.: 새로운 일을 하기 위해 기존 일을 잘 마무리
짓다.

Bar scene: 혼자 가서 짝을 찾아 즐기는 그런 술집
Face-saving statement: 남의 기분을 상하게 하지 않는 말
He's upstairs.: 죽었다

다람쥐 쳇바퀴 돌 듯: 사전을 찾아보면 다람쥐는 squirrel, 쳇바퀴는
The frame of a sieve이다. 그렇다면, '다람쥐 쳇바퀴 돌 듯'은 'It looks
like a squirrel in the frame of a sieve.'이 되어야 하는데, 실제 미국식
표현은 'It looks like a gerbil in the exercise wheel.'이다.

## Tongue twister(발음하기 어려운 말놀이)

She sells sea shells at the seaside.
She shows the short shoes to Sherry.
How much wood would a woodchuck chuck if a woodchuck could
chuck wood?
'경찰청 창살 쇠창살, 검찰청 창살 철창살'과 같은 식의 영어 표현.

각 나라의 언어는 이와 유사한 말놀이 문화가 대개 다 있다.


## 무슬림(회교도)의 이해

미국인들은 대부분 개신교 신자이지만 요즘은 인종이 다양해지는 만큼 종교도 다양해져 있다. 미국내 무슬림 교도들은 알게 모르게 차별을 받고, 일반 미국인들의 경계대상이기도 하지만, 그들과 대화하고 이해하려면 그들의 종교에 대한 약간의 상식은 매우 중요하다.


FARAZ(Five pillars of Muslim): 무슬림의 5대 의무(must do)

  1) EMUN: Believe in one God without seeing him

  2) SALAT: Pray five times a day

  3) RAMADAN: One-month fast day time for purification

  4) HAJ: The capable people visit Meka

  5) ZAKAT: Help poor people

SUNNA: 무슬림에게 권장사항, 수염기르는 것 등, 의무는 아님
       (better to do)

WAZIB: 하면 좋고 안 해도 그만인 것(good to do)

## The Stella Awards

미국사회는 '변호사 천국' 아니 '변호사 지옥' 이다. 미국에서 가장 못 믿을 사람에 대한 여론조사를 한 적이 있는데, '1위가 자동차정비사 (Mechanic), 2위가 변호사(Lawyer), 3위가 정치인(Politician)이더라'는 얘기가 있다. 1992년 'Stella Liebeck'이라는 할머니가 맥도날드에서 커피를 무릎에 쏟아 화상을 입었는데, 뉴멕시코 배심원은 그녀에게 2.9백만 달러(약 30억원)를 배상하라는 판결을 내렸다. 이 소송에서 유래하여, 'The Stella Awards'는 악명 높은 가짜 사건을 포함하여, 말도 안 되는, 너무나 충격적인 소송사건을 의미하게 되었고, 매년 선정한다. 미국에서 소송을 걸면, 소송당사자의 변호사들만 돈을 버는 경우가 허다하다.

여기 2015년 Stella Awards 우승자 중 1, 2, 3위를 소개한다.

(1위)
오클라호마에 사는 머브 그래진스키(여)는 32피트짜리 캠핑카 (Winnebago motor)를 사서, 첫 운전으로 풋볼 게임을 보러 가기 위해 고속도로를 탔다. 시속 70마일로 '크루즈 콘트롤'로 셋팅해놓고, 샌드위치를 만들려고 운전석을 벗어나 뒷칸으로 갔다. 당연히 차는 고속도로를 벗어나 쳐 박히고 뒤집어졌다. 머브는 '크루즈 콘트롤 시에는 운전석을 벗어나서는 안 된다는 조항이 매뉴얼에 없다'고 캠핑카 회사에 소송을 걸었고, 오클라호마 법원은 '$1,750,000(약 20억 원)과 새 캠핑카를 주라'고 판결을 내렸다. 그 후 캠핑카 회사는 매뉴얼을 보완했다.

Mrs. Merv Grazinski, of Oklahoma City, Oklahoma, who purchased new 32-foot Winnebago motor home. On her first trip home, from an OU football game, having driven on to the freeway, she set the cruise control at 70 mph and calmly left the driver's seat to goto the back of the Winnebago to make herself a sandwich. Not surprisingly, the motor home left the freeway, crashed and overturned. Also not surprisingly, Mrs. Grazinski sued Winnebago for not putting in the owner's manual that she couldn't actually leave the driver's seat while the cruise control was set. The Oklahoma jury awarded her, are you sitting down? $1,750,000 PLUS a new motor home. Winnebago actually changed their manuals as a result of this suit, just in case Mrs. Grazinski has any relatives who might also buy a motor home.

(2위)

델라웨어 주 그레이몬트에 사는 카라 월튼은, 집 가까이 있는 나이트 클럽 화장실에서 변기커버 교체비용 3.5달러를 안 내려고 화장실 창문을 넘어 나오다 떨어져서 앞니 2개가 부러졌다. 카라는 나이트클럽을 상대로 소송을 걸었고, 법원은 '그녀에게 $12,000(1천3백만 원)과 치아 치료비를 배상하라'고 판결했다.

Kara Walton, of Claymont, Delaware sued the owner of a night club in a nearby city because she fell from the bathroom Window to the floor, knocking out her two front teeth. Even though Ms. Walton was trying to sneak through the lady's room window to avoid paying the $3.50 cover charge, the jury said the night club had to pay her $12,000.... oh, yeah, plus dental expenses.

(3위)

펜실베니아 랑카스터에 사는 엠바 카슨은 식당에서 청량음료(soft drink)를 남자친구에게 던졌다. 약 30초 후에 그녀는 마루바닥에 있는 soft drink에 미끄러져서 꼬리뼈를 다쳤다. 엠바는 식당을 상대로 '바닥에 soft drink가 있었다'는 이유로 소송을 제기했고, 법원은 '그녀에게 $113,500(1억2천5백만 원)을 배상하라'고 판결했다.

Amber Carson of Lancaster, Pennsylvania because a jury ordered a Philadelphia restaurant to pay her $113,500 after she slipped on a spilled soft drink and broke her tailbone. The reason the soft drink was on the floor: Ms. Carson had thrown it at her boyfriend 30 seconds earlier during an argument. What ever happened to people being responsible for their own actions?

# Wine에 관한 미국인들의 생각

- Alcohol is not the answer, it just makes you forget the question.
  (알코올이란 답이 아니라 문제를 잊게만 할 뿐이다)

- Coffee keeps me busy until it's acceptable to drink wine.
  (커피란 내가 와인을 마실 수 있을 때까지 나의 무료함을 달래주
  는 것이다)

- It doesn't matter if the glass is half empty or half full.
  (술잔이 반이 찼는지 반이 비었는지는 아무런 문제가 안 된다)

- There is clearly room for more wine.
  (와인을 더 먹을 배는 항상 있다)

- At my age I need glasses.
  (내 나이가 되면 몇 잔 필요하다)

- Wine, cheaper than botox and paralyzes more muscles.
  (와인은 보톡스보다 싸지만 보톡스보다 더 많은 근육을 마비시킨
  다)

- Wine, now cheaper than gas. Drink, don't drive.
  (이제는 와인이 가솔린보다 싸 졌다. 운전하지 말고 마셔라)
  * Don't drink and drive.: 음주운전 하지 마라

- I drink wine, because I don't like to keep things bottled up.
  (내가 와인을 마시는 이유는 나를 귀찮게 하는 것이 뭔지 남에게
  털어놓고 싶기 때문이다)
  * to keep things bottled up: I don't tell other people what is bothering
  me.

- Red bull gives you wings, alcohol gives you 4x4.

  (Red Bull을 마시면 날아갈 듯한 기분이고 와인을 마시면 힘이 솟는다)

  * Red Bull은 에너지 드링크 상표명이고 4x4는 Four Wheel Drive를 의미함

- I tried cooking supper with wine together. Didn't go so well. After 5 glasses I forgot why I was even in the kitchen.

  (와인을 마시면서 저녁을 준비하려고 했는데 잘 되지 않았다. 다섯 잔을 마신 후에는 내가 왜 부엌에 있는지 잊어버렸다)

- The secret of enjoying a good wine:

  (와인을 즐기는 비밀)

  1. Open the bottle to allow it to breathe.

  (병을 열어 와인이 숨 쉬게 한다)

  2. If it does not look like it's breathing, give it mouth-to-mouth.

  (숨 쉬는 것 같지 않으면, 구강 대 구강 심폐소생술을 실시한다)

  * mouth-to-mouth 는 CPR (Cardiopulmonary Resuscitation: 심폐소생술) 용어.

- Wine 시음 법 (5S)

  See(본다), Swirl(빙빙 흔든다), Smell(냄새 맡는다), Sip(맛본다), Say(평가한다)

# 'UP'을 좋아하는 미국인

There is a two-letter word that perhaps has more meanings than any other two-letter word, and that is "UP."

It's easy to understand UP, meaning toward the sky or at the top of the list, but when we awaken in the morning, why do we wake UP? At a meeting, why does a topic come UP? Why do we speak UP and why are the officers UP for election and why is it UP to the secretary to write UP a report?

We call UP our friends. And we use it tobrighten UP a room, polish UP the silver, we warm UP the leftovers and clean UP the kitchen. We lock UP the house and some guys fix UP the old car. At other times the little word has real special meaning. People stir UP trouble, line UP for tickets, work UP an appetite, and think UP excuses. To be dressed is one thing but to be dressed UP is special.

And this UP is confusing: A drain must be opened UP because it is stopped UP. We open UP a store in the morning but we close it UP at night.

We seem to be pretty mixed UP about UP! To be knowledgeable about the proper uses of UP, look the word UP in the dictionary.

In a desk-sized dictionary, it takes UP almost 1/4th of the page and can add UP to about thirty definitions. If you are UP to it, you might try building UP a list of the many ways UP is used. It will take UP a lot of your time, but if you don't give UP, you may wind UP with a hundred or more. When it threatens to rain, we say it is clouding UP. When the sun comes out, we say it is clearing UP.

When it rains, it wets the earth and often messes things UP.
When it doesn't rain for a while, things dry UP.

One could go on and on, but I'll wrap it UP, for now my time is UP, so……. Time to shut UP!

So, Now, what's UP with you?

## 영어 속담(Idioms from Ancient history)

Eagles don't catch flies.
독수리는 파리를 잡지 않는다.

Early birds catch the worms.
일찍 일어나는 새가 벌레를 잡는다.

Easier said than done.

행해지는 것보다 말해지는 것이 더 쉽다. 말하기는 쉬우나 행하기는 어렵다.

East or west, home is best. (= There is nothing/no place like home.)

동쪽에서나 서쪽에서나 집이 최고다. 집 같은 곳은 없다.

Easy come, easy go. (= Soon got/gotten, soon gone/spent.)

쉽게 얻은 것은 쉽게 나간다.

Empty vessels make the most/greatest sound/noise.

The worst wheel of the cart creaks most.

빈 배가 가장 큰 소리를 낸다. 빈수레가 요란하다. 가장 나쁜 바퀴가 가장 삐걱거린다.

Enough is as good as feast.

배부름은 진수성찬이나 마찬가지다.

Even a worm will turn.

Tread on a worm and it will turn.

벌레조차도 꿈틀할 수 있다. 지렁이도 밟으면 꿈틀한다.

Every bean has its black.

모든 콩은 검은 부분이 있다. 모든 사람/물건에는 결점이 있다.

Every cock crow in its own dunghill.

모든 수탉은 그 자신의 거름더미 안에서만 운다. 자기 집 안에서만 큰 소리 치기.


Every dog has his day.

견공들도 한때가 있다. 쥐구멍에도 볕들 날이 있다.


Every Jack has his Gill.

모든 남자는 그의 짝이 있다. 헌 짚신도 짝이 있다.


Every man for his own trade.

Every one to his trade.

모든 사람은 그 자신의 장사를 위해 있다.(장사에는 각각 전문이 있다.)


Every man has a fool in his sleeve.

모든 사람은 그의 소매 안에 바보를 가지고 있다. 약점 없는 사람은 없다.


Every minute seems like a thousand.

매분이 천 분과 같다. 일각여삼추(一刻如三秋).


Every rose has its thorn.

모든 장미는 가시를 가지고 있다.

Every why has a wherefore.
핑계 없는 무덤 없다.


Everybody's business is nobody's business.
모든 사람의 일은 그 누구의 일도 아니다. 공동 책임은 무책임


Everyone has his own standard.
제 눈에 안경


Everyone has a skeleton in his closet/cupboard.
모든 사람은 그의 찬장 속에 해골을 가지고 있다. 털어서 먼지 안 나는
사람 없다.
모든 사람에게는 감추고 싶은 비밀이 있다.


Everything comes to those who wait.
모든 것은 기다리는 자에게 온다. 기다리는 자에게 때가 온다.


Everything has a beginning.
모든 것은 시작이 있다.


Everything has its match.
헌 짚신도 짝이 있다.

Example is better than precept.

Practice is better than precept.

본보기를 보이는 것이 가르치는 것보다 낫다.


Experience is the best teacher.

경험이 최고의 스승.


The grass is greener on the other side of the fence.

남의 집 잔디가 더 푸르다. 남의 떡이 커 보인다.


Walls have ears.

벽에도 귀가 있다. 낮말은 새가 듣고 밤말은 쥐가 듣는다.


The pot calls the kettle black.

가마솥이 주전자보고 검다고 말하다. 똥 묻은 개가 겨 묻은 개를 나무란다.


Talk of the devil and you'll hear the flutter of his wings.

악마에 대해 말하면 너는 그의 날개치는 소리를 들을 것이다. 호랑이도 제 말 하면 온다.


To teach a fish how to swim.

물고기에게 수영하는 방법을 가르치기. 공자 앞에서 문자 쓴다.

Time and tide wait for no man.
시간과 조류는 사람을 기다리지 않는다. 세월은 사람을 기다리지 않는다.

Birds of a feather flock together.
같은 깃털을 가진 새끼리 같이 모인다. 유유상종.
가재는 게 편. 과부 사정은 홀아비가 안다.

The sparrow near a school sings the primer.
학교 가까이에 있는 참새는 라틴어 입문서를 노래한다. 서당개 삼 년에 풍월 한다.

A loaf of bread is better than the song of many birds.
빵 한 덩어리가 수많은 새들의 노랫소리보다 낫다. 금강산도 식후경.

A stitch in time saves nine.
제 때의 한 바늘이 아홉 바늘을 던다. 쇠뿔도 단김에 빼라.

Mend the barn after the horse is stolen.
소 잃고 외양간 고친다.

Go home and kick the dog.
집에 가서 개나 걷어차다. 종로에서 뺨 맞고 한강 가서 눈 흘긴다.

Rome was not built in a day.

로마는 하루 아침에 이루어지지 않았다. 첫술에 배 부르랴. 천리길도 한걸음부터.


Face the music.

자진하여 책임을 지다. 당당히 비판을 받다.


Casting pearls before swine.

돼지 앞에 진주를 던지기. 돼지발에 편자.


It's no use crying over spilt milk.

우유를 엎질러 놓고 울어봤자 소용없다.


It takes two to tango.

탱고를 추려면 둘이 필요하다. 손뼉도 마주쳐야 소리가 난다.


Kill two birds with one stone.

돌멩이 하나로 새 두 마리 죽이기. 일석이조. 배 먹고 이 닦기. 도랑 치고 가재 잡기.


Ignorance is bliss.

무식은 축복. 모르는 게 약이다.

You've cried wolf too many times.
계속해서 늑대를 부를 수는 없다. 같은 거짓말을 반복할 수는 없다.


Nothing ventured, nothing gained.
모험이 없으면, 얻는 것도 없다. 호랑이 굴에 들어가야 호랑이를 잡는다.


One rotten apple spoils the barrel.
하나의 썩은 사과가 한 통의 사과를 상하게 한다. 미꾸라지 한 마리가 온 웅덩이를 흐린다.


A friend in need is a friend indeed.
곤경에 빠졌을 때의 친구야말로 참다운 친구이다.


A picture is worth a thousand words.
천마디의 말보다 한 번 보는 게 더 낫다. 백문불여일견.


No smoke without fire.
불 없이는 연기 날 수 없다. 아니 땐 굴뚝에 연기 나랴.


Every cloud has a silver lining.
모든 구름은 은색 테를 가지고 있다. 괴로움이 있으면 즐거움도 있다.

The early bird catches the worm.

일찍 일어나는 새가 벌레를 잡는다. 부지런해야 성공한다.


A leopard can't change his spots.

표범은 자기의 반점을 바꿀 수 없다. 세 살 버릇 여든 간다. 제 버릇 개 못 준다.

제2부

# 만화로 배우는 미국,
# 미국영어

미국식 영어를 제대로 한 번 배워야겠다고 여러가지 방법을 시도했다가, 우연히 신문에 연재되는 만화에 흥미를 가지게 되었다. 미국문화와 미국식 사고 그리고 미국식 유머에 익숙치 않은 나로서는 이해하기 힘든 부분이 많았다. 자격증 가진 영어선생님과 주1회, 한 시간씩 영어공부를 할 때에도 신문만화를 많이 접했고, 평소에 정말 이해가 안될 때는 직장 동료들에게 그 의미를 물어보면서 함께 대화할 기회도 늘렸다. 만화는 의외로 미국과 미국영어를 이해하는 데 큰 도움이 되었다. 여기에 내가 공부했던 만화들(Cartoons)을 몇 가지 카테고리로 묶어 소개한다. 만화가(Cartoonist)의 이름은 밝히지만, 제목을 보고 실제의 만화를 기대하시는 분들도 있을 텐데, 만화 자체는 그대로 옮기지 못하고, 만화의 내용을 한글로 설명할 수밖에 없어 좀 아쉽다. 미국과 미국영어를 이해하는 데 도움되기를 바란다.

# 1장

## 주제별 만화

### 'Play on Words'를 사용한 만화

영어에는 하나의 단어가 여러가지 의미를 가지는 경우가 정말 많다. 이러한 단어들을 사용하여 교묘하게 말장난하는 것을 'Play on Words' 라고 하는데, 몇 가지 사례들을 보자.

- 골퍼: "I've been told I have a very fluid golf swing!"
(Whack: 휘두르는 소리)
(Splash!: 물에 퐁당 빠지는 소리)
캐디: "No comment!"
  * 'Fluid'는 1) '부드럽게 휘두르다(Smooth swing)'라는 뜻도 있고 2) '액체 (Liquid water)'라는 뜻도 있다

- 뚱보남편이 바지를 입으면서 힘들게 지퍼를 올리고는 아내에게
"It's a good thing you wear the pants in the family, because I can hardly fit into 'em anymore!"(이제 바지를 입기가 힘들다)
아내: "You can still wear the sweat-pants in the family."
  * 'wear the pants'는 1) '바지를 입다'라는 뜻이지만 2) '가족 안에서(in

the family) 주도권을 쥐고 있다'라는 뜻도 있다. 같은 의미로 'top dog, dominant authority'라고도 한다.

• 서점에서

"The campus bookstore is huge!"

"How on earth are we supposed to find all the books we need?"

　(복도에 세워져 있는 'All books shelved by author'라는 간판을 보고는)

"WOW! It's not enough that they write the books, they have to shelve them, too?"

　　* 'Shelve'는 1) '선반이나 서랍에 정리해 넣다'라는 뜻도 있고, 이 경우는 2) '작가
　　의 이름순으로 정리되어 있다'는 의미이다.


• 식당 앞에 줄 서 있는 손님들

"I hear this place is great!"

"It better be."

The popularity of the restaurant resulted in customers becoming waiters.

　　* 'waiter'는 1) '종업원, 웨이터'를 뜻하지만, 여기서는 2) '기다리는 사람'이란 뜻


• 아빠: "I can't find my cell phone."

"I know it's here in the house someplace."

(Cell-phone으로 계속 text를 보내고 있는 아들에게)

"Norman, do me a favor and call my cell phone!"

아들: "Hey, cell phone!"하고 외친다.

* 아빠는 'Call'을 1) '전화를 걸다'라는 뜻으로 사용했고 아들은 2) '부르다'라는 뜻으로 이해했다.

• 아빠:(손목시계를 보며)

"…17 minutes, 31 seconds… 17 minutes, 33 seconds…"

"I'm never going to make it!!": I can't do this.

아들: "What's wrong with Dad?"

엄마: "He's having a physical tomorrow morning."

(Physical – exam)

"The doctor told him to fast for 12 hours!"

아들: "Why do day call it a fast' when the time goes so slow?"

* 엄마는 'Fast'를 1) '굶다'라는 뜻으로 사용했고 아들은 2) '빠르다'라는 뜻으로 이해

• 운전을 하고 있는 중

아빠: "Oops! we needed to turn around, Penny! That street has no outlet!"('NO OUTLET'이라는 sign을 보고는)

딸: "No outlet?"

"Where do they plug in their curling irons?"

* 아빠는 'Outlet'을 1) '출구'라는 뜻으로 말했고, 딸은 2) '벽의 소켓'으로 이해.

* 'curling iron'은 헤어 아이론

• 비행기의 이코노미석 중간 좌석에 앉은 젊은이, 양옆 좌석에는 체격이 건장한 대학 풋볼팀 코치들이 앉아 있다.

"This is the last time I fly coach."

> * 'Coach'는 1) 코치 2) 마차
> * 얼마나 불편한지 '다시는 안 타겠다'고 생각

- 홈 팀과 원정 팀 1:1 동점상황

The soccer match in Bangkok was 'Thai Game'

> * Thai 와 Tie 대비

- 4:4 동점인 채로 깜깜한 시각에 16회 inning을 경기하고 있는 야구 선수:

"It's so late. I wish I was in bed."

The player on the third base was anxious for the game to be over and wanted to go home.

> * 'go home'은 1) '집에 가다'라는 뜻이지만 2) '홈 플레이트를 밟다'라는 뜻도 있다.

- Buy 1 get 5 free!

A: "Wow! This is big."

B: "This is our biggest sales week of the year."

The 4th of July caused sales at the fireworks stored to "Skyrockets"

> * 'Skyrocket' 은 1) '급등하다'는 의미와 2) '폭죽이 로켓처럼 하늘로 솟아오르다' 는 두가지 의미를 포함

- Congratulations on one million!

사장: "Great job everyone! We did it!"

직원들: "Yes! Way to go! This is so exciting!

After selling their one million batteries, everyone at the battery factory was charged up.

> * 'charge up'은 1) '배터리를 충전하다'라는 뜻도 있고, 2) '흥분하다'라는 뜻도 있다.

• 묘지에서

여자: "This is our plot, but that's on my husband's name!"

남자: "I can't believe this! This is a serious blunder."

The mix−up at the cemetery was a(grave mistake): 묘지에서의 혼란은 심각한 실수였다.

> * blunder: 실수(mistake, error)
> * 'Grave'는 1) 명사로는 '묘지(place where dead person is buried)'라는 뜻이지만 2) 형용사로는 '심각한(serious)'이란 뜻이다.

• 서점에서

A: "Can you pick out a good biology for me to read!"

B: "Let me get this straight, you want me to "get a life" for you?"

> * 'get a life'는 1) '다시 한 번 기회를 얻다'라는 뜻도 있고, 2) '인생 그렇게 살지 마, 바보같이 굴지 마.'라는 뜻도 있다.

• 히피족 같은 사람이 "FREE TIBET"라고 적힌 피켓을 들고 있다.

지나가던 부유해 보이는 여자가 다가와서 하는 말

"I'll take one."

> * Free Tibet: 티벳에 자유를!

* Free: 1) '자유'라는 뜻도 있고 2) '공짜'라는 뜻도 있다

• All Oak 80% OFF! 매장에서

판매원: "This is our best price of the year."

손님: "Oh, my gosh! It's like you're giving this away."

When he saw the price of the hardwood, he was floored.

> * floored: 1) 아주 놀라다(slang, very surprised), 2) 나무로 된 마루(flooring physical floor).

• 소시지를 먹으면서 BBQ 통구이를 상상한다.

A: "I smoked a shoulder for 14 hours. It was so moist;it just fell apart. Now, ribs are a different story."

B: "You don't want them too lean."

The guys at the pig roast – chewed the fat.

> * lean: 1) 기울이다 2) 군살이 없는(ribs no fat on meat).
> * chew the fat: 오래 담소를 나누다(men talking)

• 양떼에게 cell phone bell 소리가 울리자 하는 말

"It's for ewe":

> * ewe는 you와 발음은 같지만 뜻은 암컷 양(female sheep)
> * 수컷 양(male sheep)은 ram

• Employment Counselor

"Why did you write 'sitting in a chair' and 'polka-dot, Extra-large'?"

Interviewee: "It asked for 'Present position'and brief description'"

* Present position: 현재 지위, 면접 받는 사람은 '현 위치'라고 이해

* brief description: 간단한 설명, 면접 받는 사람은 briefs(속옷, under wear) 이라고 이해

## '미국인의 생각과 유머'를 이해하는 데 도움되는 만화

• Snax(food and drink 자판기) 안내문

'This machine accepts what it cannot change'

* Proverb saying Prayer에 이런 말이 있다

'May I change the things I can, accept the things I cannot change, have the wisdom to know the difference.'(내가 할 수 있는 것은 변화하게 해 주시고, 내가 변화시킬 수 없는 것을 받아들이게 해 주시고, 그 두 가지의 차이를 아는 지혜를 주시옵소서)

• 데이트 중인 남녀, 여자의 등 뒤에 "Best if married by 7–19–09":

* 우유 등 식료품 유효기간 표시 'Best if … by…' 비유

• State fair(주 박람회)에서

"You won a ribbon in the eating contest? What for?"

"Honorable munchin'!"

* Contest에 이긴 사람에게는 Ribbon(Blue, red, white)을 달아준다.

* Honorable mention은 '가작'이라는 뜻(you didn't do well enough to win 1st, 2nd, 3rd prize, but had a great effort),

* munch는 '우적우적 먹다'라는 뜻

• 무더운 여름날, 주인이 간이 pool에 물을 받고 있다.

개 한 마리가 물을 조금 마시고 하는 말:

"Could I have that with ice?"


• Demographics society(인구학):

−The population is still moving to the west

−Ah, they're occident−prone

　　　* occident: 서양, 서양의

　　　* accident−prone(사고를 잘 당하는)과 대비


• IV(Intravenous: 정맥주사)를 꽂은 환자가 Health care 직원(링거액 대신 지갑을 꽂고 있다)에게

"Isn't that my purse?"

　　　* Ringer's solution: 소금물(Saline solution, fluids)


• 물 위에는 한 사람이 판자에 걸터 앉자 물놀이(?)를 하고 있는데, 물 밑에서는 고래(Killer Joke Whales) 두 마리가 대화 중

"OK, Ready on the count of three… 1…2…."

　　　* Killer Whales은 범고래


• 미국과 멕시코 접경 철조망, 멕시코 쪽에 붙은 간판 "No Immigration" 밑에 새로운 간판이 하나 매달려 있다.

"and no sneezing"

　　　* sneeze: 재채기

• 어른들이 귓속말하는 것을 본 애들이

"The best way to get a grown-up to listen to you is to whisper in their ears."


• 몸을 여러 번 꾸부린 긴 뱀이 조그만 뱀에게

"I answered one of those 'enhancement' ads."

    * enhancement: 성형, 가슴확대 등


• 식당에서 데이트 중인 남녀, 원시인 복장을 한 여자는 음식을 게걸스럽게 먹고 있고 이를 바라보는 남자

"Well, I gotta admits. She DID say in her profile that she's an old-fashioned girl!"

    * 아마 Internet Chatting에서 만난 듯


• 하늘나라 천사들의 Snowflake design dept에서

"It's ironic, but we have a lot of burnouts in this department."

    * Burnout: 극도의 피로, 연료소진

    * 'snow'와 'burn'대비


• 남자가 벽에 뚫린 구멍을 통해 얼굴을 내민 사슴에게 먹이를 주면서, 사람들에게 하는 말

"We always wanted to have a mounted deer head but loathe the thought of animals being harmed."

    * loathe: 혐오하다(hate, dislike)

• 돼지 장례식에서 관을 땅에 묻기 전 마지막 기도에서 목사 돼지가

"Wally was a total pig, and I mean that in the best way possible."

 * Total pig

 1)정리 잘 안 하는 messy한 청소년

 2)대식가(a person who eats too much).

 3)실제 돼지세계에서는 a very positive, successful, fine pig

• 꼭두각시인형극, 꼭두각시(puppet)들이 식당에서 와인을 마시면서

"I'm not religious, but I do believe in a higher power."

 * higher power: 1) 일반적으로는 God, 2) puppets에게는 puppeteers(인형
 을 부리는 사람)

• 남자가 어린 나무에 해먹(hammock)을 매어 놓고 나무에 물을 주고 있다. 아내가

"Oh, any other thoughts on a long-range retirement plan?"

• 걸어가다 탁자모서리에 발가락이 부딪힌다(Wham!)

비명: GAAAAAHHHH! 개가 와서 핥아준다.

아이: "Whenever I get hurt, the dog's always comes to me with concern! The cat, on the other hand, just looks at me like I'm an idiot!

That's why dogs are better than cats!"

개: "Actually, I just came over to see if he dropped any blood!"

• 나이 많은 사람이 막대기(stick)에 당근(carrot)을 매달고 젊은 사람을 후려치고 있다.

젊은이: "Hey! I'm getting mixed signal!"

　　* carrot or stick: 당근과 채찍

　　* 여기서는 or 대신 and이니까, Carret and stick은 mixed signal이다.

• Volatile stock market

A: "Lots of people have lost their shirts in the stock market."

B: "That's why they're feeling bare-ish."

　　* volatile: 변덕스러운

　　* bare: 벌거벗은(셔츠를 잃었으므로)

　　* Bear market(하락장세)와 대비, 상승장세는 Bull market

• 과일, 버섯 등이 그릇에서 나와 마구 흩어지는 정물화를 그리고 있는 화가

"I call it "Still Life with Mushrooms?"

　　* Mushroom: 마약(drug)

　　* Still Life with Mushrooms: 마약에 취한 정물

• Golf swing이 마치 투원반 또는 투포환 자세 같다

FWUP! FWUP! FWUP! FWUP! FWUP! FWUP! FWUP! FWUP!

"He always tees off like that. He used to throw the discus in college."

　　* Discus: 원반, Weight: 포환

• 수술실: Scratch −n− dent pacemaker sale! 40% off

    \* pacemaker: 심장박동 조율기


• 소파에 다정하게 앉아 있는 엄마, 아빠를 보고 키타를 든 딸이 와서
"If you really cared about my future songwriting career, you'd get divorced and develop drinking problem.s"


• A: "When you retire from the post office do you get a gold watch?"

B: "No, a letter sweater."

    \* Letter sweater: 기념 T−shirts(우체부는 letter 배달)


• 사무실 책상은 물론이고 천정까지 온통 거울이 설치되어 있다.
"Thanks to an elaboratesystem of mirrors. Every employee at Vecon Industries had a window view."

    \* elaborate: 정교한, 정성을 들인


• 어느 회사

A: "This is one of the biggest companies around and you paid no taxes."

B: "We're too big to file."

    \* 'too big to fail(대마불사)'과 대비

- 거대한 물고기 등을 섬으로 알고 올라 앉아 있는 표류자

"Well, let's look at the bright side…How much worse can it possibly get?"

- 북극사람이 유람선을 보며

"Is this another global warming sign? We never used to be a cruise ship port of call."

　　* Ship port: 기항지, 들르는 곳

- 사막을 기어가고 있는 두 사람

A: "To heck with global warming… I'm moving to Alaska!"
B: "This is Alaska!"

- Useless things…

'A screen door on a submarine': 잠수함 스크린 도어
'Teats on a boar': 수퇘지의 젖꼭지
'A pogo stick in the Sahara': 사하라 사막의 포고(포고;기다란 막대기 아랫부분에 용수철이 달린 발판이 있어 콩콩거리며 타고 다닐 수 있는 놀이 기구)
'A handle on a snowball': 눈덩이의 손잡이
'A jobless recovery' to: 구직자(구직자는 일이 필요하므로)

- OCD/C라는 band 그룹, 노래는 하지 않고 계속 마이크 test만 하고 있다. …test…test …test…test…test…test …test…test…test…test

test···test···test···test ···test···test···test···test test···test···test···test ···
test···test···test···test ···test···test···test···test ···test···test

* OCD: 강박병, 강박 장애(obsessive compulsive disorder)

• Indian이 불을 피워 연기가 하늘로 오르자 추장이
"Reply all…."

* Smoke signal: 연기신호, 봉화

• 벽을 바라보고 있어야 하는 벌을 받는 아이가
"My dad's got a problem, and he thinks it's me!"

• 항공기 조종석에서의 대화
"We caught someone smoking in the rest room…"
"OK, remember, there's a fee PER cigarette."

• 괭이를 든 일곱 난장이가 컴퓨터를 하고 있다.
"Data mining."

* 동화 속 난장이는 miners(광부)
* Data mining: bring up to date what do today, cultural references

• 체중을 재고 있는 아줌마
"I just read somewhere that 160 pounds is the new 135!"

• Store 주인에게 전보(telegram)가 왔다. 내용은 'Due to your recent

delinquent accounts, we hereby request that you turn over all your assets immediately.' 상점 주인은 Store를 뒤집어 엎었다.

> \* delinquent: 채무를 이행하지 않은
> \* Turn over: 1) 새로 시작하다, 2) 뒤집다

• 야구장에서 아들의 경기 모습을 보고 있는 부모
"Crack!": 깨지는 소리
"It's fly ball to Patrick in right!"
정작 선수는 글러브를 땅에다 두고 휴대폰으로 Texting을 하고 있다.
부모: "It used to be, when a kid was "all thumbs" in the outfield, it meant something way different!"

> \* All thumbs: 서툰, 재주가 없는(Not very coordinated, awkward, can't catch a ball)

• 법정에서 춤추는 사람: "I'd like to make this motion, your honor!"
재판장: "Motion denied."

> \* Motion denied: 재정신청 기각

• 검사: "Your Honor, the witness continues to be evasive."
판사:(증인에게) "This is your final warnings, young lady. Remember, I have the power to pronounce you two man and wife."
(선고하다)

> \* evasive: 회피하는
> \* I pronounce you man and wife: 주례자가 '두 사람이 부부가 되었음을 선언합니다.'

- 아더 왕과 원탁의 기사들

아더 왕: "Another grail of ale, Sir Bedivere?"

기사: "It's good to hang out with you again, Your Majesty."

After he retired, King Arthur opened a "Knight Club"

  * Grail: 성배

  * Ale: 맥주의 일종

  * 'Night Club'과 대비

- (눈이 내리는 것을 보며)

눈사람: "Look! Stem cells!"

  * stem cells(줄기세포)와 snow flakes(눈송이)의 building block(구성요소)가 비슷

- King Kong attended Yankees games because he was a huge fan.

- 감기로 누워있는 환자에게: "Good morning! How are you feeling today?"

환자: "I'm ready for this flu to go away."

After having the flu for a week, she was sick of it.

  * sick of it: 진절머리가 난다

- 아파서 학교를 가지 않고 누워 있는 애의 체온을 재 본 엄마가

"As I suspected, acute pretendicitis."

• 엄마: "You know, if you got a job, you'd be able to afford to leave the house once in a while."

아들: "No, thanks. I'm good."

Her attempt to make her teenage son get a part-time job was not working.

* not working: 소용없다.


• 아울렛(Outlet )매장 선전 간판

Buy immediately!

Purchase now!

Act quickly!

지나가는 운전자: "We should stop there."

The billboard featured ad verbs.(광고판은 광고 동사들로 꽉 채웠다)

* ad: 광고(advertisement)

* 'ad verbs'와 'adverbs' 대비


• (테니스) 무명선수에게 진 유명선수: "I can't believe he won! This is ridiculous!"

무명선수: "Yes! I can't believe I won!"

When the top-ranked player lost in the first round to an unranked player, it was upsetting.

* Tennis: set, Baseball: inning, Basketball: quarter

* 'upsetting'과 'set' 대비

• 외진 곳의 별장 주인(Casper): "I like the seclusion."

주위의 귀신들: "I just love it out here."

Casper bought a cabin in the woods so that he could live in the boo-nies.

    * seclusion: 은둔(isolated, quiet place)

    * boonies: 벽지, 오지(in the middle of nowhere, boondocks)

    * boo: 남을 놀래키거나 위협할 때의 소리

• 정원을 손질하면서

엄마: "These shrubs are overgrown."

아들: "They've really taken off."

The shrubs needed trimming because they were too bushy.

    * shrub: 관목

    * something is taken off: 아주 인기 있는(become very popular).

• 등산객이 곰을 만났다.

"Oh, my~ we can't get through."

Their hike in Alaska was going along just fine until they ran into a bearier.

    * 'barrier'(장애물)과 'bearier' 대비

• 늦잠 잔 부부

남편: "How can it be 7:15? I thought I set the clock for 6:00. Sorry about that."

아내: "I'll be fine. Traffic isn't so horrible on Wednesday."

　　* She woke up late, but she wasn't this alarmed.

　　* alarmed: 불안해하는


• 로마시대 검투시합에 출전한 기사에게 서기가

"You're right. There was a typo It's jouster. You can go back and sit with the king."

　　* jouster: 마상 창 시합

　　* jester: 어릿광대


• 점원이 가위로 신용카드를 자르려고 한다.

점원: "I'm sorry, your card has been declined and I have to destroy it."

아내가 남편에게: "What! you can't buy me the purse? Are you breaking?"

　　* 돈이 있어야 아내에게 체면이 서지, 가난해서야 원….


• 아내:(야구장비를 가리키며) "Don't you have these at the stadium?"

야구선수:(Thread mill에서 운동을 하며) "Yep, it's just easier to work out here."

The baseball player bought a treadmill for 'Home Run'
   * work out: zym에서 운동하는 것을 총칭


• Hiker1: "What a great path."

Hiker2: "I think it's coming to the end."

Their hike through the forest was great until their path trailed off.
   * Trail off: 점점 작아지다


• Olympic badminton(배드민턴)에서 일부러 져주기

Putting 'bad' in badminton


• Not a typo.

Siamese Twin(샴 쌍둥이)가 옷가게에 와서

"We'd like to buy a pair of a pair of pants."
   * typo: 타이핑 에러


• 아내: "Myfriend Kathy is under the weather."

"She lost her voice! She hasn't said a word for two days! Can you imagine?"

남편: "Maybe you should go pay her visit!"(한 번 가 보는 게 좋겠어)

아내: "Good idea!"

남편: "Try to shake hands with her a lot!"(악수를 여러 번 해)
   * under the weather는 '컨디션이 안 좋은'이란 뜻.
   * 남편은 평소 아내의 잔소리에 지쳐, 이번 기회에 감기 옮아오기를 바라고 있다.

• A: "Would you care comment on our global situation?"

B: "Certainly, I think Jupiter's storm is nothing more than a childish attempt to upstage Saturn's rings."

A: 취재판을 B의 머리에 쳐 박아놓고는 가버린다

　　* 말도 안되는 설명에 화가 나서


## '미국 사회와 문화' 를 이해하는 데 도움되는 만화

• Commodities Exchange/Metal 상점의 안내문

"Tin items or less"

　　* Ten item or less counter: 마트에서 계산을 하려면 통상 길게 줄을 서야 하
　　지만, 10개 이하의 소량 구매 고객은 별도로 self 계산대가 있다.


• BANKS라는 넥타이를 맨 사람이 TARP, US treasury $ 같은 돈 바람 속에 묻혀 행복하게 웃으며 하는 말 "What, me stressed?"

　　* TARP: Troubled Asset Relief Program(부실자산 구제 프로그램)

　　* 미국정부가 시행하려는 "Stress tests on big banks" 정책(은행이 얼마나 유
　　보자금이 있는지, 경제가 더 나빠질 경우에도 살아남을 수 있는지를 Test해보
　　려는 제도)과 실제로는 은행에 엄청난 지원(bailout)을 해주고 있는 정책의 모
　　순


• 리포터가 과학자에게 인터뷰 중

"Can you tell us the breaking news about how you cured cancer?"

이때 'and the OSCAR goes to…'라는 얘기가 들리자 리포터는 인터

뷰를 중단하고 그곳으로 가버린다. "Excuse us gotta run"(빨리 가봐야
해요)

    * OSCAR: 오스카상(아카데미상 수상자에게 주는 작은 황금상)


• TV에서 서민 1: "With all the bailouts and bonuses — I'm mad as
hell and I'm not gonna take it anymore!"
TV를 보고 있는 서민2: "Unless I have to do something about it…
like write my congressman, protest or even get off my couch!"

    * I'm mad as hell: 아주 화가 난(very very angry)

    * I'm not gonna take it anymore: 여기서 anymore라는 단어는 '과거에 경
       험이 있기 때문에 더 이상은 하지 않겠다'라는 의미가 아니다. 그냥 '나는 그러
       지 않는다'라는 뜻이다. 즉, I will no longer accept the behavior put up
       with situation, I'm going to do something differently about it.


• GM과 Crysler라는 두 거지가 Uncle Sam에게 구걸하고 있다.
"Oh, Great. He comes the government to screw things up by telling
us how to run our business."

    * Uncle Sam은 미국정부 또는 미국인, John Bull은 영국인 지칭


• Costco 같은 Bulk club membership discount warehouse에서,
'Well, now that I've had a hot dog, a polish sausage, a slice of pizza
and a churro, it's time to do a little shopping!'
'The food court prices are so cheap. I don't know how bulk club
makes any money!'
'They sell a lot of those economy-size stomach antacids'

* stomach antacid: 제산제, AIKO seltzer, over the counter remedies
  for stomach aches
* AIKO는 상표명, seltzer는 '탄산수'라는 뜻

• 부부가 소파에 앉아 TV를 보고 있다. TV에서는
"Come with us to a place of unspeakable horror. A dark, forbidden
place where evil lurks. A place so forgotten for so long that."
이를 듣고 있던 아내가
"That reminds me… I have to clean behind the refrigerator."
  * 미국 여자들은 냉장고 뒷면 청소를 잘 안 한다.

• Medical Insurance new policies
"It'll cost you an arm and a leg…and their reattachment would be
out-of-pocket."
  * cost an arm and a leg: 큰돈이 들다
  * Out-of-pocket: 현금지급의(limit on insurance policy up to $2,000)

• 탐지견들이 U.S. Govt를 냄새 맡고 있다(sniff, sniff).
Govt 관리: "Go find 'em boys! Go find those lyin', cheating' deceivin'
no-good crooks that messed up our financial system! Not me! that
way!!"
  * 관리들이 그렇다는 것을 풍자

• A: "Megan and I are going to Acapulco for a little romantic getaway."

B: "How's your Spanish?"

A: "Why? We're going to Mexico, not Spain."

B: "Right. But in Mexico they speak Spanish too."

A: "Confusing. Maybe we should just go to California."

B: "Again, Spanish."

> \* California는 원래 멕시코 영토였으나, 1846-1848 미·멕시코 전쟁에 이긴 미국이 California를 병합했으며, 현재 California에는 멕시칸 인구가 많고 스페인어도 공용어로 사용되고 있다.


• 달 표면에 찍힌 커다란 발자국을 쳐다보며,

"After 40 years, it's good to know that giant leap made such a big impression"

> \* 1969, 암스트롱 'A small step for man, a giant leap for mankind.'


• 한 사람이 수영장 다이빙대에서 점프하면서 Ring fire를 통과하고, 도끼, 볼링 핀, 사과를 저글링하고 있다.

"Some men who go through midlife crises have affairs, some buy expensive sports cars, some climb mountains….."

> \* 중년의 위기를 풍자


• 밥 먹으면서

아내: "Is it too much to ask to have a little conversation with dinner like we used to?"

남편: "We never did that."

아내: "Yes, we did."

남편: "No, we didn't."

아내: "Yes, I'm sure we did."

남편: "We did not."

아내: "Did too."

아내: "There now, see? Isn't this better?"


• 나이 든 부부가 누워서 하늘을 쳐다보며

"That cloud looks like our depleted 401K account."

"That cloud looks like our underfunded pension plan."

"That little cloud looks like our saving account."

"That big cloud looks like the looming social security crisis."

"Look! Here comes our retirement!"(비가 와 우산을 쓴다)


• 엄마가 "I want you guys to help me clear the table."라고 말할 때, 애들은 "I want to remove all the joy from your lives while everyone else in the world has fun."이라고 듣는다.

애들의 대답: "again??"


• 캠핑 출발할 때,

엄마가 "Come on! We're going to be late! Time to lose something!" 이렇게 말하면,

애들은 "I can't find my shoes!" 이렇게 듣는다.

• Democrats Health care reform 매장에는 $1 trillion짜리 고급 자동
차가 전시되어 있다. 코끼리 신사가 Uni cycle을 하나 들고
"It's not as big and it won't go as far. But our new Republican model
is much, much more affordable."

> * 미국 민주당의 상징은 당나귀이고, 공화당의 상징은 코끼리이다.
>
> * Uni Cycle: 외바퀴 자전거

• Foreclosures continue 상황에서 많은 노숙자들이 노래를
"I'll be homeless for Christmas"

> * Foreclosures: 담보권 행사, 압류
>
> * I'll be home for Christmas는 유명한 노래

• Christmas season이지만 온갖 포스터들은
'Buy war bond',
'Let's all fight.',
'I gave a man, will you give just 1% of your pay to a war surcharge
tax?'.,
'I want you to pay for the wars in Iraq and Afghanistan.',
'Keep us flying! With a 40c per gallon gas tax.',
'Doing all you can, brother? War isn't free.' 같은 것들이다.
선물꾸러미를 든 한 사람: "Bah! Humbug."
스크루우지가 하는 말: "I don't like Christmas."

> * Bah! Humbug: 흥! 사기야!

- Christmas에는 Congress(국회)로부터 Healthcare reform(건강보험 개혁)이라는 선물을 받고 좋아했는데, 1월에는 그에 따른 Bill(청구서)을 받고 놀란다.

- 컴퓨터 모니터들이 Bark! Bark!라고 짖으며 우체부를 물어뜯으려 하고 우체부는 도망치고 있다.
  * Saturday not delivery 풍자

- U.S. Mail을 상징하는 독수리의 날개에서 Saturday delivery라는 깃털이 떨어져 나가고 있다.
  * Saturday not delivery 풍자

- 남편이 지폐 한 장을 최대한 늘리고 있다. Bill(청구서)을 보고 있는 아내는
"Keep stretching⋯."

- 소방차가 불을 오히려 키운다. 소방호스에서는 물 대신 'Social security & medcare costs' 와 'Tax cuts for the rich & wars'가 나온다.

- New California flag: 마리화나를 피우는 곰이 하늘을 날고 있다.
  * Roll a joint to smoke marijuana
  * 곰은 캘리포니아를 상징하는 동물, 캘리포니아는 마리화나를 합법화시킴

• 구직을 위해 줄 서 있는 사람들

"If my third-grade teacher could see me now"

바로 뒤에 서 있는 layoff된 Teacher: "I'm right behind you"


• 개에게 새 침대를 사 주려는 엄마

개의 Trial: "Too big", 'Too small', 'Too soft', 'To hard'.

결국 엄마의 이불에 함께 누운 개: "Just right"

엄마: "Why am I surprised?"


• Free way 갈림길 Last throes of summer로 가는 1개 차선은 Traffic jam인데, Real Life 로 가는 4개 차선은 텅 비어 있다.

    * Throes: 격심한 고통

    * 미국의 Labor day는 9월 첫째 월요일인데, Labor day weekend는 여름의 끝(the end of summer)이라 보면 된다.


• Med school mascots

- The Burhan State Medical School: Screaming Scalpels(수술용 칼, 메스)

- The S.B.A. Medical College: Mighty Defibrillators(세동제거기(심장 박동을 정상화시키기 위해 전기 충격을 가하는 데 쓰는 의료 장비))

- The Huntington Medical College: Fighting Femurs(해부) 대퇴골

- The S.K. Robb College of Medicine: Raging Colons(해부) 결장(結腸)

• Walmart(Chinese product center)

"Don't think about the fact that China just replaced America as the world's biggest manufacturer, think about all the good buys!"

실업자: "Good-bye income, Good-bye savings, Good-bye home."


• Golfing with OBI-WAN-KNOBI

"May fours be with you on the par five"

> * OBI-WAN-KNOBI: 스타워즈(Star-wars) 주인공, "May force be with you"라는 대사로 유명


• Raccoon을 통째로 삼킨 암컷 뱀이 수컷 뱀에게

"Okay, be honest… Does this Raccoon make me look fat?"

> * 암컷은 수컷의 칭찬을 기대한다(looking for a compliment)


• Internet Slang

LMAO: laughing my ass off

LOL: laughing out loud

LMFAO: laughing my fucking ass off

ROFL: rolling on the floor, laughing

ROFL OL: rolling on the floor laughing out loud

ROFLMAO: rolling on the floor laughing my ass off

ROTFL: rolling on the floor laughing

ROTFLMAO: rolling on the floor laughing my ass off

• 팔이 여러 개 달린 집안의 전통 가문(家紋)을 보여주며

"Our family's coat of arms is a coat of arms of course."

> \* coat of arms:(가문, 도시 등의 상징인) 문장(紋章)
>
> coat of arms[coat-of-arms]: 문장(紋章)이 든 덧옷
>
> Papal Coat of Arms: 교황 문장
>
> a family coat of arms: 가문(家紋)
>
> the royal coat of arms: 왕실의 문장

• 신하가 왕에게 "Today is your speech on budget and taxes."

왕: "Let's hope the speech writer threw in a few good jokes."

왕:(군중에게 연설) "The budget is like a pie, with each slice presenting vital government services. The goal is to use each slice of the pie efficiently⋯."

왕: "Any Question?"

군중: "What kind of pie is it? Can I have blueberry?"

"Do I get more slices? I've got 10 kids. Can I have blueberry?"

"Is it gluten free? Can I mine a LA mode?"

왕: "Listen to me⋯ There is no pie! You got that? Nobody is getting any pie!"

군중: "No pie? No wonder they can't balance the budget."

> \* 군중의 실제 심리를 나타냄(demonstrate true nature of people)

• 감옥소 공중전화기

뒤에서 기다리는 사람들: "Hurry up! I'm only in here for 10 years.

Wrap it up!"

전화하고 있는 사람: "That's great, honey. Could you putJunior on the phone?"

    * The phone at the prison featured(call waiting)

    * 'AT&T telephone serviced' 전화 한 번 하려면 최소한 30분은 기다려야 한다 (call waiting). 이 상황과 교도소 call waiting를 대비.


• 미국 국경 검문소 직원이 전화로 어디엔가 통화하고 있다

"You mean we have to let him back in?"

리무진 차 안에 탄 사람은 대통령을 만나러 가는 국빈 같아 보인다:

"What!!! I need a passport?!!!"

    * 새로운 법: 모든 사람(시민권자 포함)은 Passport를 제시해야 함.


• Context

감옥(jail cell)에 있는 죄수의 texting:

'we r bustin out 2nite @10 pm!!'

    * context: 원래 의미는 Situation, 여기서는 Con(Convict: 죄수)의 text

    * bust out: 1) 싹트다, 2) 도망치다(to escape from jail)


• The strain(Eye strain)

The early years(초등학교 시절)

선생님: "You need to stop looking out window and focus on your work."

The later years(늙어서)

의사: "You need to look out the window and stop focusing on your work."


• What happened?
It comes a box → with lots of tiny pieces → and non-verbal instructions → It takes hours to assemble:
이런 것에는 두 가지 종류가 있다. It's fun → Lego. It's hell → Ikea.
    * Ikea에서 구매하는 모든 제품은 직접 조립해야 한다.


• The point of travel
부모: 경치를 보며, "Scenery…."
애들: Notebook을 보며 "Screenery…."


• The layoffs
사무실 책상 위, 바위(Rock)가 가위(Scissors)에게
"Life's been dulled since the office went paperless."
    * 보(Paper)가 없어서 심심하다.


• The next morning after Halloween, Jack o' lanterns의 대화
A: "My head hurts, my throat's scorched, and I have a terrible taste in my mouth."
B: "Man, we got lit last night."
    * Jack o' lanterns: 호박등(호박에 얼굴모양으로 구멍을 뚫고, 안에 촛불을 꽂은 등)

* to get lit: 취한(drunk)

• The Wreck

나무를 들이박은 차량운전자: "I haven't had anything to drink."

경찰: "So you teetotaled it?"

　　* teetotal: 절대금주

　　* totaled: total loss(전손)를 줄여서 쓰는 표현. 자동차가 값보다 수리비가 더
　　　나올 정도로 부서진 상태


## '미국식 영어 표현'을 이해하는 데 도움되는 만화

• "The sun's coming up, could we talk about this in the evening."

　　* Let's talk about this in the morning: 내일 아침에 얘기하자

• 'Union'이라는 받침대 위의 'Auto industry'라는 로켓이
'Profitabil-ity'라는 곳으로 발사되려고 하고 있다.

조종사: "I'm no rocket scientist, but I don't think this thing can fly."

　　* It's not rocket science: 단순한(pretty clear and simple)

　　　예) You don't have to be a rocket scientist

• 남자친구에게 아가씨 두 명이 다가온다.

남자: "Hi Sara, Hi D'ijon. What's up?"

여자 둘: 동시에 수없이 지껄이고는 떠난다

남자: 하나도 알아듣지 못하고 "This is way I'm strictly a 'nod n smile' guy."

> * nod n smile: 형식적으로 고개를 끄덕이고 웃다

- Barack 31 Robbins 아이스크림 가게에 온 손님:

"I'm seriously thinking of a double-dip, Mister."

> * double-dip: 연금과 급료를 이중으로 받다
> * double dip: 더블의 아이스크림 콘

- 엄마: "Alice! Time to put some ointment on your rash."

Kid: "Tee Hee."

엄마: "Now hold still, dear."

Kid: "Ha! Har Ha!"

엄마: "Alice!"

Kid: "Ointment is funny."

엄마: "Please no topical humor."

> * rash: 발진(Skin irritation)
> * Tee Hee: 간지러워서(feel a tickle) 웃는 소리
> * topical: 1) 시사와 관련된, 2)(의학) 사람 몸에서 국소의
> * 여기서 'topical humor'는 'on top of your skin, current event'이고, 원래
> 는 'Topical issue'가 바른 표현이다.

- Hook 선장: "I've been doing this too long. It's the retiree's life for me."

부하: "You have lost your step."

The pirate was ready to retire because he was(on his last leg).

Peter pan— character Captain Hook

* Peg leg: wooden stick for part of leg
* 'On one's last leg': 끝부분(almost gone, at the end of the rope).
* hasn't got a leg to stand on: 증거 없음(no evidence for claim)
* The tail between your legs: 기가 죽다(feel defeated, ashamed)

• 사장: "Our corporate structure is so complicated that I have no idea where our money even comes from. I think it comes derivatives or offshore accounts or maybe goodwill."

중역: "Or maybe customers give us money."

사장: "I hope not. I like to feel beholden."

* derivatives: 파생상품
* offshore accounts: 해외에 있는 계좌
* good will: 영어권(어떤 회사의 수익력에 유리한 요소로 작용하는 무형자산)
* beholden: 신세를 진, 은혜를 입은(indebt)

• 캡슐 속에 들어있는 세 사람: "Nicely done, Mr. Scott."

Control Board를 조작하는 사람: "Yes! I've got you! You're safe now, Captain."

After Scotty successfully transported everyone out of danger, he was beaming.

* beaming: 행복한(happy)
* Beam me up Scotty:(SF 영화에서) 올려 달라(shoot me up, transport me up)

• 여자1:(너무 많은 쇼핑을 해 와서는)

"I have to figure out how to get this bill paid. I have got to cut back on shopping."

여자2: "This is so cute. I'll buyit from you if that will help."

She tried to make a dent in her credit card debit. But she couldn't (budge it)

> \* budge it: 움직이다(move it). 즉 she lacks skill in managing money, cannot stick to budget.
>
> \* to make a dent in her debit: 빚을 줄이다(lessen her, reduce her debt)

• A: "How was your trip to Vegas, Jake?"

B: "Not so good, I gambled away the car."

A: "The Herz people were furious!"

> \* 'gamble away'는 '도박으로 날리다'라는 뜻
>
> \* Hertz는 렌트카 회사이름

## 변호사에 관한 만화

• Lawyer(변호사)에 관한 생각

"How you can tell if a lawyer is lying? His lips are moving."

"Yuppie lawyers don't cry – They just sob."

> \* Yuppie: 여피족(도시에 사는 젊고 세련된 고소득 전문직 종사자, 흔히 못마땅함)
>
> \* sob: 흐느끼다

• "What is the difference between a dead skunk and a dead lawyer in the middle of the road?"

"There are skid marks in front of the skunk."

> \* 스컹크를 보고는 브레이크를 밟았지만, 변호사를 보고는 브레이크를 밟지 않았다.

• "A jury is a collection of people gathered together to decide which side hired the better lawyer."

(배심원이란 어느 쪽이 더 좋은 변호사를 고용했는지 결정하기 위해 함께 모인 사람들 무리를 말한다)

• 야구장에서 catcher가 pitcher에게 다가와서

"See the guy in the fifth row, red shirts? Do me a favor and nail him with a fastball. He's my ex-wife's lawyer."

> \* nail: 정확히 맞히다(hit)
> \* 미국변호사들에 대한 인식: 탐욕, 바가지, 집요, 도둑놈 심보

• "One lawyer in a small town will starve to death, but two can make a pretty good living."

(조그만 마을에 변호사가 한 면 있으면 굶어 죽지만, 두 명 있으면 둘 다 제법 잘 살 수 있다)

• 고양이 한 마리가 온 집안을 난장판을 만들고 있다.

부부: "Our lawyer says we may be able to sue the catnip company."

* catnip:(식물) 개박하(고양이가 좋아함)

• Getting lawyers to smile for a picture.
사진사: "Say fees!"
　　* 'Say cheese'와 대비


• Why unemployed lawyers have trouble getting sympathy.
실직한 변호사가 팻말을 하나 들고 구걸을 하고 있다.
팻말에는 'Will bill you for my time watching you walk by'
　　*내가 지나가는 당신을 쳐다본 내 시간에 대해 청구서를 보내겠다.


• The Dawn of Billable Hours
Tablet을 들고 있는 모세가 하느님에게,
"Well, OK···, but I'm telling ya right now. Lawyers are gonna have a
field day spinning the generalities here···."
　　* Billable Hours:(수임료 따위의) 청구 대상 상담 시간: 미국의 변호사는 보통
　　　시간당 bill을 청구한다
　　* A field day: 야외행사일


• Definition of flagrant waste(명백한 낭비란 무엇인가)
A busload of lawyers going off the edge of a cliff, and there is one
empty seat.
(변호사를 가득 태운 버스 한대가 낭떠러지로 굴러 떨어지고 있다. 차
안에는 빈 자리가 하나 있다)
　　* busload: 버스 한 대에 탄 사람들

# 가솔린 가격에 관한 만화

• 주유소 주인이 기름 넣은 운전자에게 빈 현금보관통을 열어주며
"Fill'er up."

> * 'Fill her up'의 원래 뜻은 '가득 채워 주세요'이다.

• 주유요금으로 팔 하나를 떼어주는 사람에게 주인이
"I'll need your leg as well."

> * cost an arm and a leg: 큰돈이 들다

• Back yard에 풀 뜯어먹는 양을 키우고 있는 사람
"They were cheaper than buying gas for the mower."

• 경찰이 그린 몽타주에는 주유기가 그려져 있다.
"Police artist sketch of robbery suspect."

• Loan officer를 찾아온 손님에게
"So, you want to buy a tank of gas?"

• 주유기에 붙여져 있는 글씨
"Send your tax refund here."

• Towing을 위해 렉카를 부른 사람
"Oh, I'm not broken down. I just thought you'd be cheaper than

buying gas⋯."

- 구걸하고 있는 사람
"Wife and 2 cars to feed"

- 강도를 당한 현금수송차량(BRINKS) 주인이 경찰에게
"No, they left the money, but they siphoned all our gas."
> \* siphon gasoline from a tank: 사이펀으로 탱크에서 휘발유를 빨아올리다

- FreakingNews.com에 있는 Shell 주유소 간판:
At the pump financing, no application refused,
Regular 2707 9/10, Plus 3217 9/10, V-Power 4229 9/10

- 캐나다 고속도로 주유소 간판
Unleaded: LOL 9/10, Plus: OMG 9/10, Premium: WTF 9/10
> \* LOL:laugh-out-loud 크게 소리 내어 웃다
> \* OMG: Oh My God
> \* WTF: What a fuck?

- 방금 약혼한 couple
"⋯and we're registered at Shell, Mobile, BP, and Texaco."

- 경매: 'The next item in our catalog is a can of Premium
Unleaded.'

- 87 Octane 대신 Chanel No 5를 주유하고 있는 사람

"No, I'm not kidding. It's cheaper…."

- Hybrid car에 주유하고 있는 사람은 휘파람, 큰 트럭 운전자는

"Oh, shup up."

Reg: Lots, plus: More, Super: Don't ask

- 비행기가 이륙하기 위해 주유소에 간다.

"As the flight attendants pass down the aisle, please have your gas money ready…."

- 개스 값이 엄청 올랐다. 주유소의 안내문

"Free Valium with Fill-up": 가득 채우면 바륨 무료

　　* Valium은 정신안정제


## 골프에 관한 만화

- Golf장에서 풀을 뜯어 바람에 날려보는 골퍼에게

A: "What are you doing?"

B: "Checking the wind direction for my next shot."

　(이 골퍼의 뒤에는 풍차가 있다)

A: "Can't you just use the windmill?"

• Golf장에서 공을 자세히 들여다보던 사람이

"Yep, it's mine. I marked it…see? I always mark my balls clearly prior to each round."

동반자가 "Neat, what do you use to mark them?"

그러자 그 사람의 대답 "Tree bark mostly"

　　* 'Tree bark'는 '나무 껍질'이라는 뜻


• Golf장 그린, 자동차 같은 카트에 클럽이 실려 있고, U-Haul 같은 차량도 대기하고 있다. 그린에는 책상, 의자, 캐비닛 등 사무실 집기가 배치되어 있고,

한 사람이 퍼팅자세를 취하고 있다.

"He got so accustomed to putting in his office that he can't sink a putt unless there is furniture around."


• 샷(shot)하려는 골퍼의 발을 땅에 파묻으며 코치가

"There you go. NOW you'll keep your feet planted."

　　* Shot하는 자세 교정 중, 발 움직이지 마라


• Golf장 Water Hazard에 자동차를 몰고 들어가서 물에 빠진 공을 건져서

"I found it"이라고 소리친다.


• 상점 점원이 조그만 물건 하나를 건네며,

"This nifty little device will ensure a perfectly accurate golfing score."

손님: "Fantastic! How many have you sold?"
점원: "None."

* 미국인들은 일반적으로 golf score를 잘 속인다.

• 팔에 Golf볼 모양의 문신을 한 골퍼

'To add more speed to his swing, Burt had golf ball—like dimple patterns surgically implanted into his arms.'

* dimple은 Golf공에 파인 옴폭 들어간 홈

• 전신화상을 입고 천국에 온 골퍼에게

"We sent you THREE warning lightning bolts to get off the course, but you kept playing! We finally just got fed up and nailed you."

* (v) to lighten: 가볍게 하다(to make less heavy)
  (n) lightening: 번개
* to get fed up: 아주 못마땅한(very frustrated)
* to nail someone, something: 정확히 맞히다(to get a specific person, to get the exact cause or solution, to hit a target)
* make a bull's eye: 표적을 맞히다

• Golf장에서 앞 팀을 앞질러가려고 하는 골퍼

"Fellas, I have a bit of an emergency! My wife is in labor! Mind if we play through?"

* In labor: 애기를 낳는 중

• Golf장에서 한 Player가 가마(palanquin, sedan chair)를 타고 이동하고 있다.

"Here comes that pompous jerk Phil Wanzer! Gets an eagle on Number 5 and it goes straight to his head!"

    \* goes to his head: 우쭐대다(pompous, superior, proud, 젠체하는, 거만한)

• Tee box에서 남자 골퍼 두 명이 앞 팀의 play를 보고 있다.

"Oh. Brother. We're right behind the Women's 85-and-older-With-Walkers League."(보행보조기를 끌고 다니는 85세이상 할머니들의 경기)

    \* 고생 좀 하겠다. 미국의 Golf장은 캐디가 없어 Play를 재촉 당하지 않는다.

• Golf Player:(Golf볼을 발로 툭 차 낸다–kick)

Cart를 타고 있는Course marshal:

"Hey! You can't kick it out of the rough! Add a penalty stroke!"

Player: "Steinbauer! You're the course marshal?? Just when I thought you couldn't get any more obnoxious!"

(marshal이 간 후)

Player: "Hey, you just ran over my ball!"

Marshal:(멀리서) "No yelling on the course! Add another penalty stroke!"

    \* Obnoxious: 아주 불쾌한, unpleasant

• Golf 경기중 한 Player가 Ball에게

"Don't be afraid! You can do it!"

"You were born to fly high and straight! Don't ever forget that!"

옆에서 보고 있는 친구: "I've heard of a horse whisperer, but I've never heard of a golf ball whisperer!"

Player: "C'mon, baby! I believe in you! Find the fairway!"

* Horse whisper: 말 조련사


• Golf를 치고 오는 아빠에게

아들: "What was your score, Dad?"

아빠: "72!"

아들: "Really?"

아빠: "Well, Sort of…"

아빠: "I hollered 'FORE' 18 times!"

개: "I don't get it!"

* holler: 소리지르다

* Fore: 공을 잘 못 쳐서 엉뚱한 곳으로 날아갈 때 혹시 다른 Player가 공에 맞을지 모르니까 조심하라고 소리치는 말. 한국인들은 "볼"이라고 소리치는 것 같은데 fore가 맞는 말이다. 오른쪽으로 심하게 날아가면 'fore, right!"


• 꼬마 형이 동생에게 Golf채를 휘둘러 보이며

"Golf's pretty easy. You just hit the ball, then lean to the side and say 'FORE!'"

• Golf 연습장에서

(아빠가 휘둘렀으나 볼은 바로 앞에 톡 떨어진다)

아빠: "Hitting golf balls is a great way to take out my frustrations!"

아들: "What makes you frustrated?"

(다시 휘둘렀으나 역시 볼은 바로 앞에 톡 떨어진다)

아빠: "Hitting golf balls!"


• Golf Player: "My head tells me to use a 4—iron…"

"But my gut tells me to use my 5—wood."

"I always follow my gut!"

Caddy: "That's for sure!"

   * gut: 소화관, 내장


• Golf장, 한 사람이 어려운 퍼팅을 성공시키자

캐디: "Great putt, Ernie."

Player: "A par is born!"

   * 뉴욕 Broadway에 공연중인 Famous Play "A star is born."과 대비


• Golf shop에서

손님: "I need a ball that comes with distance, accuracy, and a tiny little life jacket."

   * Life jacket: 구명조끼
   * 공이 물에 빠질 때 건져 나오려고.

• 골퍼가 죽어서 천국에 오니, 천국 입구에 Golf채가 하나 박혀 있다.
천국문지기: "Remember that club you threw last month and couldn't find."

• Golf 치러 가는 젊은이를 보며
A: "I hear he discovered petroleum in his back yard!"
B: "Yeah, and he took an oily retirement!"
    * oily: Early의 뉴욕 악센트

• The perfect executive assistant
실내에서 Golf 스윙을 연습하고 있는 사장에게 보고하고 있는 비서:
"I ordered your wife's anniversary gift, got the S.E.C. investigation postponed, and that slice is due to your hands being turned too far to the left…"

• Golf course, 뒤에 따라오는 팀은 Golf채 대신 낫(Sickle)으로 공을 치는(THWACK!) Grim Reaper들이다. 동반 player에게
"I say we let them play through!"
    * Play through: 먼저 치고 나가다

• Grim Reaper가 Golf장에서 Scythe를 휘두른다.
코치: "Hmm… I think I've figured out why you're slicing…."
    * Scythe(큰 낫)의 생긴 보양이 공을 치면 슬라이스가 날 수밖에….

• The Natural Selection Process in Golf

물에 빠진 Golf공을 주우려고 손을 뻗치는 Golfer,
공은 악어의 콧잔등에 얹혀 있다:

　　* Natural Selection: 적자생존(Survival of the fittest, evolution theory)


• Golf Lesson을 찾아온 여자

"My husbandwould like to hit the ball as far as he can throw the clubs."


## 뚱뚱한 사람에 관한 만화

미국은 비만인구가 인구 전체의 70%에 달할 정도로 비만은 큰 사회적 문제가 되고 있다. 콜라, 햄버거 등 페스트 푸드를 좋아하고, 대식가들도 정말 많다. 마트 같은 곳에 가면 눈을 어디에다 두어야 할 지 모를 정도의 뚱뚱한 사람들(주로 여자)이 너무 많아 날씬한 한국사람들은 그들을 도저히 이해할 수가 없다. 여기에 유명한 시사만화가인 Jimmy Hart, Dan Piraro, Kevin Fagan, Bob Thaves, Jim Davis, Dick & Chris Browne, Bruce Tinsley, Mike Peters, Wiley Miller 등이 비만에 대해 풍자한 만화들을 소개한다.


• 도로변 '사슴주의' 표지판에 그려진 사슴을 보며 암사슴이 뚱뚱한 수사슴에게

"Kinda looks like you 20 years ago, huh, herb?"

* 20년 전에는 당신도 저렇게 날씬했었지.


• 뚱뚱한 여자가 날씬한 여자에게 하는 말

"Being overweight makes me stressed."

"And when I'm stressed, I overeat."

"All in all, it's a pretty good system."


• 배에 복근이 있는 엄청 뚱뚱한 남자에게 여자가

"Have you ever considered working on something other than your 'abs'?"

* abs: abdomen muscles(식스 팩, 초콜릿 복근)


• 아주 뚱뚱한 비둘기에게 다른 비둘기가

"You gotta start eating out of a different parking lot."

* 통상 주차장에는 비둘기들이 많다


• 지붕 위에서 뚱뚱한 근육질 비둘기가 날씬한 비둘기에게

"I didn't know they were steroids. My trainer told me they were peanuts."

* 헬스클럽에서 운동하는 근육질 남자들 중 많은 사람이 스테로이드를 복용


• 뚱뚱한 천사가 "Too much soul food"

* soul food: 미국남부 흑인들의 전통음식

• 뚱보 A: "What's new, no-neck?"

뚱보 B: "My doctor says I need to slim down."

"But, instead of going on a diet, I've decided to just hang around people who are more out of shape than I am!"

"So where are we going now?"

A: "Will you leave me alone?!!"

(A가 B보다 더 뚱뚱해 보인다)


• 더 뚱뚱해진 환자에게 의사가

"No, I suggested you might benefit from 'pilates'… pies and lattes aren't going to help you at all."

  * Pilates: 필라테스(an excise program developed by a dancer, popular in the U.S.)
  * 환자는 pies and lattes로 생각


• 가정용품(housewares) 판매점에 talking scale이 있다.

뚱뚱한 사람: "I used to have a talking scale, but every time I stepped on it, it couldn't breathe to speak."

  * Talking Scale: 몸무게를 말로 얘기해 주는 체중계
  * 체중계가 숨을 못 쉴 정도로 뚱뚱


• 의사가 아주 뚱뚱한(obese) 환자에게

"Let's just say that in the battle of the bulge, your rear flank is well supported."

* Battle of the bulge(발지 대전투)는 2차대전 말 Pattern 장군이 이끈 연합군과 독일간의 최후의 큰 전투, 여기서 왼쪽 측면, 오른쪽 측면 등의 부대 배치와 본대의 지원군배치 등과, 뚱뚱한 사람의 옆구리살, 히프살 등을 대비.

• 뚱뚱한 사람이 벤치에 앉아
"I'm very comfortable in my own skin——— It's not too snug."
* snug: 옷이 꼭 맞는(closely fitting)

• 의사가 비만환자에게
"No, you don't need to be 'Glutten-free' I said 'Gluten-free'."
* Glutten: 대식가(overeats).
* Gluten-free: 밀가루가 없는
* 미국에는 글루텐 알러지가 있는 사람이 많아 Gluten-free 식품이 많다.

• 공원 벤치에 허름한 옷을 입고 있는 뚱뚱한 두 사람의 대화
"It's been so long since I made ends meet, they probably wouldn't even fit together anymore."
* 'Make ends meet'는 1) '가난하다'(Poor)라는 뜻도 있고, 2) '허리띠가 안 메어질 정도로 과체중(too over weight for the buckle not to meet together)'이라는 뜻도 있다.

• 뚱뚱이: "I've been working so hard I haven't gone to the gym in ages."
친구: "You've been trying to make ends meet and forgot about the middle."

• 해수욕장에서, 헐렁한 바지를 입은 뚱뚱한 사람이 애인과 함께 있는 친구에게

A: "Does this swimsuit make me look heavy?"

B: "No, your birthday suit does!"

> * 태어날 때는 아무것도 입지 않은 상태이므로 birthday suit는 그냥 맨몸을 뜻함.


• 아가씨가 뚱뚱한 사람에게

"I'd like you to meet my parents. They're always complaining that I'm too picky about the men I date."

> * You're too picky: 까다로운(difficult to please)


• 엄청난 스낵을 먹고 있는 뚱뚱한 사람

"I've never seen the point of resealable snacks."

> * Resealable: 재 밀폐가 가능한


• 청춘남녀가 지나가는 걸 보며 뚱뚱한 할아버지

"I'm okay with youth being wasted on the young… …what I resent is how age has been waisted on me."

> * Youth is wasted on the young: 젊을 때는 젊음이 얼마나 소중한 건지 모르고 젊음을 낭비한다.
>
> * waisted: 허리 살이 찐다


• Menswear fitting room에서 뚱뚱한 사람:

"Every time I buy pants, I find I'm in a new slacks bracket."

* 'Slacks'은 1) '캐주얼한 바지'(casual trousers)라는 뜻도 있고, 2) '느슨하다'라는 뜻도 있다.

* Tax bracket: 소득에 따른 과세율표

• 머리는 크고 몸은 삐쩍 마른 고양이: "Nope."

머리는 작은데 몸이 뚱뚱한 고양이: "Nope."

적당한 체형을 가진 고양이가 거울에 자신의 몸을 비춰 보면서 "Oh, Yeah!"

• 뚱뚱한 사람에게 "Hagar, may I ask a question?"

Hagar: "Sure!"

"How can someone who eats three square meals a day look so round?"

* Square meat: 충분한(well balanced or enough)

• 누워서 전화를 받고 있는 뚱뚱한 남자

"Please remain on the line… we are currently experiencing the same larger-than-usual call volume that we always tell you we're experiencing…."

* 실제로는 Call 대기자가 별로 없는데 상습적으로

• 뚱뚱한 슈퍼맨이 Potato couch가 되어 있다. 아내가 전화로

"Mother, he took the buyout from the newspaper."

* Potato couch: 소파에 앉아 TV만 보며 많은 시간을 보내는 사람
* Buyout: 퇴직 시 퇴직금을 일시불로 인출하는 제도


• How human nature works

엄청 뚱뚱한 사람이 'Don't worry, you still have lots of time.'이라는 피켓을 들고 지나가고 있다.

이를 보고 있는 사람들: "OK. Now I'm worried."

* 통상은 "Repent, the world ends Nov 21, 2030"같은 피켓


• 병원에서

뚱보: "I think of my body as a temple!"

의사: "I think you should decrease the building fund."

* Biblical scripture(성경): 내 몸은 하나님이 거하는 전(Temple)이라…
* Building Fund: 건축자금
* 'Temple 건축자금을 줄여라'는 결국 '살 빼라'


• 뚱보: "I need to get in shape. I'd go jogging, but it's so boring."

친구: "A lot of people jog with cell phones or ipods…"

"Take something with you makes it more enjoyable."

뚱보: "Good idea!"

(뚱보는 Mini donuts를 먹으며 뛰고 있다)


• 뚱보 아빠가 'cannonball'이라 외치면서 water tube에 들어가려고 하니 물이 겁나서 tube 밖으로 도망간다.

애들: "Dad's the only person I know who can scare water."

　　* Cannonball: 포탄, 다이빙 경기에서 양 무릎을 껴안고 뛰어들기


• Gym(헬스클럽)에서

트레이너가 "Now we're going to work on your abs."

뚱뚱한 사람의 대답: "I think they prefer unemployment."

　　* abs: 복근(abdominal muscles)


• The problem with a memory foam mattress:

뚱뚱한 사람이 들어오자 침대가

"Ugh. You again."


• 길거리 walk way를 가득 메운 뚱보들을 바라보며

"Is it just my imagination, or did American sidewalks used to look wider?

　　* 미국의 심각한 비만문제(Obesity problem in U.S)를 풍자


• 뚱뚱한 사람이 GYM 'Try out boot camp classes'을 나서면서

"I was dishonorably discharged!"

# 병원에 관한 만화

미국의 병원은 참 불편하다. 예약의 어려움, 긴 대기시간, 비싼 진료비, 최악의 서비스, 비싼 보험료 등 한국과는 비교할 수 없을 정도로 의료시스템이 잘못되어 있다. '의사 기다리다 죽든지 병이 낫든지 둘 중 하나다'라는 말도 있고, '보통 사람이 큰병 걸리면 파산하고 알거지가 된다'는 말도 있다. 미국의 의료시스템에 관한 얘기는 필자의 다른 책에서 상세히 나와 있으니, 여기서는 의료시스템과는 큰 관련은 없으나, 시사만화가 Dan Piraro, John Mcpherson, Kevin Fagan, Bob Thaves, Gary Larson, Bill Hoest, Wiley Miller 등의 병원에 관한 만화를 모아보았다.

• 식구들이 회의를 하고 있다.

"First we'll fly to Nairobi to get Tommy's braces. Then on to Gdansk for Rachel's knee surgery. Dad's triple bypass will be done in Chiang Mai…."

'With health costs soaring in the U.S., many Americans are going to other countries for their medical care.'

   * Braces: 치아교정기
   * Triple bypass는 Heart surgery의 일종

• 병원에서 환자가 의사에게

"No offense(화를 내는 게 아니라), but I'm going to seek a third opinion."

* 의사들의 Second opinion(2차 소견) 풍자

• 머리모양이 김이 모락모락 나는 커피잔처럼 생긴 대기자에게 병원 Clerk

"The doctor will see you now, Mr. Coffee."

• 병원에서 수술 후 마취(anesthesia)에서 깨어나는 환자에게 친구들이 악마 복장을 하고 문병 왔다.

"He's coming to! Ed, It's just Ray and the guys from the office! We were at a costume party."

* 'He's coming to'는 'consciousness'가 생략된 형태로 마취에서 깨어나는 상황

• Veterinary(동물병원)에 찾아온 불만 가득한 손님에게,

수의사: "I'm sorry, does that say $777? It should be $111. I mistakenly calculated your bill in dog dollars."

* Dog age compared to human age: 개 나이 다섯 살이면 사람으로 치면 35세 정도(5 dog age equivalent to 35 years in human age)

• MRI 촬영에 들어가는 환자에게 직원이

"Everything is going to be fine, Mrs. Witzer! An orderly is getting a can of Crisco and a winch, and we'll have you out of there soon!"

* Medical orderly: 병원의 잡역부

* Crisco: 상품명(윤활유)

* 잡역부가 윤활유와 윈치를 가지고 들어가는데 괜찮을 거라고??

• 병원 Reception Desk 아가씨가 밖에 대기하고 있는 많은 환자들을 향해

"Mrs. Cranley! You need to sign this HIPPAA privacy form before the doctor can look at those warts on your stomach!"이라고 외치고 있다.

    * wart는 사마귀

    * HIPPAA는 confidential(비밀)


• 간호사가 수술 후 누워있는 환자에게

"Dr. Gormley will remove your stitches as soon as you pay your bill." 수술로 꿰맨 자국은 $12,000처럼 보인다.

    * 미국의 비싼 병원비 풍자


• 'Free Eye Exam' 이라는 간판이 붙어 있는 안과병원(Optometry) 안에서

의사: "Your eyes are fine, Mr. Drabble!" "That'll be $75!"

손님: "Your sign said 'Free Eye Exam'!"

의사: "That's right! The other eye costs $75."

    * 'Free Eyes'가 아니라, 'Free Eye'니까 한쪽 눈만 공짜다.


• 병원에서 몸무게를 재고 있는 사람에게

의사: "It just doesn't work like that… you can't make yourself 'too big to fail'."

    * Too big to fail: 대마불사

• 병원에서 의사가 "We fixed your leg. It's all healed."

환자: "I stand corrected!"

> \* Stand correct: 1) 바로 서다, 2) I have been corrected by you or your
> information

• 병원에서 벽에 걸린 자격증을 보며

"What exactly is a "Medical school equivalency diploma?""

> \* 'equivalency'는 '동등하다'는 뜻이니까 결국 이 말은 '사이비 의사(Quack,
> Fraud, imposter)'라는 뜻

• 병원을 나오면서

사람: "I'm feeling sluggish, so they did a battery of tests."

로봇: "When I feel sluggish, I get a test of batteries!"

> \* A battery of test: 일련의 테스트(a group of test).
>
> (Ex: I had to go in hospital for a battery of tests.)

• 주인의 차를 타고, 외출하려는 개가 이웃집 정원에 앉아있는 개에 게 하는 말

"Ha ha ha, Biff. Guess what? After we go to the drugstore and the post office, I'm going to the vets to get tutored."

> \* 미국사람들은 개에게 동물 병원에 사서 주사 맞힐 일이 있으면 '주사 맞으러 가
> 자'고 하지 않고, tutoring처럼 다른 핑계를 댄다. 일반적으로 개들은 동물병
> 원에 가는 걸 싫어한다.
>
> \* This dog is bragging his going to outside, because another dog is
> going to stay in home.

• 한 사람이 병원으로 왔다. 그의 뒤에는 코뿔소(Rhinoceros, Rhino) 한 마리가 뿔로 그의 등을 찌르고 있다.

의사: "Wait a minute here, Mr. Crumbley. ··· Maybe it isn't kidney stones after all."

> * How he doesn't know behind him, being so absurd makes you laugh.

• 병원을 찾은 손님에게 접수창구 간호사가

"Your visit is important to us··· your waiting time is 45 minutes."

• 아내와 함께 병원에온 남편이 의사에게

"Do you mean good condition for the age she is or the age she admits to?"

• 병원식을 받은 환자에게 의사가

"No matter what you think, Mr. Lockhorn. It's our professional opinion that this is roast beef."

> * 형편없는 병원식과 의사의 'professional opinion'

• 병원에서 찍은 개의 사진이 선명하지 못해 코가 엄청 커 보인다.

Doctor: "It's the worst case of swollen pixels I've ever seen."

> * pixels:(컴퓨터) 화소

* Swollen tonsils(부은 편도선)과 대비

• 병원에서 의사가

"It looks like you have nothing to worry about. But rest assured, pharmaceutical research is doing everything it can to put an end to that."

* Rest assured: 걱정하지 마라(Don't worry).
* 새로운 약에 대한 과잉선전

• 병원 수술실에서 수술복을 입은 의사들이 바닥에 엎드려 뭔가를 찾고 있다.

"How the heck would we lose a $14,000 pace maker?!"

* pacemaker: 심장박동 조율기
* pace maker: 마라톤의 페이스 메이커

• 병원 침대에 뇌가 하나 숨쉬고 있다.

의사: "All your signs look great. We're just waiting for a donor body now."

* Donor: 기증자

# 2장

## 작가별 만화

### 게리 라슨 만화 'The Far Side'

Gary Larson은 미국의 만화가이면서 환경운동가이다. 'The Far Side' 라는 그의 작품은 전세계적으로 1,900개의 신문에 배포되었다. 아래 내용은 필자가 그 책의 만화중 영어표현과 미국문화 이해에 도움되는 일부를 발췌한 것이다.

• 경찰이 고양이를 체포해 간다. A woman said to her dog, "And I suppose you think this is a dream come true."

　　* 개와 고양이는 앙숙

• A little dog tells its mother dog; grandfather dog is reading newspaper.

"You gotta help me, Mom. … This assignment is due tomorrow, and Gramps doesn't understand the new tricks."

　　* 미국 속담: You can't teach an old dog new tricks.(늙은 개에게는 새 기술
　　을 가르치지 못한다)

- 식탁에서 아내가 서 있는 남편에게

"For crying out loud, Patrick - sit down. ⋯ And enough with the 'give me the potatoes or give me death' nonsense."

  * For crying out loud: 무슨 일이야?(What's matter with you? You should know the better. frustrated with someone)
  * Patrick Henry: "자유가 아니면 죽음을 달라(Give me liberty or give me death)"와 대비


- 개 한 마리가 아세틸렌용접기로 쓰레기통을 불어내고 있다.

아내: "Veron, That light! ⋯ The Jeffersons' dog is back!"

  * 개가 쓰레기통을 잘 뒤진다
  * 이웃집 개가 쓰레기통을 못 뒤지도록


- 수술 중, 의사가 환자의 머리 어느 부위를 누르자, 환자의 한쪽다리가 들어올려진다.

"Whoa! That was a good one! Try it, Hobbs - Just poke his brain right where my finger is."

  * 의사들도 주먹구구식이다.


- When potato salad goes bad

냉장고 문을 여니, potato salad가 권총으로 catchup, pickle을 위협하고 있다.

  * go bad: 1) 상하다, 2)죄를 짓다(become a criminal)
  * 감자샐러드는 잘 상한다.(Potato salad spoils quickly)

• Boneless Chicken Ranch라는 목장에 닭들이 죽은 것처럼 누워 있다.

> * 사람들이 뼈 없는 닭 가슴살을 많이 산다.(Many people buy boneless chicken breast.)

• Bowler's hell
보울링 선수가 지옥에 갔다. 양 옆에 한 개씩 split 된 pin이 있고 중앙에는 이글거리는 화염이다. 뒤에 앉은 Devil 이:
"Whoa! Another split? What a bummer!"

> * bummer: 실망
> * 그러한 Split는 bowler에게는 지옥이나 다름없다.

• 남편: "Blast it, woman! … Have you seen my reading glasses?"
아내는 남편 얼굴 모양의 밀가루 반죽(dough)을 하고 있고, 안경이 반죽 위에 놓여 있다.

> * 남편은 독재자(아내를 woman이라 부르고, 욕을 하고, husband is mad), 아내는 말없이 복수(revenge) 중

• 사냥꾼이 그가 쏘아 연못에 빠진 새를 가리키고 있다. 악어 떼가 그 새를 노리고 있는 상황에서, 한쪽 다리를 다친 것 같은 사냥개가 다른 사냥개에게
"You're up, Red."(너 차례야): '너가 다칠 차례다'라는 의미

• 지옥에서 두 친구가 벤치에 앉아 있다. 한 친구가 하는 말

"I hate this place."


• 한 할아버지가 나무 둥지 구멍에 빠져 있고, 주위에는 다람쥐들이 들락거리고 있다. 할머니가 꼬마에게, "Andrew, go out and get your grandfather. …The squirrels have got him again."

> \* 영리하고 약삭빠른 다람쥐와 행동이 굼뜬 할아버지(Squirrels are very aggressive. Normally they collect nuts to store away for the winter. The grandfather is a little nutty.)


• 원주민 축제, 모닥불(Flame)을 피워 놓고, 백인 제물(Sacrifice)을 묶어 놓고 가면을 쓴 원주민들이 창을 들고 춤을 추고 있다. 주위에는 다른 원주민들이 북, 피리 등 악기를 연주하고 있다.

"Suddenly, throwing the festivities into utter confusion, Ujang begins to play Stardust."

> \* 'sacrifice' 와 'Stardust'를 대비
> \* Stardust: 프랭크 시나트라가 부른 노래(romantic song sung by Frank Cynatra instead of drums.)
> \* throwing something into confusion: 어느 순간부터 모든 것이 바뀌어 혼란됨(Everything is in confusion)


• 암컷 여치 한 마리가 이웃집 여치에게 찾아가 수컷 여치를 찾는다고 하는데,

이웃집 여치: "I don't know what you're insinuating, Jane, but I

haven't seen your Harold all day – besides, surely you know I would only devour my own husband!"

> \* 이 여치는 불륜을 의심
>
> \* Insinuating: 넌지시 빗대어 말하다(imply)
>
> \* Devour: 먹어 치우다

• 두 귀신이 호른(horn)을 손에 들고 어느 집 계단을 걷고 있다.

귀신: "This is just not effective. … We need to get some chains."

> \* Charles Dickins의 소설 Christmas Carol을 보면, 남자 주인공은very stubborn, unfriendly, stingy, mean man이다. He has not Christmas spirit, not generous. Three ghosts visited him X-mas past, X-mas present, X-mas future. They have ball and chains on their feet of which sounds make people scare.
>
> \* Chains 대신 Horn 소리를 내니, 아무도 두려워하지 않을 것 같다.

• 개구리 Bar에서 여러 개구리들이 술 마시고 담배 피우며 앉아 있다. 무대 위에는 개구리 악단이 연주하며 노래 부르고 있다. 가수 개구리가 부르는 노래는,

"My baby's left my lily pad, my legs were both deep-fried, I eat flies all day and when I'm gone, they'll stick me in formaldehyde…Oh, I got the greeeeeens, I got the greens real baaaaad…"

> \* Two types of music originated in America, Jazz and Blues
>
> Blues는 이별, 슬픔, 고통, 역경 등 슬픈(Blue: 우울) 음악을 의미한다. I got the blues라고 하면 general type of sad music이다. 개구리의 색깔은 green이기 때문에, 개구리는 I got the greens라고 슬픈 노래를 부른다.

* lily pad: 개구리들이 올라가서 노는 연꽃 잎 같은 것


• 로봇 마스크를 하고, 거미줄을 친 거미(spider)가 거미줄을 뽑으며 줄기를 타고 올라온 다른 거미에게 하는 말

"Hey, Bob ··· did I scare you or what?"

* 사람도 너무 놀라면 바지에 지리게 된다.(When somebody is so frightened, he wets his pants.)


• 나무 위에 원시인들이 올라가 있고, 나무 아래에는 곰 두 마리가 있다. 이미 cave man 몇을 잡고 있는 곰이 나무를 흔들려고 하는 곰에게 하는 말

"Let's see ··· I guess your brother's coming over, too — better give it one more shake."(동생이 오고 있으니, 한번 더 흔들어라)


• 비행기 조종석에서, 조종사(pilot)가 하는 말

"The fuel light's on, Frank! ~ We're all going to die! ··· Wait, wait. ··· Oh, my mistake — that's the intercomlight."

* intercom: 구내전화
* 멍청한 실수(stupid mistake)


• 북극곰 세 마리가 ESKIMO THIGHS라고 적힌 아이스케키 통 같은 박스 뚜껑을 열고 있다.

* 'Eskimo Pies'와 'Eskimo thighs' 대비 (Eskimo pies는 유명한 얼린 디저트 (안에 초콜릿과 바닐라 아이스크림이 들어있다)의 브랜드 이름)

• 무인도에 한 사람이 표류해 있다. 바로 옆 무인도에는 오리 한 마리가 표류해 있다. 오리가 사람에게 하는 말

"Boy, there's a lot of sharks around here, aren't there? ··· Circling and circling. ··· THERE GOES ANOTHER ONE! ··· Killers of the sea··· yes siree···."

   * Siree: sir

   * 이 사람은 배가 고파 오리를 잡아먹고 싶은데, 오리는 말로써 자신을 방어하고 있다.(The man is hungry and trying to catch the duck, the duck is defending himself.)


• 여러 마리의 곰이 장례식을 치르고 있다. 이때 죽었던 곰이 관 (casket to bury the dead) 뚜껑을 열고 나오면서 하는 말

"For crying out loud, I was hibernating! ··· Don't you guys ever take a pulse?"(맥박을 안 재 봤어?)

   * For crying out loud: 무슨 일이야(What's the matter with you? You should know the better) 라는 뜻. 장례식에서 곡을 한다는 의미는 전혀 없음. 미국의 장례식은 엄숙하고 슬픔을 표시하긴 해도 곡은 없음. 때로는 고인을 추모하면서 생전의 고인이 행했던 에피소드를 소개하며 일부러 Jokes를 하기도 함.


• 마차가 낭떠러지를 향해 질주하고 있다. 주인이 말 고삐를 놓고 (dropped the reins), 옆에 앉아 있는 토끼에게 하는 말

"Go ahead and jump, Sid! Hell, I know you're thinkin' it!"

   * 위급상황일 때는 생각보다 행동이 먼저

- 샤워실에서 고양이 한 마리가, 물이 나오는 샤워기는 없고, 대신에 혓바닥 모양의 물건에 등을 대고 있다. 제목은 'Cats shower.'
  * 고양이는 물을 싫어하고 혓바닥으로 핥아 세수한다.(Cats don't like water and clean by licking)

- 술집(Bar & Grill)에서 아랍인 복장을 한 세 사람이 앉아 있는데, 웬 덩치 한 명이 그의 패거리와 함께 다가와 하는 말
"Oh yeah? More like the three wise guys, I'd say."
  * 'three wise guys'는 동방박사 세 사람(three wise men)에 빗댄 말.

- 중세 목선의 노를 젓고 있는 광경(rowing at the bottom of the boat).
한 사람이 감독관에게 하는 말
"Mr. Mathews! Mr. Mathews! I just came back from the restroom and Hodges here took my seat! ⋯ It's my turn for the window seat, Mr. Mathews!"
  * 애들을 데리고 수학여행 같은 관광버스 여행을 갈 경우, 창측을 선호하는 경우가 많아 한 시간마다 자리를 교체하는 경우가 많음.

- 한 사람이 머리가 부스스한 채 침대에서 걸터 앉아 벽에 커다랗게 걸린 쪽지를 바라보고 있다. 쪽지에는 First pants, THEN your shoes 라고 적혀 있다.
  * 어떤 사람들은 아침에 일어나면 정신이 좀 멍해지는 경우가 있는데(When some people first wake up, they are groggy and don't think well in the morning.), 이 경우는 진짜로 좀 모자라는 사람을 위해 할 일을 적어 놓은

것 같다.

• Wrecking ball 운전자가 자신의wrecking ball에 맞아 뒤로 꼬꾸라
지고 있다.
  * 미국에는 낡은 건물을 철거할 때 Wrecking Ball을 사용하여 부순다.
  * This guy didn't drive properly; Ball came back to him.

• 서커스 단에서, 한 동물 조련사(animal trainer)가 입 마개(muzzle)
를 한 곰 한 마리에게 외발자전거(one wheel bike)타는 법을 훈련시키
고 있다. 옆에 있는 두 마리의 곰 중 입마개가 벗겨진 곰이 하는 말
"Well, hey … these things just snap right off."
  * 입마개가 벗겨졌으니 조련사를 공격할지도 모른다. He is in dangerous
    position now. 여러 마리의 곰이 달려들지도 모른다.
  * Gang up: 여러사람이 한 사람을 공격하다(a group of people attacks
    somebody.)

• 짐을 싸서 집을 나가려는 아내가 소파에 앉아 신문을 읽고 있는 남
편에게:(남편의 얼굴은 새머리를 닮았다)
"I'm leaving you, Frank, because you're a shiftless, low-down, good-
for-nothing imbecile … and, might I finally add, you have the head
of a chicken."
  * 결혼할때는 돈을 보고 했는지 모르지만 살아보니, 성격도 성격이지만(lazy,
    no-motivation, not-honest, stupid, 아무짝에도 쓸모없는), 못생긴 얼굴
    이 더욱 싫다.

• 자전거 가게 앞에서 아빠가 아들에게 하는 말

"Okay, Jimmy, you can have that new bike if you can answer just one question: What's the average rainfall in the Amazon Basin?"

아빠는 기다리고, 아들은 아무 반응없이 자전거만 구경한다. 잠시 후 아빠는 "Time's up."이라고 하고, 아들은 아무 불평 없이 아빠를 따라 가게를 떠난다.

> * How many times have you been with your children for this kind of situation? 아빠는 자전거를 사 주기 싫어서 적당한 핑계를 대고, 아들은 하도 많이 당해봐서 모든 걸 알고 있다는 듯 무관심. He knows and is not crying.

• METAL SHOP 302라고 적힌 교실(High school or vocational school),

아주 게을러 보이는(Probably mean teacher) 선생이 소파에 돌아 앉아 있고, 등 뒤에는 한 학생이 거대한 로봇을 세워 놓고 하는 말

"My project's ready for grading, Mr. Big Nose. ⋯ Hey! I'm talkin' to YOU, squid brain!"

> * 선생님 이름 대신 별명(Big Nose: 호랑말코)을 부르고 새대가리(squid brain: tinny brain, fish brain)라고 부르는 걸로 봐서 평소에 감정이 아주 안 좋았던 모양, 선생이 돌아보는 순간 깜짝 놀라게 해 주겠다는 복수의 저의가 있다. He is wishing to get back to the teacher. Universally human wish to revenge to the boss.

• 외출하려는 어린 곤충에게(A beetle going out for date) 소파에 앉아 있는 어미 곤충이 하는 말 "Hold it right there, young lady! Before you go out, you take off some of that makeup and wash off that gallon of pheromones!"

* Hold it: 움직이지 마라(don't move, teenager)
* Pheromones: 향, 냄새, 유인물질, 사람이면 perfume을 썼겠지만 곤충이므로
* typically teenager 가 adult로 되어가는 과정에서는 유혹적으로(seductive) 보이게 하려는 경향이 있다.


• Karate School에서 훈련에 여념이 없을 때, 바깥에서는 UFO가 착륙하여 사람들이 달아나고 있다. UFO의 문이 열리고 나무로 된 외계인이 내려오고 있다(aliens coming out). The class abruptly stopped practicing. Here was a chance to not only employ their skills, but also to save the entire town.

* Employ: 해보다(try out, use)
* You had enough practicing, now it's the time you use it.(가라테 배우는 사람들인데 나무로 된 외계인쯤이야.)


• "Despite his repeated efforts to explainthings to her, Satan could never dissuade his mother from offering cookies and milk to the accursed."

지옥에서 꼬리 달린 아줌마가 사람들에게 다과를 주고 있고,
악마: "Mom, No!"라고 외치고 있다.

* Mother is always mother, still wants to serve even at hell.


• 진공청소기를 든 여자가 소파 청소를 위해 소파방석을 들어내고는

그 밑에 파묻혀 있는 남편과 그 옆에 머리빗을 발견하고는,

"Andrew! So that's where you've been! And good heavens! … There's my old hairbrush, too!"

> \* Many husbands lie down on a couch watching sports all weekend(called couch potato), many wives are very upset. 소파내부 청소는 아주 간혹 하는 일이므로 얼마나 오랫동안 이 여자는 남편에 관심이 없었는가 알 수 있다. He is nothing to her, she ignored him for a long time, even the hairbrush lost a long time ago is more important to her than her husband.

• FOSTER MEAT 회사의 한 직원이 회사 안으로 들어가고 있다.
바로 옆 숲속에는 늑대(wolf)가 FOSTER MEAT 회사직원 복장으로 변장(disguise)을 하고 있다. 늑대 한 마리가 변장한 늑대에게 하는 말
"Okay, let's take a look at you."

> \* 이 말은 'Let me see if you look like a real employee'와 같은 뜻이다.

• 수캐가 정원 수도꼭지에 호스를 연결하여 물을 drinking하고 있다, 발 밑에는 물이 overflowed or dripped 되어 흥건하다.
암캐: "So! Planning on roaming the neighborhood with some of your buddies today?"

> \* Roaming: cruising "온 동네에다 싸고 돌아다닐 거냐?"
> \* 개는 오줌을 싸서 영역표시를 한다.(Dogs mark their territories by pissing)

• "Tethercat"

두 마리의 개가 Tetherball 놀이를 하고 있다. 줄 끝에는 ball 대신 고양이가 매달려 있다.

> * Tetherball은 막대 끝에 기다란 줄을 매고 줄 끝에는 ball을 매달아 두 사람이 서로 볼을 쳐서 줄이 막대에 감기게 하는 놀이로서, 상대편 쪽으로 다 감기게 하면 이긴다. 여기서는 Dogs and cats don't like each other을 표현

• 배가 불룩 나온 곰이 지나가는데, 두 마리의 곰이 쳐다보고 있다.

"Although impolite, the other bears could never help staring Larry's enormous deer gut."

> * 앞 배가 엄청나게 불룩 나온 사람을 beer gut(beer belly)라고 부르는데, 여기서는 deer gut이라 빗대었다.

• 놀러 온 곤충 두 마리가 소파에 앉아 밤이 깊었는데도 갈 생각을 않는다. 주인집 곤충이 하는 말 "Crimony! Talk about overstaying your welcome! ··· John, open the door and turn the porch light on – see if that get rids of them."

> * Talk about: 예를 들어보자(Talk about an example)
> * Overstaying your welcome···: 너무 오래 있어서 이젠 지쳤다. 가주었으면 좋겠는데 차마 면전에서 가라고 할 수는 없고.
> * 곤충은 불빛을 보고 모여든다, she is clever.

• 개 한 마리가 복잡한 차도를 무사히 건너왔다. 미리 와 있던 개들이 하는 말

"All right! Rusty's in the club!"

* Anybody who wants to join a gang club has to perform a dare devil(test). The dog passed the test.

• 지옥에서 악마들이 제안함(Suggestion Box) 안의 Suggestion들을 꺼내서 읽으며 웃고 있다.
> * 일반적으로 Suggestion Box는 better customer service를 위해 운영된다. 지옥에서 "air condition을 설치하자." 등의 Suggestion Box를 운영하다니 웃기는 얘기다.

• 어미 닭이 아파 누워있는 닭에게 Chicken Soup을 끓여주며 하는 말
"Quit complaining and eat it! ···Number one, chicken soup is good for the flu, and number two, it's nobody we know."
> * 미국 사람들은 Chicken Soup이 감기에 좋다고 생각한다. 특히 이 장면에서는 우리가 아는 chicken을 잡아 끓인 게 아니라는 데 묘미.

• 농부가 소젖을 짜고(milking the cow) 있다. 줄을 서서 대기하고 있는 소 한 마리가 다리를 꼬고 손을 허우적거리고 있다.
농부: "Hey! I'm coming, I'm coming – just cross your legs and wait!"
> * 어린애들(little kids)이 길을 가다 오줌이 마려우면 'I have to pee, mommy, I gotta a pee'라고 조른다. 이때 엄마는 'Cross our legs and hold it until we find a restroom'이라고 하는 경우가 많다.

• 밤에 늑대로 위장한 사람이 침입해왔다. 늑대의 습격을 받은 사나

이는 늑대에게 권총을 쏘는 순간 늑대가 맨 넥타이가 낮에 총포상에서 총알을 살 때 총포상 주인이 메고 있던 넥타이와 같은 것을 보고는 총포상 주인이 하던 말 "Oh, yes! I guarantee these bullets are pure silver."이 생각났다.

> * Were wolf story: a person who sometimes changes into a wolf, specially at the time of full moon.(Dr.지킬 and Mr.하이드처럼)

• 두 마귀할머니가 얘기하고 있다.

"Oh, Helen! You're pregnant? That's wonderful! ··· At first, I was taking you quite literally when you said had one in the oven!"

> * have one in the oven 은 두 가지 의미, 1)임신하다, 2)마귀인 경우 실제로 (literally: actually) oven에 애 하나를 삶고 있을 수 있다.

• 'Deer Xing'이라는 교통 표지판이 있는 도로를 늑대들이 탄 차량이 지나가고 있다. 차량의 앞부분은 심하게 찌그러져 있다.

> * The front of the car is all crunched up by a number of collisions.
> * 미국서는 차와 야생동물이 부딪히는 사고가 빈번하다.

• Bobbing for poodles

악어들이 커다란 물통에 머리를 쳐 박고 있다.

> * Bobbing for apples: 할로윈 날에 큰 물통에 사과를 넣어 놓고 애들로 하여금 입으로 물어서 꺼내게 하는 게임

• 두 아메바가 소파에 앉아 있고, couch potato 같은 아메바가 하는 말

"Hey, I got news for you, sweetheart! ···I am the lowest form of life on earth!"

* 암컷 아메바가 아마 complaining 했을 것 같다. 'You low life, lazy, couch potato'
* Lowest form: 단세포동물(one cell animal, ameba)


• 지하창고에서 난장판을 벌이고 있는 poodle을 보고 집안구경을 시켜주는 손님이 주인에게 하는 말

"And down here we keep Fluffy. ··· We're afraid he may have gone mad."

* 처음 방문한 손님에게 집안 구경(tour of the home)시켜주는 것이 관례. Poodle is a dainty, fancy, prissy type of dog. Pit bull, mean dogs, rough looking, tough dogs.


• Sheep health classes

양들에게 털 깎이는 모습이 담긴 슬라이드를 보여주고 있다. 맨 뒷자리의 양은 의자에 누워 자고 있고, 주위의 양들이 그를 쳐다보고 있다.

* Sheep shearing: 양털 깎기(taking their wool off)


• Bob's Gallery

모든 그림이 삐딱하게 걸려져 있다. Bob의 고개도 삐딱하다.

* Pictures frames are not hung straight; they are off center. The reason of it that Bob has a neck problem


• 말들 속에 황소처럼 뿔이 난 암소가 앉아 수학수업을 받고 있다.

말들: "Her answer off by miles, Sheila's 'cow sense' was always a target of ridicule."

* Off by miles: 전혀 정확하지 않은(not accurate at all)
* A target of ridicule: 우습게 하는(making fun)
* 황소처럼 뿔이 난 암소: unusual, deformed cow, horns not match with her.

• 법정에서 재판상황을(The case at the court) 중계하는 리포터:
"In this dramatic turn of events, testimony against Mr. Pumpkineateris about to be given by his sister, Jeannie Eatszucchini."

* Nursery rhyme에 이러한 노래가사가 있다.
  '--- --- pumkineater, had a wife, and couldn't keep her….'
* Pumpkin eater: 유명한 미국 드라마(노래) 제목
* eats zucchini: 애호박을 먹다

• 이른 아침, 개 한 마리가 의자 위에 올라가 ESPRESSO coffee를 뽑고 있다.
"While their owners sleep, nervous little dogs prepare for their days."

* Little dogs는 하루 종일 쉬지 않고 살살거리며 돌아다니는데, 그 에너지가 어디서 나오는지 궁금하다. Where the little dog has his nervous energy, it's from high caffein coffee.

• 성 위에서 방위하던 중세 기사가 엉덩이에 여러 개의 화살을 맞고(He got arrows in his bottom) 들 것에 실려 내려오고 있다.
"So, then I say to Borg, 'You know, as long as we're under siege, one

of us oughta moon these Saxon dogs."

> * Under siege: 포위되어 있다(surround)
> * Moon: 엉덩이를 까 보이다. Insult the enemy, crack in your buttocks bottom.
> * Saxon: 앵글로 색손(Anglo Saxon)
> * 놀려 줄려고 하다가 엉덩이에 정통으로 집중화살을 받았다.

• 밀림에서 부부 탐험대, 뱀 한 마리가 남편의 코를 물고 있고, 아내는 Field Guide 라는 책을 들여다보고 있다.

아내: "This dangerous viper, known for its peculiar habit of tenaciously hanging from one's nose, is vividly colored.'… Oo! Murray! Look!… Here's a picture of it!"

> * Viper: 뱀(snake)
> * Peculiar: 이상한(strange, different)
> * Tenaciously: 끈질긴(persistent, don't stop holding something easily)

• 꼬마가 알라딘의 마술램프에서 나온 거인(genie)에게 하는 말 꼬마의 'Mom and Dad'는 이미 병 속에 갇혀 있다.

"Gee, whiz … you mean I get a third wish, too?"

> * 아빠, 엄마가 갇혀 있는 것만으로도 만족, 다른 소원은 없다.(He has no idea for the genie, he is already happy enough with his two wishes.)

• 'ACME Mannequin Co.'라는 로고(logo)가 붙은 배가 침몰해 있고 많은 사람들이 물에 빠져 있다. 상어 떼(sharks)가 물에 빠진 마네킹 다리를 물고 있다.

"What is this? ⋯ Some kind of cruel hoax?"

    * Cruel hoax: 속임수(trick)


• 개구멍(pet door: in and out freely on its own)을 안에서 대못질
(barricade)을 해놓고, 뚱보 아줌마가 바깥에 있는 개를 부르고 있다.

"Here, Fifi! C'mon! ⋯ Faster, Fifi!"

    *The dog maybe knocked out down, terrible owner, revenge


• 맥주집에서 마주 앉은 두 사나이, 한 명이 자기 팔뚝을 가리키며,
얼굴에 칼자국이 여러 개 있는 사람에게:

"Hey, you wanna see a real scar? Check this baby out!"

    * 거의 보이지도 않는 scar를 가리킨다.

    * He is drunk, little tipsy(술 취한)


• 양(Sheep)들의 파티장에 늑대(wolf) 한 마리가 들어오고 있다. 양
한 마리가

"Henry! Our party's total chaos! No one knows when to eat, where
to stand, what to ⋯ Oh, thank God! Here comes a Border collie!"

    * 양떼들은 대체로 양치기가 없으면, 들판에서 뭘 해야 할지 잘 모르고, 잘 조
      직화되어 있지도 않고, 좀 멍청한 편이다. Sheep think a Border collie is
      coming, but a wolf is coming in.

    * a Border collie: 양몰이 전문 개


• 공룡(Dinosaurs)들의 식탁, 어린 공룡이 MEATIES라는 잡지를 보
고 있다. 표지에는 'FREE KID INSIDE!'라는 글귀가 있다.

엄마 공룡: "Randy! Just sit down, eat your cereal, and look for the thing later!"

> * Wheaties라는 아주 유명한 시리얼(cereal)이 있다. Every kid tends to find toys in the Wheaties.
> * Meaties와 Wheaties를 대비

• Maneaters Anonymous

곰 한 마리가 자기소개를 하고 있다.

"My names Elmo. Well, it all started rather innocently⋯ killing socially, y'know⋯ A game warden here, a tourist there⋯ impressing the other guys, y'know⋯But then I just couldn't stop⋯ Sometimes I'd even stash an extra one in the crotch of a tree."

> * '12step program' 이라는 중독자 치료 program이 있다. Alcohol Anonymous, Gamblers Anonymous, Overeaters Anonymous 등
> * Stash: 숨기다, 간수하다
> * crotch: 갈래, 잔가지

• 철조망(barbed wire fence)에 걸터앉은 소가 다른 소에게

"Look, if it was electric, could I do this?"

그런데 집안의 사람은 철조망에 연결된 전선의 두꺼비집을 올리려 하고 있다.

• 소떼 속에서 한 마리의 소가 공중전화 booth에서 전화를 걸고 있다.

"Listen, Mom⋯ I just wanted you to know I'm okay. The stampede seems about over  –  although everyone's still a little spooked. Yeah, I know … I miss the corral."

   * stampede: 놀라서 우르르 몰림
   * spooked: 겁먹은
   * corral: 울타리
   * Adult-children(어른 같은 어린이) is little scary and often seeking mom and dad.


• Ms. Gibson's CANINE OBEDIENCE SCHOOL

Ms. Gibson은 결박되어 있고(tied up their instructor) 복면을 쓴 (wearing the mask) 몇 마리의 개가 단상에서 Ball 하나를 손에 들고 외치고 있다.

"And I say we go outside and we play with this ball."

   * CANINE OBEDIENCE SCHOOL: 개 훈련소
   * Ball: catching and bring it back(주인의 명령에 복종하는 훈련용)


• Junior high gorillas의 locker room에서

고릴라: "Wow… That guy's already a silver back."

벽에는 NO Brachiating in the Locker Room이라 쓴 문구가 보인다.

   * Brachiate: 양팔로 번갈아 매달리며 건너가다
   * Junior high(고등학교 저학년) 때는 특별한 친구와 비교, 잘나가는 친구에 대한 부러움과 질투가 심할 때이다.


• Scene from Dinner on Elm Street

개 가면을 벗어 든 닭이 식탁에서 고기를 뜯고 있는 주인 가족들에게

"No, I'm not your little dog Fifi! I'm the chicken you thought you fixed for dinner! Would you like to know where your little Fifi is? Ha ha ha ha ha!…."

> \* 주인 가족은 닭 대신 개를 잡아먹은 것 같다.

• 지하실험실에서 파리 머리 모양을 하고 실험에 열중인 남편에게
아내: "Lunch is ready, Lawrence, and … what? You're still a fly?"

> \* 남편이 파리로 바뀌었다가 다시 인간모습으로 돌아왔을 거라 생각했는데, 실험이 계속 진행 중

• 한 할아버지가 소파에 앉아 나무로 된 한쪽 다리에 구멍을 뚫어 놓고, 구멍 주위에 올가미를 들고 있다. 옆에는 두 아줌마가 앉아 있다.
부인: "Good heavens, Bernie! We've got company!… And you're never going to catch that stupid squirrel anyway!"

> \* We've got company: we have a guest
> \* Squirrel are very smart animals and eat bird seed. Many people don't like squirrel and they are trying to get rid of it. This guy is so frustrated and trying to catch it.

• 한 사람이 거대한 물소(water buffalo)앞에서 사진을 찍고 있다. 그 뒤에는 원주민 한 사람이 에~롱하고있다.

> \* Sticking his tongue: 놀리다(Making a face, tease)

• 과학자들이 돌고래들이 어떤 소리를 내는지 관찰하고 있다.(Investigating the dolphin's own language. Dolphin is very friendly to human)

칠판에는 Kay pas-uh(13회), aw blah es spanyol(8회), be-in fago(12회), bwayno dee-us(5회)라 적혀 있고, 계속Count를 하고 있다.

한 과학자: "Matthews … we're getting another one of those strange 'aw blah es spanyol' sounds."

> \* Kay pas-uh: What's happening?
> \* aw blah es spanyol: Do you speak Spanish?
> \* bwayno dee-us: Good morning

• Nursing Home(양로원)에서, 한 노파가 낡은 의자에 앉아 쟁반위에 수프를 올려놓고 졸고 있다. 등 뒤에 걸려 있는 stuffed moose head(직접 사냥한 걸 자랑하기 위해 무스의 머리부분만 박제를 해서 벽에 장식용으로 걸어 둠)에서 눈알이 하나 빠져 soup 속에 떨어져 있다.

• Big dogs having fun with helium

개들이 헬륨 가스를 마시고 yip yip yip yip yip yip 하면서 놀고 있다.

> \* teen agers를 풍자

• 몸집이 거대한 우주인(alien) 둘이서 자전거를 타던 인간 둘을 잡아 병 속에 넣어두고 있다.

"Now, don't forget, Gorok! … This time punch some holes in the lid!"

> \* Children 놀이: 곤충을 잡아 병 속에 넣고 숨구멍을 뚫어주는 행위를 빗댐.

• 선반 위에 범퍼가 찌그러진 자동차 앞부분이 마치 박제처럼 걸려있다. 암컷 늑대가 손님 늑대에게:

"Don't listen to him, George. He didn't catch it. the stupid thing swerved to miss him and ran into a tree."

> * He didn't catch it: 직접 잡은 게 아니라
>
> * the stupid thing swerved: 그 차가 빗나가서 나무를 들이 박았다.


• MIDVALE School for the gifted

한 학생이 'PULL'이라고 쓰여진 문을 열기 위해 힘껏 밀고 있다.

> * The gifted: 영재, 천재(very smart child)


• 고 · 신생대 시절, 공룡 한 마리가 바위에 걸려 넘어지고 있고 (tripping over a rock), 시조새 한 마리는나무 둥지에 머리를 부딪치고 있다(ancient bird fly into a tree and hit head).

"Although it lasted only 2 million years, the Awkward Age was considered a hazardous time for most species."

> * Awkward Age는 보통 11~13, 14세 정도의 2~3년 동안이다.
>
> * The age of dinosaurs is 20 million years이므로only 2 million years라 표현.


• Time machine을 타고 Age of Dino(공룡시대)로 가버린 사람이 Time machine에서 나와 Gas를 구하러 가고 있다.

"He went back so many thousands of millions year and he ran out of gas."

• 개들이 자동차를 타고 출발하는데 한 마리는 목줄을 맨 채로 타서, 자동차가 달리니 목 줄 맨 개는 자동차에서 튕겨 나간다.

"Careening through the neighborhood with reckless abandon, none of them suspected that Tuffy was still tied up."

* Careening: 달리다(Driving fast through the neighbor)
* with reckless abandon: not carefully
* Young teen ager 풍자: cruising, joy ride, no destination, they just want to do

• 로마시대(around the time of Rome), 배를 저어가는데(rowing), 한쪽 편에는 힘 센 사람(oarsmen)만, 다른 쪽에는 약골들만 젓고 있다.

"We've got it, too, Omar … a strange feeling like we've just been going in circles."

• Around the time of Dino
한 여자가 건조기에 빨래감을 말리려 하고 있다. 주위에는 공룡들이 호기심으로 쳐다보고 있다.

"Disaster begins Professor Schnabel's cleaning lady when she mistakes his time machine for a new dryer."

* Time machine 시간을 잘 못 눌러 공룡시대로 와 버린 모양

• 막대 끝에 해골(Skull)을 매달고 있는 원주민(primitive tribe)마을에 숲속에서 머리가 엄청나게 큰 사람이 걸어 나오고 있다

"Unwittingly, Palmer stepped out of the jungle and into headhunter folklore forever."(자신도 모르는 새, Palmer는 정글에서 나와 전설적인 headhunter 이야기의 일부가 되었다)

    * Unwittingly: 부지불식간에

    * Into: became a story


• 유괴범(kid napping) 비슷한 사람을 고문(Torture)하고 있다. 형사가 줄에 매달린 당근을 갖다 대며

"Well, we've tried every device and you still won't talk – every device, that is, except this little baby we simply call 'Mr. Thingy.'

    * Thingy: 거시기(이름 모를 때 쓰는 말)


## 댄 피라로 만화 'Bizarro'

Dan Piraro는 미국의 유명한 화가, 작가 겸 만화가로서 1985년부터 Bizarro라는 제목의 만화를 신문에 연재하고 있다. Bizarro는 유별나고 과장된 괴짜의 캐릭터를 갖고 있는데, 색다른 코믹만화로 대단한 인기를 누리고 있다. Bizarro를 보면 미국인의 유머, Play on words, 미국문화, 미국영어의 맛을 배울 수 있다.


• Bumper Sticker(차량 뒤 범퍼에 붙이고 다니는 스티커)

'My son goes to Penn State'

'My other son is in the State Pen'

* Penn State: Pennsylvania State University

* State Pen: 주 교도소(Pen= prison, jail)


• 노아의 방주에 들어가려고 사람들이 끝없이 줄을 서 있다.

"Sorry, only two corrupt CEOs per bankrupt firm."

　　* 부패 CEO가 너무 많아…


• 노아의 방주

"Dang, I just noticed that both of the aards are male and both of the varks are female."

　　* aardvark: 땅돼지


• 집안에 장난감 가구들을 잔뜩 사다 놓은 남자가 여자에게

"Once I pay off my student loans, I'll be able to afford larger furniture."

　　* 지금은 돈이 없어 실제 가구 대신 장난감 가구로

　　* Student loans: 일부 한국인 부모를 둔 사람을 제외하고, 대부분의 미국대학
　　　생들은 학자금을 대출받고 졸업 후 갚아 나간다.


• 천국의 Soul Sorting center

　(Paradise 재활용센터에서 일하고 있는 두 천사)

여자천사: "Buddhist? Hindu? Lutheran? Krishna? Catholic? Agnostic?"

남자천사: "Recyclable. Recyclable. Non-recyclable. Yep. Nope. Flip a coin."

• Ye olde curiosity shoppe에 고양이들만 모여들고 있다
   * curious as a cat: 고양이는 호기심이 많다

• 서부개척시대 순례자들이 산타클로스를 위협하며,
"Who are you and what are you doing here before Thanksgiving?"

• 담장 옆 뱀이 똬리를 틀고 앉아 있다 'Pitiless'
   * Pit: 뱀 굴
   * 사람이 그렇게 앉아 있으면 'Homeless'

• 부모들이 어린애를 안고 애들에게 축구를 시키고 있다.
보고 있는 사람: "Do you ever wonder if we're putting too much
pressure on them at this age?"
   * 조기교육의 문제점 풍자

• 다쳐서 병상에 누워 있는 Super man(슈퍼맨)에게 의사가
"You're going to be fine. It was only a mortal wound."
   * Mortal: 치명적인, 죽을 수밖에 없는
   * Superhero는 죽지 않기 때문에(immortal, never die) 치명적인 상처라도
     별 거 아니다.

• 현상범 수배(The most wanted) 포스터에 개 한 마리의 사진이 포
함되어 있다.

FBI 요원이 상관에게,

"Look, I can't even think about catching criminals until I get my Roscoe back!"

　　* 잃어버린 자신의 개(Roscoe)를 찾기 전에는 범죄자를 안 잡겠다.


• 가석방을 원하지 않는 죄수

"I can't get paroled. I'll lose my health coverage."

　　* 출옥할 경우 의료보험 걱정


• 꼬마가 Telephone Can(깡통으로 만든 장난감 전화)으로

"No. Thanks. I'm perfectly happy with my current long-distance provider."

　　* 장거리 전화 Provider 선전에 어지간히 시달렸나 보다.


• 경찰이 피해자에게 장난감(그림 그리는 판)을 내밀며,

"We lost our artist in the latest round of budget cuts. Can you create a likeness of the assailant?"

　　* Police Sketch(몽타주)를 그리는 화가를 해고시킨 모양


• 멕시코만에 유출된 Oil을 수거하며,

"We've been hearing for years about 'alternative energy', but I had no idea it would be seawater."


• 술집에서 스모선수가 아가씨에게

"I'm huge in Japan."

> \* Huge는 '거대하다'는 뜻도 있고 '유명하다'는 뜻도 있다.

• 항공사 check-in 창구에 신사복을 입고 나타난 타조(ostrich)에게,

"The disguise is a nice touch, but you know very well you're on the No-Fly List."

> \* 타조는 날지 못한다
> \* 본래 의미의 No Fly List는 탑승불가 명단

• Impatient Butterfly collector: 나비 대신 번데기를 수집해서 벽에 걸어 둔다

> \* 진짜 참을성이 없다

• 대머리 할아버지가 공원 벤치에 앉아 새 먹이를 주고 있다. 새 한 마리가 대머리 위에 앉아 있는 새에게

"You're wasting your time. That thing never hatches."

> \* hatch: 부화하다

• Home Wrecker's Depot에서 shopping하고 있는 남자에게 묘령의 아가씨가

"Can I help you find something, big fella?"(남자를 유혹하고 있다)

> \* Home Depot는 미국 내 각종 집안수리기구를 파는 큰 마트이다
> \* Home Depot 대신 Home Wrecker's(가정파탄, 이혼) Depot

• 한 사람이 친구에게 하소연

"As a Jewish Chinese-American, I don't know when to celebrate the New Year."

> \* 유대인, 중국인, 미국인의 New Year는 다 다르다

• Bar에 앉아 있는 어미소와 새끼소
"What part of "MOO"do you not understand?"

> \* What part of NO don't you understand? 애들이 뭔가를 사 달라고 계속 조르고 부모의 대답은 항상 "NO"였는데, 애가 또 사 달라고 할 때 하는 말.

• 'A place 4 out of 5 American high school students hope to visit'
South America 대륙을 'Europe'이라고 표시해 놓았다.

> \* 많은 미국사람들은 세계지리에 정말 무식하다

• 엄마: "Anything else for Salvation Army, Clark?"
아들:(옷장에서 Superman 복장을 보고 있다.)

> \* Salvation Army: 구세군
> \* Clark이라는 아들은 좀 어리버리한 애 같다.
> \* Clark Kent: 영화 슈퍼맨에 나오는 어리버리한 신문사 기자

• 남자 눈사람에 비해 짧은 코와 올려붙인 눈 섶, 턱밑 처진 살을 깎아낸 여자 눈사람
"While I was in for the nose job, I got an eye lift & a chin tuck, too."

> \* 성형을 풍자

- 과거(Then): 프랑켄슈타인이 화난 사람들에게 쫓겨 다닌다.

현재(Now): 프랑켄슈타인이 계약을 위해 업체와 얘기하고 있다.

업자: "$9 million per season for 5 years with a $3 million signing bonus."

  * 프랑켄슈타인: Famous star를 지칭


- 300lb. man+48lb. bag, 100lb. woman+54lb. bag

"Ask an airline representative which one gets charged for extra weight"


- 여자가 제비족같이 생긴 남자에게

"While I'm certain the police consider you a person of interest, I assure you, I do not."

  * Person of interest: 용의자


- 숲 속의 호랑이

"It wasn't the taste of human flesh that made me a maneater. It was reading headlines."

  * 신문의 헤드라인에는 통상 온갖 Bad News로 장식


- 도로표지판: 사슴이 총을 겨누고 있고 'Cross Deer'라 적혀 있다.

  * 여기서 'Cross'는 '화가 난'(Angry, irritated)이란 뜻
  * 통상의 표지판Deer Crossing Sign과 대비

• 동물원 코끼리 우리 안에서 청소하고 있는 직원에게 코끼리가

"So random people can stare at me for 45 seconds. What are you in for?"

　　* 우리 안을 감옥이라 생각


• 호랑이가 곰에게 인터뷰

"I understand you recently had a baby."

"Yes, it was delicious."

　　* 호랑이는 곰에게 '임신했냐?'라고 물었는데, 곰은 어린애를 잡아먹었다고 대답.


• Bar에서 남자가 여자에게

"Want to go to a bar where the music is louder & we won't be able to hear each other talk?

　　* seduction: 유혹

　　* pick up line: 여자를 꼬시는 말


• Downside of cloning

쌍둥이 A가 쌍둥이 B를 보며

"Good lord! Do I really sound like that? I look so fat from behind! Stop slouching, stand up straight!"

　　* Downside: 불리한 면(disadvantage)

　　* slouch: 축 늘어지다


• Seats in the nosebleed section

Boxing 경기에서 Ring 안에서 구경하고 있는 관중.(운 나쁘면 코피 터

지는 수가 있다)

　　* Nosebleed(코피) Section: 아주 높은 관중석


• 청혼하러 온 남자가 장인 될 사람에게

"I'd like to ask for your daughter's hand in marriage. If that works out, I'll be back for the rest later."

　　* hand in marriage: 혼인을 승낙하다


• 장대만 한 담배 한 개피를 둘러메고 출근하는 사람

"I've cut myself down to one cigarette per day."


• Goat check counter에서 손님

"I don't have my ticket, but he answers to 'Eddy'"

　　* Coat check service(의류보관): coat와 goat를 대비


• Bar에서 ipod를 보여주며 수작 걸려는 남성에게 여성이

"Fascinating, do you have a 'Drop Dead' app?"

　　* drop dead: 깜짝 놀라게 하는


• 가전센터에서 4D TV를 판매하는 점원

"In addition to a 3-D picture, you can smell what's on the screen."
나이 많은 고객: "I dunno. I watch a lot of wrestling."


• Farmacy에서 주인이 손님에게 양배추 하나를 건네며

"Take one a day with tomato and cucumber."

 * Pharmacy(약국)와 Farmacy를 대비


• 비둘기에게 모이를 주고 있는 Car wash 주인

"All right, guys ――― eat up & then get out there and drum up some business."

 * drum up: 선전하다, 알리다(create or find), 즉 많이 먹고 차 위에 똥 싸라.


• 태양열로 작동하는 전기 톱을 들고 있는 삼림 벌목공

"The solar powered chainsaw makes me feel less guilty about deforestation."

 * deforestation: 산림파괴


• 돌망치를 들고 있는 원시인(Cave man) 의사가 환자에게

"As soon as the anesthesiologist gets here, we'll get started."
(저쪽에서는 누가 큰 몽둥이를 들고 오고 있다)

 * Anesthesiologist: 마취의사


• 'J'자 모양의 전화기로 통화하고 있는 여자

"Really? She's still using an iPhone?"

 * 이 여자는 iphone 이 아니라 jphone을 사용 중


• 남자: "Where did we go wrong, Nora?"
여자: "I'm not Nora."

* 'wrong'과 'not Nora'를 대비

• 난폭운전을 한 차를 한 대 잡고

교통경찰: "You were swerving"

운전자: "Got into an argument with my GPS & she grabbed the wheel."

* Swerve: 자동차가 갑자기 방향을 바꾸다[틀다]

• 사장이 신입종업원에게 청소용 밀대를 건네 주며

"You have just won a million dollars. You will be paid in hourly installments of $8 and you must be present to collect."

* 시간당 $8씩, 백만$를 다 받으려면 몇 살까지 살아야 하나?

• 모든 자동차 지붕위에 풍력발전용 풍차가 설치되어 있다.

"Of course, as technology improves, the windmill will get smaller."

*언젠가는 가능할지도

• A: "I'm sorry about your loss."

대머리B: "Who died?"

A: "I was talking about your hair."

* Loss: 부고, 사망, 여기서는 머리카락이 없는 상황

• 아담이 나무에서 MS Window를 따먹으려 하자, 사과(Apple)나무에 몸을 감고 있는 뱀이 "Try this one— it's less buggy."

* Micro Soft vs. Apple
* bug는 1) 벌레 2) 컴퓨터 버그


- Psychiatrist를 찾아온 앵무새

"I want more than a cracker, but I don't know how to ask for it."

  * 앵무새에게 말을 가르칠 때 항상 "Polly, want a cracker."라고 가르친다.


- Judith has a senior moment and heads to the Prom

할아버지가 무도회복을 입고 밖으로 나가려는 할머니를 바라보고 있다.

  * Senior moment: 건망증(sometimes, you forget a name, a place, a word)
  * Prom: 고등학교 졸업전에 갖는 댄스 파티


- 네 발로 다니는 유인원마을에, 한 유인원이 두 발로 걷는 여자 한 명과 함께 나타나자, 다른 유인원들이 "Trophy wife!"

  * Trophy wife: 나이 많은 남자의 젊고 매력적인 아내


- TV 모 채널 뉴스 리포터가 무표정한 얼굴로

"Breaking news— this statement just in from the White House

'No matter what you do, most people are going to complain'"


- 주인은 새장안에 묶인 채로 갇혀 있고 앵무새(parrot)은 Door를 향해

"False alarm, officers. Sorry for the bother."

  * 알람이 울려, 문밖에 경찰이 온 상황


• 마야인 A:(마야 달력을 보이며) "I only had enough room to go up to 2012."

마야인 B: "Ha! That'll freak somebody out someday."

  * freak: 기급을 하다


• Attack of the vegetarian zombies

채식주의 좀비가 사람을 공격하면서:

"Not want brains! Got Bran?"

  * Bran: 겨(high fiber, outer skin of grain, healthy food)

  * Brain과 Bran 대비


• Smile 표시가 있는 셔츠를 입은 우울한 남자가 셔츠를 보며

"Lying shirt!"

  * 거짓말하는 셔츠


• 잠옷(nightwear)과 슬리퍼를 신고 출근하는 재판장에게 법원 직원이

"Happy casual Friday, Your Honor."

  * 통상 금요일은 캐주얼 차림 허용


• 식탁에서 식사중인 식구들이 밥 먹다 말고 휴대폰으로 문자를 주고 받고 있다.

아들: BOL(Burp out loud)

아빠: EY!(Excuse you!)

엄마: EOTT(Elbows off the table)

    * Burp: 트림하다

    * 언제 어디서나 휴대폰이 우선인 세태


• Perils of the beehive hairdo

올림머리를 하고 있는 아내가 잠자리에서 일어난 후, 남편이 침대 머리맡을 보며,

남편: "There's honey on your pillowcase again."

    * Peril: 유해함, 위험

    * Beehive: 1) 올림머리, 2) 벌집

    * Hairdo: hair style


• 함께 도시락을 먹으려는데, 한 아이는 Box에 닭 한 마리를 사 가지고 와서 칼로 닭을 잡으려 하고 있다.

"My mommy insists all our food be local, organic, and totally fresh."


• Origami for beginners

종이 한 장 눕혀 놓으면 Rug, 세워 놓으면 Door, 비스듬히 세워 놓으면 Ramp

    * Origami: 종이 접기


• Hearse(장의 차: Car. Limo to carry dead) 가 고장나서 멈춰 섰다.

엔진을 점검중인 정비사: "I'm afraid it's dead, too."

- 자신에게 수갑을 채우려는 경찰에게 힙합바지를 잡고 있는 불량청
소년이

"If you cuff me, who's going to hold up my pants?"

    * cuff: 수갑 채우다

- Newton's 5-second rule of gravity

뉴턴이 1..2..3..세면서 살금살금 기어가서 떨어져 있는 사과를 주워
입으로 깨문다(CHOP!)

    * 5-second Rule: 떨어진 음식을 재빨리 주우면 먹어도 괜찮다.

- Inventor of the pop-up book

한쪽 눈에 붕대를 붙이고 있다.

"I came across the idea accidently, actually."

    * pop-up book: 그림이 튀어나오는 책

- Fly swatter(파리채)를 들고 있는 Grim Reaper 앞에서 늙은 Mayfly가

"Oh well, I've lived a good, long life of over 29 days."

    * Grim Reaper: 저승사자
    * Mayfly: 하루살이

- Adam and Eve(아담과 이브)

"I've got it! We'll call it 'Forbidden Fruit'. Nobody can resist something that's forbidden."

* Forbidden Fruit: 금단의 열매

• 집으로 들어오는 남편에게 아내가 전화기를 손에 들고

"Your old boss just called to congratulate you for being named Unemployee of the Month."

* Employee of the Month(이 달의 사원)와 대비

• Zen Birthday Card

"Not thinking of you."

* Zen: 선, 선종(禪宗)

• 투표장표시를 따라 쭉 가보니 Voting Boothe에 붙어 있는 Sign

'Abandon hope all ye who enter here'

* 어디에 투표하든 그 나물에 그 밥

• Minnie's new implant

Micky Mouse의 여자친구 Minnie가 큰 귀를 뽐내며 서 있다.

* Implant라 하면 한국에서는 치아(Teeth) 임플란트를 연상하지만 미국에서는 일반적으로 가슴(Breast) 임플란트를 뜻한다.

* Minni는 귀를 임플란트한 모양이다

• 전화로 얘기하고 있는 남녀

남자: "We need to text."

여자: "We've texted this to death. It's time to unfriend."

* Texted: talked

* (Twitter) new verb in language: Friend, unfriend

• 새들의 대화

"Just ate the juiciest worm!"

"This breeze is awesome."

"Anyone else tried of flying?"

"Enough with the tweeting."

　　* 새들도 tweet(짹짹)로 대화하는 모양

　　* twitter와 tweet를 대비

• 고양이 세계, 남편고양이가 죽어 보험금관련 상담하러 온 고양이에게

"I'm sorry, ma'am, but the fine print clearly states that your husband will have to die 8 more times before you can collect on the policy."

　　* A cat has 9 lives: 고양이는 9개의 생명을 가지고 있다(U.S saying because cats can live after dangerous falls often land on their feet.)

• 어깨 위에 앵무새(parrot)를 올려놓고 있는 환자에게 치료사가 고무줄 새총(sling shot)를 겨누면서

"I think I can get rid of those voices in your head."

　　* 환자는 '머리에서 무슨 소리가 난다'고 찾아온 모양

• Homeless: will work for food

Unprincipled: will work for jerks

　　* Unprincipled: 타락한 정치인

* Jerk: 역겹고 비도덕적인(offensive, unethical)

- 식당에서 식사 도중 전화를 받고 있는 남자

"Hold on, I'm going to put you on speaker phone so everyone can hear what I have to put up with."

　　* 어지간히 화난 모양

- Greece 시대, 월계관을 깔고 앉아 있는 동료에게

"Excuse me, but you're resting on my laurels."

　　* Rest on one's laurels: 이미 얻은 영예[승리]에 만족하다, 성공에 안주하다

- Future Wall Street Executive

방안을 난장판으로 만든 애가 엄마에게 신경질 내며 하는 소리

"But increased regulation will stifle my growth!!"

　　* Stifle: 숨막히게 하다

- 식당에서 주문받는 사람

"Would you like sparkling water, bottled water, tap water, tap water from France, or dew collected from flower petals in Fuji?"

　　* 미국식당에서 주문 제대로 할 수 있다면 영어가 상당한 수준이다.

- Blind dog이 다른 개를 만나 코에 냄새를 맞고 있다. 'sniff, sniff', Blind dog을 몰고가는 Seeing eye man: "Other end"

　　* Other end: 머리 쪽이 아니라 꼬리 쪽을 냄새 맡아라

* Seeing eye dog(인도견)
* 통상은 안내견이 장님을 안내하지만, 여기서는 사람이 눈먼 개를 안내

• Lunch with Karl & Carl
Karl은 Ketchup을, Carl은 Catchup을 먹고 있다

• 통조림을 따고 있는 새가 전화를 받으면서
"Oh, not much. Just opening up a whole new can of worms."
* a whole new can of worms: 귀찮은 일이 한꺼번에 왕창 쏟아지다.

• 하루살이(Mayfly)들이 감옥 안에서
A: "Two consecutive life sentences or 60 days, whichever comes first, you?"
B: "Armed robbery— 3~5 minutes."
* Two consecutive life sentences: 두 번 무기징역

• 귀를 떼 놓고 책을 읽고 있는 남편에게 아내가
"You think you're pretty clever with those removable ears, don't you?"
* 아내의 잔소리가 얼마나 심했으면..

• 애꾸눈에다 얼굴에 자상상처가 많은 사람이 다른 사람에게
"My mother stopped smoking during pregnancy, but she wouldn't give up sword."

* swallowing: 마술 쇼 같은 데서 볼 수 있는 입으로 칼 삼키기 묘기
* 어머니 직업은 swallowing을 전문으로 하는 마술사


• 해변가 인어(Mermaid)상 머리위에 앉아 있는 새
"Don't know what I did to get so famous, but people sure are taking a lot of pictures of me."


• 거지가 모닥불에 양말을 던지며
"I've darned these socks too much. Time to damn them."
* darn(꿰매다) 와 damn(빌어먹을)의 발음


• 서부개척시대 사막에서 만난 두 사나이, 말 안장 위에 엄청나게 큰 K2(CHAW) 통을 실은 사나이에게
"I reckon somebody's been to Costco."
* K2(CHAW)는 씹는 담배, Costco는 염가 대량 판매하는 마트


• 저승사자(a messenger of the other world, 미국에서는 Grim Reaper: 죽음을 의미)가 stand-bar에 앉아 술 한잔 시켜 놓고 바텐더에게 하소연을 하고 있다
"I'm being sued for age discrimination."
* 미국에서 금지되는 차별(discrimination): 인종(race), 성(sex), 나이(age), 종교(religion)


• 'Eye of the beholder beauty salon' 내부에서 손님은 머리모양이 마

음에 들지 않는 표정인데, 미용사는

"Well, I think it's GORGEOUS and that's all that matters."

* Beauty is the eye of the beholder: 美는 보는 사람에 따라 다르다.
* beholder: 보는 사람, 구경꾼


• 사파리 같은 평원, 사자 둘이 사냥은 않고 water cooler에서 물을 먹으며

"Catch the game last night?"(어젯밤 게임 봤어?)

* Water cooler는 유대관계 돈독 장소(friends making, bonding activity)


• 경찰서 취조실에서 '오즈의 마법사'에 나오는 Tin man을 취조하고 있는

형사 A: "So you set fire to the Scarecrow and sold the Cowardly Lion to a circus."

형사 B: "I thought you had a heart, Tin man."


• At the atheist café

"I can't believe how good this is."

"I can't believe we haven't been here before."

"I can't believe these prices!"

* Atheist: 무신론자


• Dentist: "Helium?"

환자: "Will it kill the pain?"

Dentist: "No, but when you scream, it's funny."

- 불은 도망가고 있고 뒤쫓아오는 소방관은

"Quick! It's heading for the fire escape!"

* fire escape의 원래 의미는 화재 시 비상탈출구

- 돼지가 번호판이 'H1N1'인 차량을 운전하면서

"The cops never stop me since I got these vanity plates."

* Vanity plate: 장식번호판(돈을 더 주고 원하는 글자대로 만든 차량번호판)
* H1N1: 신종 인플루엔자 A

- 어느 건강염려 망상자의 묘비

Bruno Christoff

Chronic Hypochondriac

1950 – 1990 1993 1995 1998 2002 2004 2005 2008 2011 2013 2015

* Chronic Hypochondriac 만성적 심기증환자(건강염려증)

- 서부개척시대, 마차가 지나가고 있고, 이것을 보고 있는 산 위의 인디언

"Forget war parties. If we build a casino, they will hand over their money faster than we can pour drinks."

* War party: 1)일대의 진군하는 북미 인디언, 2)호전파 정당

- 죽어 하늘나라에서 천사가 된 친구를 만나

"Some friend you turned out to be! I was at your funeral, why weren't you at mine?"

- New from Apple: 귀에 peapod(완두 꼬투리)을 꽂고 있다
    * ppod: ipod와 대비

- 'Interest-Free Checking'이라는 Sign이 있는 은행창구
손님: "I'd like to open an account."
창구직원: "Who cares?"
    * Interest: 1)이자, 2)관심

- 도심 빌딩거리에 엄청 큰 광고판 'Jenifer, will you marry me? - Mike'
빌딩 위에 띄워진 광고용 애드벌룬 'Not a chance -Jen'

- 'No Dogs Allowed'라고 적힌 가게 앞에서 개 두 마리가
"Let's go in anyway & just pretend we can't read."

- 수술실(operation room)에서 나온 의사가 밖에서 기다리고 있는 Devil가족에게
"I'm afraid I have some good news."
    * Patient lived: 환자가 살아난 것이 Devil에게는 좋은 소식이 아니다

- Vegetarian Vampire가 blood orange를 먹고 있다.

* Blood Orange: 과육이 검붉은 오렌지

• Beethoven's second fifth: 베토벤이 피아노에 엎드려 자고 있다.
피아노 위에는 양주병과 악보가 놓여 있고..

* Fifth: 1)5번 교향곡 운명, 2)1/5 gallon(알코올 음료단위)

• 후보자 TV 토론회 사회자
"As a gubernatorialcandidate, what kind of guber would you be?"

* gubernatorial: Governer(주지사)의,

* guber: nut(바보, 괴짜): not so rational, nut case

• 화장실 표식의 남녀가 식탁에서 차를 마시며
남: "We've worked together for so many years, it's a wonder we never
hooked up before."
여: "Speaking of which, we should be getting back to the restrooms."

* hook up: 데이트하다

* get back: 돌아오다

• If puns are outlawed, only outlaws will have puns
빵을 배달하는 Bakery 차 운전기사에게, 길다란 빵조각을 마치 총인
것처럼 겨눈 강도: "Gimme all your dough!"

* Gimme: Give me

* pun: 동음이의(week 와 weak는 같은 발음)

* outlawed: 불법의(illegal)

* outlaws: 무법자

* dough: 1)가루 반죽, 2)현금


• 썰렁한 장례식장에서

"He had over 2000 Facebook friends. I was expecting a bigger turnout."

* Turn out: 나타나다(show up)


• 사냥개(Pointer 종)가 컴퓨터를 보고 있다.

사냥꾼: "She's a Power Pointer."

* Power Pointer: 미국 MS가 개발한 프레젠테이션용 도표 따위의 작성 소프트 웨어


• 수술실에서 나오는 수의사가 밖에서 기다리는 개를 향해

"Great news, Bella! Rocky went to the country to live on a farm!"

* 죽었다는 말을 완곡하게 표현
* Euphemism: 완곡어법


• 거지가 들고 있는 종이: 'I beg to differ'

* I beg to differ: 동의하지 않는다.


• 어린애에게 처음으로 개를 선물한 아빠가

"You can name her whatever you like, but be sure it's something you can remember. You'll be using it as a security question answer for the rest of your life."

* What was your first pet name? 컴퓨터 사이트에 access할 때 가장 자주

- Fence에 "Be aware of Dog"라는 간판이 붙어 있다. Fence 안에 있는 개:

"I'm not dangerous. I just appreciate the occasional nod of acknowledgment."

  * 개 조심이라는 간판은 'Beware of Dog', 'be aware of'는 '알고 있다'라는 뜻


- Bellybuttons
  * Innie(들어간 배꼽), Outie(나온 배꼽), Audi(네 개의 배꼽)
  * Audi는 차 brand


- 카운터에 주차확인 도장을 받으러 온 손님

"Will you validate my parking?"(주차권 확인 좀 해 주세요)

Counter 직원: "You did a great job. Evenly spaced, at nearly a perfect right angle."

  * 직원은 손님이 주차를 얼마나 잘했는지 평가하고 있다.


- GPS-Robber edition: "Go! Go! Hang a right! Cut through that alley!"
  * robber: 강도
  * Hang a right: 우회전 하세요(Turn right)
  * Cut through that alley: 지름길로 가세요(Take a short cut)

• 다정한 부부

"The ice in my wife's vein has melted! Thanks, global warming!"

   * cold hearted person: 인정이 없는 사람


• Science Projects Due Day에 커다란 악어를 들고 온 꼬마

"My homework ate my dog."

   * My dog ate my homework와 대비

   * 미국 학교에서 선생님이 '숙제를 왜 안 해 왔느냐'라고 물으면, 애들이 "I did,
     but my dog ate it."이라고 변명하는 경우가 많다.


• Bowling 옆 lane에서 경기하는 Devil

"Suddenly Mick realizes he's in league with the devil."

   * To be in league with: 나쁜 목적으로 함께 비밀히 작업하다(to be working
     together secretly for a bad purpose)

   * To be in a different league from: 훨씬 좋다(be much better)


• 컴퓨터로 speed dating을 하고 있는 젊은이에게 어른이

"In my day, 'Speed dating' meant something completely different."

   * Speed dating: 독신 남녀들이 애인을 찾을 수 있도록 여러 사람들을 돌아가며
     잠깐씩 만나 보게 하는 행사


• 독수리문양의 의사대(통상 미국대통령 상징, 한국에서는 봉황)에서

"We can't afford another generation raised on handouts! I move that
we ban Santa Clause!"

   * Handouts: Social security, Medicare 등 정부부담 기부

* I move that: 공식 상정합니다(formal meeting): I bring this motion
* Robert's rule of order(로버트 회의법): '회의진행법'(會議進行法). 국회법이
나 교회법 등 우리나라 공공 기관이나 교회의 모든 회의법은 '만국통상법'(萬國
通商法)으로 불리는 '로버트 회의법'(Robert's rule of order)을 토대로 만들어
졌다. 이 회의법은 다수의 결정권, 소수의 발언권, 결석자의 안전권을 보장하
는 데 기초를 두고 있으며, 예의 · 질서 · 절차를 대전제로 하고 있다.

• Lenny always treats 'Concentrate'as a verb

Orange juice concentrate를 컵에 따라 놓고 뚫어지게 쳐다보고 있다.

* Concentrate: 1) 농축, 2) 집중하다

• 접시안테나(Dish antenna)를 머리에 메단 토끼가 다른 토끼에게

"And I can't believe you still have rabbit ears."

* Rabbit ears antenna: 재래식 와이어 안테나

• 약사: "Yes, we carry placebos, but you'll need a fake prescription."

* placebo: 가짜 약
* fake prescription: 가짜진단서

• A: "It's raining out."

B:(막 컴퓨터를 켜고 녹화해 둔 것을 보려고 하던 차)

"I TiVo'd yesterday's weather forecast. Thanks for ruining it for me!"

* TiVo: 예약녹화 장치

• 목장에서 큰 소들이 어린 소를 보며

"Who's the new heifer?"

"Never seen herbivore."

> \* Heifer: 어린 암소
>
> \* Hervivo: 초식동물(her before와 발음이 비슷함)

• 서점 counter점원

Two 'Math for Dummies' at \$16.99 each. That'll be \$50.

> \* 미국인들은 계산기가 없으면 아무것도 계산하지 못한다

• Helium gas와 사과를 넣은 풍선을 들고 있는 사나이

"Wanna pop over to Newton's place and watch him freak?"

> \* pop over: 예고없이 잠깐 들르다(drop in unannounced, visit somebody's home for a short time)
>
> \* freak out: 흥분하다(go crazy)
>
> \* 뉴턴이 사과와 함께 헬륨가스를 마시면…

• 요란한 복장을 한 신참형사가 고참형사에게

"Come on, Lieutenant! What do I gotta to get promoted to plainclothes detective?

> \* plainclothes detective: 사복형사

• 약사가 손님에게 약을 건네면서 손을 내민다.

"Your money or your life."

- The Divisiveness continues

Washington으로 들어가는 고속도로 진입로 표시판

Washington A.C. – left lane

Washington D.C. – right lane

 * Divisive: 분열을 초래하는


- 비행기 내 안내방송

"We're ready for takeoff, so leave your cell phones on, keep your tray tables down and recline your seats as far as possible. Thanks again for flying Rebel Air."

 * Rebel: 반대자
 * Rebel Air이기 때문에 뭐든지 반대로


- 아빠가 아들에게

"When I was young, we pushed kids around just fine without computers!"

 * Cyber Bully: 약자를 괴롭히는 사람


- 약국에 온 아줌마

"I have an overwhelming desire to operate heavy machinery. Is there a pill for that?"

 * 약 복용 시 주의사항: 'Do not drive or operate heavy machinery while taking these pills…'

- The Blister Pack Avenger

물건 포장이 잘 뜯기지 않아 짜증이 나는 사람에게 가위를 들고 짠~
나타난 Hero

"Dry your tears, good citizen. I shall open it for you!"

> \* Blister Pack: 알약 같은 것을 기포같이 생긴 투명 플라스틱 칸 안에 개별 포
> 장하는 것

- 여자가 전화기에 대고 하는 말

"Then I say I'm low on minutes, I mean that life is too short to
waste talking with you."

> \* 얼마나 싫었으면

- 간호사: "Says here you're a type O."

환자: "That must be a typo."

> \* typo: 타이프 잘 못 친 것. 오자

- Scarescarecrow

새를 쫓는 허수아비 앞에 허수아비보다 훨씬 큰 새모양의 허수아비가
허수아비를 쏘아보고 있다.

> \* '허수아비'는 Scarecrow

- Beginner Palindromist

"Anal was I ere I saw Lana."

> \* Palindromist: Palindromes을 쓰는 사람
> \* Palindromes: 앞에서부터 읽으나 뒤에서부터 읽으나 동일한 단어나 구.

예: madam, nurses run(우리말에도: 여보게 저기 저게 보여)

- The weather or not channel

'As usual, tomorrow's weather is pretty much anyone's guess.'


- 술집 Bar에서

손님: "Nine dollars for a beer?"

직원: "Sorry, pal, it's crappy hour."

  * Crappy: 쓰레기 같은, 형편없는
  * Happy Hour(술집에서 정상가보다 싼 값에 술을 파는 보통 이른 시간대)와 대비


- 스님들의 시위

선창자: "What do we want?"

군중: "Mindfulness!"

선창자: "When do we want it?"

군중: "Now."

  * 완전히 모순이다


## 딕 브라운 만화 'Hagar The Horrible'

Hagar The Horrible 은 1973년에 Dik Browne이 연재를 시작했으나, 1988년에 Dik이 갑자기 사망하여 그의 아들 Chris가 이어받아 계속 연재하고 있다. 바이킹시대의 자유로운 해석을 통해 현재의 미국생활

을 평하는 작품이다.


• 말을 탄 중세기사가 긴 창으로 한 바이킹의 몸을 콕콕 찌르며
"We don't like Vikings here in England, stranger…. Do you get my
point?" 라고 하자, 그 Viking이 친구에게: "I have puns, don't you?"

  * pun: 1) 찌르다, 2) 동음이의 말장난(two interpretations),


• 사막 한가운데를 걷고 있는 두 사람
A: "Hum, hum, hum, da dee."
B: "Will you please stop humming 'Row, row, row your boat'?!"


• 판사 앞에 사람들이 줄을 서서 대기하고 있다. 맨 앞에 서 있는 사
람은 등에 화살이 3개가 꽂혀 있다.
판사: "What's your name?"
A: "Lucky Eddie"
판사: "No, seriously… what's your name?"
A: ???


• 무인도에 조난된 두 사람
A: There's always a silver lining in even the worst of situation.
B: What's the silver lining here?
A: I didn't pay my six-month bar bill before I left home!

  * Silver lining: 구름의 흰 가장자리
  * Every Cloud has a silver lining: 아무리 안 좋은 상황에서도 한 가지 긍정

적인 측면은 있다.

    * A silver lining: 불행 속의 한 가닥 희망(the bright side of a problem).

• 모두가 줄에 매달려 있는 벌을 받는데, 한 사람만 줄에 매달리긴 했지만 발판 위에 서서 벌을 받고 있다. 줄에 매달린 사람 중에 한 명이

"They say he has friends in high places."

• 판사가 Viking에게

"You have looked and taken over many English castles, distributed people's lives and forced them to leave their homes!"

"Are you sure you were never in the banking business?"

    * Bank를 Viking에 비유

## 마이크 피터스 만화 'Mother Goose & Grimm'

Mike Peters는 시사만화가(Editorial Cartoonist)로서 풀리처상을 수상했으며, 대표작은 1984년부터 연재한 Mother Goose & Grimm이다. 캐릭터들은 'Grimm'이란 이름의 Bull Terrier(목이 두껍고 코가 길며 털이 짧은 개)와 의인화된 거위 Mother Goose, 또 다른 개(Ralph) 한 마리, 고양이(Attilla) 한 마리다. 주제는 인기있는 문화나 뉴스 위주이다.

• Road kill(차에 치여 죽은 동물)을 먹고 있는 vultures(독수리, 콘도

르)

독수리 한마리가 다른 독수리에게

"Tell me… what did we eat before they invented cars?"


• 컴퓨터에 뭔가 문제가 있어 씨름하고 있는 사람에게

"What's wrong with him?",

"Puss 'N' reboots"

> * Puss and Boots(TV에 나오는 유명한 Cartoon 이름)와 대비


• 옥수수들의 대화

"Oh… in one ear and out the other… How about you?"

> * in one ear and out the other: 마이동풍(don't pay attention)
> * ear는 '옥수수 알'이라는 뜻도 있다. 알갱이 하나는 kernel, 옥수수 한 개는 an
>   ear of corn.


• 중세, 왕의 머리모양의 인형을 들고 있는 jester(joker: 중세 왕후 귀
족들이 거느리던 농담을 하는 사람, 광대)에게 왕의 시녀가 하는 말

"The king doesn't mind a few jokes at his expense, but quit while
you have a head"

> * jokes at one's expense: 농담의 대상이 되는 사람
> * Quit while you are ahead(정상에 있을 때 물러나라)와 대비


• 할아버지가 든 피켓: Repent
로봇이 든 피켓: Reboot

* Repent: 회개하라(ask for forgiveness, start over again)

　　　* Reboot: 부팅을 다시하다(similar to Robot)


• 심리치료를 받고 있는 조지 워싱턴(George Washington) 대통령

"It's that tea party group, no matter what happens they say 'Blame Washington.'"

　　　* Tea party group: 보수주의자

　　　* Blame Washington: 모든 원인을 대통령 탓으로 돌린다


• 한 사람이 집안으로 들어오며 "I'm here to fix the dog"이라고 하니, 이를 들은 집안의 수캐가 졸도("THUD☆")한다.

들어오던 사람: "Just kidding…the dishwasher."

집 주인: "I thought just girls fainted."

　　　* fix: 거세하다(neuter)

　　　* girls fainted: 암캐가 기절했다


• 지옥에서 여러 사람이 전화를 걸고 있다.

악마: "And this is the final ring of hell … Tele-marketers."

　　　* Dante의 신곡(La Divina Commedia)의 제1부 지옥편(the Inferno)에 나오는 the final ring of hell: 지옥 중 최악의 레벨(the worst level of hell)


• 애완견: "Why don't people ever take cats to church?"

고양이: "Cause cats don't like dogma."

　　　* Dogma: 종교적 신조, 교리

• 애완견:

"I think we're due for another vacation… you're almost out of motel soap."

> \* 주인은 여행가면 모텔비누를 잘 가져오는구나

• OZ in 2018: Can man은 Artificial Heart를, 허수아비는 Computer Brain을, 사자는Courage 약병을 들고 있다.

> \* 오즈의 마법사(The Wizard of OZ, 1939) 에는 '두뇌가 없는 허수아비, 심장이 없는 양철나무꾼, 겁쟁이 사자가 나온다.

• 1인용 배를 타고 양손을 깁스를 한 상태로 Carpal tunnel을 차례로 통과하고 있다.

> \* Carpal tunnel syndrome: 팔목터널 증후군

• Acme Thesaurus Co.에서 사장이 직원에게

"Simpson, you're fired, canned, discharged, downsized, sacked…"

> \* Thesaurus: 유의어

• 성문을 지키는 병사가 성 앞에 있는 목마를 보며

"It's from the Greeks…they say it's an economic stimulus package."

> \* Economic stimulus package: 경기부양종합대책

• 집안에서

A: "Strange, what happens to sour cream when it's past its expiration date?"

B: "It turns good."


• Elvis Presley가 칠판에 "You are not anything except a hound dog, You are not anything except a hound dog"이라고 두 번 썼다.

옆에 앉아 있는 선생님: "All right young man, write it again."

　　* Elvis Presley의 유명한 노래제목 'You aint nothing but a hound dog."


• 엄청나게 큰 개가 기절한 듯 누워있는 남자를 핥고 있다.

옆의 개: "Sorry about that… I think your pacemaker sounds like an electric can opener."

　　* pacemaker: 심장박동 조율기


• New York SAKS 5th Ave.에서 쇼핑을 한아름 해 온 왕비가왕에게 "It's okay, I borrowed the money from China."

　　* SAKS 5th Ave: 뉴욕 5번가에 본점을 두고 있는 패션 중심의 고급 백화점 체
　　　인


• 비서: "Bad news, Mr. Putin… the Chechens have come home to roost."

　　* Chechen 은 방사능 유출사고가 일어난 곳

　　* Chickens come home to roost(누워서 침 뱉기, 자업자득이다 )와 대비

　　* You know it is chickens come home to roost.: 누워서 침 뱉기라는 거 너
　　　도 알지?

• 원시인 Cave man, 많은 양의 커피를 들고 몸을 덜덜 떨고 있는 녀석을 보고 다른 Cave man이 "Java man"

> * Java는 커피로 유명

• 원시인이 불을 발견한 후

"Great innovation… Let's try testing it on animals."

   (옆에 누워있는 개의 눈이 동그랗게 커진다)

• 하늘 위 천사가 하프(Harp)는 없고 우체통에 편지를 부치고 있다

"I had to sell my harp… I'm still paying of my student loan."

> *Student loans: 대학 학자금 대출

• 잠을 청하는 사람에게 요정이

"Sandman? No, I sold out to a pharmaceutical years ago… care for an Ambien?"

> * Sandman: 모래를 뿌려 잠을 재워 준다는 요정
> * 미국의 배우이자 가수인 Rosemary Clooney가 부른 Popular song: 'Mr. Sandman, send me a dream.'
> * Ambien: Sleeping pill

• Sleep apnea(수면 무호흡증)이 있는 사람에게 산소호흡기를 가지고 와서 코에 대주는 요정

> * tooth fairy: 치아요정(빠진 치아를 베게 밑에 두면 헌 치아는 가져가고 새 치아를 준다)

• 개가 고양이 볼일 보는 곳(Kitty litter box)에 방향제를 뿌리며

"Let's just say I'm doing aroma therapy."

    * Aroma: 향기(Fragrance in oils, smells)


• 신문기사를 보며

"Oh dear…"

"The factory that makes trick birthday candles burned down last night."

"Firemen tried to put it out but it kept relighting."

    * Relight: 다시 점화하다(Trick Candle이니까)


• 식인종(Cannibals)들이 Dagwood(Blondie의 남편)를 잡아 놓고

"Really, I'm not kidding. We're having Dagwood sandwiches tonight."

    * Dagwood Sandwich: 여러 층으로 포갠 초대형 샌드위치


• 서부개척시대, 미국인과 인디언이 함께 말을 타고 가고 있다.

인디언: "Kimo Sabe, in most states, after 30 years, I'm your common-law sidekick"

    * Sidekick: 조수, 짝패, 동료

    * common-law marriage(사실혼)과 대비


• 주인: "Ralph, could you make me some orange juice? Just open the can and read the directions."

Ralph: "O.K."

한참이 지나도 아무런 소식이 없자 주인: "Ralph?"

Ralph:(can을 계속 들여 다 보고 있다) "It says concentrate."

* concentrate: 1) 농축액, 2)집중하다

* Orange juice made from concentrate

* Pure juice는 농축액이 없다.(No concentrate)


• 개: "Kora Kangaroo, how have you been?"

캥거루: "Oh fine… just fine, really everything is just fine."

(캥거루 뱃속에서 "BEER BONG!! 하는 소리가 난다)

캥거루: "My son moved back in with me."

* move back: 자녀가 부모집으로 다시 들어오다


• 사막에 설치돼 있는 자판기 옆에서, 갈증으로 다 죽어가는 사람이 지나가는 차량에 구걸하고 있다.

차량운전자: "Don't give him money, he'll only use it to buy a drink."

* Homeless에게 돈을 주면 술 사 먹는다고 생각


• 고대 로마시대

아내: "I'm sorry I'm late. I thought you said A.D. instead of B.C."

* 언제 어디서는 아내는 남편을 기다리게 하나보다(Wives keep husbands waiting…)


• 감자(Potato Head)가 롤러보드를 타고 계단 난간으로 미끄러져 내려오고 있다. 구경하는 짐승들이 "This is gonna end up on youtuber."

* YouTube라는 internet site와 tuber('감자'라는 뜻) 대비

* end up: 결국 ~이 되다.

• Buddhist Radio: No things considered

　　* NPR(National Public Radio)프로그램의 'All things considered'와 대비

• 슈퍼맨이 소파에 앉아 맥주를 마시면서 TV의 Football 경기를 보고 있다.

아내: "You can change the rotation of the earth, but you can't change an empty toilet paper roll?"

• 아인슈타인 흉상이 있는 공원의 이름: "MC Square"

　　* Time Square와 대비

• Hen house에서 닭들이 Fox news를 보고 있다. 어미 닭이 뛰어오면서 "I can't believe you guys are watching fox news in there!"

　　* Fox: 1)여우, 2)방송사 이름

• 식당에서 종업원이 험상궂은 인상에 불친절한 목소리로

"Have you heard today's special?"

손님: "Of course today's special. Every day is special if you approach life with the right attitude."

종업원:(돌아서며) "Freak."

손님: "I love a positive waitress."

* Freak: (못마땅할 때) 괴짜!


• Date 중인 남녀, 남자가 옆의자에 놓인 모양이 큰 의치같이 생긴 목걸이(Jewelry necklace)를 바라보고 있다.

부자인 듯한 여자, "That?... Oh, just an old family retainer."

    * old family retainer: 노복(늙은 하인)
    * dental retainer(의치, false teeth)와 대비
    * retainer: 1)변호사 의뢰비용, 2)소유물, 3) 가신(家臣)
    * family heirloom: 가보


• 아빠가 애기사진을 휴대폰으로 찍고는

"Honey, how do I send this baby picture to your mom's cell phone?"

Baby carriage에 있는 애기:

"Attach the photo to email, enter her number and press 'SEND'."


• 더러운 개에게

주인: "Gross, you're filthy! Don't you know that cleanliness is next to godliness?"

개: "Then I must be an agnostic."

    * filthy: 아주 더러운
    * Godliness: 신앙심 깊음
    * Agnostic: 불가지론자(not sure if God exist)


• 할로윈 호박(Halloween Pumpkin)에게

개A: "Hello, you've got a candle inside you. Doesn't that burn?"

개B: "Ralph, you realize you're talking to a pumpkin."

개A: "The light's on but nobody's home, if you know what I mean."

    * The lights are on, but nobody's home: '멍청하다(stupid)'라는 뜻


• '포인트'종 사냥개가 컴퓨터 자판 앞에서 쳐다보기만 하고 있다.

"He can point but he can't click."

    * Point-and-click 은 컴퓨터 사용자가 커서를 옮기는 기본 동작


• 해변에서 Oil을 뒤집어쓴 펠리컨, 펠리컨의 몸에는 조그만 Sign이 붙어 있다.

여자: "What does that little sign say?"

남자: "Wash, Rinse, Repeat."


• 여러가지 mounted game trophy heads를 가지고 있는 사냥꾼이 한 모형 코끼리 머리를 가리키며 "I bagged this one while he was walking out of Fao Schwarz."

    * bagged this one: 사냥하다(killed, shoot)

    * Fao Schwarz: 뉴욕에 있는 유명한 장난감 가게


• City morgue에 찾아온 왕자, 직원이 여자시체(공주처럼 보인다)가 누워있는 캐비닛을 열어놓고 휴대폰으로

"Get the coroner down here, some wacko wants to kiss number 42."

    * morgue: 영안실

    * coroner: 검시관

* wacko: 미친

• 감옥에 있는 죄수들, 서로의 cell phone을 보며

"Yeah, I've got full bars too."

　　* Bars: 1)교도소 창살, 2)휴대폰의 전지용량 나타내는 표시


• A: "I hope Grimmy's first day as a flight attendant went well."

B: "The airline called and said they'd drop him off here any minute."

Grimmy: 낙하산을 타고 떨어지며 "Take this job and …"

　　* Take this job and shove it: 유명한 노래, 집어서 던져라


• 거북이 두 마리

"I don't live in the Galapagos, but my family takes a vacation there every 200 years."

　　* Galapagos(갈라파고스): 에콰도르 서쪽에 있는 섬

　　* 십장생(Ten longest living things): Sun, Mountain, water, stone, cloud, pine tree, turtle, crane, deer.


• 손으로 뭔가를 더듬으며 걷고 있는 개를 보며

"He's been acting like that since I got the invisible fence."

　　* invisible fence: 남의 집 개가 못 들어오도록 하는 보이지않는 울타리


• 식당에서

"Hi, I'm your waiter Jim. This is my wife Jean, our daughter Sara, my mother-in-law Fran, her husband Bob, my mom & dad Barb and John."

• A: "I'm dating this new girl named piñata. She's from Mexico."
"But I don't think our relationship is going to last."
B: "Why not?"
A: "Guys keep hitting on her."

> \* Pinata: "주로 어린이 생일날 하는 놀이. Pinata 속에 초콜릿, 사탕 등의 선물
> 은 넣어 두고 눈을 가린 어린이들이 bet을 휘둘러 맞추면 선물이 쏟아지도록
> 되어 있다. Pinata는 나무 같은 데 매달아 놓고 어른이 뒤에 숨어서 연결된 줄
> 을 조정하여 주인공이 아닌 아이들은 헛스윙하게 한다.

## 밥 데이브스 만화 'Frank & Ernest'

미국 만화가 Bob Thaves(1924 – 2006)는 Frank and Ernest라는
comic strip을 1972년에 시작했는데, 그가 죽은 후에는 그의 아들인
Tom Thaves가 이어오고 있다. 이 만화의 특징은 '대단히 재치 있는 말
장난'(exclusively on wordplay and puns)이라 할 수 있다. Frank는 단
어 뜻 그대로 솔직하고 정직한(honest) 캐릭터이고, Ernest는 'earnest'
와 발음이 같은데 심각하고 진지한(serious) 캐릭터이다. 'Frank &
Ernest' 만화를 공부해 보면, 미국영어, 미국문화, 미국인의 생각 등에
대해 많은 것을 배울 수 있다.

• Royal furniture makers에서, 주인이 손님으로 온 왕에게 안락한 의

자를 권하며

주인: "And this model comes with a handy storage compartment.we call it a 'Throne's stone'!"

> \* Throne: 왕좌
>
> \* a stone's throw away: 돌을 던져서 닿을 거리

• 사진사가 왕과 왕비의 사진을 찍으려고 하자, 왕이 사진사에게
"Be careful. don't cut our heads off!"

> \* Cut one's head: 참수하다

• TV를 보고 있는 왕의 표정이 안 좋다, 이를 보면서
Frank: "He's upset because he tuned in to 'Tribute to the King', and it turned out to be about Elvis."

> \* Tribute to the King: 왕에게 바침

• 기자들이 왕에게
"How can you say a monarchy is better than a representative democracy?"
왕: "There's no assembly required!"

> \* Assembly: 1) 의회, 2) 조립

• The birth of free market economics(프리마켓의 시초)
(원시인 두 사람, 한사람은 돌을, 다른 한 사람은 나무막대를 가지고 있다.)

원시인 A: I wish I had a rock.

원시인 B: I wish I had a stick.


- 바위에 숫자를 써 놓고 1,5,4,7,8,6,3,2,9

원시인 A: I just invented numbers!

원시인 B: I knew we could count on you.

    \* count on: 그럴 줄 알았어. 성공 예상(you are very reliable.)


- 동굴에 벽화를 그리고 있는 사람을 보며

원시인 A: "I'm not sure which, but he's just invented either writing or vandalism."

    \* vandalism: 공공기물 파손 죄


- 원시부족들이 태양을 보며 신에게 감사하고 있다.

A: "He's making the sun stand still!"

B: "Ah, the 'brake' of the day."

    \* Break of a day: 새벽(dawn)

    \* Brake: 브레이크(stop a car)


- 원시인이 몽둥이로 사람을 후려 패 놓고는

A: "Clubs are great for instant messaging!"

    \* 몽둥이가 약


- 원시시대, 두 발로 걷게 된 사람이 여전히 네 발로 걷고 있는 사람

에게

"It's called 'Bipedalism'. I got the idea from a bird!"

   * Bipedalism: 두 발 보행


• Frank: "How did the focus group go?"

Ernie: I am not sure, it was all just blur."

   * Focus group: 시장 조사나 여론 조사를 위해 각 계층을 대표하도록 뽑은 소수
     의 사람들로 이뤄진 그룹

   * Blur: 더러운, 흐릿한


• Optometrists(검안사) Convention에서 강사가

"Okay, let's break into focus groups."

   * Focus group 1)토의를 위한 소그룹, 2) 눈의 초점을 맞추다


• 상추(Lettuce)가 사탕무(Red beet)에게

"We're all tired, and besides, it wasn't funny the first time you said 'I'm beet'!"

   * I'm beat: 피곤하다(tired)


• 야채(produce) 가게 주인

"Manage the inventory better⋯ spoilage is bankrupting me!"

손님들: "He's losing money because of all the dead beets."

   * Dead beets: 죽은 사탕무

   * Dead Beats: 몹시 지친, 게으름뱅이

• Science Fair에서 "Vegetable Growth rate"에 대한 논문이 1등으로
당선되었다.

Frank: "The winning entry studied how fast vegetables grow."

Ernie: "Clock the beet."

> \* Beat the clock: 시간 전에 마치다

• Bored Collie는 앉아서 하품을 하고 있고, Border Collie는 누워 있다.

> \* bored: 지루해하는
>
> \* Border Collie: 흔히 양치기 개로 많이 쓰이는종류의 개

• Frank's Moving Co.

Frank: "The keys to success in this business are relocation, relocation,
relocation!"

> \* 미국에는 'The keys to success in the business is location, location,
> location'이라는 격언이 있다.

• Frank & Ernie가 동료에게

"He avoids wrath, envy, lust, greed, gluttony and sloth··· the
problem is, he's proud of it!"

> \* The Seven Deadly Sins: wrath(분노), envy(질투), lust(성욕), greed(탐욕),
> gluttony(폭식), sloth(나태), and pride(자만).
>
> \* sloth는 '나무늘보'라는 뜻도 있다.

• 알파벳 철자 IOU가 함께 오고 있다. 다른 철자 EF가

"Here come those deadbeat guys again."

* deadbeat: 평판이 좋지 않은
* IOU: I owe you 와 발음이 같다


• 알파벳 Q 와 U는 항상 손을 잡고 다닌다. 다른 철자 E와 F가

"The only time I know when they've been apart is when he was in
IRAQ."

* Q로 시작되는 단어를 사전에서 찾아보면 Q 다음에는 항상 U가 따라온다.


• 인쇄체 문자(printing letters) EF가 필기체 대문자(writing letters)인
LD에게

"I never know what to expect from those guys… they're pretty loopy"

* Loopy: 1)이상한, 제 정신이 아닌(someone is not quite right mentally, not predictable, some crazy actions, ideas.), 2)고리모양의(loop: 고리)
* LD를 인쇄체 대문자로 쓰면 고리모양이 보인다.


• ULUFSE라는 순서로 줄을 서 있는 문자들에게

Frank: "Hey! Make yourself 'useful'!"

* Make oneself useful: 남에게 도움이 되다


• Medical lab에서

직원: "Ernie, we call it a 'paternity test', not a 'pop quiz'."

* Paternity Test: 친부 확인 테스트
* pop quiz: 예고없이 간단히 치는 깜짝 쪽지 시험
* pop: 1) 뻥하는 소리(팝), 2)아빠

- Bio lab에서

의사: "You crossed a stink bug with a segmented worm? What do you call it?"

Ernie: "A "sectipede"!"

* Centipede(지네)와 대비


- Biolab 연구원이 Frank에게

"At first, I didn't like bacteriology, but it grew on me!"

* bacteriology: 세균학
* grow on me: 차차 적응되었다.(I got used to it)


- Agriculture Research Lab에서 손님에게

박사: "I've come up with an onion that can be made into fuel… I call it the 'Gas leek'!"

* leek: 큰 부추같이 생긴 채소
* Gas leak(가스가 새다)와 대비시킨 유머


- 도서관에 책 빌리러온 사람이

"Toss me that copy of 'the Canterbury tales'"라고 하자,
사서가 책 한권을 던져주며 "It's a Flying Chaucer".

* Chaucer는 '캔터베리 이야기'를 쓴 작가이름
* Flying saucer(비행접시)와 대비


- 접시를 싣고 가던 트럭이 타임스퀘어(Times Suare)에서 사고를 냈다.

Frank: "That truck crashed and tea sets flew all over!"

Ernie: (휴대폰을 조작하며) "I'm tweeting… 'Flying saucers land in Manhattan!'"

　　* 날아간 접시니까 글자 그대로 Flying saucer(비행접시)


• A: "What's a twelve-letter term for an outfit with only one button?"

B: "Birthday suit!"

　　* 단추가 한 개뿐인 옷, 여기서 단추는 '배꼽'을 의미

　　* Birthday suit: 벌거벗은(naked)


• Frank: "What's a twelve-letter phase for 'modify anger'?"

Ernie: "Temper temper."

　　* Temper temper: 진정해(calm down, make less extreme)


• Frank: "I need seven letters for 'Dehydrated'. Can you help me out, Ernie?"

Ernie: "Sure, no sweat."

　　* Dehydrated: 탈수상태가 되다


• Adopt a highway 사무실 직원: "What first interested you in our program?"

찾아온 사람들: "I always wanted to say 'It's my way and the highway!'"

　　* Adopt a highway: 도로의 일부 구간을 특정회사가 맡아 청소도 하고 관리하

면서 그 회사는 자사를 광고하는 제도

* It's my way or the highway:  Frank Sinatra의 유명한 노래의 한 구절:
내 방식에 따르든지 아니면 네 맘대로 고속도로로 나가든지!


• Frank: 체중을 재고 있는 Ernest에게 "Why do you turn back the dial before stepping on the scale?"

Ernie: "It's my weigh or the high weigh!"

* 'It's my way or the highway'와 대비


• Personnel(인사부서) 사무실

담당자: We are overstaffed right now.(사람이 너무 많다)

Frank: With the amount of work I do, I'd hardly be noticed.

* 나는 일이 너무 많다


• Personnel 부서에 면접 보러 온 사람이 얼굴에 종이가면을 쓰고 왔다.

면접관: "How long have you been working in the private sector?"

* Private: 1)사적인, 비공개의, 2)민간의
* Private sector: 민간부문


• 회사 personnel dept.에서 Job interview 하는 사람

"Don't assume I'm incompetent, give me a chance to prove it!"

* incompetent: 무능한
* 무능함을 증명할 기회를 달라고??

- 직장상사를 보며

Frank: "Butter up the boss? No way! He's slippery enough already!"

  * Butter up: 1) 버터를 바르다, 2) 아첨하다(Flatter)
  * Slippery: 믿을 수 없는, 약삭빠른(Dishonest in a clever way, cunning, crafty)


- 상사에 대해 불만을 토로하는 직원

"There's no pleasing him. He tells me to go to extra mile and then complains when I'm late for work!"

  * 마태복음: Whoever compels you to go one mile, go with him two.
    (누가 너에게 1마일을 가라고 강요하거든 그와 함께 2마일을 가라)
  * No pleasing him: 아무것도 그를 즐겁게 하지 못한다(Nothing makes him happy)


- Dept. of Transportation에서 상사가 부하직원에게

"We're going to have to let you go. You're intelligent enough, but you lack street smarts.

  * let you go: 해고하다(fire you)
  * street smarts: 세상물정에 밝은(the skills and intelligence people need to be successful in difficult situations in big cities.)


- Piano tuner가 조율 중 선 하나가 끊어졌다.

Frank: "You broke a wire."

Ernie: "That'll cost a C-note!"

  * C-NOTE: 1) C 음표, 2) 100 달러 지폐

- 공원 벤치에 앉아서

Frank: "I always thought I was a pretty good guy until I googled myself."

> * google: 구글에서 자기이름을 찾아보다

- 간호사가 의사에게

"Mister Jones is back with his sore throat⋯he googled instead of gargled."

> * 의사는 가글(gargle)을 하라고 했는데 가글 대신 구글을 했으니 인후염이 낫지 않지.

- 남성복(menswear) 세일 매장, $30짜리 가격표가 달린 모자를 쓴 사람이

"Look, Ernie, there's a price on my head."

> * price on one's head: 현상금 수배자(public enemy: terrorist)

- 해변에서 새 두 마리가 물고기 등에 올라타 있다.

Frank: "Look at those birds sitting on the back of the fish!"

Ernie: "It must be a perch!"

> * Perch: 1)물고기 종류(type of fish), 2)횃대(Place where birds sit or roost)

- Frank: 새 집(birds nest) for sale,

Bird1: "And the best part is that this is a very seedy neighborhood!"

* seedy neighborhood: 1)씨가 많은, 2)평판이 나쁜

• F&E Dinner 식당에서 손님이 매워서 어쩔 줄 몰라 하고 있다.

Cook: "You asked for a hot breakfast, so I put some jalapenos in your corn flakes!"

　　* hot: 1)따뜻한, 2)매운

• 이삿짐센터 직원들이 교회에서

A: "Ever moved a church before?"

B: "The hardest part is the organ transplant!"

　　* organ transplant: 1)올갠 운반, 2)장기이식

• 간판 제작소에서 "Welcome back students"라는 간판을 만들어 놓고

직원A: This isn't right⋯ the sign for a gathering of new students!

(신입생 모집 간판인데 'welcome back'이라고 하면 틀렸어)

직원B: Yeah, but it's a chiropractic school!

　　* back: 1)돌아오다, 2)등

　　* chiropractic(척추지압사)에서는 등(back)을 마사지한다.

• Frank: "My uncle put his wife on a pedestal!"

Ernie: "He upped the auntie!"

　　* put somebody on a pedestal: 칭찬하다(admire)

　　* up the ante: 1) 판돈을 올리다(place a higher bet in poker), 2) 수요를 높
　　　이다(Make more demands)

　　* auntie(아줌마)와 ante를 대비

• 새 한 마리(Herold) 가 날아가고 있는데, 털이 빠져 날리고 있다.

새1: "Old Harold is losing his feathers!"

새2: "P–Too! And I'm getting down in the mouth!"

> * P–Too: 퇴!(sound has to spit something out of mouth)
> * Down in the mouth: 활기 없는(depressed, droopy, dispirited, discourage)
> * Down: 1)낮은, 2)새의 솜털(small, soft feathers)

<br>

• Dept of Seismology(지진학)

Frank: "The foundation is fully funding my San Andreas research!"

Ernie: "They're generous to a fault!"

> * San Andreas Fault: 북미 서해안의 대단층 이름
> * Fault: 1)잘못, 2)단층
> * be generous to a fault: 몫보다 더 많이 하다(do more than your share)

<br>

• 휴대폰(Cell phone)상점에 찾아와 Wireless Plans을 상담하는 손님에게

직원: "No, 'Rollover minutes' has nothing to do with hitting the snooze alarm and going back to sleep."

> * Rollover Minutes: 이번 달에 정해진 통화시간을 다 쓰지 않았으면 다음달로 이월해 주는 제도
> * rollover: '자명종시계를 눌러 놓고 다시 자다'라는 뜻이 있다.
> * Snooze(수잠, 낮잠, nap, doze) alarm

• 버섯에 대해 설명하고 있는 선생님을 보고

Frank: "He's been teaching a class on fungi for decades!"

Ernie: "He loves molding young minds!"

* Mold: 1) 곰팡이(biological:a kind of mushroom)

2) 형상 짓다, 인격을 도야하다(psychological)


• IRS Audits

Q: "Do you have tax records?"

A: "No, I pay about the same as most people."

* IRS(Internal Revenue Service): 미국 국세청

* Records: 1) 보고서, 2) 신기록


• A meal break in night court에 Piza 배달 온 직원에게

판사: "$29.95 for a pizza?!. This is a very serious charge!"

* Charge: 1) 요금, 2) 고발

* charged of a crime: 재판(trial)

* convicted of a crime: 유죄(guilty)


• 칵테일 파티장에서 한 남자가 한 여자에게

"Really?! You work in the theater? I had my leg in a cast once!"

* cast: 1) 깁스, 2) 캐스팅(casting)


• 날씬한 아가씨가 Ernie에게 손을 흔들며 반갑게 인사하면서 지나간다.

Frank: "How do you get dates with all those actresses?"

Ernie: "I don't say that I teach fly-fishing⋯ I tell them that I'm a 'casting director'."

* fly-fishing: 제물낚시
* Casting: 1) 투망, 2) 배역선정
* 단순히 'casting director'라고 하면, 투망으로 낚시하는 사람일 수도 있고, 연예인을 캐스팅하는 사람일 수도 있다.


• TV의 Election report를 보고 있는 사람들의 대화

A: "The political debates had huge ratings."(시청률이 아주 높다)

B: "'Dancing with the stars' was topped by 'Dancing around the issues!"

* 'Dancing with the star'는 유명연예인과 함께 춤추는 인기있는 TV 프로그램.
* 'Dancing around the issues'는 직설적으로 말하지 않고 빙빙 둘러서 말하는 것.


• Zoo dental clinic에서 의사가 곰에게

"You need to start flossing or you'll become a gummy bear."

* flossing: 치실로 치아청소하기
* Gummy Bear: 1)이빨 없는 곰, 2)캔디이름


• 'Enlightenment $5'라는 Sign을 세워놓은 산 위의 현인을 찾아온 구도자

Seeker: "Hey, I gave you twenty. Where's my change?"

Gulu: "Change comes from within!"(변화는 내부로부터 오는 것)

* Enlightenment: 깨우침
* Change: 1) 잔돈, 2) 변화

• 해변에 놀러 온 사람들이 책을 읽으며

A: "It's a good book for the beach about Thomas Edison and his most famous innovation."

B: "Ah, a little "light" reading."

　　* Light: 1) 가벼운, 2) 빛(에디슨이 전기를 발명)


• Therapist(치료사)가 Frank에게

"The first step in therapy is acknowledging your issues, or as I like to call it 'Baggage claim'!"

　　* Baggage: 1) 가방(bags), 2) 마음의 앙금(emotional problems, fixed ideas, prejudice)


• School of acupuncture(침술학교)에서 Frank:

"There's a competitive academic environment here··· this place is full of backstabbers!"

　　* backstab: 1) 바늘로 등을 찌르다(stab a person in the back with needle), 2) 중상, 험담하다


• Publishing Co.를 나오면서

Frank: "The editor rejected my novel about a group of buddies on a roadtrip···She said it had too many potholes."

　　* roadtrip: 장거리 자동차여행
　　* potholes: 1) 도로에 패인 웅덩이, 2) 잘 쓰이지 않은(not well written)

- Nudist colony(나체 촌)에서

A: "You lost the election for colony president?"

B: "Yeah, I wasn't unsuited for the job."

  * Suit: 1) 일자리에 자격이 된다, 2) 옷이 맞다, 어울린다


- 복싱 경기에서 벨트 아래를 가격해서 주의를 받고 있는 모습을 보며

Frank: "Tuba players shouldn't be boxers. they're always making low blows."

  * Tuba Player: Tuba(장중한 저음을 내는 금관악기)를 부는 사람
  * Low blow: 1) 벨트라인 아래를 치는 반칙 2) 저음


- 권투사진을 걸어 둔 변호사 사무실

Frank: "I trained fighters before I became a lawyer."

손님: "You went from boxers to briefs!"

  * briefs: 1) 팬티, 2) 준비서면(소송사건 적요서)
  * 권투선수는 Briefs를 입는다


- Dermatology Clinic(피부과 의사: Skin doctor)에서 채용면접

의사: "We're looking for somebody who can make rash decision!"

  * Rash: 1) 피부발진(skin rash treatment), 2) 경솔한, 성급한(Rapid foolish decision)


- 'Fire Exit' sign을 보고

Frank: "If there's a fire, I hope it can read!"

  * Fire Exit: 1) 화재발생 시 탈출구, 2)불이 꺼지다

• Superior 호수(미국 오대호 중의 하나)의 물관리를 담당하는 직원에게
Frank: "I think he's spent his whole career studying the one great lake just so he can say "Superior knowledge".

> \* Superior: 1) 호수이름, 2) 뛰어난
>
> \* 오대호(Great lakes)의 이름을 기억하는 방법: HOMES
>
>    (Huron, Ontario, Michigan, Erie, Superior)

• 'Home security Pat−Down' Sign
'Beware of dog'이라 적힌 집 앞에서 Frank가 "good boy" 하면서 앉아 있는 개의 머리를 토닥거려주고 있다.

> \* Home Security: 1) 국토안보, 2) 여기서는 단순히 집 지키는
>
> \* Pat−Down: 몸을 더듬으며 하는 신체검사(search, frisking)
>
> \* 개가 앉아 있다:Pet down

• 손바닥만 한 무인도에 조난된 세 사람, 그 중 두 사람이 서로 적대시하며 돌아 앉아 있다. 중간 사람이
"Stop being stubborn and shake hands⋯C'mon, guys, reach across the isle!"

> \* isle: Island(aisle과 같은 발음)
>
> \* Reach across the aisle: 의회에서 여. 야가 손잡다.

• 전원코드가 빠진 Stand light: "Everything seems so dark and gloomy."
Psychiatrist(정신과 의사): "I think you just need an outlet!"

> \* Outlet: 1) 콘센트, 2) 출구

• News : Huge factory blast

Frank: "The bathroom fixture factory blew up? What's the situation?"

Ernie: "Scattered showers."

> * fixture: 붙박이
>
> * Scattered showers: 기상예보(Weather report)에서 산발적 소나기

• 천체관측망원경을 보던 직원

Frank: "I've discovered thousands of talking birds on Pluto!"

Ernie: "Ah. Then it is a mynah planet after all!"

> * Mynah: 사람 목소리를 내는 새(minor와 같은 발음)
>
> * Pluto Planet(명왕성): 위성의 자격을 상실함(No longer qualifies as a planet)

• Frank:(악기를 연주하며) "How do you like my zither playing?"

Ernie: "Zither a way I can get you to stop?"

> * Zither 1) 악기의 일종, 2) 'Is there'와 같음

• Physical therapy(물리치료)를 받고 있는 Frank

"How do I know you're not just pulling my leg?"

> * pull one's leg: 1)다리를 당기다, 2)놀리다

• F&E Chimney Sweeps 회사 직원들

A: "These days we clean chimneys with a big blast of air."

B: "We call it a "Flue shot"!

  \* Flue: 1) 굴뚝이라는 뜻도 있고, 2) 독감을 의미하기도 함.


• Freight Elevator(화물전용 엘리베이터)를 보며

Frank: "What makes you think the elevator isn't working properly?"

Ernie: "You just said that it's 'coming down with something'."

  \* coming down: 1) 몸이 안 좋다(I'm getting sick, I'm feeling bad). 2) 내려
    오다


• 동물원에서 기린이 고개를 땅바닥으로 숙이고 있는 것을 본 수의사

"He needs a facelift."

  \* Facelift: 1) 주름제거수술, 2) 얼굴을 들다


• Ernest의 친구인 듯한 아가씨에게

Frank: "Ernie is using his smartphone to search the net for drinking establishments."

Ernie: "I'm not getting any bars!"

  \* drinking establishments: 주점
  \* Get in bars: 술집을 찾아 들다


• The carrier highlight for Washington plumbers

Department of Justice(법무부)에 온 Plumbing(배관회사) 직원

"We're here for the leak investigation"

  \* Leak: 1) 신문에 기밀 누설(Secret on confidential information given to
    the press, public), 2) 누수

• 옷을 몽땅 벗고 있는 남편에게 아내가

"I was talking about running your credit card through the machine when I said 'Strip Down'."

> * Strip Down: 1) Strip(천 조각) 부분을 아래로 향하게 하라, 2) 바지를 벗어 내려라

• 그리스 시대, 하반신이 말이 된 여자가 꽃을 들고 웃으며 다가온다. 이를 본 여자가 옆에 있는 어른들에게

"I told my friend I was looking for a stable relationship, and she fixed me up with a centaur."

> * Stable: 1) 안정적인, 2) 마구간
> * Fix me up: 만나다
> * Centaur: 켄타우로스(그리스 신화에 나오는 반인반마의 괴물)

• Lumber yard에서 한 사람이 나무 위에 앉아 있다. 일꾼들이

"He just hangs around here all day and then he tells people he has 'a seat on the board'"

> * Seat on the board: 1) 임원이 되다, 2) 나무 위에 앉아 있다

• The civil war(남북전쟁)에 대해 수업하고 있는 교실, 한 어린이가 손을 들고,

"I know! The surrender at Appomattox was made possible by a 'grant'."

> * Appomattox: 애퍼매톡스(미국 Virginia 주 중부의 도시: 남군 총사령관 Lee 장군이 1865년 4월 9일 북군 총사령관 Grant 장군에게 항복한 곳)

* by a grant: 보조금으로


• Health club massage room에서

Frank: "Ernie, you get a massage almost every day!"

Ernie: "It makes me feel kneaded!"

　　* knead: 반죽하다, 안마하다.(need와 같은 발음)

　　* It makes me feel needed(좋은 느낌, feel good)과 대비


• Grandfather's clock(괘종시계)의 대화

"I'm still hungry."

"Go back four seconds."(4초 뒤로 가라)

　　* Go back for seconds: 부페식당 같은 곳에서 '한번 더 가져와라'라는 뜻.(for
　　　와 four는 같은 발음)


• State penitentiary(연방교도소) 앞에서 간수가 휴대폰을 보며

"It's ironic, but I don't get any bars here."

　　* Bars: 1) 교도소 창살, 2) 휴대폰의 전지용량 나타내는 표시


• Pharmaceuticals warehouse(약국 창고)에서

Frank: "Has that shipment of medicated ointment left the warehouse?"

Ernie: "Balm away!"

　　* lip balm: Neosporin 연고

　　* balm은 진통제(bomb와 같은 발음)

　　* Bombs Away: 음악그룹 이름

• Ernie··· the world's greatest optimist

"My girlfriend thinks our relationship is one of for the ages···last night she said 'we're history'!"

　　* History: 1) '우린 이제 끝났어'라는 뜻, 2) 역사에 기억될 만한 일


• 바다에서 조난당한 Frank와 Ernest

Ernie가 해초(kelp)를 한 다발 들고 온다.

Frank: "Sea kelp? I said 'seek help'."


• 배 위에서 선장: "Arrgh, that's a strange device ye have there!"

선원: "Arrgh, 'tis an 'Aye-phone'!"

　　* Arrgh: 탄식(puzzled about something)

　　* Aye: 네(i와 같은 발음)

　　* i-phone: 애플사의 아이폰, Aye-phone과 대비


• 리모컨으로 TV 채널을 바꿔서 풋볼(football)게임을 보고 있는 친구에게

A: "Is that a new hi-tech remote?"

B: "Yeah, it's a real game changer!"

　　* Game changer: 바뀐 선수로 인해 게임을 반전시킨 경우, 그 선수를 일컫는 말

　　* 여기서는 리모컨이 Game Changer


• Operating Room 유머(Humer)

Frank: "Why are anesthesiologists assumed to be honest."

Ernie: "Because numb–ers don't lie!"

    \* Anesthesiologists: 마취과 의사

    \* Numbers don't lie: 숫자는 거짓말하지 않는다.

    \* numb: 무감각한, numb–ers는 무감각한 사람

    \* Numbers와 numb–ers를 대비


• 군대 정문을 나서는 의가제대병

"Double negatives have nothing to do with it, Ernie. A 'dishonorable discharge" is bad news."

    \* dishonorable discharge: 불명예 제대

    \* Two negatives make a positive(부정의 부정은 긍정)과 대비


• Frank: "It's a 'futility bill'. I have no chance of being able to pay it."

    \* futility: 쓸데없음, 무익

    \* Utility Bill(전기, 수도, 가스 등의 고지서)과 대비


• 수도원 내에서 편지를 쌓아 놓은 모습을 신부에게 들키자

A: "We've started an advice column."

B: "It's called 'Dear Abbey'!"

    \* Abbey: 대수도원

    \* 미국신문에 "Dear Abby' 라는 유명한Advice Column이 있다.


• Drug store가 도둑에게 털렸다. 카우보이 차림의 경찰들이 와서

A: "Somebody broke in, but all they took was cough drops."

B: "Must have been a hoarse thief!"

* cough drop: 기침 멎게 하는 약
* Hoarse: 목 쉰. Horse와 대비(Horse thief 은 말 도둑)

• 사방에 고릴라들이 판을 치고 있는 공원 벤치에서 두 사람의대화

"What gives with all these gorillas?"

"We're in the month of Ape-ril!"

* Ape: 유인원(April과 같은 발음)

• Frank: "The boss yells at me whenever I try to think outside the box!"

Ernie: "He's giving you some constrictive criticism!"

* Think outside of the box: 고정관념에서 벗어나다
* Constrictive: 바싹 죄는, 긴축적인
* Constructive: 건설적인(Building up)
* Constrictive: 바싹 죄는, 긴축적인(narrower, limits actions)

• Wall Street Unemployment 사무실

Agency: "Reason for dismissal?"

Frank: "Thinking outside the bucks."

* bucks는 돈
* 'Thinking outside the box'와 대비

• Science Books 전문 서점

"Do you have any books about Lepidoptera?"

"Yes, and would you like to join 'the book of the moth club'?"

* Lepidoptera: 나비 목

* Moth: 나방

* the book of the month(이 달의 책)과 대비


• 휴대폰 가게 진열장에는 Texting –Hardware, –software, –plans 같은 문구가 있다. 점원이 손님에게 "Most of our business comes from word–of–thumb!"

* word–of–mouth(입에서 입으로 전해지는 소문)과 대비


• 깨어진 Humpty Dumpty를 보며

Frank: "He just fell off the wall."

MD: "I sound like a case of 'restless egg' syndrome."

* Humpty– Dumpty: 1) 영국의 전래 동요(nursery rhyme)에 나오는 주인공으로 달걀꼴 사람, 담벼락에서 떨어져 깨져버린 달걀의 의인화, 2)한 번 부서지면 원래대로 고쳐지지 않는 것, 3)[미 · 속어] 낙선이 뻔한 후보자

* Restless: 가만히 못 있는

* 동요: Humpty Dumpty sat on a wall,

Humpty Dumpty had a great fall.

All the king's horses and all the king's men

Couldn't put Humpty together again.


• 자동차 수리소(Auto repair shop)에서

Mechanic: "I'm just taking it in for a few adjustments."

손님: "A visit to the car–o–practor!"

* Chiropractor adjustment(척추신경마사지)와 대비

• Ernie's discount clinic: 손님에게 시계를 건네 주며

Doctor: "I didn't see the need to go to medical school, I just give everybody a clock⋯ the time heals all wounds, you know."

   * 시간은 만병통치약


• Daily News Headline 부서

Editor: "Here's a story about a guy who shaved his racehorse to cut wind resistance, and the horse got a terrible sunburn."

Frank: "a pony shaved is a pony burned."

   * 속담 'A penny saved is a penny earned.'와 대비: Money that you save is more valuable than money that you spend right away.


• 뱀들의 대화

A: "I think some people don't like us just because we don't have feet!"

B: "Don't pay any attention to the lack—toes intolerant!"

   * Lactose intolerant(유제품에 대한 과민반응)과 대비


• Frank: "According to the program, cows have four stomachs so they can digest the grasses they eat."

Ernie: "You must be watching "Graze anatomy!"

   * Graze: 풀을 뜯어 먹다
   * Gray's Anatomy: 해부학 교과서
   * Grey's Anatomy: 인기있는 미국TV Show(Medical Drama)
   * 미국의 TV Show는 한국의 TV 프로그램과 같은 의미

- Soap Opera(연속극): Problem doesn't get resolve in 1 session
- TV Drama(드라마):1 hour episode: problem gets resolved
- Situation comedy(코미디)
- Documentary(다큐멘터리)
- Talking …(대담)

- **Ghost Hunters**

Frank: The spirit just pinched my backside!

Ernie: You were "polter-goosed"!

* goosed me: 뒤를 꼬집다(pinched me on the backside)
* polter goosed: 귀신의 초자연적인 힘이 사물을 움직이다(Ghost supernatural force moves objects)

- Frank: "My cousins from Barcelona showed up unannounced, and have been here for weeks!"(예고없이 와서 몇 주째 머물고 있다)

Ernie: "The Spanish Imposition!"

* Impose: 강요, 부과
* Spanish Inquisition(기독교가 아닌 사람 처형한 역사,1478-1834)과 대비

- 'Seminar Today: Making your money go further' 세미나장 (회의장에서 종이비행기가 날아 나온다.)

Frank: "It's just a tutorial on folding paper airplanes."

* tutorial: 개별지도
* Money go further: 돈을 불리다(Stretch your money)

- 교통표시판: 'Stoop – Low Creance ahead'
  * Stop 대신 Stoop
  * Stoop: 몸을 구부리다


- Frank: I'm being evicted from both my apartment and my office!"
Ernie: "The evil of two lessors!"
  * Evict: 쫓겨나다
  * The lesser of two evils(둘 중 덜 나쁜 것 선택)과 대비


- 아주 화가 나 소리지르는 난방설비 작업자를 보며
Frank: "Is the heating contractor mad about something?"
Ernie: "He just needs space to vent."
  * "I just need to vent": 화를 풀기 위해 크게 소리치다(express, say out loud – feeling of stress anger, frustration)


- Not clear on the concept
문신가게(Tattoo shop)를 찾아온 고객: "I'd like to return this tattoo."
  * 미국의 물건반품체계는 대단히 편리하지만, Tattoo 반품은 어떻게?


- History dept. 에서 나오는 Frank에게 Ernie가
"Hi, Frank, how is life in the past lane?"
  * Life in fast lane(잘 나가던 때)와 대비


- Podiatrist(발 전문 의사)에서
조수: "The shoe repairman wants to callus removed."

의사: "Ahh, a corn on the cobbler!"

 * callus: 굳은 살
 * A corn: 티눈
 * Cobbler: shoe repairman
 * I love fresh corn on the cob in the summer.

   Corn은 옥수수, 이때의 corn은 kernels(옥수수 알갱이), cob은 corncob(옥
   수수 속대)


• Medical center에서 주차장으로 걸어 나오면서

의사: "Being a plastic surgeon, I do very well in a sagging economy!"

 * Sagging economy: 침체경제


• Animal preserve director's office에서

Frank: "I've been demoted from the primate house to the bird
sanctuary!"

Ernie: "You've been sent back to the mynahs!"

 * demote: 강등
 * Primate: 영장류(gorillas, monkeys)
 * mynahs: 구관조(minors와 발음이 같다)
 * Sanctuary: 보호구역


• 'Question authority', 'I'm with stupid', 'I love N.Y.' 같은 logo가
새겨진 T-shirts를 입고 있는 사람들을 보며,

Frank: "What's the deal with all the message T-Shirts?"

Ernie: "It's clothes captioning!"

* Close captioning(청각장애인을 위한 TV Caption)과 대비

• 구두수선(Shoe Repair) 가게 앞에서
Frank: "Shoe Repair" --- it must be for people who have lost one shoe and want to replace it!"
　　* 'Re-Pair' 와 'Repair'를 대비

• Insurance agency에서 나온 사람이
"I couldn't get health coverage due to a pre-existing condition … I'm broke."
　　* Pre-existing condition: 기존질병, 여기서는 파산한 상태를 의미

• Robotic Inc.
R1: He's coming back to work here? I thought he was obsolete.
R2: He was retired, rewired, and rehired.
　　* obsolete: 한물간, 더 이상 쓸모 없는

• First Vegetable Savings and Loan 회사 슬로건:
'Lettuce mushroom your cabbage!'
이를 본 Frank: "Corny."
　　* 보통 Savings & Loan 회사의 슬로건: 'Let us grow your money'
　　* Corn: 곡식, corny: 진부한, 시시한

• 데파트 스토아 창고직원: "The undergarments are still back-ordered."

Frank: "Ah, late bloomers!":

   * Undergarments: 속옷

   * Back-order: 이월주문

   * Late bloomer: 만성형의 사람

   * Bloomers: 속바지


• 딱따구리를 보면서

Frank: "The woodpecker's sending that tree into bankruptcy… He's always sticking him with the bill."

   * to stick someone with the bill: 지불해야 한다(have to pay, give him the bill each time)


• When I got to the land of milk and honey, I found out I'm lactose intolerant and allergic to bees!

   * The land of Milk and Honey:(성경) 젖과 꿀의 땅

   * Lactose intolerant:(우유 속에 많이 들어 있는) 젖당에 대한 알레르기

   * Allergic to bees: 벌 알레르기


• Road Rage(도로의 분노)

고물자동차가 지나가는데 도로가 벌떡 일어나 외친다

"Hey! Your noisy muffler woke me up! "

"And fix that oil leak before coming back here again!"


• F&E parachutes 주인

"Maybe not getting any calls on our complaint line isn't a good

thing!"
<blockquote>* 사고 나면 죽었을 거니까</blockquote>

• 애벌레(caterpillar)에서 나비로태어난다. 애벌레 왈
"He's my inner child!"
<blockquote>* Inner child: 내면의 어린이(어른의 마음속에 존재하는 어린이 부분)</blockquote>

• F&E Glass co.에 찾아온 손님이 거울을 들여다 보고만 있자
주인: "I hate those days when it seems like every customer jokes that they're 'going window shopping'."
<blockquote>* Window shopping: 우리말 아이쇼핑(not buying just browsing), 여기는 유리가게이니까 실제로 유리 쇼핑</blockquote>

• Hades check in counter에 온 사람이 지옥사자를 보며, 동료에게
"Bad news, he says we're not just here for our fifteen minutes of flame!"
<blockquote>* Hades(하데스): 지옥(hell)</blockquote>
<blockquote>* 15 minutes of fame: 아주 잠깐 각광을 받고 잊혀지는 것</blockquote>
<blockquote>* 여기서는 Fame 대신 Flame</blockquote>

• Defense Contractor Inc.에서 바퀴 달린 이동식화장실을 보며
Frank: "It's a portable bathroom for navy ships."
Ernie: "Head will roll."
<blockquote>* Head in Navy: 화장실(toilet)</blockquote>

• E-book을 읽고 있는 아이들

"My mom says this story is a real 'page-turner', I have no idea what she means by that."

   * Page-turner: 책장 넘기기가 바쁠 정도로 흥미진진한 책
   * E-book에서 어떻게 책장을 넘기나?


• In box는 없고 Out box만 두개 있는 사무실 책상에 앉아 있는 직원: "In many ways this is the perfect job"

   * 'In box'는 외부에서 오는 문서 보관함, 'Out box'는 외부로 보내는 문서 보관함.


• 오늘의 설교(Today's Sermon): 'We come into this world with nothing and we leave with nothing' 이를 본 Frank가 목사에게,
Frank: "Is there any chance of bailout?"

   * bailout: 긴급구제


• Japanese cuisine 식당 내에서 요란한 소리가 들린다
"What's the matter with chef?
"He's just having a tempura tantrum."

   * Temper tantrum(울화통이 나 안달복달하는 것) 과 '덴뿌라'를 대비


• 자전거 가게(Bicycle shop)에서 주인이 'No Peddlers Allowed'라는 Sign을 만들고 있다.
이를 본 친구: "Maybe you should change that to "No solicitors".

　　　 * Peddler(마약판매원)과 자전거 페달을 대비

　　　 * Solicitors: 잡상인(salesman)


• 농장에 와서 돼지와 소를 보고 있는 Frank

"Ironically, the pig has a pulled calf muscleand the cow has a strained hamstring."

　　　 * pulled calf muscle: 종아리

　　　 * strained hamstring: 허벅지


• 카지노 뷔페 식당 'All you can eat buffet'에서 Frank

"Now here's a game where I can beat the house!"

　　　 * 음식을 엄청 많이 먹어서 casino 회사에 손해를 입히겠다.


• A: 훌쩍이며(Sniff), "My allergies are acting up and I can't find the pollen count anywhere!"

B: "Who's minding the spore?"

　　　 * Spore(홀씨)를 store와 대비

　　　 * Who's minding the store? 가게는 누가 보나? 누가 네 일을 대신해 주나? 네 일은 어떠하고 나왔나? '소는 누가 키우나?'


• Santa's accountants recommend budget cuts:

Frank가 Santa에게

"If you raise your naughty-nice standards, you'll save billions of toys this year!"

　　　 * naughty-nice standards: 나쁜 애-착한 애의 기준

- 임신한 엄마와 동생과 함께 산책 나온 꼬마아가씨

"I'm hoping a little sister⋯ I want to be majority leader!"

    * Majority Leader: 다수당 대표


- CD를 손에 들고

Frank: "One thousand hours of chamber music? Where did you get this?"

Ernie: "At the big bach store."

    * A big-box store(규모가 큰 소매점)와 대비

    * John Sebastian Bach: 독일의 작곡가 바흐


- Mega Corp pharmaceutical 신약 선전 'New! Safe and Defective!'

Frank: "Tell marketing to stop relying on spell-check."

    * 'Safe and Effective'가 바른 표현, Defective는 '결점이 있다'는 뜻


- 다림질을 하며

세탁소 주인: "During the job action, I'm making money by doing laundry."

Frank: "Ironing while the strike is hot."

    * Job Action: 두드리다(Strike, walk off)

    * Strike while the iron is hot(쇠는 달궈졌을 때 두드려라)와 대비

    * Timing: 타이밍(Action move at the right time)


- Moses and the Burning Bush

Smokey the Bear(산림화재예방운동의 마스코트)에게 모세가

"I didn't start it, I swear!"

• Investment Bankers를 수사하고 있는 FBI요원에게 취재기자가

"Hey, is this a typo?... it says 'Accounts Deceivable'."

* Account Receivable(미수금)과 대비, Deceivable 은 '속일 수 있는'이란 뜻


• F.B.I: Financial Fraud Investigation unit에서

Frank: "The accountant passed his lie detector test. Where should I file the results?"

Ernie: "In 'Account believable'!"

* Account Receivable과 대비


• 수학(가감승제)을 가르치는 선생님에게

학생: "I don't need to know any math… I'm going to be a politician."

* 정치인은 어느 나라든 정말 문제다.


• 보석상에 강도가 들었다. CSI unit에서 조사중

A: "It was a perfect theft. They didn't leave any evidence."

B: "Ah, stainless steal."

* stainless steel 과 steal의 대비

• 공원 벤치에 앉아

A: I chose the path of least resistance and have been going downhill ever since.

> * choose the path of least resistance: 차선책을 택하다(not necessary to be the best way)
> * going downhill: 나빠지다(worse)

• TV를 보면서

Frank: "Too many people post comments in the heat of anger."

Ernie: "They strike while the ire is hot."

> * in the heat of anger: 분노의 열기(all stirred up emotions, rage, anger)
> * Ire: 분노
> * Strike while the iron is hot.(쇠는 뜨거울 때 때려라)와 대비

• Pet shelter앞에서 주인이 손님에게 목줄을 건네며

"If you can't decide which dog to adopt, try taking one for a walk"

손님: "Leash to own!"

> * Lease to own(빌리는 것으로 시작해서 마지막에는 구매하는: rent and buy in the end)과 대비

• 은행에서 계좌내역(Account statement)를 보고 있는 남자

"My account doesn't give any return on my money, but a lot of my checks are coming back."

> * 이자 들어오는 건 없고 잔고부족으로 수표만 되돌아온다.

• 등껍질을 떼어 낸 snail(달팽이)이 동료 snail에게

"I thought getting rid of my shell would make me quicker, but I just feel sluggish."

    * sluggish: 게으른, 동작이 느린

    * slug: 민달팽이


• Frank: "This berry plant destroyed all my new landscaping."

Earnie: "Swept away by a strong currant!"

    * Currant: Berry의 일종

    * Swept away by a strong current.(수압 센 호스로 씻어내다)와 대비


• 신문을 보며

친구: "It says here that you sleep less as you get older."

Ernie: zzzz

Frank: "I think Ernie has found the fountain of eternal youth."

    * Fountain of eternal youth: 영생의 근원


• 두 사람이 음식을 먹으며 식탁 밑으로 많이 흘린다. 옆에 앉아 있는 개

개A: "What's for dinner?"

개B: "Leftunders! "

    * leftover(먹고 남은 음식)과 대비, 식탁 밑으로 흘리니까 leftunder?


• 'Cash for Clunkers'를 찾아온 Frank 여자친구에게

가게주인: "Sorry, ma'am, it's cars not boyfriends in the 'Cash for clunkers' program."

* Cash for clunkers: 오래된 자동차 바꾸면 현금 지원해 주는 제도
* 여자는 남자를 바꿔 달라고…


• A:(자랑스럽게 친구들에게)

"Hey, I qualified for a program that gives aid to under achieving students!"

B:(옆 친구에게) "Cash for flunkers!"

* Flunkers(낙제생)를 clunkers와 대비


• 5K Run(5 km 달리기대회), 녹초가 된 Frank에게 질문

"How'd the 5K go, Frank?"

"I only made it to 'G'"

* G → H → I → J → K: '완주하지 못했다'는 뜻.


• News, Mixed economic data를 보고 있는 사람들

A: Do you see the glass half−empty or half−full in this case?

B: Neither, all I can see is the giant crack in the glass!


• Capitol gym에서 스태프들이 몇 가지 운동기구들을 보며

"This model was designed just for politicians…it reverses direction without any warning!"

* 어느 나라든 정치인이 문제다.

• 공원 벤치에 앉아 있는 노인들

노인 A: "Life didn't pass me by… I just refused to keep up!"

　　* Life passed me by: 해놓은 일 없이 인생이 덧없이 지나갔다


• 수학자 Euclid에게

"You're working too hard, Euclid… Let's go do some angling!"

　　* Angle은 '각도'라는 뜻이지만, 여기서 Angling은 낚시(Fishing)를 뜻함


• 길거리에서 'World ends today' 라는 간판을 든 사람과 'World ends tomorrow'라는 간판을 든 사람을 보고

"Like lots of people, those two are having a tough time making ends meet."

　　* Make ends meet: 겨우 먹고 살만큼 벌다


• Junk food에 파묻혀 있는 친구들

"Have you ever noticed how well this stuff fills in the cracks between the blocks of food pyramid?!"

　　* Food pyramid 칸 안에 들어가지 않고 사이사이를 채워주는 음식?


• Book club tonight: 'The catcher in the Rye'

Frank: "What a disappointment! I thought it was going to be about a baseball player opening a Deli."

　　* The catcher in the Rye: 호밀밭의 파수꾼; J. D. Salinger의 소설(1951).

　　* Rye bread: 호밀로 된 빵

• 맥주집 안에서 두 사람이 건배를 하고 있다.

A: "My philosophy is that there's nothing so important it can't be blown off."

B: "Sneeze the day"

　　* You can blow off everything(I don't care 라는 뜻)

　　* Sneeze: 재채기하다

　　* seize the day: 내일까지 기다리지 마라.(Don't wait until tomorrow)


• Auction(경매)

Frank: "Let's start the bidding at one thousand dollars!"

Ernie: "A 'Grand' Opening!"(그랜드 오프닝)

　　* Grand: 1)1000, 2)웅장한


• Apiary(양봉장)에서

양봉업자: "I tried living in the city but didn't like the crowds, so I moved out here to make honey.

Frank: You went with plan bee!

　　* 'Plan B'와 대비


• 엄마오리가 땅바닥에서 착지연습을 하고 있는 새끼오리들에게

"No, that's not necessary…in the event of a water landing, we are flotation devices."

　　* 'flotation'은 'floatation'과 같은 말이고, 'floatation devise'는 '구명보트'(lifeboat)라는 뜻이다. 여기서는 'devices'와 'devise'를 대비

- 벌목 작업 중 나무 나이테를 보면서

작업자: "The wobbly, discovered rings are election years."

  * 나이테: Rings of growth
  * 나이테가 고르지 못한(wobble: 흔들리다)것을 보고 '선거가 있었던 년도'라고
    추측: 그럴 듯하다.


- 원자력 발전소(Nuclear power plant)에서

Frank: "The tiny computer components on this board regulate the operation of the reactor."

Ernie: "How about that! Fission chips!"

  * Fission: 핵분열
  * Fish'n chips(피쉬 엔 칩스:Restaurant menu)와 대비


- 마야 달력회사(Mayan calendar co.)가 폐업을 하겠다(Going out of business)는 Sign을 걸어 놓고 있다.

Frank: "Don't take it so hard, Ernie. It's not the end of the world."


- 동물원(zoo)에서

Frank: "It's Wednesday again… time to wash the camels."

Ernie: "I hate 'Hump'day."

  * Hump: 낙타 등
  * Humpday: 수요일


- 벌들이 벌집안에서 "I'm tired of working in a cubicle"

  * Cubicle: 좁은 방

• Frank: "There used to be a palindrome club in town and I'm starting it up again."

Ernie: "Ah, you're a reviver!"

　　* Palindrome: 앞에서부터 읽으나 뒤에서부터 읽으나 동일한 단어나 구(소주만 병만주소)

　　* 'reviver'도 하나의 Palindrome


• Faculty lounge

Ernie: "Archaeologists(고고학자) throw the worst parties－－－ we went to a field and looked for leg bones."

Frank: "It wasn't a party, Ernie. It was a 'shin－dig'"

　　* 'shin'은 '정강이 뼈', 'dig'는 '파다'라는 뜻

　　* Shindig party(떠들썩하고 흥겨운 파티)와 대비


• Famous last words ~~ Cleopatra

뱀에 물린 클레오파트라(Cleopatra)가 뱀(asp)을 가져온 시종들에게

"Idiots! I said bring me an 'Aspirin'!"

　　* Aspirin 과 asp 대비


• IRS Tax payer information에서

"I'm sorry, sir. That loophole is preserved for people in the loop."

　　* Loophole: 법의 허점

　　* People in the loop: 주류(Main stream)

　　* out of the loop: 비주류(outside)

　　* Rich take advantage of loophole(부자는 법의 허점을 이용한다)

- 병충해 방제(Pest control) 회사 직원

"I love fighting termites! They're such a bunch of gnaw–it–alls!"

   * Gnaw: 갉아먹다

   * Know–it–all: 아는 체하다(act or think they know everything)


- Frank: "It's an abbreviated guide to the Grand Canyon."

Ernie: "Cliffs Notes."

   * Cliffs: 절벽

   * Cliffs note: 1)요약(Essence, Summary), 2)미국상표: 명작요약 학습참고서
      시리즈


- 소방관 채용면접장(hiring firefighters)

"All my friends say I'm a real wet blanket!"

   * Wet blanket: 원래 의미는 '다른 사람의 장난을 망쳐버리는 사람'(person
      tries to spoil other people's fun), 여기서는 글자 그대로 '젖은 담요'라는 뜻


- 과일 병사들이 작전을 수행하고 있다. 무전병에게

"We need more men··· call up the preserve!"

   * Preserves: 보관창고

   * Reserves(보충대)와 대비


- Frank: "As the earth's temperature rises, shouldn't my heating bill
fall?"

   * 비싼 난방비 풍자

- Pet shop 안내판: 'Sale! Buy one dog, get another flea!'
  * Flea market은 벼룩처럼 잽싸게 사고 판다는 뜻에서 유래?
  * Buy one, get another free(한국의 1+1)과 대비


- Gas & Food에서 먹을거리를 잔뜩 사서 나오는 Ernest를 보고,

Frank: "To Ernie, 'Filling station' means just that!"
  * Gas Station(주유소)과 대비


- 육면체에게 세모와 원이

"Three—dimensional, eh—what makes you so spatial?"
  * Spatial: 공간의, 공간적인(relating to space)
  * What makes you so special? 과 대비
  * globe: 3 dimensions of circle


- Near great movie: 'Mutiny over the Bounty'

선장의 명령: "Swap the deck"

선원의 항명: "Captain Bligh, we refuse to swab the deck with paper towels!"
  * Bounty는 paper towel의 브랜드 이름, Mutiny about the Bounty의 의미
    이지만, 전치사 'Over'는 'On'과 비슷하다.
  * Mutiny on the Bounty: 유명한 영화이름, Bounty는 배 이름


- Medical clinic에서 부러진 팔을 치료하고 나오는 Frank

"I didn't say it was funny when I hurt my arm, I said it was a "humerus incident"."

* humerus: 상완, 상박:  humorous(우스운)와 같은 발음

• 목장에서 얼룩배기 젖소를 보면서

Frank: "Nice guess, Ernie, but 'Milk Duds' are not defective cows."

　　* Milk Duds: 카라멜 과자 이름

• Mega Corp Pictures 회사

사장: "How should we promote the disaster movie about the disease epidemic?"

직원: "A viral campaign!"

　　* disease epidemic: 유행병

　　* Viral: 바이러스의

　　* It went viral on the computer.(컴퓨터 바이러스가 걸렸다)

• 옛여자친구가 다른 남자와 데이트하는 것을 보며

Ernie: "She dumped me for a guy with a better job."

Frank: You should sue her for wage discrimination.

　　* Dump one: 관계를 끝내다(break up a relationship)

　　* Age discrimination과 대비

• Birthday card 판매대에서

Frank: "I don't know if 50 is the new 40, but apparently $4.49 is the new buck—fifty."

　　* 예전에 $1.50 하던 카드 값이 $4.95로 올랐다.

• Cable Inc.에 온 손님에게 상품을 소개하며

Frank: "This has all of the sports and entertainment channels, and none of the news channels."

Ernie: "It's called the "Ignorance is bliss package!"

　　　* 모르는 게 약

　　　* 뉴스만 보면 왜 짜증이 날까?


• 목사가 설교 준비 중

Frank: "He's rehearsing his sermon."

Ernie: "Ah, practicing what he preaches!"

　　　* Walk your talk: 말한 대로 행하다

　　　* Practice what you preach: 언행일치


• 앵무새를 파는 가게(the parrot shop)에서 주인에게

Frank: "Do you get a lot of repeat business?"

　　　* 앵무새는 무조건 따라하므로(repeat)


• 쌓여 있는 서류더미. No, this is not a "pile-it" project!

　　　* pile: 쌓다

　　　* 'pilot project'(시범사업)와 대비


• Grocery store에서 어린 콩나물을 보고

Frank: "What are these little growths on the legumes?"

Ernie: "Must be foot-umes!"

　　　* Legume: 콩과 식물

* 어린 legume이니까, leg 대신 foot로 표현


• Video game을 하는 로봇을 보고 있는 다른 로봇

A: "He's programmed to play video games all day long."

B: "Planned adolescence!"

　　　* Adolescence: 청소년기(Game을 좋아한다)

　　　* Planned obsolescence(계획적 구식화, Marketing policy)와 대비


• 사자가 기린에게

"Yeah, maybe so, but you're not higher up on the food chain"

　　　* 키로 보면 기린이 가장 높은 곳에 있다.

　　　* Food chain: 먹이 사슬, 맨 꼭대기에는 인간

　　　* Food pyramid: 음식 피라밋(꼭대기에는 fat, 밑바닥에는 grains, vegetables등 how much of each food type you should eat to be healthy를 나타내는 표)


• 의사를 찾아온 비만한 사람에게

의사: "I told you to take the stairs instead of elevators. Taking escalators isn't meeting me halfway"

　　　* To meet me halfway: 보상하다(to compensate)


• 비행기 날개 위에 허수아비(scare crow)를 세워놓고 사람들이 하는 말

"We think it will prevent bird collision."

　　　* Bird collision: 비행기가 새와 부딪혀 사고나는 것

• Toyland pool에서 여러가지 장난감들이 Pool에서 놀고 있고, 감자
는 안전요원차림으로 있다.

Frank: "Mister potato head got the lift guard job?"

Ernie: "He has lots of eyes."

　　* 감자는 눈이 많으니까


• 호숫가에서 Frank 와 Ernie

Frank: "I need a bath but that water looks really cold!"

Ernie: "It's a case of stink or swim."

　　* Stink: 냄새가 나다

　　* Sink or swim(자력으로 살아남느냐 아니면 완전히 망하느냐[죽든 살든 알아
　　　서해야] 하는 처지에 있다)와 대비


• 한 무더기의 나무와 여러가지 공구(Tools)가 있고, 'Ladder of
Success(Some assembly required)'라는 sign이 있다.

　　* Ladder of success: 출세의 계단(Build your own success)


• Frank와 Ernie가 맥주를 먹으며 얘기하고 있는 것을 본 아가씨들

A: "These two say they're a couple of Renaissance men."

B: "That's right, if they mean they're about five hundred years
behind the times!"

　　* Renaissance men: 르네상스적 교양인(특히 문학과 회화를 비롯한 여러 분야
　　　에 능하고 관심도 많은 사람

• 개가 짖고 있다. "Arf! Arf! Arf! Arf!(개 짖는 소리)"

Frank: "Why do dogs have to bark all the time?"

Ernie: "It's arf for arf's sake!"

> * 격언 "It's art for art's sake": 상업적 목적이 아닌 예술을 위한 예술, 순수예
> 술(Graphic designer vs. fine artist, poor starving artist)

• 표어: Always let your conscience be your guide.(항상 양심에 따라라)

Frank: "I let my conscience be my guide, but it's non-binding!"

> * Non-binding: 구속력이 없는

• 구름 위의 천사들의 대화

"If you're goingto flap that hard, you need to tighten the wing nuts."

> * wing nuts: 땅에서는 '나비 너트'라는 뜻이지만 천사에게는 날개 조이는 너트

• 'Dinner special with choice of side dishes'라는 Sign이 있는 식당에
서, 무엇을 주문한 손님에게

주방장: "No sir, we don't have any black-eyed peas, but we have
some pretty roughed-up lima beans!"

> * black-eyed: 멍든
> * rough up: 짓뭉갬

• Picnic을 와서

Frank: "When I said, 'Let the good times roll', I didn't mean for you
to let go of the keg."

> * Let the good times roll: 좋은 시간 갖자(let's have a good time)

* keg: 작은 맥주통(a kegger, keg of bear)

• Frank의 아들이 TV를 보고 있다.

Frank: "Seeing him in an old movie does not count as an Elvis Sighting."

* Elvis Sighting: 살아 있는 Elvis를 보다(To see Elvis alive. He never died—Legend.)
* 많은 사람들이 아직 엘비스 프레슬리가 죽지 않았다고 생각한다

• Winnie the Pooh(곰돌이 푸) stories: Bear stock in a honey pot

Frank: "I have a vague sense that I've seen the bear stuck like that before."

Ernie: "It's a case of Deja Pooh."

* Deja Vu: 데자 뷰, 기시의 환각(the feeling that you have already experienced the things that are happening to you now.

• Scentco Fragrances(방향, 향기) 공장 앞에서

직원: "The perfume plant is the only employer in this city."

Frank: "It's an ol'factory town!"

* ol'은 old를 의미
* olfactory: 후각의, 냄새의

• A: "How was your date with the architect?"

B: "I didn't fit into her plans."

* Fit into: 꼭 들어 맞다

• Eden Landscaping Dept.에 소속된 천사들이 하나님이 지켜보고 있는 가운데,

"Uh-oh. Maybe we shouldn't have put the poison ivy so close to the fig leaves."

    * Poison ivy: 옻나무

    * Fig leaves: 무화과 잎


• Mega Cosmic films(영화관)에서

직원: "It's about a squad of ninja nuns!"

손님: "Yes, we call it 'Force of Habit' Something we do over and over unconsciously."

    * a squad of ninja nuns: 닌자수녀부대

    * Force of Habit' Something: 무의식적으로 반복하다.(We do over and over unconsciously)


• Mt. Everest Museum에 Sir Edmund Hillary 사진이 First ascent(최초 등정자)로 걸려 있는 것을 보고 Frank

"Now that you mention it, it is pretty ironic that his name was "Hill"-ary."


• 매점 점원: "Ernie, You eat the same stuff for breakfast every morning!"

Frank: "He's a cereal monogamist!"

    * monogamist: 일부일처주의자

• 후버 댐(Hoover Dam)에서

안내자: "And these controls open the dam's sluice gates."

관광객: "Draining wheels!"

  * sluice gate: 수문

  * Drain: 물이 빠지다

  * Training wheels(보조바퀴)와 대비


• 탱크 그림을 걸어 놓고 설명회를 하는 사람

"Building this vehicle will create jobs and stimulate growth."

듣고 있던 Frank:

"He's given new meaning to the phrase 'The Economy's in the Tank'!"

  * 경제가 수렁에 빠졌다


• 보트에 타고 있는 남편을 가리키며, 여자가 Frank & Ernest에게

"Our nest egg hatched into a new ski boat."

  * Nest egg(모아둔 돈)로 새 보트를 구입했다


• Mr. Buck, Financial Wizard, answers your questions.

Q: "Dear Mr. Buck, What would you say is the fundamental error that led to the current economic mess?"

A: "Exceeding the greed limit."

  * exceeding the speed limit(제한속도 초과)와 대비

• 찻잔을 들고 태극권을 수련하는 사람들

"It doesn't get any better than this --- Tai Chi with Chai Tea!"

* Tai Chi: 태극권
* Chai Tea: 차이 티(아로마 향이 나는 차)


• 코끼리를 연구하는 Ernie

"Ernie's spent his entire career studying one species. He says everything else is irrelephant."

* elephant: 코끼리
* irrelevant: 부적절한, 무관계한


• 두 우주비행사가 작업을 위해 우주모선을 떠나고 있다.

한 명이 왈: "I've got stage fright."

* Stage Flight: 무대공포증


• 지옥(Hades)의 불길 속에서 두 사람이 체스를 두고 있다.

지옥사자: "Here is the grandmasters section."

보고 있던 사람: "There're chess nuts roasting on an open fire!"

* Chestnut: 밤(a type of nut to eat)
* Chess nuts: chess에 미친 사람(Golf nuts: golf에 미친 사람)


• 화가가 여자모델에게

"There's no need to disrobe anymore…I have a full-body scanner now."

* Disrobe: 옷을 벗다

• 공사장에서 다쳐서 들것에 실려가면서

작업자: "You didn't tell me how dangerous this job is!"

사장: "It's right in your contract, 'guaranteed Hospitalization'."

　　* 입원 보장


• 경찰에게 혼나고 있는 주방장을 보며

Frank: "He's in trouble… he's in charge of the mess halls abroad, and there have been lots of complaintsthat the food is too spicy."

Ernie: "He oversees the overseas over−seasoning!"

　　* over−seasoning: 양념과다


• ATM 기계에서 모자를 내밀고 지나가는 사람에게 구걸을 하고 있다.

Frank: "Things are getting bad!"

　　* Things are getting better: 1958년 캐논 볼 애덜리(Cannon ball Adderley)가 발표한 앨범


• Alice Vegan café에 안내문: 'Come on in and eschew the fat.'

　　* Vegan: 엄격한 채식주의자

　　* eschew: 피하다, 삼가다

　　* Chew the fat(오래 담소를 나누다)와 대비


• 컴퓨터 게임을 하고 있는 아들에게

아빠: "Do you think computer games are as good as real life?"

아들: "Virtually!"(가상으로)

• 낙타를 타고 사막을 걸으면서

Frank: "Look! An oasis!"

Ernie: "An Arab spring!"

> * spring: 1)샘, 2)봄, 3)스프링
> * Arab spring(아랍의 봄): 2010년 말 튀니지에서 시작되어 아랍 중동국가 및 북아프리카로 확산된 반정부 시위의 통칭

• Doggy Philosophy

Father dog이 강아지(poppy)에게

"Don't limit yourself to flowers, son. Take the time to smell everything!"

> * Stop and smell the roses: 서두르지 말고 여유를 가져라

• 요술사가 죽을 끓이면서

"It's alphabet soup. I'm going to cast a spell."

> * cast a spell:(~에게) 주문을 걸다
> * 알파벳(alphabet)과 스펠(spell)을 대비

• Frank: "Ernie, you promised a meal from your garden, but only served an omelet and a glass of water."

Ernie: "I grew eggplant and leeks!"

> * egg는 오믈렛(omelet)재료, leek(서양부추)는 leak와 같은 발음이니까.

• Judicial studies: History of organized crime(조직범죄) 수업에서

학생: "Is this required reading?",

선생 "Yes, an author you can't refuse!"

> \* an offer you can't refuse(마피아, mobster용어): 말 안 들으면 죽어
>
> \* author와 offer 대비

• Nursery(아기 방, 신생아실) 앞에서

Frank: "You ordered a pizza for your sister while she was in labor?"

Ernie: (pizza 광고지를 보며) "This says, 'Buy a pizza and get free delivery'!"

> \* delivery: 1) 분만, 2) 배달

• 경찰서에서 손에 수갑을 찬 사람이

"I've been selling all my stolen loot to the nice guy who lives next door to me."

Frank: "Ah, good neighbors make good fences!"

> \* loot: 훔치다. 훔친 물건
>
> \* Good fences make good neighbors!(속담) 좋은 울타리는 선한 이웃을 만든다.

## 브라이언 크레인 만화 'Pickles'

Brian Crane은 젊었을 때 여러 가지 직업을 전전하다가 나이 40이 되서야 '신문 comic strip 작가가 되겠다'는 어릴 적 꿈을 회고하여, 1990

년에 Pickles를 연재하기 시작했다. Pickles는 은퇴한 70대 노부부(Earl and Opal Pickles)가 딸(Sylvia), 손자(Nelson) 그리고 개(Roscoe)와 고양이(Muffin)와 함께 은퇴생활을 즐기는 내용이다.

• 할아버지: "I had a terrible dream last night."

딸: "Oh? What was it?"

할아버지: "I dreamed you put me in a lousy nursing home and never came to visit me."

딸: Oh, don't worry, dad. You know I would never do that to you."

"By the way, and this is totally off topic, I was wondering if you could help me with my car payment this month."

　　* Manipulation(교묘히 속이기)

• 공원 벤치에 앉아 있는 할아버지들

A: "The house next door to us was foreclosed on, it's been sitting empty for months now."

A: "It's sad. The place is getting really run down."

B: "That's shame."

A: "I'll say, you hate to see that happen to a place."

A: "On the plus side, it's kind of handy to be able to toss my extra trash over the backyard fence."

　　* SAYS(말)와 DOES(행동) 대비

• 어린아이들의 대화

A: "Dogs are funny, when Roscoe stands in front of the door it means he wants to go outside"

B: "Old people are funny too, when my grampa stands in front of a door it means he forgot why he came into the room."


• 손자의 머리를 깎아주고 있는 할아버지  'bzzz'

손자: "How did you learn how to cut hair, Grampa?" 'bzzz'

할아버지: "Trial and error, mostly, it's not very hard." 'bzzzz'

할아버지: "Giving someone a buzz cut is a lot like mowing the lawn."

할아버지: "Oops! I may have just run over a sprinkler head."

    * buzz cut: 까까머리

    * run over: 넘치다

    * sprinkler head: 살수기 머리(할아버지가 뭔가 잘못 한 것 같다)


• 손자: "Thanks for making spaghetti, Gramma, you're my number one!"

할머니: "Aww… that's sweet, Nelson. Thank you!"

할아버지: "I thought I was your number one."

손자: "You can't rest on your laurels, Grampa."

    * rest on your laurels: 이미 얻은 명예[성공]에 만족하다

• 할머니: "Earl, must you be so lackadaisical?"

손자: "Grampa, what is lackadaisical?"

할아버지: "It means I don't have daisies."

손자가 개에게: "My grandparents are weird."

　　* lackadaisical: 부주의한, 태만한

　　* lack daisies 와 발음이 비슷함


• Couch(소파)에 누워 있는 할아버지

"Darn it! I was really hoping to get some yardwork done today!"

"But this stupid couch grabbed me as I walked by and clutched me in its powerful grip."

"I struggled mightily to escape, but it was too strong for me."

듣고 있던 할머니: "Yeah, right!" 하면서 나가버린다.

침대맡의 개: "For what it's worth, I believe you."

　　* For what it's worth: 너를 기분 좋게 해 준다면(If it makes you feel better, If it matters to you.)

　　* A dog is a man's best friend.


• 대머리 할아버지에게 손자가: "Grampa, do you ever think about dyeing your hair?"

할아버지: "I do dye my hair, Nelson."

"Its natural color is brown, so I dye it this beautiful shade of white."

"I also trim all the thick curls off the top my head so it's easier to comb."

"Don't tell gramma, she thinks I come by these good looks naturally."


• 거울을 보고 있는 할머니 "Look at all those wrinkle!"
"They say every wrinkle tells a story."
— I can't believe got this sun—burned on a cloudy day!
— With part and labor that'll be $6,257.85
— This is your final notice that your mortgage payment is due!
— The vice principal wishes to talk about your daughter's behavior in class
— Hey, remember that funny noise the furnace was making? Well guess what.
— Oh… Well, I can always find another job, right?
할머니: "I just wish they'd shut the heck up."
　　　* Shut the heck up: 입 닥쳐!(Shut the hell up)


• 할아버지: "Back in those days you couldn't just drive across the country like you can today. But that all changed when Eisenhower started building interstate highways all over the place."
손자: (개를 보며) "I think Roscoe need to go outside."
(개와 함께 밖으로 나와서 개에게)
"You always have to have an exit strategy with grampa."

• 손자: "Grampa, are you an expert on anything?"

할아버지: "Yes, in my opinion I am the world's greatest expert on my opinion."

   * 완고하다(stubborn)는 의미

옆에서 뜨개질하던 할머니: "Ahem."

할아버지: "Correction. Second greatest expert on my opinion."


• 타자를 치고 있는 할아버지에게

손자: "Grampa, what's a memoir?"

할아버지: "It's where someone writes about everything they've done."

손자: "Oh⋯like Facebook!"

"Is it going to have funny videos of puppies and stuff?"

할아버지: "No, it'll just be words on paper."

손자: "Ahh. too bad, I don't think it's going to get very many 'likes'."

   * memoir: 자서전(life story, autobiography)
   * '좋아요'를 못 받을 것 같다


• 손자: "What are those spots on your arms, grampa?"

할아버지: "They're just bruises from working in the yard."

손자: "How come you get bruises?"

할아버지: "Well, as we get older, our skin becomes thinner and more fragile, and we bruise easier."

손자: "So you get thinner on the outside and thicker on the inside.

   * bruises: 멍

* Thick skinned: 피부가 두꺼운, 둔감한, 뻔뻔스러운

* Thin skinned: 피부가 얇은, 민감한


- 할아버지, 할머니가 집을 나선다.

손자: "Where are you guys going?"

할머니: "We're going to buy grampa a new pair of dress shoes. Do you want to go with us?"

손자: "No Thanks."

할머니: "Okay."

손자가 개에게: "That's weird, I didn't think grampa wore dresses."

　　* Dress는 여성용이다.


- 산책하고 있는 할아버지와 손자

손자: "When I grow up I'm going to be a truck driver, a car driver, a lawn mower driver and a helicopter driver."

할아버지: "Wow. That sounds like a whole lot of driving."

손자: "Do you ever drive anything besides a car, grampa?"

할아버지: "Yeah, I drive your grandma crazy."

　　* Drive someone crazy: 정말 화나게 만들다


- 신문으로 얼굴을 가리고 있는 할아버지에게

손자: "Gramma was just here looking for you, grampa."

"Are you really reading the paper or just hiding from gramma?"

이때 할머니가 "Nelson?" 하고 부르자 손자도 책으로 얼굴을 가린다.

- 엎드려 한쪽다리 들기 운동을 하고 있는 할머니에게

손자: "Can I do your exercises with you, gramma?"

할머니: "Of course, Nelson. It'd be nice to have someone to exercise with me."

손자: "I like exercising with you too!"

(한쪽 다리를 들고 오줌누는 개를 보고) "And so does Roscoe!"

할머니: "Roscoe!"라고 크게 외친다

> * 개가 오줌을 싸고 있는 모양


- 손자가 친구에게 "That's my grampa. He's a genius."

"He's the smartest person I know."

친구가 할아버지에게: "Are you really a genius?"

할아버지: "Yup. With a capital 'J'".

손자: "See? I told you."

> * Jenious: 모자라는 사람, the opposite of genious.


- 소파에 앉아 있는 부부

할아버지: "Change is part of life. Life is one long series of changes."

"We're always changing, all of us. The only constant in life is change."

"When you're through changing. You're through."

할머니: TV 리모컨을 가지고 있는 할아버지에게

"All I said was 'Can't you just pick one channel and stay with it?'"

• 구두 주걱을 보고, 손자: "What's that thing, Grampa?"

할아버지: "This? It's a shoe horn, Nelson. A lot of people don't appreciate how important a shoe horn is."

손자: "I do."

할아버지: "You do?"

손자: "Can you play me something on it?"

　　* shoehorn: 구두주걱, 손자는 악기 horn(호른)을 생각


• 할머니: "I swear this dog can tell time."

"He knows exactly when I usually feed him."

"If I'm even two minutes late with his dinner he starts making sad puppy-dog eyes at me."

할아버지: "Why doses it only work for the dog?"

　　* 내 생각은 안 해 주는 거야?


• 할아버지: "What's this?"

할머니: "Avocado dip."

할아버지: "Avocado dip? You know I don't like avocados."

할머니: "Did I say avocado dip? It's not avocado dip. It's guacamole dip."

할아버지: "Ah, good. I love guacamole."

　　* Guacamole: 과카몰리(아보카도를 으깬 것에 양파, 토마토, 고추 등을 섞어 만든 멕시코 요리)

• 할아버지: "Why can't words be spelled the way they sounds? English spelling is insane!"

"Why is "night" spelled with a "g" and an "h" in it? That's crazy!"

"Same thing with 'thought'. If the bozos who invent words put a real thought into it, they spell it 'thot'."

할머니: "If words were spelled the way they sound it would put the spelling bee folks out of work, Earl".

할아버지: "I'm okay with that."

    * Bozo: 멍청이

    * Spelling bee: 철자법 대회

    * out of work: 실직


• 할머니:(뜨개질을 하면서) "Hummmmmmm."

할아버지:(신문을 보면서) "Why are you humming?"

할머니: "Dr. Oz says humming one hour a day relieves sinus pain. (계속해서) "Hummmmmmm.."

할아버지: "Great. What does Dr. Oz say will relieve humming pain?"

    * sinus: 부비강(두개골 속의 코 안쪽으로 이어지는 구멍)

    * Dr. Oz: 건강에 관한 TV show 진행자


• 딸: "I heard you got a new cell phone, mom."

할머니: "Yes, I did, Sylvia."(할머니는 안경을 끼고 있다)

딸: "If you give me your contacts I'll put them in for you."

할머니: "Well, that is a rather strange offer, dear. But I appreciate the thought."

"Actually, I don't wear my contacts anymore. I've gone back to my eyeglasses."

* contacts: 1) 연락처, 2)콘택트렌즈


• 할머니: "What do you want to be for Halloween this year, Nelson?"

손자: "God."

할머니: "God?! Why on earth would you want to be God for Halloween?"

손자: "'cause I like him. And I think maybe it will make people want to give me a tenth of all their candy."

* 십일조


• TV를 보고 있는 노부부

할아버지: "Don't you think it's a bit sacrilegious for Nelson to be dressing up as God for Halloween?"

할머니: "Maybe, but isn't it better than dressing up as a demon or monster?"

'GOD' 복장을 한 Nelson이 다가와서 "Thou shalt not hog the remote"라고 하면서 리모컨을 뺏아간다.

할아버지: "I'm not sure."

* sacrilegious: 신성을 더럽히는

* demon: 악령
* Hog: 1)돼지, 2)독차지하다


• 할아버지: "When I was young it was my elders who knew me about how things worked and could explain it all to me."
"I looked forward to someday growing old and wise being able to explain things to young folks."
손자가 할아버지에게 컴퓨터를 가르치며 "And then all you do is click here to restart."
할아버지: "Somehow it just didn't work out that way!"


• TV를 보고 있는 할머니: "Oh my goodness! That was a dumb commercial!"
"I just spent 30 seconds of my life watching it, and I have no idea what it was advertising!"
"I couldn't tell what they were trying to sell me or what it was supposed to do."
할아버지: "Me neither."
"But I want one."


• TV를 보면서
할아버지: "Wow, that thing is amazing!"
할머니: "What thing?"
할아버지: "That thing on the TV."

할머니: "What is it?"

할아버지: "I'm not sure, but it looks really cool!"

할머니: "What does it do?"

할아버지: "I have no clue. But I want one."

　　* no clue: 모르겠다.


• 할아버지가 바지를 입으며 "Stupid trousers!"

할머니: "What's wrong with that?"

할아버지: "I can't get them to stay around my middle. They insist on riding high or low. It's either chest or drawers."

　　* chest or drawers: 가슴 또는 속바지

　　* Chest of drawers(서랍장)과 대비


• 개와 Frisbee 놀이를 하면서,

손자: "I don't like it that dogs don't live as long as people."

할아버지: "Maybe you should get a tortoise. They live a long, long time."

손자: 거북이와 Frisbee 놀이를 하는 장면을 생각(Go, get it, boy!)하다가 "I don't think that would be quite the same."

　　* Frisbee: 던지기 놀이용 플라스틱 원반


• 할아버지1: "Mark Twain said the two most important days in your life are the day you were born and the day you figure out way."

할아버지2: "I think today is the most important day of your life, because that's the only day you have any control over."

할머니: "Come on, Earl. Remember? We're going shopping today."

할아버지1: "So much for that theory."

* Mark Twain: 소설가, Homespun philosopher(아마추어 철학자)
* So much for that …: 정확하지 않은(not accurate, not true)


• 할머니: "Nelson, do you think you're strong enough to carry a gallon of milk from the car for gramma?"

손자: "No."

할머니: "No? what if I told you, it was chocolate milk?"

손자: 쌩~(Zooom!)

할머니: "Don't worry if it looks like white chocolate milk."


• 할머니: "So you think reusing my paper napkins for more than one meal means I'm cheap?"

할아버지: "Yes, I do."

할머니: "Well, you can be pretty cheap yourself sometimes."

할아버지: "What do you mean?"

할머니: "Where do you go for lunch several times a week?"

할아버지: "Free samples at Costco. What's wrong with that?"

* cheap: 인색한(stingy)
* 할아버지가 더 인색하네


• 손자: "Can you take me to the park, Grampa?"

소파에 누워 있는 할아버지: "I'm kind of busy right now."

손자: "What are you doing? "

할아버지: "Contemplating the meaning of life."

손자: "Have you tried googling it? "

    * Contemplation: 사색, 명상


- 할아버지가 손자에게: "As you go through life it's a good idea to ask yourself from time to time if you're being the best 'you'you can be."

손자: "How do I know if I'm being the best 'me' I can be?"

할머니가 다가와서: "Nelson, get in here and clean up the mess you made in the kitchen."

할아버지: "The women in your life will let you know".


- 손자: "My friend Caleb doesn't call his grandparents gramma and grampa. He calls them Meemaw and Baboo."

"I was thinking grampa sounds kind of boring. Can I call you Baboo from now on?"

할아버지: "Nix, nay, negatory, nuh—unh, no way, no how, not a chance."

손자 친구: "I think he'll like it once he gets used to it."


- 손자: "Gramma, Can I call you Meemaw instead of gramma from now on?"

할머니: "That depends."

손자: "On what?"

할머니: "Can I call you baby cakes from now on?"

손자: "Point taken."

　　　* Point taken: 알겠다. 당신 말이 옳다(Debate 용어)


• 할머니: "Nelson, your shoes are on the wrong feet."

(왼쪽, 오른쪽이 바뀌었다)

손자: "No, they are not. These are my feet."

　　　* On the wrong foot: 갑자기, 느닷없이


• 손자: "Guess what, gramma."

할머니: "What, Nelson?"

손자: "I saw a lady at the store today, and she was even fatter than you."

할머니: "Nelson, that is a very very rude thing to say!"

손자: "Oh, don't worry, I didn't tell her."


• 손자가 할아버지에게 "Where are you going, Grandpa?"

할아버지: "I'm going on a jabberwalky."

손자가 엄마에게: "What's a jabberwalky?"

할아버지와 함께 산책 나온 할머니: "…and so Donna, she is the adult who does my hair, says to me, 'Opal, you have got to try this new humectant on your hair'. And, of course, you know how reluctant I am to try new hair products, so …"

* Jabber: 지껄이다
* Jabberwocky(무의미한 말)와 대비
* Humectant: 습윤제, 보습제
* 'Jabberwalky'는 무의미한 말을 지껄이며 걷는 할머니를 지칭한 것 같네

• 할아버지가 청소기를 쳐다보고 있다.

할머니: "What are you going to do with the vacuum, Earl?"

할아버지: "Hey, I'm a grown man in my own house. Can't I use my own vacuum without being interrogated?"

할머니: "By all means. Go right ahead."

할아버지: "Thank you!"

할아버지: "Okay where's the turny-on thingy?"

* turny-on thingy: 할아버지의 발음이 이상하지만 turn-on switch를 의미하는 듯.

• 할머니:(바닥을 내려다보며) "Oh for pete's sake!"

할아버지: "What is it?"

할머니: "I decided to do my vacuuming before I put in my hearing aids this morning."

할아버지: "So, what's wrong with that?"

할머니: "I vacuumed the whole house, and then I realized I never turned the vacuum on."

* For pete's sake: 제발

• 할아버지: "Opal, where's the vacuum?"

할머니: "What do you need the vacuum for?"

할아버지: "Something."

할머니: "Something? Did you do something stupid?"

할아버지: Why do you always assume that?"

할머니: "Why do farmers always wear rubber boots when they walk in the pigpen?"

   * pigpen: 돼지우리


• 전화벨이 울리고 있다(Ring! Ring!)

할머니: "Earl, aren't you going to answer the phone?"

할아버지: "Nope, I don't answer the phone anymore. It's almost never anyone I want to talk to."

"If they really want to tellme, they can leave a message on the answering machine."

할머니: "We don't have an answering machine."

할아버지: "Even better!"


• 손자: "Do you have a comb, gramma?"

할머니: "No, I don't, Nelson. Grampa does but he probably won't let you use it."

손자: "How come?"

할머니: "Because he never parts with it."

대머리 할아버지: "You think you're pretty funny, don't you?"

* parts: 1)가르마를 타다, 2)나누어 쓰다

• 손자: "I can't brush my teeth. The battery in my toothbrush is dead."

할아버지: "You can still use it, even without a battery. It just takes a little more effort. Go try it."

"But before you do, go change the TV channel too for me, will you?"

손자: "Isn't the remote working?"

할아버지: "No, the battery is…uhh…NEVER MIND. Just go change it."


• 할아버지와 손자가 길을 걸으며

손자: "Grampa, why don't trucks ever have the answer?"

할아버지: "Huh? What do you mean? What answer?"

손자: "You know, the answer to the problem."

"A lot of them say 4x4, but they leave off the:16."

    * 4x4: four-wheel drive


• 할머니: "I found this power cord in a drawer, but I can't remember what it goes to."

할아버지: "That goes to the video camera, I think. Or the still camera, or the cell phone, or the printer, or the DVD player, or the VCR, or the battery charger, or the WII, or my electric razor."

할머니: "Well, that certainly narrows it down."(그만하면 많이 좁혀졌네)

- 집안청소를 하면서

할머니: "If I simply got rid of all clothes, food and dishes from this house, it would be so easier to keep clean."
(소파에 앉아 있는 할아버지를 보고는)
"Oh, yeah. You're probably right. He'd have to go too."

- 할머니: "So, how was your day today, Earl?"

할아버지: "How was my day? You know very well how my day was."
"I haven't been out of your sight in the last 24 hours."
"So obviously it was fantastically marvelous day."
할머니: "Good answer."

- 신문을 보고 있는 할머니

할머니: "Whoo! Whoo!"(후 후)
할아버지: "Why are you blowing on the newspaper, Opal?"
할머니: "The pages are stuck together. I'm trying to get them apart."
할아버지: "Oh, good. I thought you might try to tell me it was because it was hot off the press."

- 공원 벤치에 앉아 있는 할아버지와 손자

할아버지: "Kids today aren't as tough as when I was kid."

"When I was a kid, I was so tough I could wear out a pair of shoes in just one day."

손자: "I'm pretty tough, too. Grampa."

할아버지: "Oh?"

손자: "Whenever you take me to the park I wear you out in less than one hour."

  * wear out: 닳아 없어지게 하다

  * wear one out: 지쳐버리게 하다.


• 할아버지1: 도넛을 권하며 "Donut?"

할아버지2: "No, Thanks. I can't. I haven't had one of those since Halloween."

할아버지1: "You're on a diet?"

할아버지2: "Yeah. I can't eat certain things."

할아버지1: "Oh, is it one of those gluten-free diets?"

할아버지2: "No, glutton-free."

  * Gluten은 밀 안에 들어있는 단백질, Glutton은 '대식가'라는 뜻


• 손자: "You talk about the past a lot, don't you' grampa?"

할아버지: "Nope, not really, hardly ever, in fact."

"I can't even remember the last time I talked about pasta."

손자: "I said the past, not pasta!"

할아버지: "I wouldn't mind talking about some 3-cheese lasagna right now, though."

* Lasagna: 라자냐(파스타 · 치즈 · 고기 · 토마토 소스 등으로 만드는 이탈리아 요리)

- 누워 있는 할아버지를 보고

할머니: "Did you clean the basement up yet, Earl?"

할아버지: "Let me ask you this: If a room is a mess and no one sees it, is it still a mess?"

할머니: "Let me ask you this: If an old man is hungry and no one feeds him, is he still hungry?"

할아버지: "I'll be in the basement. Call me when dinner ready."

- Back Yard에 잔디를 깎지 않아 무성하게 자란 것을 보고

할머니: "This yard looks like a mess, Earl!"

할아버지: "Henry David Thoreau said, 'It's not what you look at that matters, it's what you see.'"

"Me? I see a wild untamed area of indigenous flora, flourishing and thriving as nature intended."(번창하는 번성하는)

할머니: "Yeah, and I see a husband who's full of baloney."

    * Henry David Thoreau(헨리 소로): 미국의 사상가 겸 문학가

    * wild untamed: 야생의 길들여지지 않은

    * indigenous flora: 토종의 식물군

    * flourishing and thriving: 번성하는

    * Baloney:(비 격식, 특히 美) 헛소리; 거짓말

• 진공청소기로 귀를 후비는 할아버지를 보고

할머니: "Earl, you cannot use vacuum to get that cotton swab out of your ear."

"I'll get it out with some tweezers."

할아버지: "What's wrong with using the vacuum?"

할머니: "It's too risky. You could suck your brain out."

　　* tweezers: 핀셋
　　* 귀이지가 아니라 뇌가 빨려 나올까 봐


• 진공청소기를 만지며,

할아버지: "Isn't there some sort of attachment for this thing to reach into tight spots?"

할머니: "Yes. It's right here. You just attach it to this hole link this."

할아버지: "Good, that ought to do the trick."

할머니: "What trick is that?"

할아버지: "I need to suck out the tip of a cotton swab that came off inside my ear."

할머니: "Of course you do."

　　* swab: 면봉


• 할머니: "Did you read this, Earl?"

할아버지: "What is it?"

할머니: "It says researchers have identified the keys to a long−lasting marriage. These include caring, long−term commitment, imgreite, and togetherness."

할아버지: "If they don't have 'two TVs' on that list, they're full of hooey."

　　* Hooey: foolishness(바보같은)


• 할머니: "Did you put those towels in the bathroom cabinet for me, Nelson?"

손자: "Yes."

할머니: "Did you fold those T–shirts of yours that were in the dryer and put them in your dresser?"

손자: "Uh Huh. I think I'll go help grampa now for a while."

할머니: "Help grampa? What's He doing?"

손자:(행 나가면서) "Nothing."


• 할아버지: "Okay, Nelson, why are you staring at me?"

손자: "I don't think you look like either one of those animals."

할아버지: "What animals?"

손자: "I heard gramma say you're as pigheaded as a mule."

　　* as pigheaded as a mule: 완고한(Stubborn)


• 할아버지: "Back in 1952, Gasoline cost 20 cents a gallon. When you pulled up to the pumps, three guys came up and checked your oil and your tires and cleaned your windows."

손자: "This must be that thing they call 'senility'"

* senility: 노망(Common misspelling of senility)

- 할아버지: "Did you see this? An 82-year-old woman was arrested for shoplifting."

할머니: "Oh, that's too bad. Poor dear!"

할아버지: "I've heard that old people generally have the stickiest fingers."

할머니: "Probably poligrip residue."

* Sticky finger: 손버릇이 나쁜, 도벽이 있는(steal something)

* Poligrip residue: 입안에서 틀니(false teeth)를 잡아주는 접착제(glue that holds dentures in the mouth.

- 할머니: "Listen to this, Earl… This article says that children benefit from being around their grandparents."

"It says, 'children are a composite of all the people they interact with, so it's important for us, from one generation to the next, to leave a piece of us!"

이 때 할머니, 할아버지 앞으로 다가오는 손자가 바지춤을 끌어 올리며,

손자: "Dagnabit! My darn skivvies keep ridin' up on me."

할아버지: "Mission accomplished."

* Dagnabit: 빌어먹을(dagnabbit: Damn)

* Darn: Damn

* Skivvies: 내복

• 할머니 친구: "Someone once said, 'Age is a very high price to pay for maturity'."

할머니: "Yes, I suppose that's true."

할아버지: "Hey, ladies! What's cookin'?"

(할아버지가 사라지자)

할머니: "Earl paid the price, but he hasn't gotten his money's worth."


## 브래드 앤더슨 만화 'Marmaduke'

미국 만화가 Brad Anderson(1924-2015)의 대표작은 1954년에 신문연재를 시작하여 죽을 때까지 그린 Marmaduke이다. Marmaduke는 Winslow 가족과 함께 사는 Great Dane 종(털이 짧고 몸집이 아주 큰 개)의 이름이다. 이 캐릭터는 지저분하지만 사랑스럽고(messy but lovable), 또 탐욕의 표상(a very large example of the breed)이다.

• Marmaduke는 눈을 막고, 큰 애는 귀를 막고, 작은 애는 입을 막고 있다. 아빠가 아내에게 "I don't think I want to know."

   * See no evil, hear no evil, speak no evil.: 뭔가 잘못을 저질러 놓고 '본 적도 들은 적도, 말한 적도 없다'고 딱 잡아 떼기.
   * Blind for 3 years, Deaf for 3 years, Dumb for 3 years.

• Garage sale을 하려고 진열해 놓은 신발들 앞에 Marmaduke가 지키

고 있다. 안주인이 손님들에게 "Sorry, sorry. Apparently, those shoes are not for sale."

 * Marmaduke에게 신발은 물어뜯고 노는 장난감이므로 팔리면 안된다.

• 꼬마가 Marmaduke에게 먹이를 주며
"Everyone calls him Marmaduke, except the guy at the pet store calls him Gold Mine."

• 망원경으로 길거리를 관찰해 놓고는 모른 체하고 있는 Marmaduke에게
"Have you been spying on the cat across the street?"

• Marmaduke가 손목에 찬 시계를 주인에게 보인다.
주인: "Yes, I see. It's time for your walk."

• 개가 우체통을 넘어뜨려 물어뜯고 있다. 집안에서 이를 보고 있는 주인:
"On the other hand, it may cut down all the junk mail we get."

• 개가 소파에 누워 TV를 보고 있다. 남편이 아내에게
"I wish I'd never taught him to sit"

 * Who is the owner, dog? Or man?

• Marmaduke가 뭔가를 열심히 먹고 있다. 'Crunch, Crunch,

Munch, Crunch, Munch, Crunch'
TV news에는 "and the pet food industry has done well despite the tough economy"


• 공원 벤치에 앉은 주인이 먹을 것을 Marmaduke에게 던져주며
"Remember, when we get home, pant like we've been running for an hour."
    * pant: 헐떡이다


• Marmaduke가 야구 글러브를 물어뜯고 있다.
꼬마: "He doesn't care who wins or loses as long as he gets a glove."


• Marmaduke와 놀고 있는 꼬마:
"We don't have a three-second rule. Food's never on the floor that long."
    * 바닥에 떨어진 음식물을 3초내에 다시 집으면 먹어도 된다.


• 신문뭉치가 입에 붙어 있는 Marmaduke에게
"You don't fetch the newspaper while chewing gum."
    * fetch: 가지고 오다


• 쏜살같이 달리는 Marmaduke의 끈을 잡은 주인
"I said I'd take you for a walk⋯ not a marathon."

• Marmaduke가 앞에서 달려가고 있고 leash를 잡은 주인이 힘겹게 뒤쫓아가고 있다. 외계인이 이를 보고 "The one in front seemed to be their leader."

• Marmaduke에게 줄을 매달고 거리를 달린 꼬마에게
경찰: "You clocked us going 60 miles an hour?"
꼬마: Really?

• 온 집안이 난장판이 된 가운데, 꼬마가 엄마에게
"Marmaduke caught a fly."

• 소화전에 냄새 맡는 Marmaduke를 보고
주인: "This is where he gets all of his latest gossip."

    * gossip은 얘깃거리, 개에게는 수다 대신 냄새

• 잔디에 벌렁 누워있는 개를 보고 애들이
"Naw, he's not sleeping. He's storing up solar energy."

    * Naw: 안 돼(slang term for NO negation)

• 긁어 모아둔 낙엽을 파헤치는 Marmaduke에게
주인: "No! you don't bury bones in the leaf pile!"

• Marmaduke가 음식자동 공급기에서 엄청난 양의 사료를 빼내 먹고 있다.

주인: "I got the idea from a bulk foods store."


• 사료를 먹던 Marmaduke가 뭔가를 뱉아낸다(Pyoo).

"He can separate a 5-gram fill from 2 founds of kibble in 10 seconds."

　　* fill: 약

　　* kibble: 개 사료(dog food)


• Marmaduke가 개집 안에서 호스를 물고 물을 뿜어내고 있다.

주인: "Then he got his idea he wanted a waterfront doghouse."

　　* Waterfront house(물가에 위치한 집): 비싸다


• 가구점에서 Marmaduke가 소파에 누워 있다. 점원이 개주인에게

"Your dog just bought it."

　　* 당신 개가 부쉈으니 당신이 사야 한다.


• Marmaduke가 사료를 열심히 먹고 있다 'sniff, sniff, sniff…'

남자가 아내에게:

"He'll eat now - I put some steak sauce on it."


• 주인이 Marmaduke에게

"If you're so innocent, why do I have an empty plate and you have steak-sauce breath?"

• Museum of national history에서 Marmaduke가 공룡의 뼈를 보고 침을 흘리고 있다.

주인: "Keep an eye on him."


• Marmaduke가 산책 나온 조그만 개의 냄새를 맡고 있다.

개 주인: "No, he does not run on batteries!"

    * run on batteries: 베터리로 달리다


• Halloween 지나고 나서 애들 앞에는Candy 봉지가 수북하고 Marmaduke 앞에는 개먹이가 수북하다.

아줌마: "I didn't know so many people handed out doggie treats."


• 밤에 Marmaduke 가 끊임없이 짖어 댄다 "Woof, woof, woof ……"

옆집 사람 "Marm! You're repeating yourself."


• 집안에 많은 개들이 들어와 있다.

"They aren't strays. Marmaduke went to the animal shelter and adopted them."

    * Stray dogs: 집 잃은 개


• 온 동네 개를 다 불러 모아 놓고 TV를 보고 있는 Marmaduke에게

"This isn't what I meant when I said you could help at a homeless shelter."

• Marmaduke의 얼굴에 박힌 선인장 가시를 뽑아주며 주인이
"Next time, try smell the roses."

  * Stop and smell the roses: 긴장을 풀어라


• 공원 벤치에 앉아있는 할아버지, 완전히 녹초가 된 상태로 지나가
는 Marmaduke와 주인을 보며, "Was the blur I saw earlier YOU?"

  * blur: 흐릿한(not distinct going to fast)


• Marmaduke가 세탁기에 뼈를 넣고 돌리고 있다.
꼬마가 엄마에게: "He's washing his bones. They're real dirty when
he digs them up."


• 벽에서 전기선이 연결되어 있다. 전기선을 따라 가보니Marmaduke
가 개집 안에서 전기 담요로 몸을 감싸고 있다.
주인: "So this is where our electric blankey went."


• 신발 한 켤레를 Marmaduke에게 주며
주인: "How about chewing up Phil's old slippers? I want to get him
new ones for his birthday."


• American Football 경기를 하며 놀고 있는 애들에게 Marmaduke
가 어린애 하나를 물고 온다.
애들: "You can stop recruiting, Marmaduke. We have enough players
now."

- Marmaduke에게 한 아름의 먹을 것을 주고 있는 남편에게

아내: "You forgot our anniversary, but you remember his birthday?"


## 브루스 틴슬리 만화 'Mallard Fillmore'

Bruce Tinsley는 16세 때 한 신문사의 시사만화가(editorial cartoonist)로 일을 시작했으며, 그의 대표작 Mallard Fillmore는 1994년부터 시작했다. Mallard Fillmore는 오리(Duck)를 의인화한 캐릭터인데, 정치적으로 보수적인 리포터 역할이다. 이 이름은 미국의 13대 대통령 Millard Fillmore에서 따온 것이다.


- 전화기 Answering Machine

"Thank you for holding⋯. Because we are currently experiencing larger −than−usual call volume⋯. We're dedicating this next song to you⋯."

> *  미국에서 전화로 담당자와 통화에 성공하려면, 최소한 5번 이상 시도해야 하고, 30분 이상 대기해야 한다.


- 전화기를 통해 들리는 소리

"⋯ if you'd like to speak to one of our representatives⋯"

"⋯ it probably means that you've never spoken with one of our representatives before ⋯"

• To save time, rather than give the latest unemployment figures⋯. I'm just going to read the names of the Americans who still have jobs⋯

    * 실업이 얼마나 심각했으면⋯


• TV에서 인터뷰를 하고 있는 유명인사

"Hi. I'm a celebrity, and I, like, vote, and stuff, so you should vote too⋯ so you can feel like, you know, a celebrity, and stuff! Just because I know all civilizations rise and fall doesn't mean I want a front-row seat⋯"

    * 유명인사란 대체로 이런 류다. 말도 안 되는 소리를 횡설수설하면서


• Occupy Wall Street에 쌓인 쓰레기

Q: "Who gets to pay to clean up their mess?"

A: "The same ones of us who get to pay for everything else."

    * 세금 꼬박꼬박 내는 서민이 봉


• TV news: All your rural people are against banning guns! Why can't you be more sophisticated and cosmopolitan? if you had strict gun control, like New York and C.C⋯.

시청자: "⋯You'd be as safe as people in those places!"

    * 반어법이다


• New North Korean leader Kim Jong Un will narrow his search

for a title down to "Dearest leader", "Maximum Important Leader",
and "Cutest chubby little dictator since Deng Xiaoping" ⋯

　*chubby: 오동통한

• Holiday Gift Idea: Recycle!!

"Recycling is good for the 'Planet'⋯ you know it's the right thing to
do. Just make sure the person who gets it ⋯ ain't the same one who
gave it to you."

• In other news, earlier today, Punxsutawney Phil(The groundhog)
came out his hole, saw the latest unemployment statistics⋯ and was
informed that his services would no longer be needed⋯

　* Groundhog day(Candlemas day, 2월 2일): Groundhog이 동면에서 나와
　　서 그의 그림자를 보면 다시 6주 더 자러 간다(겨울이 6주 길어진다)

• 전화 통화

여자: "Hey, it's Chantel⋯ remember when you said you'd go to the
next 'Twilight' movie opening with me?"

남자: "No, not exactly⋯ was I under anesthesia?"

여자: "It's this Friday."

남자: "Do you have a transcript on file?"

　* anesthesia: 마비, 지각 마비
　* transcript: 기록

• 깜깜한 곳에서 들리는 말

"And we will continue to be the most transparent administration in history…"

　　* Transparent: 투명한, 속이 뻔히 들여다보이는(clear, open records, not secret)


• A: "A TSA spokesperson today issued a statement regarding the agency's bullying of woman, children and the elderly…"
TSA: "In the war against profiling…. there's always going to be some collateral damage…"

　　* Bully: Intimidate(협박) cyber bullying

　　* Collateral(평범한, 부수적인) damage: 죄 없는 시민(innocent civilians)

　　* 대악 척결을 위해 사소한 피해는 감수해야 한다는 주장이나, 당하는 사람 입장 에서는


• A: "So I met this really attractive woman at Chantel's party… she works over at the Justice Department… I was just about to give her my phone number…But she already had it."

　　* 개개인정보 무단 도용 문제를 풍자


• 레스토랑 종업원이 손님에게

"Tonight, we're featuring a wild-caught, gluten-free, free-range, fair-trade halibut from Nova Scotia…… whose hobbies include swimming, eating smaller fishes, and lying around with both eyes on the same side of his head…"

* Current trend: local fresh fish

* Nova Scotia: Maine 주 동쪽, Canada 동부해안

* 가자미: a flatfish, a sole, a plaice

* 광어: a flatfish, a flounder

* 넙치: a flatfish, a left-eyed founder

• 산타가 받은 쪽지

"We regret to inform you that we no longer require your service⋯ Last month's election has made you redundant."

* Someone else is doing it.

* 선거 끝나면 정치인들이 어떻게 달라지는지 풍자

• SUV car에 짐 싸 들고 떠나며

"I know it's a long drive, but it's always worth it to have the whole family together⋯

"⋯to celebrate Black Friday Eve⋯"

* Black Friday: 추수감사절 연휴 첫 금요일, 1년중 쇼핑센터가 가장 붐비는 날

• Mallard's holiday gift idea

"Follow our government's example to stimulate our economy this year, and spend like crazy, even if you're in debt! Then⋯ send the bill to tour grandchildren.

* 나라 빚을 후손에게 물려주는 정부 정책을 비난

• Public reaction to the study that says the average congressperson speaks at a tenth–grade level has been ⋯ "amazingly awesome," according to one congressperson, who asked "like, you know, not to be, you know, identified, and stuff⋯"

  * 정치인들의 돌머리 풍자


• Mallard's Fashion tip: 허리살이 너무 쪄서 바지가 안 올라가는 사람에게,

"If the tops of your hips are trying to escape from your pants⋯ Buying tighter pants to keep them in is not the answer⋯"


• Restaurant 종업원

"Hi, I'm Kevin, and I'll be your locally sourced, organic, hormone–free server tonight⋯."


• 신문을 보고 있는 사람

" I can't say I am better off now than I was four years ago"⋯
Latest polls기사를 보고 있는 대통령: "Me either⋯"


• High School 졸업식, 학생대표의 연설1

"As we leave here, some of us will get a job in a McDonald's Drive–Thru⋯ ⋯while others of us will go on to college⋯ ⋯and then get jobs in a McDonald's Drive–Thru⋯"

  * 취업의 어려움 풍자

• High School 졸업식, 학생대표의 연설2

"… and now, with my brand-new liberal arts degree…"

"I'll be able to say 'welcome to Starbucks' in four different languages!"

   * 취업의 어려움 풍자


• News

"An appellate court says there's enough evidence that the university of Iowa refused to hire a professor because she's conservative for the case to go to Trial…"

"Meanwhile, police are investigating the sudden disappearance of all of the people who are usually outraged at the hiring discrimination…"

   * Appellate courts: 항소(상고)법원
   * Outrage: 격노


## 빌 킨 만화 'The Family Circus'

'The Family Circus'는 The Family Circle이란 제목으로 1960년도에 연재가 시작되었으며, 2011년 Bil Keane이 사망한 후에는 그의 아들인 Jeff Keane이 계속 이어오고 있다. 아빠(Bil), 엄마(Thel), 네 아이 (Billy, Dolly, Jeffy, P.J)와 두 마리의 개가 등장인물이며, 아이들의 생각과 행동을 통해 미국의 가정의 일상을 배울 수 있다. 여기서는 편의상 캐릭터의 이름을 쓰지 않고, 엄마, 아빠, 꼬마로 통일한다.

- 꼬마: "There goes Elizabeth, but we call her Liz or Beth or Lizzy or Elie or Lisa or Betsy or …"

- 할머니가 겨울 창 밖을 내다보고 있다.

꼬마: "Grandma says a lot of her friends are like the birds. They fly south for the winter."

    * snow birds: 은퇴자(retirees)
    * salaried man: 봉급생활자

- Halloween 때, 꼬마가 엄마에게

"Daddy said if I want to be something REALLY scary, I should dress up as a politician."

- 꼬마가 엄마, 아빠에게

"I can't reach the towel!",

"I can't reach the sink",

"I can't reach my coat." 하면서 도움을 요청하는데,

아주 높은 곳에 있는 Cookie는 온갖 방법을 동원해서 손에 넣는다.

- U.S. Army의 recruit 광고(손가락으로 정면을 가리키며 'I want you to U.S. Army'라고 한다)를 보며,

꼬마: "Uncle Sam's mommy should've told him it's not polite to point."

    * Uncle Sam은 미국정부 또는 미국인을 의미

• 꼬마가 식당 앞을 지나며 엄마에게

"Whenever we pass by here, my eyes make my tummy hungry."

> \* Tummy: 배
>
> \* My eyes were bigger than my stomach.

• 빵 사이에 엄청난 양의 Peanut butter를 넣은 샌드위치,
꼬마가 동생에게,

"Sorry, there was only enough peanut butter for one sandwich."

• 동생을 데리고 온 꼬마

"P. J's feelin'sad. I think two cookies might cheer us up."

• 꼬마에게 읽기를 가르치는 선생이 'cabinet'이라는 단어를 보이며,

선생님: "It's a place where we keep dishes."

꼬마: "Oh, I know – SINK"

> \* 엄마는 설거지를 잘 안 하는 모양

• 꼬마가 동생들에게 책을 읽어주고 있다.

"Moses wasn't feelin'well, so God gave him some tablets."

Tablet: 1)알약, 2)서판(書板)

• 할머니가 꼬마의 옷을 벗기고 목욕탕으로 데려가려 한다(draw ~ a
bath)

꼬마: "Grandma, you don't hafta draw me a bath. I know what they look like."

> \* 여기서 꼬마는 'draw'를 '그림을 그리다'로 생각하고..

• 꼬마가 Funny bone을 만지며, 울며

"No, I musta hit some other bone… This doesn't feel funny at all."

> \* funny bone: 팔꿈치뼈

• 숙제하고 있는 꼬마의 생각

"When I finish my homework, can I do something useless?"

• 대통령 취임식 중계를 보고 있는 꼬마

"Hurry up, Jeffy! We're gonna watch the president get inoculated!"

> \* inoculated: 접종한(vaccinated)
>
> \* inaugurated: 취임식(ceremony to mark the beginning of a term, especially The President of the U.S.)
>
> \* 국회의사당(Congress, Capitol): Senator(상원)와 The House of Representative(하원)가 함께 사용

• 아파서 침대에서 밥을 먹고 있는 아빠에게 꼬마가

"Maybe you caught your virus from our computer, Daddy."

• 추운 날, 밖으로 나가려는 아이에게 엄마가 겹겹이 옷을 입히고 있다.

아이: "Can you remember why I wanted to go outside?"

• 저녁 무렵, 난장판이 된 집안에서 친구들과 놀고 있던 꼬마가 엄마에게

"O YEAH! Daddy called earlier and said he's bringing his boss home for dinner."

• 할머니가 어린아이를 안고 흔들의자에 앉아서 흔들거리고 있다. 꼬마가 엄마에게 "Grandma says that's how she used to rock you, but how could she even LIFT you?"

　　* Rock: 1)바위, 2)앞뒤, 좌우로 살살 흔들다

• 부엌에서 엄마와 할머니가 얘기를 하고 있다.

꼬마들: "Mommy and Grandma will NEVER get those dishes done. 'cause all they do is talk."

• 울고 있는 동생, 동생의 장난감 차를 빼앗은 꼬마가 엄마에게

"He's just mad 'cause I had to recall his car."

• 해변 모래 위에 애들 이름을 쓰고 있는 아빠에게 꼬마가

"Hurry up, Daddy, before the ocean erases it!"

• 더러워진 손을 하고 집안으로 들어오며

꼬마: "I don't get it. I just washed my hands yesterday. How did they get dirty again already?"

• 꼬마가 개 두 마리를 친구에게 소개하며

"This is Barfy and Sam's favoritetime of year 'cause it's full of dog days."

　　* Dog days: 복중, 삼복더위 때, 꼬마는 '개를 위한 날'이라 생각


• 꼬마가 창 밖을 내다보며

"When the cold weather gets here, this will be one of the good 'ol days."

　　* Older people generation refers to the good old days(Maybe 20년전),
　　* 여기서는 어린애가 '겨울이 되면 여름 그때가 좋았던 시절'이라고


• 스케이트장에서 스케이트를 타고 있는 꼬마가 동생에게

"Don't worry, Dolly, there aren't any judges watching us."

　　* judges: 심판


• 꼬마가 얼음조각을 눈사람 앞에 세우며

"It's a TV set. He wanted to watch the Olympics."


• 발가벗고 있는 꼬마가 엄마에게

"'Cause it's my birthday!"


• 밖에서 놀던 꼬마가 울면서 집으로 들어오며

"I've got a humongous cut on my leg!"

"I'll show it to you as soon as I find it again."

* humongous: 기대한


• 엄마와 옷을 커플처럼 입은 꼬마가 아빠에게:

"We got matching dresses …"

"'cept Mommy's came with more curves and things."


• 공부방으로 들어오는 엄마에게 꼬마가

"Feel free to interrupt me while I'm doing my homework."


• 꼬마: "Know what, grandma? I even enjoy doing nothing with you."


• Easter day, 꼬마가 아빠에게

"How'd you like your egg this morning, Daddy? Purple? Yellow? Green?"

> * dye easter egg: 부활절에 달걀에 색칠하다
> * Easter Egg hunt: A common festive activity held at Easter, where Easter eggs are hidden outdoors(or indoors if in bad weather) for children to run around and find.


• 꼬마 "How many one-of-kinds are there?"

> * 모든 선전: 홈 쇼핑 channel 등에서 One- of - kinds


• 가게 주인이 꼬마에게 막대사탕을 하나 주자, 엄마가 꼬마에게

엄마: "What do you say?"

꼬마가 가게 주인에게: "Could I have one for Billy, one for Dolly, and one for PJ?"

> * 엄마는 'Thank you'라는 대답을 예상했는데…

- 아빠가 아이를 거꾸로 들고 있다. 꼬마가

"Now I know what it feels like to live in Australia!"

- Halloween Pumpkin 옆에 Orange로 만든 꼬마귀신이 있다. 꼬마가 동생에게

"I made him a baby out of an orange."

- 꼬마가 할아버지, 할머니, 아빠, 엄마 등에게 Kiss를 하면서

"Boy, we're lucky! We've got a LOT of people to kiss good night!"

- 바닥에 누워 울며 앙탈을 부리는 동생을 보며 꼬마가

"You should save it for later. Mommy is outside."

- Back yard에서 저녁을 먹으려는 가족, 놀러 와 있는 이웃집 아이에게 엄마가

"Shouldn't you go home now, Bobby? We're going to have dinner."

꼬마: "That's okay, I'll just stand here and watch."

• 꼬마가 Mud pie를 만들어서 아빠에게 주며

"It's good for you!"

"It has no sugars and is all natural ingredients."

• 피자를 먹고 난 후 부스러기(crust)를 접어들며,

꼬마: "All that's left of my pizza are the bones."

• 남자아이: "Morri twisted his ankle and can't walk right."

여자아이: "Can he still go left?"

　　* right: 1) 옳은, 바른, 2)오른쪽

• 여자애가 남자애에게

"Boys have an Adam's apple, so girls have an Eve's apple."

• 아빠의 무거운 서류가방을 들어 옮기며 꼬마:

"Gosh, Daddy! They sure gave you a lot of homework today."

• 아빠의 서류가방 옆에 선 꼬마

"Daddy, don't they make a BRIEFER case than this?"

　　* Brief case: 서류가방

• 개가 동생의 얼굴을 핥고 있다.

꼬마가 엄마에게: "We save a lot on napkins with Barfy around."

- 샌드위치를 먹고 있던 꼬마가 곁에 온 고양이를 보고,

"Who told Kittycat we were eating tuna sandwiches?"

- 나팔을 들고 있는 꼬마가 동생에게

"Wanna hear the bugle call they use to wake soldiers up?"
"It's called Ravioli."

    * bugle call: 집합나팔

    * Ravioli: 저며서 양념을 한 고기를 얇은 가루 반죽에 싼 요리

    * reveille(기상신호)와 대비

- 비싼 장난감 가게에 온 꼬마가 엄마에게

"I won't cost you any money, Mommy. You can just pay with a credit card."

- 피구게임을 하면서 꼬마가 동생에게

"Remember, Jeffy. If the dodgeball hits you, you'll be illuminated."

    * Dodgeball: 피구, dodge는 escape, avoid라는 뜻

    * illuminated: 불빛이 환한

    * you'll be eliminated(:out of the game)라고 해야 하는데….

- 꼬마가 사과를 먹으며 동생에게

"Apples are a healthy snack, but I like 'em anyway."

    * 애들에게는 Healthy food가 대체로 맛이 없다

• 아빠: "What are they teaching you in history these days, Billy?"
꼬마: "The 1980s."

• 꼬마의 숙제를 도와주던 아빠가 아내에게
"Want to hear something depressing?... The year 1988 is in this HISTORY book!"

• 짧은 머리스타일의 할머니가 애들에게
"I used to wear my hair in a bun"
애들: "What kind, hot dog or hamburger?"
　　* Hair in bun: 머리 쪽을 찌다. 올림머리를 하다
　　* Bun: 빵

• 퍼 질러 앉아 있는 동생에게 누나가 "Did you hurt yourself?"
동생 대답: 'No, but if Mommy was here I'd really cry up a storm."
　　* up a storm: 극도로

• 카드놀이를 하고 있는 꼬마
"These cards have kings, queens and jacks. Where are jills?"
　　* Jack and Jill Nursery rhyme(유치원 노래):
　　　Jack and Jill went up the hill
　　　To fit a pail of water
　　　Jack fell down and broke his crown
　　　and Jill came tumbling after

• 흙을 잔뜩 묻힌 꼬마가 키 큰 아빠에게

"You'd be a lot dirtier too if you were this close to the ground."

• 아빠가 꼬마에게 역사책을 읽어주고 있다

"On Dec. 17, 1903, Orville Wright made the world's first flight. It lasted for 12 seconds!"

꼬마: "I hope the passengers got their seat backs and tray tables into an upright position!"

• 아빠: "I've decided to make dinner tonight."

꼬마: "Great! So, what are you microwaving?"

• 편지를 받은 할머니: "How nice! Bob and Mary named their baby after me."

꼬마: "They named their baby 'Grandma'?"

    * name after: …의 이름을 따서 이름 짓다

• 아침에 일어나 몸에 열이 나고 있는 아이와 이를 체크하는 엄마를 보고

꼬마: "Maybe Mommy will have to take Billy into the shop."

    * 자동차가 고장 나면 "go to the shop"

• Sink 대 배관을 수리하는 아빠를 보고

꼬마: "Daddy's helping the sink clear its throat."

• Boston Red Sox의 홈구장 Fenway Park에 온 꼬마

"We're wearing WHITE socks, Mommy! Is that OK?"


• 아빠가 벽난로(Fire place)에 장작(Logs)을 넣고 있는 것을 보며 꼬마가,

"Christmas is coming, Daddy. Instead of logs shouldn't we put some pillows in there?"

    * 굴뚝으로 들어올 Santa를 생각하며


• 피아노 앞에서 꼬마가

"How come piano letters stop at 'G'? There's plenty of keys to go all the way to 'Z'."

    * 피아노 한 옥타브는 7음: 도레미파솔라시: ABCDEFG


• 남자 꼬마가 엄마에게

"How come I never get a top to my bathing suit like Dolly always gets?"

    * Top: 상의(여성의 옷)
    * Dolly는 여동생


• 아빠가 애들에게 'Goldilocks and 3 bears'라는 동화책을 읽어준다. 꼬마가

"Why didn't they have her booked for illegal entry?"

    * Goldilocks: 1)금발의 마녀, 2)너무 뜨겁지도 너무 차갑지도 않은 적당한 상태

* Goldilocks and the three bears: 영국의 전래동화
* 무단 침입죄로 체포하다


• 애기에게 Goldilocks and the three bears를 읽어주고 있는 엄마에게 꼬마가

"No way! I was watchin' 'Animal Planet' and they didn't say anything about bears eating porridge."

> * Porridge:(美 주로 oatmeal)(특히 英) 포리지, 오트밀(귀리(oats)에 우유나 물을 부어 걸쭉하게 죽처럼 끓인 음식. 특히 아침식사로 먹음)


• 꼬마가 부엌서랍을 열어보며

"If you don't know where something belongs, it belongs in this drawer."

> * 대부분의 미국 부엌 서랍은 온갖 물건들이 정리 안 된 채로.


• 식당 종업원이 주문받을 때

종업원: "Ranch, Italian, or Blue cheese dressing?"

꼬마: "How 'bout chocolate dressing?"


• 꼬마: "At what age do my calves turn into cows?"

> * Carve: 1)종아리, 2)송아지


• 차 뒷좌석에 앉아 다투는 꼬마

"Knock it off! Mommy can see you in her review mirror."

* Knock it off: Stop it
* review mirror는 Rear View mirror의 잘못 발음한 것

- 새 한 마리가노래를 부르고 있다.

꼬마: "Mommy, which do birds do − chirp, whistle or tweet?"
   * chirp: 짹짹거리다(short high pitched sound)
   * Whistle: 휘파람 불다(high musical)
   * tweet: 짹짹거리다(small bird, short)

- 어질러진 방을 나무라는 엄마에게 꼬마가

"But I thought you told me you weren't gonna ask me to clean up my room again."

- 숙제를 하고 있는 꼬마

"Will there be less homework if the Democrats win or the Republicans?"

- 어른들이 거실에서 얘기하고 있는데 방에서 놀고 있는 꼬마들이 이 모습을 보며, "We/re not S'POSED to understand. They're talking politics."

- 아빠가 슬리퍼를 신고 소파에 앉아 다리를 높인 채 TV를 보고 있다. 아빠 앞에 앉은 꼬마는 아빠의 발 때문에 TV가 잘 안 보인다

"Daddy, your new fuzzy slippers are nice, but…"

- 알파벳이 적힌 주사위같은 장난감을 가지고 놀고 있는 동생을 보고 꼬마가

"Look! PJ is texting."

- 꼬마가 동생에게 집안에 진열된 백과사전을 보이며

"They're encyclopedias. When Daddy was a kid, he used them to find out stuff."

   * 요즘 애들은 모든 것을 휴대폰으로

- 독일산 셰퍼드를 데리고 있는 꼬마에게 다른 꼬마가

"Do you talk to your German Shepherd in English?"

- 벽 높이 걸려 있는 Thermostat(온도조절기)를 쳐다보면서 꼬마

"That little box can heat our whole house.

- 꼬마가 저금통을 열어놓고 엄마에게

"I have $7.35 in my bank, Mommy. Do you think I should get a financial advisor?"

- Box 안에 들어가 그림을 그리고 있는 꼬마가 놀러 온 꼬마에게

"I can't play with you till I'm finished workin' here in my cubicle."

- 바깥에서 옷을 더럽혀 집으로 돌아오는 꼬마

"Mommy, was tonight gonna be a bath night?"

• 방학이 시작되는 날, 하교길에 꼬마

"I'm gonna spend all summer not missing school."

> \* Summer school

• X-mas Tree 주위에서 선물을 찾고 있는 꼬마들을 보며 부모:

"They won't know till they're grown, but their BEST gifts are the memories they're making."

• 무거운 가방을 옮기고 있는 꼬마

"Somebody better help me. My fingers are just holdin'on by their tip-toes."

> \* tip-toe: 발가락으로 서다

• 하모니카 부는 누나가 북 치는 동생 꼬마에게

"No, I don't like drums. They only play one note."

• 꼬마: "Can I put my tooth under Eric's pillow? His Tooth Fairy pays more than ours."

> \* Tooth fairy: 뽑은 이빨을 베게 밑에 두면 요정이 선물을 준다.

• 꼬마가 책을 읽으며 "Books are better than TV."

" …If you fall asleep while reading, you don't worry miss the ending."

> \* 책은 다음날 또 읽으면 되니까.

- 비 오는 걸 보고 있는 꼬마

"I wish it would get cold enough to snow. You can't build anything out of rain."

- 캠핑 와서 꼬마가 아빠에게

"Where can I buy a postcard? Grandma said to be sure to send her one."

- 꼬마가 신문을 읽고 있는 아빠에게

"Well SURE they call a dead person 'the late.' If you're not alive, you can't get anywhere on time."

    * The late name of person, 꼬마는 'late'를 '늦다'라는 뜻으로만 알고 있다

- Guitar, horn, bell 등으로 연주준비 중인 꼬마들이 아빠에게

"Get your video camera, Daddy. We're gonna try to go viral!"

    * go viral: 엄청난 히트를 기록한 internet U-tube

- 야구공으로 유리창을 깬 아이에게

엄마: "What do you have to say, young man?"

꼬마: "Does our homeowner's insurance cover it?"

- 촛불이 하나뿐인 아빠의 생일케이크를 보며 꼬마가 동생에게

"You know you're old when you only get the one for you good luck!"

- 꼬마가 역사책을 보며

"If George Washington was the father of our country, was Uncle Sam his brother?"

> * George Washington은 미국 건국의 아버지이고, Uncle Sam은 미국인을 뜻하지만, 꼬마 생각에는 Uncle(삼촌)이니까, Uncle Sam이 George Washington의 동생.

- 동생을 때려 울게 한 꼬마에게 엄마가

"Dolly! Why did you do that?"

꼬마: "I think it was self-defense."

- 꼬마가 밖에서 뛰어들어오며

"MY economy is improving! I just found a penny."

- 꼬마가 동생들에게 책을 읽어주며

"It starts with 'Once upon a time' 'cause nobody was wearing a watch."

- 빗자루를 들고 있는 꼬마

"OK, I'm done cleaning my room! Come look quick 'cause I'm ready to start messin' it up again."

- 꼬마가 아빠에게 "Daddy, did you ever know any caveman?"

- 망치질하고 있는 꼬마를 보며 다른 꼬마가

"The only kinda nails Billy hits are thumb and finger."

 * thumb and finger: 다섯 손가락


- 샌들(flip-flop)을 신은 꼬마가

"Mommy, which of these is my flip and which is my flop?"


- 낮잠 든 동생을 엄마에게 일러바치며 꼬마가

"PJ's takin' a nap without bein' told. Is he allowed to do that?"


- 방안을 온통 어질러놓은 꼬마가 엄마에게

"But the ceiling's clean!"


- 올림픽 시상식을 보고 있는 꼬마

"Oooooh! I like their National Anfem. I hope they win more gold medals."

 * National Anfem: 'Anthem'(국가, 國歌)이라 해야 맞는데 꼬마니까)


- 꼬마가 Winter Olympics를 보며

"How come spring and fall don't have Olympics, too?"


- 두껍게 옷을 입은 꼬마가

"I'm too warm. Can I bundle down?"

 * Bundle up(두둑하게 입다)과 대비

• 꼬마들이 동계올림픽 봅슬레이(Bobsleigh, Bobsled) 경기를 시청하며

"I wonder if all their sleds are named Bob."

    \* Sled: 썰매

• 여러 꼬마들 중 제일 큰 꼬마가 어른에게

"No, I'm not the oldest in the family – Daddy is."

• 동생이 책을 마구 찢으며 놀고 있는 모습을 보고, 꼬마가 엄마에게

"Is this the year PJ being gonna be old enough to know better?"

• 맛있는 과자를 만들어 주는 엄마에게 꼬마가

"MMMM, that's it! When it's my turn to be president…"
"I'm gonna put you in charge of cookies for the whole country!"

• 'House for Sale'이란 간판을 보고 있는 꼬마가 동생들에게

"It's a HOUSE right now. When people move in it'll be a HOME."

• 꼬마가 계산기를 들고는 엄마에게

"Know what? In four thousand, two hundred and six days I can get my driver's license."

• 동물원 구경을 마치고 나오면서 아빠가

"Which was your favorite animal?"

꼬마: "The hot dog!"

• Tool box와 각종 공구를 들고 있는 꼬마

"I'm ready if anybody wants to break something."

• The tolerance for pain is in direct proportion to the proximity of
the mom.

(아픔의 정도는 '엄마와 얼마나 가까이 있는가'에 정비례한다)

야구하다 다쳤을 때,

감독이 "I think that way need stitches"(몇 바늘 꿰매야겠다)라고 하면

꼬마는 "Okay"라고 하는데,

엄마가 "I think you snagged a hangnail on your sweater"(손 거스러미
가 옷에 걸린 것 같네)라고 하면,

꼬마는 'AAAGGGGGGGGHH! OW! OW! OW! OW! OW!
OW!' 라고 비명을 지른다.

• 경치구경을 하고 있는 아빠에게 꼬마가

"Can you do anything with scenery besides look at it?"

• 계산기를 두드리고 있던 남편이 아내에게

"By my calculations, their Christmas lists so far will cost $15,631.87."

• 아빠가 애들과 함께 눈사람을 만들고 있다. 당근으로 코를 붙이고
입에는 파이프를 물린다.

꼬마: "No, daddy! Let's make him a NON-SMOKER so he'll last longer!"

• 꼬마가 친구와 함께 집안으로 들어오며
"This is MY house, but my parents and brothers live here too."

• 꼬마가 개에게
"You're lucky! You never have to remember where you left YOUR shoes!"

• 방안에서 동생들과 놀던 꼬마가
"Mommy, can we borrow the dustpan, bloom and maybe some glue?"

• 꼬마가 엄마에게 새끼손가락을 가리키며
"Why does this finger forgottin' to grow as much as the rest?"

• 꼬마가 방에서 나오며
"Good news, Mommy. I outgrew this shirt I never liked."

• 눈 밭에서 눈으로 도넛 모양을 만든 꼬마가 다른 꼬마에게
"Look, I made you a snownut."

• 국회의사당을 쳐다보며 꼬마들이 엄마에게
"Can we go in there and see if our senators are doin' any work?"

• 꼬마: "Grandma, when you were little, what kinda music did you play on your iPod?"

• 남자애가 여자애의 허리둘레를 재면서
"Yep! You're a perfect 20−23−25."

• Thanks Giving 다음날, 학교에서 돌아온 꼬마가 엄마에게
"Nobody trades lunches today. EVERYBODY had turkey sandwiches."

• 책을 읽고 있는 꼬마
"Was Robin Hood the daddy of Red Riding Hood?"

    \* Little Red Riding Hood(빨간 모자): 유럽 아이들 교육용 동화

• 꼬마 누나가 동생에게
"Mommy's new blouse was made by two ladies − Polly and Esther."

• 꼬마가 럭비공을 들고 엄마에게
"What's the least breakable room in our house?"

• 긴 담뱃대를 들고 있는 인디언 조각상을 구경하고 있는 꼬마

"He might've lived longer if he didn't smoke that pipe."

• 아빠가 다리를 꼬고 책을 읽고 있다. 이 자세를 그대로 흉내 내고 있는 꼬마가 동생이 그 자세를 흉내 내려고 하자,
"Stop it, PJ!... Stop coping me!"

• Geese migrating(거위무리의 이동)을 보고 있는 꼬마
"The birds in front must have the map."

• 향수 냄새를 맡게 하는 누나에게 꼬마가
"Sorry, the only perfume I'd like would like a chocolate-chip cookie."

• Halloween 물건을 내다버리는 엄마에게 꼬마가
"While we're puttin'this Halloween stuff away, we might as well get out the CHRISTMAS decollations."
    * 미국 풍습 풍자

• 낮잠을 자다 말고 일어난 꼬마
"Mommy, which is shorter – a 'CAT nap' or a 'PEOPLE nap'?"

• 해변에서 Sun 로션을 손에 든 꼬마가
"Mommy, will you put some of this sunSCREEN-SAVER on my back?"

- 케첩, 양파 등이 없는 핫도그를 들고 있는 꼬마

"Mommy, you left my hot dog blank."

- 아빠의 그림을 친구에게 보여주며 꼬마가

"These are some of my dad's drawings. We call it 'POP art'".

    * pop art: 대중 미술(pop)

    * POP: dad, father

- 꼬마가 괘종시계를 쳐다보며

"Grandma's clock is always tick-talking."

    * tick-tock: 똑딱똑딱

- 꼬마들이 신문을 보고 있는 할머니를 바라보며,

"Mommy said 'no' and Daddy said 'yes'. We need to get Grandma to break the tie."

    * break the tie: 동점을 깨다

- 야외 캠핑 중 꼬마가 아빠에게 바람 빠진 Air mattress를 가지고 와서

"My mattress has a flat!"

- '얼굴에 묻은 오물을 씻어라'고 엄마가 비누와 타월을 주고 있다. 꼬마가

"Daddy's lettin' his whiskers grow. Why can't I let my dirt grow?"

* whiskers: 구레나룻

• 비행기에서 밖을 보며 아빠가

"There she lies, everybody… the City of Boston."

엄마 머리 속 상상: Paul Revere, Tall ships, quaint light, cape cod

(미국 독립혁명 당시 우국지사, 대형 범선, 진기한 빛, 케이프 코드 반도)

꼬마 머리 속 상상: Celtics, Red Sox, Bruins

　(농구팀, 야구팀, 아이스하키팀)


• 'Icecream' 차량이 아니고 'I Scream' 차량안에서 도깨비가 꼬마에게

"Whatsamatta, kid? Never seen an I scream Truck before?"


• 4월 15일(Tax return 신고 마지막일), 꼬마가 아빠에게

"Why did you wait the last minute to do your homework?"


• 날아가는 기러기 떼를 보며 꼬마

"I wonder if birds fly in any other letters than a 'V'?"


• 산타에게 꼬마가

"You know when I've been bad or good?! What! Did you get that from wikileaks?!"

　* 산타는 착한 아이에게 선물을 준다

　* WIKILEAKS: 정부 및 기업 비리, 불법 행위 고발 사이트, 사진, 동영상, 문서

자료 등 제공.

• 무릎이 까져 들어오는 애에게 엄마가: "Oh, you scraped your knee."

꼬마: "No, the sidewalk did it!"

• 꼬마가 비누를 가지고 밖으로 나가며 엄마에게

"We filled the birdbath but forgot the soap."

    * Birdbath: 새 목욕용 물 대야

• Digital Camera를 가지고 있는 아빠에게 꼬마가

"Since your new camera never runs out of films, does it run out of digitals?"

• 꼬마가 애기의 젖병을 마구 흔들며 엄마에게

"I figured PJ would rather have a milkshake!"

• 꼬마가 'Be the life of your party. Vote!' 라고 적힌 종이를 엄마에게 보이며,

"The only homework my teacher gave me was to make sure you and Daddy read this."

• Terrier(테리어 개) 한 마리가 으르렁(GRR!) 거린다. 꼬마가 동생에게,

"Watch out, Jeffy! That's a terrirIST!"

* -er는 비교급, -ist는 최상급

## 빌 호스트 만화 'The Lockhorns'

'The Lockhorns'는 대립이란 뜻으로 미국 만화가 Bill Hoest가 1968년에 시작한 연재만화로서 1988년부터는 Bunny Hoest가 대를 이어 연재하고 있다. 주인공인 Leroy와 Loretta 부부가 모든 일에 끊임없이 의견이 맞지 않는 캐릭터인데, 이 만화를 통해 일상의 미국생활에 사용되는 표현을 많이 익힐 수 있다.

• 집으로 찾아온 젊은 친구에게
Leroy: "I don't know how much it costs to get married. …I'm still paying."

• 팔등신 미녀가 서빙해주는 식당 간판을 보며
Leroy: "I hear the food is really good here."

• DMV에서 줄을 서서 기다리며
Leroy: "Whenever I feel life is moving too fast, I come here."
    * DMV(Department of Motor Vehicles)는 장시간의 대기시간으로 악명

• 아내는 무어라 소리지르고 있고, 빗자루를 든 남편은 이웃에게

"Unfortunately, Loretta has an unlimited calling plan"

  * Calling Plan: 전화요금제


• Loretta: 연기가 자욱한 부엌에서 나오며

"Good news, Leroy··· Dinner is about 90% contained"

  * Contain: safe, under control, 화재진압 시 90% contained라는 의미는 불
    길이 90% 잡혔다.


• Loretta가 Leroy에게

"I'm not looking for life in the fast lane, Leroy··· I'd just like to leave
the parking lot."

  * Life in fast lane: 잘 나가던 때
  * related idiom 'Mover and Shaker': 실력자, 유력자


• 시리얼(Cereal)로 아침을 먹으며 Loretta가 Leroy에게

"When you promised me the moon and the stars, I didn't think
they'd be made of the marshmallow."

  * 연애할 때 '별도 달도 따 주마'라고 했던 모양


• Loretta의 청력을 검사하려는 Audiologist에게 Leroy가

"If you really want to test her hearing, whisper some gossip out in
the hall."

  * Selective hearing: 듣고 싶은 것만 듣는다

- Marriage counselor앞에서 Leroy가

"I am not stubborn… when I get my way."

    \* stubborn: 완고한


- 청소기를 돌리고 있는 아내가 귀를 막은 채 TV를 보고 있는 남편에게

"Sorry, Leroy… unlike your appliances, mine don't have mute buttons."

    \* your appliances: 귀 막은 것을 비유


- Loretta가 Leroy에게

"Don't use our anniversary as a password. You can never remember it."


- 차 사고를 내고 집으로 돌아온 Loretta

"I learned a valuable lesson today, Leroy… how much it'll cost to replace the car.'


- 대기실, 주위에 있는 사람들이 모두 일어나 가슴에 손을 얹는다.

남편: 휴대폰을 손에 쥐고 있다

아내: "When did you switch your ring tone to 'The star-spangled banner'":

    \* The star-spangled banner은 미국 국가(National Anthem)

- 월드컵에서 자국팀이 진 후 Frown(mad) face로 회사에 전화를 하려는 Leroy에게, Loretta: "You can't call in sick because your team lost."

- 옷 가게에서 셔츠를 입어 보고 있는 Leroy가 점원에게
"You're right. It fits like a glove… unfortunately, I'm looking for a shirt."
  * Fit like a glove: 딱 맞는

- 남편이 아내에게 진공청소기를 선물로 주고는 으쓱댄다.
아내: "A new vacuum cleaner. I didn't think you could top the iron you gave me last year."
('지난해 내게 준 다리미가 최고였다'고 생각치 않았다.)

- 은행에 온 부부에게 창구직원이
"Our new policy is 'the customer isn't always right… the computer is."

- 의사에게 환자가 "I have a beef with this diet. It doesn't let me have any."
  * Have a beef with: 속상하다(upset about something)

- Scrabble game 중 아내가 Leroy에게
"Remember, it's your word against mine."

* Scrabble: 철자가 적힌 플라스틱 조각들로 글자 만들기를 하는 보드게임


• Leroy가 Doctor에게 "My headaches started when I joined my HMO."

* HMO: 미국 보건 기관(health maintenance organization)


• Leroy가 Loretta에게

"'Final notice' does not mean that they've finally given up."


• 낚싯대를 사려고 하는 Leroy, Loretta가 친구에게

"..but teach a man to fish, and he'll be back every year for new equipment."

* If you give a man a fish, he will eat for a day. If you teach a man to fish, he will eat for a lifetime.(물고기를 주면 하루에 먹어버리지만, 물고기 잡는 법을 가르쳐 주면 평생을 먹는다)
* 그런데 Leroy는 물고기 잡는 법을 가르쳐 주면 매년 새 장비를 장만한다.


• Loretta가 늦잠자는 Leroy에게

"I'm pretty sure casual Friday doesn't mean showing up to work at eleven."


• Couch potato 인 Leroy를 보며, Loretta 가 친구에게

"The government should hire Leroy as a consultant···nobody uses less energy than he does."

• Loretta가 친구에게

"I definitely married 'Mister Right'… Leroy never admits that he's wrong."

> * Mister Right: 결혼 적임자(The right person for you to marry. Right man for me)


• Parking lot에 Security manager 자리, Purchasing manager 자리에는 차가 있는데, Pay roll manager 자리에는 차가 대어져 있지 않다. Leroy가 친구에게 "Nobody ever steals that space."


• 식당에서 식사하는 남녀, 남자가

"This should be in the Michelin guide…the tire company."

> * 'Michelin guide'는 restaurant guide book


• 아내가 남편에게 stand lamp를 가리키며,

"I don't need feng shui to know this should be moved to the basement."

> * feng shui: 풍수


• Cocktail party에서 얘기 중인 부부

"We wanted to make a killing in the market, but our broker turned out to be a pacifist."

> * make a killing in the market: 많은 돈을 벌다(make a lot of money)
> * pacifist: 평화주의자

- Loretta가 Leroy에게

"I saw your old girlfriend today and she looked great…wrinkled, overweight, gray…"

- Financial advisor가 Leroy 부부에게

"The good news is you won't need identity protection."

    * identity protection: 신변보호

- Loretta가 Leroy에게

"I do have a balanced diet…I have a pound of white chocolate and a pound of dark."

- 남편이 아내에게

"You introduce so many new bills, you should be a member of congress."

    * 입법제안

- 남편으로부터 봉급봉투(Payable check가 들어있는)를 건네받은 아내: "At least you won't need a police escort when you take this to the bank."

남편 표정은 모욕당한(insult) 기분

- Doctor를 찾아온 Leroy에게 접수간호사가

"I scheduled you for 4:45 P.M. because he told me you were the last person he wanted to see."


• Loretta가 Leroy에게

"Wouldn't renewing your gym membership come under throwing good money after bad."

  * 쓸데없는 데 돈 낭비
  * Come under: within category


• Leroy가 친구에게, 화장하고 있는 아내를 소개하며

"This is my wife Loretta… some assembly is required."


• 침대에서 책을 읽고 있는 Leroy에게 아내가

"I hope you've learned your lesson, Leroy…never judge a book by its movie."

  * Never judge a book by its cover(표지만 보고 책을 평가하지 마라)와 대비


• Leroy 부부가 원룸에서(Studio apartment)

"We need to start thinking outside the box or we'll be living in one."

  * think outside the box: 객관적으로 냉정히 생각하다


• Soap opera를 보고 눈물을 흘리는 Loretta에게 Leroy가

"Maybe you won't feel so bad if you remember she's getting paid $25,000 an episode."

  * 연속극 주인공은 한 편 당 $25,000 받는다

- 쇼핑해서 들어오는 아내를 보고 Leroy가 친구에게

"When Loretta's father gave her away, I didn't know about the hidden costs."

  * Father gives away the bride: 아빠가 딸을 신랑에게 넘겨주다.(Marriage ceremony)


- Loan 상담을 하러 온 부부, loan 담당자가 전화하면서 웃고 있자, 아내가

"I guess he's checking our credit score."


- 모페드 가게에 있는 부부, 남편이:

"I think I'll start exercising by getting one of these and work my way down to a bicycle."


- 아내가 쇼핑을 잔뜩 해 가지고 오면서Leroy에게

"I got a whole new outfit to go with the tie I bought you."


- TV 밑의 VCR을 점검하고 있는 Leroy에게 아내가

"Just as well the VCR is obsolete… you never did learn how to program it."


- It was okay, but nothing to twitter home about it.

  * To write home about: 주위 사람들에게 추천하다

• 새 옷과 새 구두를 사려고 하는 Loretta에게 Leroy가

"Why can't you ever buy an outfit that you already have shoes for?"


• 보석가게에서 팔찌를 사서 나오는 Loretta가 Leroy에게

"This should teach you about nodding when you're really not listening."

    * 평소 Leroy는 잘 듣지 않고 건성으로 고개를 끄덕이는 모양


• 반지 감정하러 온 Loretta에게 보석감정사(Jewelry appraisals):

"So far, I haven't even found it listed on the periodic table."

    * Periodic table: 주기율표

    * 결국 가짜라는 뜻


• 집 밖 나무에 거울을 걸어 놓고 Bird bath fountain물로 면도를 하고 있는 Leroy, "Loretta has convinced me that we need another bathroom."


• 식탁에 앉은 Leroy가 Loretta를 보며

"Ahh…. Remember airline food?"

    * 지금의 음식이 맛이 없었던 기내식과 비슷한 모양


• Book revue(book review)에서 책을 고르고 있는 Leroy

"Mountain climbing for dummies… I'll agree with that."

    * 등산을 싫어하는 Leroy

• Loretta의 생일파티에서 Leroy가

"I don't have to wish Loretta many happy returns··· she returns everything I give her."

• 오래된 차에 왁스칠을 하고 있는 Leroy가 Loretta에게

"Waxing the old heap is silly?... I don't say anything when you put on makeup."

• Loretta가 친구에게

"When I say Leroy's heart is in the right place, I'm speaking anatomically."

    * anatomically: 따뜻한 마음을 가진, 해부학적으로

• 사람을 만나고 나오는 Leroy

"I like them better as Facebook friends than actual friends."

• Marriage counselor 앞에서

Leroy: "Loretta is becoming increasingly judgmental."(Loretta는 손에 gavel을 들고 있다)

    * gavel: 의장, 판사, 경매진행자가 쓰는 작은 망치
    * judgmental: 판사처럼 행동하는(acting like a judge, critical)

• Marriage counselor를 찾은

Leroy: "Loretta would have made a great seismologist···she always finding faults."

* seismologist: 지진학자
* Fault: 1) 잘못, 2) 단층

• 쇼핑을 하면서 물병을 하나 집어 들고

Leroy: "When did water start being more expensive than wine?"

• 남편은 면도도 하지 않고 팝콘을 먹으며 TV 앞에 앉아 있다. 아내
는 전화를 받으며

"The same… the rich are getting richer, the poor are getting poorer,
and Leroy is getting Leroyer."

• Leroy는 소파에 앉아 자고 있고, Loretta는 집으로 놀러 온 친구에게

"Leroy says his love for me is undying, but it never shows any vital
signs."

• Loretta는 소파에 앉아 신문을 읽고 있고, Leroy는 달력을 확인하
면서 친구에게 전화를 하고 있다.

"Thursday's no good, Herb…it's Loretta's annual 39th birthday
party."

* Loretta의 나이는 39에 고정

• 가발가게(Hair Apparent) 앞에서 Loretta가 Leroy에게

"Forget it Leroy… if I can't have a new fur, neither can you."

• Leroy가 수염도 깎지 않고, 잠옷 차림으로 온 방을 어질러 놓은 채 TV를 보고 있다. Loretta 가 친구에게

"This is Leroy's retirement Plan."

• 컴퓨터와 씨름하고 있는 Leroy를 보고 Loretta가

"Leroy doesn't swear by technology…he swears at it."

    * swear by: 믿다(rely on, believe in)

    * swear at: ~을 욕하다


## 스캇 아담스 만화 'Dilbert'

Dilbert는 미국 만화가 Scott Adams가 1989년부터 신문에 연재한 코믹 strip(4단짜리 만화)이다. 주제는 엔지니어인 Dilbert가 사무실 내에서 겪는 화이트칼라와 Micromanagement(소사한 것까지 세세하게 관리하는 쫌상 관리)이다. 이 만화를 보면 미국직장 내의 생생한 일면을 잘 알 수 있다.

• 직원이 비서에게

"Have you heard any rumors about what is driving our boss's decision lately?"

비서: "He's thwarting a rival within the company by offering only prohibitively expensive engineering solutions."

직원: "My work have meaning, but it's not the good kind."

* thwarting: 좌절시키다(frustrate)

* rival: 경쟁자(opponent, competitor)

* prohibitive: 엄두도 못 낼 정도로 높은


• 상사: "Your engineering experience looks great, but your social media score is nearly zero. You have no friends, no followers, and no social influence whatsoever."

부하: "Because I focus on my work!"

상사: "No, I'm pretty sure you're dead."


• 상사: "We've been using the Dogbert offsite document storage service for five years, and frankly, I'm concerned."

"Your service trucks look suspiciously like garbage trucks."

"I would cancel service if I could find the contract."

애완고양이: "It's in storage."

　　* 자신의 Storage를 마치 Garbage처럼 해 놓고 남 탓


• 비서: "Management experts say fat leaders are viewed less favorably than athletic ones. That's why I didn't order any donuts for your meeting."

상사: "Or did you just forget to do it?"

비서: "I can't take you seriously looking like that."

　　* because you are fat 라는 의미

- 부하: "My motivation is low today. I understand it's your job to fix that situation."

"An intensive attaboy or a fake interest in my life would be enough."

상사: "Drop dead and let the fries eat you."

부하: "I set the bar too high."

  * intensive attaboy or fake interest: 실제는 안 그러면서 굽실대고 아첨하는 것
  * Drop dead: 급사(急死)하다


- 오랜만에 업무에 복귀한 직원에게

상사: "I'm concerned because you've been out of work for such a long time."

직원: "It's like riding a bicycle. Once you learn, you always know how." (뒤로 넘어진다.)

상사: "Are you okay?"

직원: "Did chairs always swivel?"

  * swivel: 돌리다


- 사장이 애완고양이에게 말하고 있다

"The media is saying I'm overpaid compared to other CEOs. That's crazy."

"Do a benchmark study of executive pay, including the sultan of Brunei, Larry Elision and God."

"Make sure my pay ends up somewhere in the middle so it doesn't look suspicious."

> \* 자신의 Pay를 부루나이국왕, Lawrence J. Ellison(Oracle 창업자), 하느님
> 과 비교하고 있다.

- 상사: "Would you be my mentor?"

사장: "It's better for me if none of my underlings are qualified to take my job."

부하: "I think you just taught me something."

상사: "Gaaa!!! I hate it when I do that!"

> \* Underlings: 아랫사람들
> \* 이런 류의 상사는 자신이 아는 것을 부하에게 잘 안 가르쳐 준다

- 부하직원에게

상사: "Carol. Why did you send me a link about people who like to dress in animal costumes?"

직원: "It's called the furry life style. I thought you might want to try it out."

상사: "I'll take a look."

동료직원: "What's your end game?"

직원: "If the furry thing sticks, I'll try to get him to go on a safari."

> \* furry: 털로 덮인
> \* end game: 최종단계

# 윌리 밀러 만화 'Non Sequitur'

Wiley Miller의 만화는 비꼬는 식의 위트(wry wit)와 정곡을 찌르는 사회풍자(trenchant social satire)로 유명하다. 1991년 연재를 시작한 Non Sequitur는 스페인어로 'it does not follow'라는 의미이며, 대단히 정치적인 내용이 많다.

• The four horsemen of annoyance
네 명이 말을 타고 가면서 짜증나게 하는 행동을 하고 있다.
-The incessant Facebook updater: 끊임없이 페이스북을 업데이트하는 사람
-The constant whisper: 계속 휘파람을 부는 사람
-The public nose-picker: 사람들 앞에서 코 파는 사람
-The gym grunter: Gym에서 운동하면서 툴툴거리는 사람
   * annoyance: 짜증
   * The four horsemen of apocalypse: [성서] 요한 계시록의 네 기사(백·적·흑·청색 말에 탄 4명: 각각 질병·전쟁·기근·죽음을 상징함)
   * apocalypse: 종말

• 신생아실을 들여다보고 있는 사람들
"I wonder why they're all crying so much."
신생아실 출구에 warning: 'Life is unfair past this point'
   * Maternity Ward: 분만실, 부인과 병동, 산과 병동

• 식탁에서 Pet Foods Can으로 식사를 하고 있는 노부부

"I miss the days when being a cat-person or a dog-person had something to do with having a pet."

> \* cat-person or a dog-person: 고양이를 좋아하는 사람, 개를 좋아하는 사람

• 양쪽으로 힘을 합쳐 노를 젓는 배 안에서 크게 울고 있는 애기

"So much for the things-can't-possibly-get-any-worse theory."

> \* Can't get any worse: 더 이상 나빠질 수는 없다
> \* '비행기 안에서 계속 우는 애기'와 대비

• 입간판 'No unicycles beyond this point'를 보고 있는 시민

"Y'know…up until now I never had the urge to ride a unicycle"

> \* urge: 욕구, 충동
> \* 사람심리: 하지말라면 하고 싶어진다

• And the great mystery remains unsolved

'Chicken XING' sign board가 있는 건널목에서 할아버지 부부:

"No, that just tells us where, not why…"

> \* 'Why chicken cross the road?'(병아리들은 왜 도로를 건너는가?): a common riddle joke

• 줄을 서서 길을 건너는 오리(닭) 무리를 보며 부부

"No, I didn't know chickens can't resist a conga line, but now we have the answer to that old question…"

* Conga: 길게 줄을 서서 각자 앞 사람을 잡고 빙글빙글 돌아가며 추는 빠른 춤.

* Old question "Why did the chicken cross the road?"

* Answer: To get the other side.

• Biology 101 class 교실에, '우주인이 유인원에게 Alien DNA Beam
을 쏘아서 그 유인원이 사람으로 진화되었음을 설명하는 그림'이 붙여
져 있다.

찾아온 교장에게 선생님이

"Hey, I'm not the one who insisted on presenting an alternate
explanation."

* Usual alternate explanation: 창조론(Creationism)

• Genesis of the Trial Attorney(소송변호사의 기원)

시나이산(Mt. Sinai)에 모세(Moses)가 서 있고 그 아래에 군중들이 있
다.

한 사람이: "Ok… you say 'Commandments', but I hear 'Recomm-
endations'".

* Genesis: 1) 창세기, 2) 기원

• 술집 선전 간판 'No politics 6-7 PM'

술집 주인: "We call it very happy hour."

* Happy Hour: 술집에서 정상가보다 싼 값에 술을 파는 보통 이른 시간대

- How to make debates watchable

(토론자 두 사람이 얼굴에 Pie를 뒤집어쓰고 있다: pie in the face of both candidates)

MC: "Well, gentlemen, it appears our fact-checker has found a problem with both opening statements."

&ast; fact checker: 사실확인팀

&ast; 'pie in the face'는 '어리석은 사람'이란 뜻


- 곰이 낚시꾼들을 보고, 잡아먹을까 말까 고민하며

"It's a real struggle to stay on a healthy, omega-3-rich diet when junk food is so readily available."

&ast; 곰에게 사람은 Junk food


- 천국의 입구에 'No guns allowed'라는 간판이 세워져 있다.

천국의 문지기: "yeah, you'd think it'd be given, but apparently it needs to be pointed out to Americans."

&ast; 미국의 총기소지 문제점 풍자


- Closing arguments on dessert

식당에서 디저트를 주문하려는 부부:

"If 60 is the new 40, that would make 200 pounds the new 120 pounds, right?"


- Blind Duck을 데리고 나온 친구 사냥꾼에게

사냥꾼: "No… I said it was your turn to bring a buck blind."

　　* Blind Duck: 눈이 안 보이는 오리

　　* Duck Blind(사냥꾼이 숨을 만한 위장처)와 대비


• Humpty Dumphty, the later years.

담장 아래서 머리가 깨진 채로 구걸하고 있는 Humpty Dumpty:

"I didn't 'fall'! I was pushed by a government conspiracy!"

　　* the later years: 늙어서

　　* Humpty‑ Dumpty: 영국의 전래 동요(nursery rhyme)에 나오는 주인공으로 달걀꼴 사람

　　* 다른 사람을 비난하고 방어적인 캐릭터(blaming others, defensive character)

　　* Conspiracy: 음모(secret planning by a group of people to do something illegal)


• 하늘나라에 온 부부

"How do you know this is heaven?"

"Well, to begin with, I don't see any campaign signs…"

　　* 정치 캠페인 Sign이 없으니 천국


• Pioneer 시대, 마차(wagon)를 타고 가다가, 길에서 음식을 해 먹고 있는 개척자들

"First, we could never taste the difference. Second, everything out here is free‑range."

　　* Can't taste the difference: 맛의 차이를 느끼지 못하다

* Free-range: 놓아 기른

• Optimist section과 Pessimist section으로 구분되어 있는 식당에 온 부부
"It means we either sit separately or we don't talk about the economy."

• 술집 앞에서 집으로 전화 거는 남자
"Hi, Honey⋯ Hey, don't wait up. It looks like another long meeting⋯"
술집 간판에는

    Happy hour: 5-7 PM

    Fix the economy hour: 7-10 PM

    Mideast crisis resolution hour: 10PM - 1 AM

    Call a cab hour: 1-2 AM

• Mel presents his traditional post-election wrap-up
집 앞에서 노인이 'Now everyone shut up and get a life'라는 Picket을 들고 있다.

    * wrap-up: 마무리

    * get a life: 따분하게 굴지 마라

    * '선거 끝났으니 일상으로 돌아가라'는 뜻

• '4th Amendment Lost & Found' booth에 있는 Information 안내판에

'You were there' 지점, 'You are here' 지점, 'We know you want to go there' 지점이 표시되어 있다.

손님: "See? I told you there was a practical reason for all that data mining."

> \* Data Mining: 데이터 마이닝(컴퓨터를 통해 대규모 자료를 토대로 새로운 정보를 찾아내는 것)

- Worst bucket list ever 코끼리 배설물 치우는 사람
  1. Fill it.
  2. Empty it.
  3. Fill it again.
  4. Empty it again.
  5. Repeat 1-4.

- 경찰이 Metropolice café 앞에서 슈퍼맨을 단속하고 있다.
전신주에 붙어 있는 Warning: 'Laws of physics strictly enforced'

> \* Law of physics: 물리학 법칙
>
> \* Super man은 물리학 법칙 위반

- Last words cemetery, Men's' dept.(남자들의 묘비 글)
"Let me show you the old-school way to do it."
"Hey, it looks sturdy enough to me."
"Don't worry. I can two things at once."

> \* Old-school: 구식의, 전통적인

　　* sturdy: 튼튼한

　　* Safety에 관한 경고성 묘비 글이다

• 하늘나라에서 하느님이 지구를 보며, 천사에게

"Truth be told, if it wasn't for dogs, I would have blown it up years ago…"

　　* Truth be told: 사실을 말하자면

　　* 개가 아니었다면 지구를 날려버렸을 거야


• The free market celebration of Labor Day

휴일에 해변에 놀러 와 보니

'Life guard on duty somewhere in India'라는 Sign이 세워져 있다


• Job creation update

주유소 주유기 바로 옆에 Scottish bag pipe로 자동차타이어에 공기를 넣어주는 직업 등장.


• 아이: "Hey, the calendar says today starts the Chinese new year, and that it's the year of dragon…what does that mean?"

어른: "That means it's an election year, so it'll seem to drag on longer than usual."

아이: "I better update Wikipedia on that…"

어른: "I'm sure they'll appreciate it."

　　* Drag on: 질질 끌다

　　* 'Dragon'과 'drag on' 대비

• The direct male market에서
Genuine emotion greetings 코너에는 birthday, wedding, miss you,
get well, anniversary등 많은 종류의cards들이 진열되어 있는데,
Feigned sincerity greetings 코너에는 "sold out"

　　* Genuine: 진심
　　* Feigned: 허위(pretend)
　　* sold out: 매진


• 사람들이 줄을 서서 Grim Reaper(저승사자)가 타고 있는 배로 들
어가고 있다.
"What did I tell you? There's always a catch to those bargain internet
travel fares…"

　　* 굉장히 싼 것처럼 보이나, 실제 가보면 형편없고 바가지 씌우는 여행상품


• The Vatican's H.R Manager 책상 위에는 frocked(성직에 취임한)
서류와 defrocked(성직에서 박탈된) 서류가 거의 비슷하게 쌓여 있다.

　　* hypocrite(위선자), so-called Christian


• Elevator 앞, Botton에는 – Down –Way Down –You really
don't want to know 세 개 밖에 없고 올라가는 표시는 없다. 정부관료
인 듯한 사람이 기다리며:
"Looks like it's still going to be a while to get the old confidence
back…"

　　* confidence back: 신뢰회복

• Idle Hands Financial Corp.의 회의실,

한 사람이 추이(Trends)를 나타내는 그래프를 설명하며

"No… it's an E.K.G. of our investors."

> \* Idle hands: 게으른 사람
>
> \* EKG: 가슴이 미어질 듯한(Heart beating, Electrocardiograms, electrocardiograph)


• Open Casket Funeral Service에서, 고인이 소파에 기댄 채 TV를 보고 있고, TV 위에는 맥주 캔이 놓여 있다.

조문객: "Yeah…. But maybe there's such a thing as looking too natural…"

> \* open casket: 관을 열어 놓음(closed casket)


• The Shortest Retirement in History

퇴직하고 집으로 돌아온 남편이 청소하고 있는 아내에게,

"That's it. Honey. I'm done! Now I can stay home and micromanage whatever it is you do all day!"

> \* The shortest라는 제목을 보면 실제로는 며칠 못 갔다는 얘기


• TV를 켜며(click),

할아버지: "OK, now… Amuse us!"

(TV에서 별 재미있는 게 없자)

할머니: "I don't think that's how the 'On-Demand' program works, dear."

남자: "Well, it should be!"

    \* Amuse me: 나를 재미있게 해봐(Make me laugh, entertain)

    \* On Demand program: 원하는 시간에 방영되도록 하는 기능


• Chocolate co-op Inc. Research and Development

상사: "Look, half the work is done! All you need to do is fill in the top part so we can legally say the bottom part."

부하직원은 보고서를 쳐다보고 있다.

Top part: Data(공란)

Bottom Part: 결론(Conclusion): Eating chocolate will make you look younger and thinner.


• 재판정(Judge's Chamber) 배심원석에는 사람 대신 개들이 앉아있다.

판사: 'We've found they're a better judge of character than the usual pool of jurors…'

    \* Attorneys(원고측 및 피고측 변호사 합의 하에) choose and agree on 12 people among 100, usually neutral jury

    \*개들이 배심원이니까 확실 중립(neutral)


• Bert makes a fashion statement

Bert라는 남자가 집 앞에 Teen Agers들의 힙합패션을 싫어한다는 간판을 세워놓고 있다.

'You look like an idiot!'

'Pull up your pants!'

'That thing on your nose looks like booger!'

'Turn your hat around!'

   \* Booger: 코딱지


• 무인도(deserted island)에 조난된 사람이 구조용 불을 피워 놓고 있는데,

Grim Reaper가 배를 타고 오고 있다.

"Well, the good news is, our signal fire seems to have worked…"

   \* Grim Reaper: 저승사자


• The bittersweet meeting of perception and reality

고무보트를 타고 무인도에 도착한 사람, 무인도에서 조난당해 있던 사람, 두 사람이 동시에 외친다.

"Yay! I'm saved!!"

   \* Bittersweet: 씁쓸하면서 달콤한


• 천국(Heaven)의 입구에 두 개의 출입문이 있다. 왼쪽은 'Wrong religion entrance'. 오른쪽은 'Right religion entrance'. 왼쪽으로 들어가는 사람은 아무도 없고, 오른쪽 입구로는 길게 줄서 있다. 이를 보고 있는 천사가

"The funny thing is, none of them ever get the joke…"

• The men-only cemetery의 묘비명들

'Yes, I know what I'm doing'

'Hey, trust me'

'It's the black wire to the red wire, right?'

'What's the worst that can happen'

'That doesn't look so hard to do'

'Don't worry, I've done these a million times'

'Pull my finger'

　　* 남자들의 허세 표현


• 피라미드 건설 공사장에서, 역 피라미드를 건설 중에 있는 광경을 보며,

이집트 인: "I can't quiet put my finger on it, but something tells me that this is some sort of scheme."

　　* put one's finger on it: 정확하게 지적하다

　　* Pyramid scheme(Ponzi scheme): 피라미드 방식, 폰지형 사기방식


• Why engineering and philosophy aren't always a good mix

Elevators 옆에 안내문구: 'There is no up or down, only the presence of where you are at the moment'

그 문구 밑에 있는 쓰레기통에는: 'Another man's treasure'

　　* One man's trash is another man's treasure.


• 감옥소에서 양손과 양 발에 쇠사슬을 채운 채 거꾸로 매달려 있는

사람이

"They gave me a choice … it was either this or watch political debates."

    * 정치토론(political debates)을 얼마나 싫어했으면


• Climbing the new ladder of success

Confused Homeless Drunker가 'Fund Rasing Chart' 같은 걸 세워놓고 구걸하고 있다

Help me reach my goal!

1단계: Babbling wino * babbling: talking nonsense, wino: 싸구려 와인

2단계: Prophet of doom * 종말 예언

3단계: Blowhard in Bar * 허풍

4단계: Blowhard on Radio * talk show host, Rush Limb rough

5단계: Donald Trump * 재력가, 허풍으로 미국대통령에 당선된 사람.


• 항공기 날개 위에 고양이 한 마리가 앉아 있다. 조종석에서 이 고양이를 쳐다보면서 조종사:

"All I know about the new bird avoidance system is that it's supposed to be the latest in green technology… why do you ask?"

    * Green technology: 환경보존을 위한 녹색기술

- Moses invents the top 10 list

하나님이 모세에게 엄청나게 많은 tablets를 보여주자 모세가:

"Whoa, whoa, whoa… trust me, that's waaaaay too much information."

* Ten Commandments: 십계명


- 'This way to Utopia'라는 팻말을 따라 좁은 길, 바위산을 기어오르고, 사다리를 타고 드디어 도착한 곳에는 "No cell or WIFI reception here"라는 팻말이 세워져 있다


- 궁전 같은 사무실에서 왕처럼 군림하는 회사 사장이 직원에게

"Sorry, we have to let you go, Bob, but it's just a matter of budget priorities."

* Let one go: 해고하다


- 'Complete, corporate, control is near!'라는 피켓을 들고 다니는 사람을 보고,

행인: "Now that's what I call a doomsday prophecy."

* Doomsday prophecy: 최후의 심판일 예언


- 숲속 동물들의 재판정. 판사석에는 사자, 증인석에는 사슴 등등…

사람: "Quiet, everyone…we're about to witness firsthand the awe and majesty of the law of the jungle…"

* Firsthand: 직접

* awe and majesty: 경외감과 장엄함
* The law of the jungle: 정글의 법칙(약육강식, 성공하기 위해서는 다른 사람들을 해칠 각오를 해야 하는 상황)

• The Final Reward for a Writer…

묘비명(gravestone epitaph)에 R.I.P. 'At Last, a Deadline I can live with!'

* R.I.P: Rest in peace(평화롭게 잠들다)
* Deadline: 마감기한

• Litigators' Heaven

한 Litigator(소송자)가 지옥의 계단을 내려가면서,

"Would you look at this? No handrails! Man. Someone is just asking for a big, fat lawsuit. And don't get me started on the heating system…"

* 지옥은 소송자에게는 천국

• 술집 'La Taverne Tranquille' 안내문

'Nobody wants to hear what you think, 5–8 pm'

찾아온 손님: "It's nice to see a place that really puts an effort into making happy hour happy."

* the tranquil tavern: 조용한 술집

• The intricate mechanics of government

-'Public Entrance'는 쥐구멍 같은 곳으로 기어 들어가는데, 안쪽은 미

로로 되어 있어 결국 담당자에게 가는 길은 없다(no way to reach 담당자).

－Lobbyist Entrance: direct way to 담당자
* Intricate: 복잡한


• 개썰매를 타고 있는 Eskimo인, 상어 떼가 있는 무인도에 고립된 사람(Stranded on a deserted island), 사막에서 지쳐 있는 사람 등이 모두 한 곳에 있다

"Ok… one of us is having the mother of all hallucinations…"
* Hallucinations: 환각


• 사무실에 염소들이 서류를 씹어 먹고 있고, 어린아이도 있다.

직원: "Um, Bob? The memo specially said this is bring－your－kid－to－work day."
* kid: 1)아이, 2)새끼염소


• The First Writer and Editor
원시인이 동굴 벽화를 그릴 때, Editor가 이것 저것 지적을 하자
Writer가 Editor에게

"Take out that part? Are you nuts? How is the stampede scene at the end of the cave going to make sense without it?"
* Stampede: 무리 지어 우르르 움직임(Group of animals moving fast, trample what is in the way).
* Trample: 밟아 뭉개다

• iPhone 을 쉴 새 없이 하며(tap,tap,tap,tap,tap…..) 해안가를 운전하고 있는 Teen의 twitter:

'During down the coast. Was about to complain about ugly offshore oil drilling platforms. Then I remembered: I'm DRIVING.'

  * oil drilling platforms: 해양 시추설비


• The Big Picture

기업체 중역회의 의장: "The meek may inherit the earth, gentlemen, but we'll still own congress."

  * Meek: 온순한 사람
  * Biblical the mount sermon(산상수훈) on the board of directors. 온유한 자는 복이 있나니 저희가 땅을 기업으로 받을 것임이요…
  * 그러나 우리는 여전히 의회를 장악하고 있다.


• 부두에 정박해 있는 'MISSPOKE'라는 배를 보며

"My guess is, it belongs to a politician…"

  * Misspoke: 실언하다(특히 Bill Clinton 전 대통령의 거짓말)


## 존 맥퍼슨 만화 'Close to Home'

John McPherson의 'Close to Home'이란 신문만화는 1992년부터 연재되었는데, 주제는 결혼, 자녀, 학교, 일, 스포츠, 건강, 가정생활 등 다양하다. 1990년대 최고 인기를 끌었으며, 2021년 현재는 전세계 약

700개 국 신문에 연재되고 있다. 'Close to Home'이라는 동명의 영화와 TV 시리즈도 있으며, 만화에서는 역시 미국사회의 현실적인 모습을 배울 수 있다.

• 공항 체크인 카운터

여자손님: "Listen, you ignorant little twit! I need a connecting flight to Vienna for my return trip or heads will roll here!"

직원:('send bags to Mongolia' button을 누르고 있다)

　　* ignorant little twit: 모욕, modern insult
　　* Heads will roll: 목을 쳐 버리겠다
　　* 직원은 이 손님을 몽골로 보내 버림으로써 복수하고 있다.

• 자동차정비공장에 차를 맡긴 사람에게 정비공(Mechanic)이,

"Let's see… new couch in the den, $800… piano lessons for the kids, $300… new golf clubs, $600…", "I'd say you're looking at about $1,700."

　　* cynical point of view: 자기이익만 생각하는
　　* 미국의 자동차정비공(Mechanic)은 못 믿을 사람 1위

• To be more convincing when he faked a sick day, Bill liked to actually feel lousy(거실에 벌집을 두고 상의를 벗은 채 벌에 쏘여가며 회사에 전화를 하고 있다)

"… um, yeah, Mr. Croger. I've got a horrible headache, chills, and sharp, stinging pains all over."

• Wine을 따니 코르크마개가 병을 가득 채우고 Wine은 몇 방울만나 온다.

"What a rip-off!"

  * rip-off: 바가지

 

• Elementary School 학생들이 광고판을 하나씩 매고 하교한다.

교장: "At $50 a sandwich board per week, multiplied by 800 students, it'll really help balance the school budget this year."

  * 미국에는 길거리에서 광고판을 매고 아르바이트하는 어린 학생들이 많다.

 

• 바닷가에 놀러 온 가족, 남편은 모래로 사무실 책상, 의자, 컴퓨터 등을 쌓고 있다(쌓는 소리: Pat, pat, pat, pat…)

아내: "For cryin' out loud! Can you forget about work just for one day?"

  * For crying out loud: 무슨 짓이야(What's the matter with you, what's wrong?)

  (You are crazy, strange, odd)

 

• 방안에서 스프링 위에 놓인 서핑 보드를 타면서 TV를 켜고 있다.

"With a little ingenuity, Howie was able to feel like he was truly channel surfing."

  * Chanel surfing: TV channel을 이리저리 돌려봄

 

• Garage Sale에 내놓은 Thead Mill을 보고

"That treadmill was used only one time, I swear."

* 대부분의 사람들이 작심삼일

• 경찰차가 Flash lights를 켜고 이동 중, 경찰관은 운전하면서 도넛, 핫도그, 음료수를 먹으면서, 무전기로

"I've got a ··· cough! " 'scuse me, a ··· mmphl ··· 1143, texting—while—driving, license plate 876—FFK··· grrgl··· I'm. um, in pursuit."

　* 발음이 제대로 될 리가 있나?

• County coroner가 시체를 집에 가지고 와서 검시를 하고 있다. 아내가 친구에게

"I hate it when Bill brings work home."

　* coroner: 검시관

• 의사가 환자에게

"The virus attacks part of your brain and makes you extremely gullible, I'll see you on Monday, and don't forget to pay your $30,000 co—pay on the way out."

　* gullible: 잘 속아 넘어가는(naïve)

• 약국에서 약사가 손님에게

"Now, these AREN'T covered by your insurance, and they do cost $700. But they will COMPLETELY cure you of being too gullible."

• Drugs(마약류) 판매 상점에서 직원이 손님에게

"Like to sample an antidepressant, sir?"

"Brighten your day a bit? Free antidepressant, mama?"

 * Antidepressant: 우울증 치료제


• 앰뷸런스에서 환자가 침대와 함께 차 밖으로 떨어져 차문에 매달린 채 끌려가고 있다. 운전사: "Yeah, I hear the squealing noise too. Probably just a bad wheel bearing."


• 죽은 줄 알고 Morgue(영안실)에 안치된 사람이 살아있다.

직원들: "Anyway, to make a long story short, the medical examiner who performed your autopsy was fired."

 * Autopsy: 부검, 검시


• 'Tastee time Donuts'라는 Sign을 단 차량이 경찰에 과속으로 잡혔다.

경찰: "I clocked you doing 67 in a 45, but maybe we can work something out."

 * 67 in a 45: 시속 45마일 도로에서 67마일로 달렸다

 * 어느 나라든 경찰은 뇌물을 좋아하는가 보다


• Monarch airlines에서는 '$25 per bag handling fees' 정책을 시행 중. Check-in 하러 온 승객 엄청 큰 가방을 가지고 와서'

"Yep, that's right. Just the one bag for the five of us."

- How many teens see their parents
  * 청소년들에게는 부모가 ATM 기계로 보인다

- Santa replaces Rudolph's nose with a state-of-the-art GPS system.
  * state-of-the-art: 최신의

- Never wanting to share a seat on the train
뱀, 전갈 같은 혐오동물 모양의 옷을 입고 좌석에 앉아 있다
'Barry always wore his special commuting suit.'
  * 혼자 편하게 앉아 가려고

- Mapquest를 보고 길을 찾아온 운전자, 막다른 골목에 붙은 안내표지:
'Fake out! You are 300 miles from Dulles airport. Ah! Ha! Ha! Signed, the mapquest pranksters!'
  * Mapquest는 Google처럼 지도 길 안내 서비스를 제공하는 미국회사
  * prankster: 장난꾸러기

- 상점 음료판매기 앞에서 여자가 턱걸이를 하고 있다.
"Instead of passing the fat tax on soda, the government requires that people do 10 chin-ups before the cooler will open."
  * chin-ups: 턱걸이

• 아내가 손뼉(Clap! Clap!) 을 치자 전등이 켜진다(click!), 동시에 남편이 쿵(Wump!) 하고 쓰러진다.

"Claire discovers that the Clapper operates on the same frequency as Don's pacemaker."

　　* pacemaker: 심박조율기


• Mike Tyson. Age: minus three months

임산부가 Punching bag 앞에 서자, 뱃속의 태아가 punching bag을 친다.

'Bappity, bappity, bappita!'

　　* Punching bag: 샌드백


• 트림하고 있는(URP!) 남편을 데리고 자동차 딜러에 찾아온 여자에게

직원: "I'm sorry, ma'am, but the Cash for Clunkers program is good only for vehicles, not loser, deadbeat husbands."

　　* Cash for Clunkers: 노후차량 보상프로그램

　　* Deadbeat: 게으름뱅이, 사회의 낙오자


• 비행기 좌석사이 통로에 serving용 카트가 길을 막고 있고, 어떤 사람이 카트 밑으로 림보 통과하는 자세로 뚫고 나오려 하고 있다.

'As a world limbo champion, Dave could make it an airplane's rest room, even when the beverage cart was in the aisle.'

- 도서관에서 'Learn to levitate'라는 제목의 책들이 공중에 떠 다닌다.

  * levitate: 공중에 뜨다

- 서점 Information Desk에서 한 사내가 점원에게 소리치고 있다.
"Watha matter? You got lard in your ears, fathead? I TOLD YOU, I'm lookin' for the book 'How to Win Friends and Influence People'!"

  * Lard: 돼지기름(looking fat)
  * Fathead: 멍청한 사람(a stupid person)
  *그런 책 안 읽어도 되겠다.

- Oct.17, 1938: Evel Knievel is born
태어나는 아기가 엄마 뱃속에서부터 바로 sliding table을 점프하면서 세상밖으로 나온다.(Fooosh!)

  * Evel Knievel was an American daredevil(무모한 사람) who became an icon in the 1970s for his incredible motorcycle stunts.

- 식당에서 손님에게Empire State Building 모양의 음식을 내놓으며
종업원: "…and here's your Manhattan clam chowder, sir."

  * Clam chowder의 종류: Manhattan clam chowder(red, tomato base)
  New England clam chowder(white sause)

- In the year 2030. 상점 앞을 지나며 엄마가 애에게
"That? That's a store, Hon. In the olden days people would buy

things in stores instead of online."

    * Hon: Honney


• 학교 교장실 문 앞 안내판

'Please wait to be yelled at': 꾸중 듣다

    * 식당에 들어가면 흔히 볼 수 있는 안내판 'Please wait to be seated' 와 대비


• Game Town에서 온갖 Video game들을 다 때려 부수고(smash! bam!) 있는 여자들을 보고

"They say they're speaking out against violent video games."

    * Using violence to denounce violence: 폭력을 비난하기 위해 폭력을 사용


• 두 작업자가 콘크리트 파쇄기로 열심히 일을 하고 있다. 작업감독관이 보스에게

"We just have them drink 10 cups of espresso each morning and VOILA! Energy-free jack-hammers!"

    * Viola: 감탄사

    * Jack-hammer: 착암기


• 사무실로 아주 작은(tiny) 여자가 들어오고 있다.

직원: "Oh, brother! Here she comes to micromanage me again!"

    * Micromanage: 사소한 것까지 꼼꼼히 따지는 관리자


• 'The latest in shopping cart technology': Water soluble carts that don't need to be returned.

비 오는 날 'Super-Duper Foods' 라는 Grocery store에서 쇼핑하고 나
오는데 빗물에 녹아내린 쇼핑 카트가 이곳 저곳에 있다.

    * Super-duper: 기막히게 좋은


• 양말 한 짝이 소파에 앉아 TV를 보고 있다. 화면에는 Match.com


• Yard sale이라는 간판을 걸어 놓고 진짜 Yard를 팔려는 집주인이 지
나가는 사람들에게 "You folks missed a heck of a sale!"

    * Yard sale 또는 Garage sale은 자신의 집에서 사용하던 물건을 싸게 판매
    * Heck of: 대단한, 엄청난, 터무니없는


• 심장박동조절장치를 부착하고 있는 환자에게

간호사: "Your new pacemaker comes with 50 million free beats! You
can buy additional beats at pulsemore.com."

    * Cash 충전 등 최근의 Technology 풍자


• Hippy 부모가 정상적으로 자란 애를 보며

"You know, I just feel like somewhere along the line we have failed as
parents."


• Skier들이 스키를 타고 있고, 한 사람이 ski pole에 가슴이 찔려서
누워 있다.

한 사람이 마이크를 들고

"Yoooo-hooo! Has anyone seen a ski pole that I dropped when I was on the chairlift?"


• TV 위에 애가 올라 앉아 물고기를 한 마리 물고 뛰어내리려는 자세를 취하고 있다. 소파에 앉아 커피를 마시고 있는 엄마가 옆에 있는 이웃집 아줌마에게

"We're very proud of Todd. He just became an Eagle Scout!"

　　* Eagle scout: 최고의 Scout 단원

　　* The apple falls close to the tree: 부전자전(Like son, like father)


• 강도가 총을 들이대자 휴대폰으로 사진을 찍으며

"Hold on. I just want to put on Facebook that I'm actually in the process of being mugged, then you can have my BlackBerry!"

　　* BlackBerry: 상표명


• 비행기의 앞부분은 늑대 얼굴, 날개에는 짐승 발 모양

'To prevent flocks of geese from flying toward its.Jupiter Airlines made some key design changes.'

　　* 새가 비행기와 충돌하는 사례가 빈번하다


• 항공사 Check-in Counter 앞에서 부부가 싸움을 하고, 애기는 바닥에 앉아 울고 있다.

광고벽보에는 'Tranquility Airlines where kids fly in our cargo hold play zone!'

\* tranquil: 고요한, 평온한(calm & peaceful)

• 시험일, 선풍기를 의자 뒤에 설치해서 틀어 놓고 있는 학생(whirrr! 선풍기 돌아가는 소리).

'Garrett knew it was important to keep his brain from overheating during big tests.'


• 야구, 주자가 도루하다 슬라이딩 태그아웃(Sliding tag out)되자

Coach: "Whoops, sorry, Steve. That wasn't a steal sign. I had an itch on my stomach."


• Things you don't want to hear on a blind date

남자: "Hey! I made that license plate!"

   \* Blind date: 미팅

   \* 차량번호판 제작은 보통 죄수들이 하는 일


• UFO를 타고 나타난 외계인이 집 앞에 착륙해 있다.

남편이 아내에게

"Relax! They just want to know if we have jumper cables."


• 비행기가 활주로에서 급정거한다(Screech)

"Steve! Watch out! Runway models!"

활주로에는 여자 모델들이 워킹을 하고 있다.

   \* Runway: 1)활주로, 2)패션쇼 장의 런웨이

* Screech to halt: 브레이크를 밟다(put on brakes).

• 사람들이 관을 메고 허들달리기를 하고 있다.

"It was his last request. He was a track star in college."

• National Bank and Trust 건물 앞에서 Bob이 전화를 받고 있다.

전화: "Bob, it's Dr. Zimmel! Great news, you're not dying after all. We mixed up your chart with another patient's!"

'Bob wished he had gotten this call BEFORE he gave all his money to his favorite charity.'

• An avid text massager, Katie Hunter started using fewer vowels in her everyday speech.

"···so, then I got a jb wrking fr a majr lw frm in bstn···"

  * avid: 열심인

• 은행창구직원이 손님에게 권총을 겨누며

"The bank is all out of money, Mrs. Clagner. Hand over everything you've got!"

  * 은행에 돈이 없단다

• 땅굴을 파서 감옥을 탈출해서 나온 곳은 호랑이 우리 안

"Lou, we did it! Twelve years of tunneling, but we're finally FREEEEEEE!!!"

• 컴퓨터에서 스타벅스(Starbucks)를 주문하고 enter를 치면 책상 옆에서 주문한 커피가 따라져 나온다

'Starbucks doubles its sales by devising a way to sell coffee over the internet'


• 'Swim with the Dolphins!'라는 간판을 걸어 둔 풀(Pool) 장에 사람들이 돌고래가 아닌 Football 선수들과 놀고 있다. 수영장에서 나오는 사람들이

"What a Rip-off"

 * Dolphins는 Miami Dolphins Football Team 이름

 * Rip-off는 바가지


• Garage에는 자동차가 수리가 불가능하도록 분해되고 망가져 있다.

작업자: "The rust problem turned out to be more extensive than we expected"

 * 미국에서는 자동차 수리비가 너무 비싸기 때문에 자기집 Garage에서 스스로
  수리하는 사람이 많다.


• Computer mail: Memo to employee Lyle Zincott:

'Please disregard this morning's termination notice, which was sent to you in error.'

Unfortunately, Lyle had already sent nasty e-mails to his boss, three vice-presidents and the CEO.

 * Nasty: 끔찍한, 형편없는

• 유리구슬(Crystal ball)을 보고 있는 점쟁이(Fortune Teller)가 고객에게

"You are being completely duped by a stranger! She says she can foretell your future, but she is just a con artist…"

    * dupe: 속이다

    * con artist: 사기꾼

    * 이 점쟁이는 자기 자신의 얘기를 하고 있다


• 달표면에 착륙해 있는 우주인(Astronaut)에게 소 한 마리가 'mooooo!' 하면서 달려 든다. "Kent! Watch out"

    * Nursery Rhyme(유치원 노래)에 'the cow jumped over the moon'이라는 가사가 있다

    Hey diddle diddle,

    The Cat and the fiddle,

    The Cow jumped over the moon,

    The little Dog laughed to see such sport,

    And the Dish ran away with the Spoon.


• Winery에서 채용면접을 하고 있다.

간판에는 'All-nature wines made the old- fashioned way' 라 쓰여 있다.

발이 엄청나게 큰 응시자에게 면접관이

"Harry, you have impeccable qualifications. I'm pleased to offer you the position of Master Wine Maker."

    * 전통적인 Wine 제조법: 포도를 사람이 직접 발로 밟아서

• Job Interview for Books for Dummies Publishing에서 면접관이 멍청해 보이는 지원자를 보며

"Hmm···he is remarkably dumb! He would be perfect for our new test-marketing position!"

> * Dummies Publishing: 아무것도 모르는 초보자를 위한 생초보도서(Very Basic Books) 출판

• Early snooze buttons

원시 Cave man이 'Cockadoodledoo!'라고 우는 닭을 향해 돌을 던져 맞춘다(Clonk!)

> * snooze button: 아침에 잠이 깬 뒤 조금 더 자기 위해 누르는 타이머 버튼

• 운전 중 Navigation 안내를 듣고 있는 운전자(Driver)

"I see what you are up to! You're heading to that tramp Lori Bertwald's house! Turn left on Elm St. NOW!"

'Kenny's new GPS system was programmed with his mother's voice and directional information.'

• Chinese Restaurant Misfortune cookies

A yak will fall from great heights and crush you flat.

> * 중국식당에서는 fortune cookie를 준다.
> * yak: 야쿠자

• 여자가 물속에서 일어나는데, 물고기 한 마리가 여자의 귀를 물고

있다.

물가에는 남자가 뜰채를 가지고 있다.

"Unbeknownst to Charlene, the new earrings that Burt gave her were actually bass lures."

　　* Unbeknownst to: 모르는 사이에

　　* Lure: 가짜 미끼


• Gommet Airline Check-in Counter에서

"It's $15 to check a bag and $25 if you want it to arrive at your destination."

　　* Gommet: 초보


• 휴대폰이 돌아다니면서 잔디를 깎고 있다.

"I got a new lawn-mowing app for my cell phone."

　　* 하도 새로운 어플리케이션이 많이 나오다 보니…


• Glue stick(딱풀)을 온 몸에 붙인 사람이 사무실 동료들을 놀래킬려고 하고 있으나, 동료들은 아무런 반응없이 무덤덤하다.

"Every now and then, Doug liked to get glue sticks out of the supply closet and do his porcupine impression"

　　* porcupine impression: 고슴도치효과, 심리적 거리효과(온 몸이 가시로 덮여 있는 고슴도치는 추운 겨울에 서로 몸을 따뜻하게 하기 위해 가까이 다가가지만 가시 때문에 가까이 다가갈수록 서로를 찌르게 된다)

• 에스컬레이터(Escalator)를 타고 내려오던 아이가 지하로 빨려 들어가고 있다.

엄마: "Don't expect sympathy from me! I TOLD you your shoe was untied!"

(신발끈 풀렸다고 얘기 했잖아!)


• Dan had some concerns about the new secretary

비서가 엎드려서 책상서랍을 열려고 하고 있다.

"Uh··· when I said 'Face down', I meant the documents should be face down on the copier, Ms. Camelli."

* face down: 복사할 때 내용이 적힌 부분을 아래로 향하게
* face up: 팩스 보내거나 스캔할 때 내용이 적힌 부분을 위로 향하게


• 방청소를 하기 위해 진공청소기를 돌리는 아줌마, 벽에 붙여 놓은 글귀,

Sounds that various toys make when they are vacuumed up

SCHLANK! – Lego

PROODLE FLOMP! – Barbie head

KACHUNG KACHUNG – K'nex

PLBBP! – Silly putty

CLINK-TUNK – Bionicle

CLANKSMASH – Hot wheel

SCHKLUFF – Clayon

• Mortuary stones and Toilet Paper을 함께 취급하는 상점을 보고 있는 사람에게

주인: "Yeah, I've been lucky. My business is pretty darned recession-proof."

    * Mortuary stones: 묘비석

    * recession-proof: 불황을 타지 않는


• 고속도로 Quick pass lane을 어떤 차가 후진으로 통과한다.

"Josh tests his theory that by driving backward through a quick-pass toll lane, he can get money ADDED to his credit card amount."


• 마트에서 안경을 낀 남편이 빗(Combs) 진열대를 보고 있다. 안경 진열대 앞에 있는 아내: "Stuart, those are combs. The reading glasses are over here"


• 약국에 온 노인에게 약국직원들이 크게 환영하고 있다.

"Congratulations, Mr. Gimler! You're our Patient of the Year!"

    * 이 달의 모범직원, 올해의 모범 직원 등은 있어도 올해의 환자라니…


• TV Channel 광고

""Don't miss the all new Violence Channel! 24 hours of brain-splattering carnage! All violence, all the time!"

    * Brain-splattering carnage: 골수가 낭자하는 살육

    * Splatter Movie(Film): 유혈낭자한 영화

• Before going out on a first date, Tanya always checked for wedding ring tan marks.

여자가 남자의 손가락을 들여다보며

"So… what's the pale circle around your ring finger, Steve?!"

　　* 다른 여자를 만날 때는 반지를 빼는 모양


• 여성학교 강사가 남자에 대해 강의하고 있다.

What guys say → 　What they mean

—I need some space → I'm moving in with two Swedish gymnastics

—Your new hairdo loos, um, great → For a water buffalo

—I've grown a lot since we dated before →I move out of my parents' basement and into cousin Bobby's RV.

　　* 남자의 말은 믿을 게 못된다


• 양로원 앞에 세 할아버지가 흔들의자에 앉아 있다.

"So, did you hear? They say that 97 is the new 92!"


• 아버지와 새로 사귄 남자친구가 소파에 앉아 터무니없는 장난을 치면서 놀고 있다. 이를 보고 있는 여자:

'Although Danielle hoped that her dad and her new boyfriend would hit it off, this was not what she had in mind.'

　　* Hit it off: 죽이 맞다

# 존 하트 만화 'B.C.'

B.C.는 선사시대 몇 명의 원시인(Peter, B.C, Thor, Jane, Wiley 등)과 지질시대의 여러 의인화된 동물(거북이, 새, 뱀, 공룡, 개미, 늑대 등) 이 등장하는 만화이다. 만화가 Jonny Hart가 1958년에 시작하여 현재 는 여러 신문에 연재되고 있다. 작가가 캐릭터를 Cavemen으로 정한 것은 'Cavemen이 단순하고 사상의 원천(A combination of simplicity and the origin of ideas)'이라고 생각했기 때문이다.

• Riddle(수수께끼)

A: "The one who buys it doesn't need it. The one who needs it doesn't buy it. The one who makes it doesn't want it. What is it?"

B: "It's a coffin!"

A: "Nope. A campaign promises."

  *정치인들이 얼마나 쓸데없는 짓만 하고 다니는지

• Jake: "Harv has been spreading vicious lies about you."

(악랄한 거짓말을 퍼뜨리고 다닌다)

친구: !!

친구가 Harv를 찾아와서: "Jake says you're spreading rumors about me!"

Harv의 대답: "I told him you were an excellent cook."

(뛰어난 요리사라고 했는데)

• Nudist colony(누드 족 집단거주지)에 모두가 옷을 입고 있다.
Sign up 카운터에 앉은 안내인: "It's casual Friday."

   *주중에 정장을 입고 근무하는 직장인들이 금요일에 캐주얼한 복장으로 일한다.


• 술집에서 취한 사람:
"Well, boys, it's time for me to hit the ol'road."라고 하고는 쿵(Fump!)
바닥에 넘어진다.
잠시 후 큰 개 한 마리가 주인 취객을 끌고 간다
손님들: "A designated driver."

   * ol': old

   * Designated driver: 술을 마시지 않는 지정운전자


• 개미핥기(anteater) 가 "Oooh. A beetle!" 하면서 삼켰다(ZOT! 삼
키는 소리).
땅속에 있는 개미: "Do we have insurance on the Volkswagen?"

   * Beetle의 원 뜻은 딱정벌레

   * VW car는 딱정벌레처럼 생겨서 'Bug 또는beetle'이라고도 한다.


• A: "Well, well, well."
"What do we have here?"

   * 실제로는 두레박 우물(Well) 3 개가 있다


• 코치와 선수들의 대화
"Men, I'm changing our team's name to 'the possums!'"

"Why, coach?"

"Because we play dead at theme and get killed on the road!"

 * 'possum(opossum)'은 '주머니 쥐'라는 뜻

 * 'Play opossum'은 '죽은 체하다'라는 뜻


• Tavern(선술집) 안에서의 대화

A: "How was your trip to Vegas, Jake?"

B: "Not so good, I gambled away the car."

"The Hertz people were furious!"

 * Hertz는 Rent car 회사 이름

 * Rent car를 도박으로 날려 먹었으니 당연히…


• The cure(치료제)

환자: "I feel like my life has no purpose."

치료사: "To concoct the cure, you must bring me the sleepy-eye crust of the fruited yak."

환자: "Ok, thanks."

이 광경을 본 사람: "Will that really cure him?

치료사 대답: "As long as he never finds it."

 * 'concoct'는 '만들다'라는 뜻

 * sleepy-eye crust of the fruited yak: 이런 것은 세상에 없다

 * 의사는 결국 환자에게 삶의 의미를 주었다.


• 손님: "I have a question regarding meat."

Meat 주인: "Hit me."(말해 봐)

손님: "What's the best way to smoke ham?"

Meat주인: "Replace the cigar filling with a slice of bacon."

> * 'Smoke ham'의 뜻은 'BBQ처럼 훈증기(smoker)에 요리하다'라는 뜻
>
> * 'cigar filling'은 Cigar의 속, 내부
>
> * 손님은 햄 요리하는 방법을 물었는데, 주인은 smoke를 '담배 피우다'로 받아들임

<br>

• 아들: "Dad, I think I'm starting to notice girls."

아빠: "Wonderful! You're on the precipice of life's greatest journey – that which explores the magnificent splendor that is woman!"

아들: "How long will it last?"

아빠: "Right up until your wedding day."

> * 'Precipice'은 '절벽, 벼랑'이라는 뜻

<br>

• 들판에서 한 Diviner(점쟁이)가 Divining stick을 땅에 꽂는다 (FUNK: 꽂히는 소리).

Divining rod는 땅밑에 개미부부의 스파에 박힌다.

개미: "So much for our romantic evening"

> * 'So much for something'은 '끝장이군!'이라는 뜻이다(ending of that, not gonna happening)

<br>

• 수거북이가 암거북이에게

"Hey there, darlin', did you just wax your shell? …'cause I can see myself in it!"

등껍질이 뜯겨 나온 거북이에게 새 한 마리가

"What happened to you?"

수거북이: "Never use lousy pickup lines on a snapping turtle."

> \* 'lousy pickup lines'은 수작 거는 작업
>
> \* 'snapping'은 '친하지 않은'이라는 뜻(not friendly)

• 높은 전망대에서 망보는 사람에게 "lookout"이라고 소리친다. 망지기가 "Yes?" 하면서 내려다보는데, 뒤에서는 큰 바위가 망루로 굴러 내려오고 있다.

> \* 'lookout' 은 1)명사로는 '망보는 사람'이라는 뜻이지만, 2)동사로는 '조심해'(watch out) 이라는 뜻이다. 외친 사람은 조심하라고 경고한 것인데, 망지기는 자기를 부르는 줄 알고 대답을 했군.

• 손님이 Soup를 한 그릇 받아 들고는

"You say this chicken soup is 100% organic?"

요리사: "That's right."

"All the organs are still in there."

(손님이 Soup을 쏟아버린다)

> \* 'organic'은 1) '화학비료를 쓰지 않은 유기농'이라는 뜻이지만, 'organic' 또는 'organs' 은 2)'내장, 장기'라는 뜻도 있다.

• Pharmacy(약국)에서

손님: "What do you take for pain?"

약사: "Me? Nothing, but keep that between us."

손님: "Why don't you want people to know?"

약사: "Would you trust a vegan butcher?"

  * 'keep that between us'는 '우리만의 비밀로 하자'라는 뜻
  * Vegan은 완벽한 채식주의자, Butcher는 정육점주인


• 시력검사

의사: "Okay, what's the smallest thing you can read?"

손님:(시력검사 차트의 맨 밑부분에 깨알처럼 작게 적힌 글씨를 읽어낸다)

"Distributed by Acme eye chart company, LLC"

의사:(돋보기로 확인하면서) "…Above that, showoff!"

  * 'showoff'는 '자랑하다, 과시하다'라는 뜻


• 벌레들의 대화

A: "My dad was a real class clown in school."

B: "So was mine… sort of."

A: "Sort of?"

B: "He was a cut up in biology class."

  * 'Class crown'은 '광대처럼 재미있는'이라는 뜻(funny like a clown)
  * 'cut up'는 '개구리를 해부하다'(dissect a frog)라는 뜻인데, 글자 그대로의 의미는 '조각조각 자르다'(cut apart in pieces)라는 뜻


• 앞발이 아주 짧은 공룡을 채용 면접하는 면접관

"I see you have a degree in shorthand."

* 'shorthand'는 글자 그대로는 1) '짧은 손'이란 의미지만, 2) '속기'(shortcut writing code)라는 뜻도 있다.

• 낚시바늘에 물린 미끼를 본 물고기 한 마리가 Sucker fish(빨판 상어)에게

"Hey, fellas! There's some good eats over this way."

Suckers: "Wow" "Thanks" 하면서 그 쪽으로 간다

물고기: "Suckers"

* 'Sucker'는 '잘 속는 사람'이란 뜻

• Bar에서

A: "Hey, Thor, how was the hunt?"

Thor: "Terrible, spent all day chasin' a doe – just to come up with nothin'!"

A: "That's the second time I've heard that tonight."

(옆 자리에는 수사슴(Stag) 한 마리가 한잔하고 있다.)

* Doe: 암사슴

*아마 수사슴에게 같은 얘기를 먼저 들었던 모양

• Tavern(선술집)에서

A: "Maude tricked me into the opera."(속아서 오페라를 보러 갔었다)

B: "How'd she do that?"(어떻게 속였는데)

A: "The gun she put to my head wasn't loaded."(장전 안 된 총이었다)

* 'put a gun to my head'는 '머리에 총을 겨누다'라는 뜻인데, 여자가 총으로 협박해서 강제로 데이트를 한 모양

• 야구공에 눈을 맞아 다친 선수를 의사에게 데리고 온 사람

"I told him to keep his eye on the ball."

> * 선수는 코치가 시키는 대로 볼을 끝까지 쳐다본 죄.


• Thor's Diner 식당에서 메뉴판을 보며 주문을 받는 웨이터에게,

손님: "I've found that the best way to keep from overeating is to avoid food that taste really good."(과식하지 않는 가장 좋은 방법은 맛있는 음식을 피하는 것)

아무 것도 먹지 않고 포크만 들고 있는 옆테이블 손님이 이 말을 듣고 는,

"Hence, my continued patronage."

> * 'continued patronage'는 '지속적인 후원'이라는 뜻


• 새 털옷을 입고 있는 친구에게

A: "Wow, nice coat! Where'd you get it?"

B: "Let's just say I borrowed it while the owner slept."

세 마리의 짐승 중 털이 몽땅 뽑힌 한 마리가 다른 두 마리에게

"You guys feel a draft?"(너희들은 좋아?)

> * 'Draft'는 '시원한 공기'(cool air, breeze)라는 뜻
> * 주인이 안 보는 사이에 짐승 털을 몽땅 뽑은 것 같다.


• 한 여자가 Job interview를 하고 있다.

면접관: "Can you handle a flagman's job?"

여자: "What do I have to do?"

면접관: "Tell people where to go."

여자: "… and you're gonna pay me to do this?"

면접관: "Yep."

여자(혼자 생각): "must have passed away sometime in my sleep…"

   * 'Flagman'은 도로공사시 '차 통제하는 사람'

   * 사람들에게 시키는 일만 하는데 돈을 준다고? 여자는 정말 이게 꿈인지 생시인
     지…


• Pet 상점에서 앵무새 한 마리를 보이며

주인: "Check out this parrot, he was once owned by an infamous mobster."

손님: "Hey there, fella, do you talk?"

앵무새: "I'm a parrot, not a stool pigeon."

   * 'mobster'는 조직폭력배

   * 'Do you talk?'는 '말해 봐라'는 뜻이지만, 조직폭력배에게는 '정보를 대라'가
     맞을 듯

   * 'stool pigeon'은 '미끼 새, 밀고자'


• 여자: "You're a big fat liar! I'll never believe a word that comes out of your mouth again!"

남자: "That dress really brings out your eyes."

여자:(좋아하면서) "… Really?"

   * 'bring out'은 '드러나게 하다'라는 뜻

   * 하여간 여자란….

• 카지노에서 예쁜 여자 딜러가 남자에게

"Wanna play Chinese checkers?"

남자: "Nah."

여자 딜러: "Why not?"

남자: "An hour after a game I feel like I have to play again."


• 두 사람이 나무집을 짓고 있다. 한 사람은 고슴도치로 못을 박고 있다. 다른 사람은 털이 다 뽑힌 고슴도치를 던져버리며

"My nail gun is empty, toss me another"

다른 고슴도치들은 달아난다.


• 보석(Jewelry) 가게

손님: "This ring you sold me is way too big."

주인: "Let's see what we can do for ya."

(몽둥이로 손님의 손가락을 내려친 후)

주인: "Try it now."(이제 한 번 껴보세요)


• 기자: "Coach, are you going to have a good team this year?"

코치: "Not likely, we're already referring to the cheerleaders as grief counselors."

　　* 'Grief counselor'는 '슬픔극복 상담사'


• 64: 7로 게임에 진 팀에게

기자: "How do you feel about your team's execution today?"

Coach: "I'm all for it."

  * 'All for it'는 '완벽히 찬성하다'라는 뜻


• 할 일 없는 두 사람

A: "Sometimes I think we are put here for no real purpose."

B: (A를 한 번 쳐다보고는) "You're certainly doing your part."


• A: "What's the difference between an old gaffer and an old geezer?"

B: "A gaffer sees a pretty girl and recalls his youth with a smile."

B: "A geezer does the same thing but has no idea why he's smiling."

  * 'Gaffer'는 '시골할아버지'라는 의미인데, 늙었지만 생각이 있는 사람(old + has memory). 'Geezer'는 '괴짜할아버지'로 번역하고, 늙고 정신없는 사람(so old + no memory, very old – sort of stupid)을 뜻함


• Watchdog(경비견) 판매점에서

고객: "I'd like to return this so-called watchdog."

주인: "What's the problem?"

고객: "A bugler came into my cave, and all he did was watch!"

주인: "OK… let's try that once more from the top."

  * 'From the top'은 '처음부터'(from the beginning)라는 뜻


• 선생: "Okay, class…I want you to write a detailed essay telling me what you did this summer."

학생:(Essay를 선생에게 제출하며) "Here ya go."

선생:(학생의 Essay 내용을 읽는다)

"In the interest of our mutual convenience, please refer to my Facebook page."


• A가 B에게 다가서며

"Ahem"(어험)

"Do you know my girlfriend left me for a guy just like you?"

B: "Nope… But if you find me an accordion, I'll wing it."

> \* 'My girlfriend left me for a guy just like you'는 유명한 Country Song.
>
> \* I'll wing it: 잘 못 하지만 한 번 시도해 보겠다


• 침대에 누워 게임을 하고 있는 아들

'zabeep, shahoop, zocca, blak, zocca, zzup'

아빠: "You kids today with your video games.I never had anything like that."(아빠가 game을 하려고 하니 'bip' 하면서 꺼져버린다.)

아들: "What did you play when you were a kid?"

아빠: "The horses."

> \* Play the horses는 '경마에 돈을 걸다'라는 뜻(bet on a horse race)


• 물 속을 들여 다 본 남자가 "spawning season"이라고 하면서, 물가에 'Do not disturb'라는 팻말을 세운다.

> \* 'spawning season'은 '물고기가 짝짓기하는 계절'이라는 뜻(mating season for fish)

- Mammal whisperer(동물과 소통하는 능력을 가졌다고 주장하는 사람)

"Dog training is about establishing dominance. If the animal is subordinate, I will reflect in his posture. I'm doing a free seminar tomorrow."

막상 그 다음날 세미나에 가 보니 개가 주인 머리 위에 올라 앉아 있다.

"Hey, thor."

　　* thor는 there 와 같은 말


- 수수께끼(riddle)

거북이: "What has holes in its top, bottom, middle and sides, but still holds water?"

새: "A sponge?"

거북이: "Nope……. the Titanic."

　　*침몰한 관광선 타이타닉


- 원시인이 늑대(wolf)에게 구운 고기를 주며

"I wonder what I should name you?"

늑대가 한 입에 꿀꺽 삼키는 소리(WOLF!)를 듣고는

"That's it! I'll call you wolf!"


- 체벌의 일종으로 아이를 방에 가두고 나서, 한참 후

아내: "I think junior has been in his room long enough— go talk to him."

남편: "OK."

아빠: "Well son, have you learned your lesson?"(반성 좀 했니?)

아이: "Yep- Next time you break your neighbor's window, don't twitter about it."

> *다음에는 이웃집 유리창을 깨도 트위터에 올리지 말 것

• Dr. Peter(Head shrinker: 정신과 의사)

의사: "When did you first realize you were in this terrible rut?"

환자: "When I started writing my diary two weeks in advance."

> * 'Rut'은 '쳇바퀴 도는 삶, 판에 박힌 생활'(Do same thing over and over again)이란 뜻으로 환자는 '2주 후의 일기를 오늘 미리 쓸 때부터'라고 한다.

• 영화관 매점에서

관객: "I'll have a small popcorn."

점원: "That's $10.00, you want a receipt?"

관객: "No, thanks-. I'd rather not be reminded of this purchase."

> * Popcorn이 너무 비싸다는 뜻

• 사막 한 가운데에 있는 사람 발자국을 보며 조그만 벌레들

A: "Humans occupy this planet."

B: "How can you tell?"

A: "This thing is 100% carbon."

> * Carbon foot print(탄소발자국): 개인 또는 단체가 직접 · 간접적으로 발생시키는 온실 기체의 총량. 일상 생활에서 사용하는 연료, 전기, 용품 등이 모두 포함된다.

• 아침에 일어난 원시인(Cave man)과 개가 동시에 하품한다(yawn). 동굴 앞 물가에서 사람은 빗으로 머리를 손질하고, 개는 몸을 흔든다(shake shakily shakily sake). 몸을 흔드는 것만으로 개의 털은 이미 완벽히 손질이 되었다.

Cave man: "If only it were that easy."


• 물고기 무리(school of fish)가 Sunfish schools이나 Marine schools 등으로 떼 지어 가고 있는 데, 유독 한 마리만 Harvard, Yale로 가는 Grad schools로 가려 하고 있다. 다른 물고기가 "You really get a kick outta yourself, huh, Bob?"

　　* 'You think you are a big deal.'은 '네가 대단하다고 생각해?'라는 뜻으로 모욕(insult)적인 표현.

　　* 'I get a kick out of you!'는 '넌 좀 특이하고 나는 너의 그런 특이한 것을 보고 즐기고 있다'라는 뜻(You are different and I enjoy your antics, craziness, your funny.)

　　* 'To kick someone out of here'는 '쫓아내다'라는 뜻


• 은행에서

손님: "What do I need to get a credit card?"

직원:(거울을 건네며) "Breathe on this mirror."

　　* 죽은 사람이 아니면 OK라는 뜻


• Free style skiing 경기

누워서 타는 사람, 뒤로 타는 사람, 물구나무서서 타는 사람, 굴러서

내려오는 사람…

스포츠 중계자: "This is just ridiculous."


• 스키 가게에서

손님: "What can I put on these skis to make them go faster?"

주인: "Endorsement logos."

　　* 'go fast'는 '스피드를 내다'라는 뜻

　　* Endorsement: 항공사간의 항공권의 권리를 양도하기 위한 이서(또는 배서)


• 몽둥이를 든 원시인 남자 'Wonk' 소리가 난 후 한 여자를 끌고 나간다.

이를 본 사람: "Have a nice time, you two."

잠시 후 다시 'Wonk' 소리가 들리고, 이번엔 여자가 남자를 끌고 들어오면서

"We went dutch."

　　* 'wonk'는 몽둥이로 후려 패는 소리

　　* 'go dutch'는 '비용을 나누어 내다'라는 뜻


• 바닷가에서

A: "What are you doing?"

B: "I'm putting ice cubes in the ocean to help fight global warming."

A: "Nice… Where do you get the ice cubes?"

B: "From my ice cube machine."

(Ice cube machine은 엄청난 매연을 배출하고 있다)

- 애완견을 데리고 나온 주인: "Pet at your own risk."(조심해)

친구:(개를 쓰다듬으며) "Why, does he bite?"

주인: "Not directory."

(개가 꼬리를 흔드니 빈데 같은 것들이 친구에게 옮아간다. ping, pig, ping)


## Wiley's Dictionary

- Cured: Good news for people – bad news for pig.
    * Cured의 원 뜻은 보존을 위한 가공


- Mammoth: the mother of all butterflies(모든 나비, 나방의 어머니)
    * Mammoth의 원 뜻은 매머드(멸종한 코끼리과의 포유동물, 거대한)


- Faux pas: deadbeat dad
    * Fraux Pas는 불어로 실례, 무례라는 뜻이나 영어의 Foe Pa처럼 들린다
    * 'Deadbeat dad'는 '자녀들을 돌보지 않는 아버지'라는 뜻(wouldn't see his children, or provide financial support)


- Sublime: Shady spot under a citrus tree.(감귤나무 아래의 그늘)
    * Sublime의 원 뜻은 Wonderful, great


- Pro.gram: official stance on the national lobby for the metric system

* Pro: for Pros and cons: for and against(찬성 또는 반대)

* Gram: g(그램)

* Official stance: Official position

* National lobby: 의회, 정부등에 정치적인 압력행사

- Roller Derby: competition for the fastest house painter.(가옥도장업자의 경쟁자)

    * Roller Derby의 원 뜻은 롤러게임 상표명

- Bulldozer: Matador with a tranquilizer gun(마취총을 가진 투우사)

    * Bulldozer의 원 뜻은 불도저

- Peanut: a fanatical bean farmer(광적으로 콩을 좋아하는 농부)

    *Peanut의 원 뜻은 땅콩

- Stakeholder: 'the most important person at the barbecue'(바비큐에서 주요역할자)

    * steak와 대비
    * Stakeholder의 원 뜻은 주주

- Rebate: put another worm on the hook.(낚시바늘에 다른 벌레를 끼우다)

    * re-bait와 같은 발음
    * Rebate의 원 뜻은 할인, 리베이트

• Secondhand smoke: a pawn shop on fire(전당포 화재)

    * 원 뜻은 간접흡연


## 짐 보그먼 만화 'Zits'

Comic strip인 Zits는 만화가 Jerry Scott와 삽화가 Jim Borgman이 함께 만든 작품으로 1997년에 연재가 시작되었다. Jeremy라는 청소년(Teenager, 17세의 고등학교 학생)을 통해 Teenagers의 생각과 행동, 부모와의 갈등 및 미국사회의 단면을 잘 배울 수 있다.


• Teen agers 용어 때문에 Dictionaries would be a lot lighter.
Mom: "C U 4 DINR?" (See you for dinner?)
Teen: "IDK. LUV U Bye."(I don't know. I love you. Bye)


• Teen: "Mom! The fridge is making a funny noise!"
Mom: "A noise? What kind of noise?"
Teen: "Well, it's not really a noise, I guess… it's more of an echo."
Mom: 냉장고 문을 열어보고 텅 비어 있자, "I just went shopping yesterday!"


• 화초에 물을 주고 있는 엄마의 머릿속엔 온통 Worry, worry, worry……
cell-phone으로 texting하고 있는 아들의 머릿속엔 온통 Un-worry,

unworry, unworry….

아내가 남편에게: "Jeremy and I don't just disagree… we totally cancel each other out."

    * Cancel out: 상쇄되다


• 수업시간에 졸고 있는 Teens

"Basically, I look at school as a seven-hour interruption in my sleep cycle."


• 어머니가 Jeremy의 어질러 놓은 흔적을 따라 가서 숨어 있는 그를 발견한다.

Teen: "How do you always know where I am?"

Mom: "I call it debris-based intuition."

    * debris-based intuition: 부스러기에 기반을 둔 직관


• Teens 둘이 끊임없이 texting을 하고 있다.(Tap! Tap! Tap! Tap! Tap!……)

Teen A: "My dad says being 'all thumbs' used to be a bad thing."

Teen B: "I'd trade my toes for more thumbs."

    * all thumbs: 서툴다(clumsy, drop things, fall down frequently)

    * texting을 할 때는 주로 엄지손가락을 사용한다.


• Teen: "Here is a list of colleges that I want to visit."

Mom: "Let's see. Hmm…"

Dad: "Interesting choices. Basically, all of the top party schools."

Teen: "You always said I should aim high."

    \* Top college party school: 사회생활이 최고(social life best)


• 차를 타고 있는 Teen에게 차 창문으로 음식을 건네며

Mom: "Okay··· Two breakfast burritos and two bananas. Here you go."

Teen: "Thanks, Mom."

친구: "You have the awesomest mom."

Teen: "It's cool that she understands everything tasters better served through a window."

    \* drive through에 빗댐


• Pizza 배달 아르바이트를 하는

Teen: "I'm home."

Dad: "Hi Jeremy. How much did you make in tips tonight?"

Teen: "About half a tank."

    \* 차에 주유할 가솔린 가격(Gas price)


• Teens이 Pizza를 먹으면서 여자친구 혼자 수많은 사소한 얘기를 끊임없이 하고는

Girl: "So, how was your day?"

Boy: "Like yours, but with less detail."

• Teen의 휴대폰에서 엄마가 하는 얘기

"Jeremy— I recommend this book… it's a classic!"

Jeremey 가 Computer로 searching Interesting articles!

www.someboringblah.com

www.stupefyingstudy.com

www.uselessblather.com

휴대폰에서 들리는 엄마의 목소리 "Cute kitten pics! Link Link Link."

친구: "I checked. There's no 'Unsubscribe' for moms."

    \* Stupefy: makes you feel surprised

    \* Unsubscribe: 구독 해지


• 아빠와 아들이 하루 종일 한 집에 있다. 마주칠 때나(Bop! Bip! Boop! Bip! Bip! Boop!)  밥 먹을 때나(Bip! Boop! Bip! Bip! Bip! Bip!), TV를 볼 때나 아들은 쉬지 않고(Bip! Bip! Bip! Bip! Bip! Bip! Bip! Bip!) Game기 인지 휴대폰인지를 손에서 놓지 않고 있다.

밖에서 아내의 전화 "So how is it with just you and Jeremy at home?"

남편 대답 "A lot like being alone, only lonelier."


• 친구와 함께 온 아들이 엄마에게:

"Hey mom… do you have any jobs we could do to earn some money?"

"We're open to anything as long as it doesn't involve lifting, cleaning, painting, mowing, or ecessive mental exertion."

"Plus, it has to be fun."

친구: "and preferably dangerous."

• Same DNA, different chemistry
부모와 Teen이 TV를 보고 있는데, 부모가 깔깔 웃으면 Teen은 무반응, Teen이 깔깔댈 때 부모는 무반응

• 소파에 불량한 자세로 누워 휴대폰을 갖고 놀고 있는 Teen-ager가 신문에 난 기사를 보며 얘기하고 있는 부모를 보며
"How is it possible two people to be so consistently wrong about everything?"

• 차를 뒤에서 들이받은 여자친구에게
Jeremy: "Sara?? You're the one who just rear-ended me?"
Sara: "Jeremy, I am so sorry! I'm a really good driver, but some bozo had sent me about ten texts in a row and I just glanced down to see who it wa."
"YOU!?"
   * Bozo: 멍청이
   * rear-end: 차량이나 운전자가(다른 차의 뒷부분을) 들이받다, 추돌하다

• SWAT, RIOT polices, HazMat 등이 총출동한 가운데
음악연주를 연습하고 있던 하고 있던 Teen:
"Okay, maybe we should try it once with the garage door shut."
   * SWAT: Special Weapons and Tactics or Special Weapons Attack

Team(특별기동대)

* Riot Police: 폭동진압경찰

* Hazmat: 위험물질

• (키타 치고 놀고 있는 Teens)

Teen A: "Oh My Gosh! I totally forgot that I was supposed to pick my dad up at 5:00!"

Teen B: "It's understandable."

"I was supposed to pick my dad up yesterday and it completely slipped my mind, too."

Teen A:(차를 타며) "Was he mad?"

Teen B: "I'll let you know."(아직도 안 갔다는 의미)

* slip one's mind: 잊어버리다

• School cafeteria에서

Teen A: "I think I'll try the fried rat brains."

Teen B: "Steamed leeches, please."

험상궂게 생긴 요리사 종업원을 보고는,

Teen A: "We remain comedically ahead of our time."

Teen B: "Wait— I think I got what I ordered!"

* leeches: 거머리

• 엄청 크고 긴 샌드위치(sandwich)를 먹고 있는 Teen

"Dinner isn't for another two hours. Make yourself a snack."

• Teen: "Dad, Can I drive your car?"

Dad: "Why? Is there something wrong with the van?"

Teen: "No, I just think that it's good for me to drive a variety of vehicles to keep my skills sharp."

"Your cars have features that mine doesn't, like an automatic transmission, cruise control, ABS…"

Dad: "… gas."

Teen 친구: "He's on to us."

    \* on to us: 눈치채다


• 친구: "Do you ever think about where you want to go to college, Jeremy?"

Jeremy: "Not really."

"Well, sorta."

"You know…"

"In general"

"Someplace outside the parental orbit, but still within wallet range."

    \* orbit: 궤도, 영향권


• Teen: "Mom, have you seen a blue scrap of paper laying around anywhere?"

"I might have written a really important phone number on it and I can't remember where I put it."

Mom: "I threw it away."

Teen: "Mom!! How could you be so careless??"

• 컴퓨터로 음악을 듣고 있는 아들에게

Mom: "Who are we listening to Jeremy?"

Teen: "Psych 101"

Mom: "I like it!"

Teen: "Good to know."

아들은 그 음악을 'delete'시켜 버린다.

• Mom: "Jeremy! Are you listening to me?"

Teen: "Of course, mom."

"I can hear your stomach growling, and your right knee cracks when you shift your weight."

Mom: "I meant, are you listening to what I'm saying?"

Teen: "Oh. Then No."

• Teen ager, 소파에 함께 앉아 있는 부모에게

"What's wrong?"

"Is it the apocalypse?"

"Is dad going to prison?"

"Are we moving?"

Mom: "No. we just wanted to sit with you and watch some TV."

Teen:(GROAN! 신음소리) "It's always worse than you think."

* apocalypse: 세상의 종말(end of world)

• 난장판이 된 소파에 비스듬히 누워 있는 Teen, 간식을 가져온 엄마에게 "Sure, sit anywhere."(앉을 데가 없다)

• Mom의 생각
애기 때 발가락을 세어주던 기억: one, two, three, four.
어릴 때 lego block 놀이를 하던 기억: one, two, three, four.
Teen ager가 된 지금의 one, two, three, four! 는 친구들과 Band 하는 모습
Mom: 'sigh'(한숨)

• 치워야 할 쓰레기봉투를 쌓아 놓고 소파에 앉아 게임에만 열중하는 Teen ager가 엄마에게 "Not procrastinating, strategizing"
(꾸물거리는 게 아니라 전략을 세우는 중이야)

• Teen A: "I kinda sorta think that I might maybe possibly consider exploring the concept of looking into the idea of an east coast college."
B: "Okay, but could you get a bit more non-committal about it."
A: "Maybe— but don't hold me to it."
　　* Committal: 어물쩍거리는, 애매한
　　* don't hold me: 너무 기대하지 말라.(I may change my mind.)

• Mom: "Good luck with the S.A.T., Jeremy!"
Dad: "Knock 'em dead, Son!"

Mom: "No pressure!"

Teen:(등에는 엄청난 중압감을 지고가면서) "Heaven forbid."

　　* Crushing expectations(참담한 기대) weight on his back

　　* knock 'em dead: 파이팅

- 아빠와 Teen

Dad: "Vietnam, Watergate, Civil Rights."

Teen: "Iraq, WMDs, Immigration."

(서로 쳐다보다가 돌아서며)

Dad: "Well, our music was better."

Teen: "We know how to get it for free."

　　* WMD: Weapons of Mass Destruction: 대량파괴무기

- 지각한 Jeremy가 "Sixth row, fourth desk!"라고 외치자, 학생들이 머리 위로 손을 올려 Jeremy를 자기 자리에 운반한다.

Jeremy: "I thought these large class sizes would be a problem, but it's actually kind of fun."

- Teen Ager가 엄마에게

"I'm not arguing. I'm just offering a relentlessly contrary point of view."

　　* relentlessly contrary point of view: 가차없이 정반대되는 관점

- 옷가게에서 아들이 "Dad, what do you think of these jeans?"

Dad: "I like 'em."

아들: "Good. Okay. Thanks."

(점원에게) "I'd like a pair of the opposite of these."


• Teen ager 남: "Can I use your bathroom, Sara?"

여: "Sure."

남: (수많은 종류의 샴푸, 린스 종류를 보고는)

"I know that just you and your mom live here, but how many people wash their hair here?"


• 두꺼운 옷을 입은 아빠가 팬티 차림의 아들에게 "Aren't you freezing?"

아들: "No, 'Cool'is the best insulator."

   * insulator: 절연재


• Mom: 다락방에 있는 아빠와 아들에게 "Are you two hiding from me?"

아들: "Sorta."

Mom: "If you didn't want to scrapbook, you should have just said so!"

"Besides, our time can be better spent on more important things like alphabetizing the spice drawer". * 양념통을 알파벳 순서대로 보관

아빠와 아들:(Washer and dryer 속으로 숨는다.)

• Teen A: "Dude! My parents are going to be out of town until tomorrow morning!"

"You know what that means, don't you?"

Teen B: "You're going to have a party?"

Teen A: "I was picturing it more like an apocalyptic realignment of the earth's tectonic plates, but I suppose 'party 'works."

　　* apocalyptic: 종말론적인

　　* tectonic: 구조상의


• 세탁기에 너무 많은 세탁물을 넣은 Teen이 아빠에게

"What do you do when there's no room for the detergent?"

(세제 넣을 공간이 없을 땐 어떡하죠?)


• Mom: "What's that?"

Teen: "A stack of paper that should be full of words."

"We were supposed to keep a journal of daily reflectionsfor English class, and I kind of forgot."

Mom: "Since when?"

Teen: "September."

Mom: "When is it due?"

Teen: "Tomorrow."


• Dad:(다락방에 숨어 있는 아들에게) "What th…! Jeremy, what are you doing here?"

Teen: "Hiding out."

"It's a snow day, none of us can go anywhere, and mom is in full—on project mode."

Dad: "Don't be ridic—"

엄마가 아빠에게:(scrap할 일거리를 잔뜩 쌓아 놓고) "You know if the three of us really hunkered down, I'll bet we could get a ton of scrapbooking done!"

Dad: 다락방으로 올라와 아들에게: "Move over."

    * What th..: What the hell!

    * Snow day: 눈이 너무 많이 와서 쉬는 날

    * hunker down: 쪼그리고 앉다, 태세를 갖추다

    * Mover over: 저리 비켜줘(나도 숨게)


• 커피잔을 들고 신문을보고 있는 엄마의 독백: "My schedule has really changed since Jeremy got his driver's license."

"I used to spend most of my time driving him places."

(이때 걸려온 전화를 받고는)

"OK, I'll be right there."

"Now I spend most of my time bringing him stuff he forgets when he drives himself places."


• (전화벨 소리)

Mom: "Jeremy, why aren't you answering your phone?"

Teen: "Huh? Oh, it's probably nothing."

Mom: "How do you know? What if it's important?"

Teen: "If it was important, they'd text me."

    * Current culture


• Teen A: "How much sleep do you get at night, Jeremy?"

Jeremy: "Not enough."

"Five or six hours at most."

"But I supplement that with several power-nap opportunities throughout the day…"

"Otherwise known as lecture classes."


• Teen: "I put all the clean dishes in the dishwasher away"

Mom "Jeremy, that's…"

Teen: "And I left my dirty ones in the sink."

Mom "… typical."

Dad: "The light's not on yet., but it's flicking."

    * '배워가고 있는 중'이란 뜻


• Mom: "I can't believe I lost my phone again!"

Teen:(문자를 보내며) "It's the third time this week, Mom."

Mom: "I could have sworn that I put it down right here!"

Teen: "Well, there's your problem."

Mom: "I'm absent minded?"

Teen: "You put your phone down."

* Teen은 휴대폰을 절대 손에서 놓지 않는다.


• Teen A: "So you got popped for texting while driving, huh?"

B: "Yeah. And I'm grounded for two weeks."

"Plus, they took my phone away."

A: "(Gasp!) for two weeks?"

B: "I know, right?"

A:(엄지 두개를 펴며) "What are you going to do with your thumbs?"

　　　* Popped: caught

　　　* Grounded: 외출 금지시키다


• Mom의 헐렁한 옷을 걸쳐 입은 Teen ager 친구:

"Most desperate", "laundry day", "ever!"

Teen: "Dude, is that your mom's maternity shirt?"

　　　* maternity shirt: 출산복


• Teen: "There's a spider in my shower,"

"But I took care of the problem on my own…"

Mom: "Thanks, Jeremy. That shows real matur−"

Teen: "… I traded bathrooms with you."

Mom: "−ity."

　　　* 거미를 잡은 게 아니고 목욕탕을 바꾸었다고


• 뒹굴거리는 Teen에게 엄마가

"Jeremy, I found an empty carton in the ridge,"

"An empty cereal box in the pantry,"

"And an empty Doritosbag under the sofa cushion!"

"I don't think a person could get lazier than you!"

Teen: "Thanks for believing in me, Mom."

Mom: "That was not a compliment!"

    * carton: 음료수 통

    * Doritos: 나초 칩의 한 종류

    * compliment: 칭찬


• 비서: "Do you need a ride home, Dr. Duncan?"

Duncan: "No, Jeremy is picking me up at 5:00."

"He should be here any minute."

한밤중이 되어도 Jeremy는 오질 않고

Duncan: "A-a-a-a-a-n-y minute…"


• 집 앞 차도에 자리 깔고 놀고 있던 Teen, 차가 지나가기 위해 경적을 울리자,

"Some people just can't get into the spirit of summer vacation."


• 남편: "Is Jeremy home?"

아내: "I have no idea. He never tells me when he comes or goes anymore. I just have to see if his van is here."

남편: "What if he leaves on foot?"

아내: "If he's going further than the fridge, he drives."

• Teen's sneeze 'WAA-CHOOO!' 하자마자, 곧바로 그의 i-pod에
는 'Gesundheit' 'Gesundheit' 'Gesundheit' 'Bless you' 'Gesundheit'
Teen: "It's possible that I'm too connected."라고 하면서 소매로 코를
훔친다. 즉시 i-pod: 'Use a tissue'

    * Gesundheit:(원래는 독일어) 재채기 한 사람에게 '몸 조심하세요'
    (영어: God bless you 와 같은 말)


• Teen: "What's for dinner?"
Mom: "Pot roast, salad, crab."
Teen: "Hold on, Sara."(texting)
Teen: "Mom, can't you see I'm in the middle of a conversation?"
Mom "I don't know what a conversation looks like anymore."
Teen: "Sheesh."
 전화기 속: "I know, right?"

    * sheesh: My goodness
    * face to face 대화는 사라지고 texting만 있는 세태


• Teens 대화
Teen A: "The only problem I have with school is that it's so ⋯ you
know⋯"
Teen B: "Daily"


• 약국에 온 Mom: "Do you carry an antidote for this energy
drink?"

* Antidote: 해독제
* Energy Drink: Teens이 너무 energy가 넘치는 것이 Red Bull 같은 Drink 제 영향이라 생각.


• 엄마가 아들을 꼭 껴안는데, 아들은 차렷 자세로 뻣뻣이 있다.

Mom: "Jeremy, I don't hug you so you'll hug me back…I hug you so you'll hug your kids."

* telling why she hugs
* so: because
* you'll: future 애들은 부모가 하는 것을 보고 배운다.


• Teen: 냄새나는 옷을 들고 와서 "Mom, Can you wash this shirts?"

Mom: "I just hung it in your closet an hour ago."

Teen: "I know but…"

Mom 냄새를 받아보고는 'GAAAK!'

Teen: "These sweat glands should be registeredas lethal weapon."

* sweat glands: 땀샘
* Lethal: 치명적인


• Teen: "Mom, do you think you can sew up this hole in my jeans?"

Mom: "Let me see it. Yes, I think I can handle that."

Teen: "Great. And then can you rip a new one right here?"

* sew up: 꿰매다(mend, fix the hole)
* rip: 찢다

• 늦잠자는 Teen에게 Mom: "Jeremy, it's a beautiful day! Get up and go outside!"

잠이 덜 깬 상태로 밖으로 나온 Teen: "So this is what I've been missing. Sunlight. Big whoop."

현관 밖에서 신문을 보고 있는 Dad: "I've had enough of your sarcasm. Go to your room!"

다시 침대에 누운 Teen: "And that's the beauty of the two-parent system."

　　* whoop: 와 하는 함성
　　* sarcasm: 빈정댐


• 남녀가 춤을 춘 후,

남자 Teen: "Pretty much all my dance moves come from dodging Sara's ponytail."

　　* Dodge: 피하다
　　* Ponytail: 묶은 머리


• 슈퍼마켓에서 만난 이웃집 사람: "Connie, let me just tell you that your son Jeremy is amazing!"

"I don't think I've ever met such a poised, polite and centered kid in my whole life!"

Connie: "Really? I don't think I've ever met that kid, either."

　　* 집 안에서는 천하의 말썽꾸러기, 집 밖에서는 예의 바른 아이

• Mom: "Jeremy, you seem rather disconsolate this morning."

Dad: "Very perspicacious, dear."

Mom "Would some blueberry pancakes make you feel more sanguine"

Dad: "The granola is ambrosial!"

Mom: "Is he cogitating?"

Dad: "I'd say chafing."

Teen: "This S.A.T. prep is going to kill me."

> \* disconsolate: 슬픈(sad)
>
> \* perspicacious: 총명한(clever)
>
> \* granola: 아침식사용 시리얼의 일종
>
> \* sanguine: 쾌활한
>
> \* ambrosial: 신의 음식
>
> \* cogitating: 숙고하다
>
> \* chafing: 초조
>
> \* S.A.T. prep: 대학수능시험 자율학습

• 남편: 돼지가 날아다니는 것을 본다. 'Snot'

아내: "Jeremy cleaned his bathroom without being threatened!"

남편: "That explains it."

> \* 해가 서쪽에서 뜬다: Condition A will not happen until pigs fly.

• Teen: 엄청나게 빠른 속도로 기타 연주, 엄청나게 빠른 속도로 Texting, 엄청나게 빠른 속도로 typing, 눈을 치울(shoveling snows) 때 는 엄청나게 느린 속도로

Mom: "That's as far as you've gotten?"

Teen: "All my speed is from the wrist down."

    * wrist: 손목


• Jeremy로 부터의 전화 Message: Running late. Won't be home 4 dinners.

Msg 2: Finished early. Will be home 4 dinners after all.

Msg 3: Eating at Hector's. go ahead without me.

Msg 4: Menudo at Hector's. Bringing him home for dinner.

Msg 5: Got invited for burgers with Pierce. Chowing there instead.

친구들과 햄버거를 먹고 있는 Jeremy에게 부모가 보내는 msg:

 From now on, only text us if your plans aren't changing.

친구1: "Is it me, or are parents getting crabbier as we get older?"

친구 2: "It's them."

    * chow: eat

    * crabby: 까다로운(easily annoyed)


• Teen: "mhnoifrgcuyc"

Mom: "What?"

Teen: "nbkiu4g8uq4g 9ut"

Mom: "Jeremy, I can't understand a word you are saying!"

"Can you just talk slower?"

Teen: "Can't you listen faster?"

• Old Memories: 아침 5:00에 아기가 자고 있는 엄마 등에 올라타 깨우려고 했는데,

New Realties: Noon에 엄마가 자고 있는 Teen등에 올라타 깨우려고 한다.


• 남편: "Why is Jeremy out there sitting in the van?"

아내: "You mean hasn't left yet? I asked him to go to the market twenty minutes ago!"

Teen:(엄마에게) "What part of 'assembling the perfect playlist for driving on a Wednesday' don't you understand?"

　　* What part of X don't you understand?: 우리가 지금 무슨 얘길 하고 있는 지 이해를 못 한단 말인가?


## 케빈 페이건 만화 'Drabble'

미국의 만화가 Kevin Fagan은 22세 때인 1979년에 Drabble이란 제목으로 신문 Strip에 데뷔한 이래 여러 신문사에 판매하고 있으며, Drabble Facebook의 팔로워도 상당히 많다. 주제는 주로 그의 대학시절 이야기들이 많다.


• 아내: "You need some exercise, Ralph!"

남편: "What are you talking about? I'm getting plenty of exercise! My head's spinning, my heart's racing and my stomach's churning!"

- 아빠: "This is ridiculous! I can't go 12 hours without food or drink!"

아들: "Dad, I know it seems hard, but it's important to follow the doctors' orders!"

"You can do it, dad! I'll help you every step of the way!"

"It'll be a piece of cake!"

아빠: "CAKE?!!"

> \* A piece of cake: 식은 죽 먹기

- 남자가 회사에 전화를 건다

"Hello, boss. It's me, Drabble. I won't be at work today."

"I'm dealing with a nagging cold."

이때 침대에 누워 있는 아내가 "Ralph! I need another box of tissues!" 라고 소리친다.

남자: "There it is now!"

> \* 'nagging'은 1)'잔소리하다, 바가지 긁다'라는 의미도 있고, 2)'아주 심해서 치료하기 힘든'이라는 의미도 있는데, 남자는 두 가지 의미를 함께 사용하고 있다.

- 아들: "Here's my report card, dad!"

아빠: (Sigh: 한숨)

아들: "Just remember times have changed. A 'D-plus' is the new 'B-minus'."

> \* 'Seventy is new fifty' 같은 얘기를 성적표에 갖다 붙인다.

- 식당에서 밥을 먹고 있는 남녀

남: "Let's see what my fortune cookie says…"

'A partner's hip will prove to be exciting'

여자: (먹고 있던 스파게티를 남자 얼굴에 뒤집어 씌운다)

남: "Oh, my mistake… 'A partnership…'"

  * '파트너쉽'을 '파트너의 엉덩이'라고 했으니…


- 개:

"I don't understand it."

"It kind of bugs me."

"Dogs are man's best friend!"

(높은 곳에 있는 새장을 보며)

"So how come your place is cooler than mine?"

새: "Women do the shopping!"

  *개는 수컷이고, 새는 암컷인 모양이다


- 집으로 돌아온 주인: "We're home!"

개: "You're home! You're home! You're home!"

(반가워서 뛰고, 돌고, 난리 났다.)

앉아 있는 고양이: "They were gone?"

  * 일반적으로 개는 주인이 나갔다 돌아오는 데 엄청난 관심을 보이지만 고양이는
    관심 없다.


- 아내가 잠들어 있는 동안 남편은 살금살금 냉장고 문을 연다.

냉장고에서 '찰칵(flash)' 사진이 찍힌다. 아침에 남편사진을 들고,

아내: "Well, look who raided the ridge last night!"

남편: "I'm pretty sure this is unconstitutional!"

　　* Raid: 1)급습, 2)훔쳐먹다

　　* be unconstitutional: 위헌이다, 헌법에 위반이 된다


• 아들: "Mom, dad… I've decided to live at college this semester!"
"I need my independence! Don't worry, I'll come home for holidays."
"…and weekends….and when I have laundry…and whenever you
cook something good for dinner! Farewell!"

엄마: "Our little boy is growing up!"

아빠: "I wish he'd hurry!"

아들: "Oops, I almost forgot my blanky!"

　　* Blanky: 어린애들이 잠잘 때 껴안고 자는 담요(a blanket that kids go to
　　　sleep with)


• 애들이 부업으로 팔고 있는 'Lemonade $1.0'에는 아무도 없고,
'Ask about our senior discount'라는 Sign을 붙여 놓고 있는 'Program
your Cell Phone $1.00'에는 많은 할아버지들이 줄 서 있다.


• 컴퓨터 앞에서 책을 읽으면서 마우스를 굴린다 (roll, roll, roll)

아빠: "Hey, what's wrong with my mouse? I can't scroll down!"

아들: "You're reading a book! Turn the page!"

아빠: "Oh yeah, huh!"

- 아들: "Dad, can I borrow your comb?"

아빠: "Sure."

아들: (빗으로 이빨을 쑤시며) "I've got something stuck in my teeth!"

아빠: "You're not supposed to pick your teeth with a comb!"

(볼펜 뚜껑으로 이를 쑤시며) "You're supposed to use a cap from a ball point pen!"


- 아이들: "Trick or treat!!"

(멀뚱히 보고만 있는 집주인)

아이들: "Well?"

집주인: "Huh? Oh, sorry.  I was having a flashback to my wife's family reunion!"

아내: "Your whole life is about flashback!"

    * Treat or trick: 할로윈 날 애들이 사탕 얻으러 다닐 때 하는 말

    * flashback: 회상, 환각의 재현

    * 예전에 처가식구들이 와서 어지간했던 모양


- 남편: "Honeybunch, I have a stupid question…"

아내: "There's no such thing as a stupid question, Ralph!"

남편: (헐렁한 바지를 보이며) "Are these my sweat-pants or yours?"

(바지를 얼굴에 뒤집어쓰고는) "There may be no stupid questions, but there are certainly ill-advised ones!"

    * Honeybunch: 부부간의 호칭 중 하나 (affectionate nickname for spouse)

• 비만환자의 체중을 재어보며

의사: "Shame on you Ralph…"

"I told you to start watching what you eat!"

"What happened?"

환자: "My eyes got tired."

   * Watch: 의사는 1)'주의하다'라는 뜻으로 말하고, 환자는 2)'보다'라는 뜻으로 이
   해

• 아들: "Have you and mom ever had your credit card stolen?"

아빠: "Yeah, once."

아들: "That must have been terrible! What did you do?"

아빠: "Nothing. The thief spends less than your mom!"

• 이웃 A: "Hi, Neighbor!"

이웃 B: "Steinbauer!!, Are you moving??"

A: "No, I'm just throwing away a box of junk!"

B: Dang!

A: "Nice to see you, too!"

   * Dang: Damn을 완곡하게 표현한 것(polite form of Damn)

• 남자: "At last! Every chore on my 'Honey-do' list is done!"

아이 1: "Dad, will you please blow up my wading pool now?"

아이 2: "Dad, when you're done with that, will you take me to the driving range?"

남자: "When the 'Honey-do's' end, the 'Do-dads' begin."

   * Honey-Do List: 아내가 남편에게 해 달라고 써 놓은 목록


- 꼬마: "Wow! What's all that?"

아빠: "I'm playing solitaire."

꼬마: "You mean people can now play solitaire without a computer??"

아빠: "These are amazing times in which we live."

꼬마: "What will they think of next??!"

   * Solitaire: 혼자서 하는 카드놀이


- 야구장비를 갖추고 어디론가 가고 있는 아이

"Well, it's the start of another little league baseball season…"

"A time when a big career is the dream of every child"

"… and quite a few of their parents!"

뒤따라가는 아빠: "Swing level, keep your eye on the ball, and remember that the average major league salary is over $3 million!"

   * 꿈도 크다.


- 컴퓨터를 하고 있는 남자:

"So, what's wrong with me?"

"Was I doing something incorrectly??"

"I'm a nice guy!"

"Why would someone 'unfriend' me??"

* Unfriend: twitter 용어, 친구관계를 끝내다


* 식빵을 다림질해서 주면서

아빠: "Perfect! One grilled cheese sandwich!"

아들: "Thanks Dad!"

아빠: "The iron chef!"

* Iron chef: 일본인 요리사가 나오는 요리방송 프로그램 중의 하나(a show where a Japanese guy bites a yellow pepper in the start)


* 엄마 뒤를 졸졸 따라다니는 꼬마가 이리저리 둘러보다가, 아빠를 찾는다.

"I don't see any warpath, Dad!"

아빠: "Mom is on the warpath."

* 'warpath'는 '출정길'이란 뜻이지만, 'on the warpath'라고 하면 '화가 나서 싸우려고 드는'이란 뜻이다.


* 아빠: "Dang" "I can't seem to tighten this screw."

아들: "Turn clockwise."

아빠: (벽시계가 걸려있는 방향으로 돌아서서) "I still can't do it."

* clockwise: 시계 돌아가는 방향


* 아빠: (휘파람 부는 시범) "And that's how to whistle, kids!"

아이들: "Cool!" "Thanks, dad!" "That's neat!"

아빠: "OK, I can cross another one off the list."

아빠의 리스트 (Things every dad should teach his kids)에는

−Be nice to people

−Pro wrestling is fake

−How to whistle

−Yo−yo tricks

−How to play Bongo

−Talk like Donald Duck


• 남자가 우체통을 열기 전에 침을 삼킨다−Gulp! 조금 긴장하고 있다(a little nervous)

(연다− click!)

우체통 안으로부터 남자의 얼굴에 청구서들이 총 쏘는 것처럼 (RATTA−TATTA−TAT) 날아든다.

남자: "It's always a little painful to get the December credit card bills!"


• 남편: "I've noticed something…The more you shop at bulk club, the more your garage starts to resemble bulk club!"

아들: "Mom, where is the cereal?"

엄마: "Aisle 5!"

　　* Bulk: (상점 앞의) 삐죽 나온 진열장[판매대](stall)

　　* 아들이 먹을 시리얼은 안 사고 쓸데없는 것들만 사고 있는 엄마

• 공부하고 있는 아들에게

아빠: "I think the correct answer is 578! ⋯ or maybe it's 12."

아들: "Dad, will you please help me with my homework?"

아빠: "Oh, yeah. Sure." 하면서 나가버린다.

아들: "Dad helps by not helping!"

　　* 안 도와주는 게 돕는 것이다.


• 건물 안의 사무실 안내표지판(directory) 앞에 서 있는 남자

'You are here X'라는 걸 보고는 고개를 갸웃하며

"How do they always know?"

　　* 간판에서 'You are here'는 현 위치 표시


• 아빠가 세탁물을 찾아와서 차에서 기다리고 있는 아들에게

"OK, I picked up the dry-cleaning! Let's go! I'm in a hurry!"

아들: "Sorry, dad. We can't leave yet."

아빠: "Why not?"

아들: "Because we parked in a space that said '30 minutes parking only'."

"We've been only been here four and a half minutes!"

아빠: "Will you start the car!!

　　* '30 minutes parking only'는 '30분 초과해서 주차할 수 없다'는 뜻


• 애들과 함께 연날리기를 하러 가는 중

아빠: "Kids today spend too much time immersed in technology."

"They don't know how to play outside anymore. That's why I'm teaching you to fly a kite."

"One day you'll thank me!"

"Although it will probably be tweeted!"

이 때 애들은 Smart phone으로 검색을 하고 있다.

"Isn't there an app for playing outside?"

　　* 스마트폰에 빠져 사는 세태를 풍자


• 도넛 가게에서

손님: "Darn! I can't find my punch card!"

"This donut should be free because I filled up my punch card, but now I can't find it."

점원: "It's OK, I'm new here, but I can certainly believe you're a regular customer!"

손님: (가게를 나오면서) "I didn't like the way she said that!"

　　* 자신이 단골고객인 것처럼 먼저 말해 놓고서…


• 할아버지가 딸과 함께 길을 걸으며

"Here's another great thing about little league season…"

"It gives us the opportunity to get to know other parents!"

"People we might not otherwise have gotten the chance to know!"

"Like that windbag down the street, or the raving lunatic around the corner, or the dirty rotten cheater across town…"

　　* 별 희한한 사람들을 만날 수 있는 기회다

• 아들이 신문을 보고 있는 아빠에게 "What's wrong, Dad?"

아빠: "My favorite comic strip looks a little strange today!"

"It's almost as if the cartoonist lost his glasses."

아들: "It could happen I suppose!"(글자가 칸 밖으로 삐어져 나와 있다)

  * Comic strip: 네 칸짜리 신문만화


• TV 리모컨으로 볼륨을 줄이려고 하는데 소리는 더 커진다.

아빠: "Why isn't the volume going up?"

아들: "You're pointing the remote backward."

아빠: "Oh yeah, huh!"


• 아들이 엄마를 찾는다.

아들: "Mom!"

"Mom!"

"Mother! June! Honeybunch!"

이때 고양이를 바라보고는 고양이 소리를 낸다. "Meow"

금방 나타난 엄마가 "Did my kitty just call me?"


• 아들: "Did you play baseball in school, dad?"

아빠: "I sure did, son!"

"I was considered a 'five-tool' player!"

아들: "Really??"

아빠: "Absolutely…. I had a hammer toe, a wrench in my back, an iron glove, a hangnail and a screwball swing!"

* Five-tool player: (야구) 5툴 플레이어 (타격, 홈런, 출루, 도루, 수비)
* He's a legit five-tool player.(그는 진정으로 5가지를 모두 갖춘 선수다.)
* 해머, 렌치, 아이론, 손 거스러미, 나사: 5 tool(다섯가지 공구)이긴 하다.


• 마을 회관에 사람들이 모여 있다.

연설자: "Thank you all for coming to our neighborhood emergency preparedness meeting!"

"Every day, we hear reports of fires, floods and earth quakes."

"But if we look out for each other, we might be able to withstand the next disaster!"

(한 사람이 늦게 도착한다)

이웃: "Hi, Mr. Stein Bauer!"

늦게 도착한 사람: "Sorry I'm late. Where are the snacks?"

연설자: "Speaking of disaster!"

* 연설에 방해되는 사람


• 레모네이드(Lemonade) 주스를 팔고 있는 아들에게

아빠: "How's the business, Patrick?"

아들: "Better than ever. I'm proud to report!"

"You've just got to give people what they want!"

'Lemonade Free WIFI'라는 간판이보인다.

* 아내: "Whenever I do the laundry, there always seems to be a few socks missing!"
"Where do they go? Why do they just disappear??"
남편: "I'll bet the dog has something to do with it!"
양말 몇 짝을 가지고 있는 개: "Dogs get blamed for everything!"

Thank you for your patience.

Hope this helps you!


Young J Sohn